MODERN CHINESE LITERATURE FROM TAIWAN

From the Old Country

MODERN CHINESE LITERATURE FROM TAIWAN

EDITORIAL BOARD
PANG-YUAN CHI
GÖRAN MALMQVIST
DAVID DER-WEI WANG, COORDINATOR

Wang Chen-ho, *Rose, Rose, I Love You*
Cheng Ch'ing-wen, *Three-Legged Horse*
Chu T'ien-wen, *Notes of a Desolate Man*
Hsiao Li-hung, *A Thousand Moons on a Thousand Rivers*
Chang Ta-chun, *Wild Kids: Two Novels About Growing Up*
Michelle Yeh and N. G. D. Malmqvist, editors, *Frontier Taiwan:
An Anthology of Modern Chinese Poetry*
Li Qiao, *Wintry Night*
Huang Chun-ming, *The Taste of Apples*
Chang Hsi-kuo, *The City Trilogy:
Five Jade Disks, Defenders of the Dragon City, Tale of a Feather*
Li Yung-p'ing, *Retribution: The Jiling Chronicles*
Shih Shu-ching, *City of the Queen: A Novel of Colonial Hong Kong*
Wu Zhuoliu, *Orphan of Asia*
Ping Lu, *Love and Revolution: A Novel About Song Qingling and Sun Yat-sen*
Zhang Guixing, *My South Seas Sleeping Beauty: A Tale of Memory and Longing*
Chu T'ien-hsin, *The Old Capital: A Novel of Taipei*
Guo Songfen, *Running Mother and Other Stories*
Huang Fan, Zero *and Other Fictions*

From the Old Country

Stories and Sketches of China and Taiwan

《原鄉、故鄉：鍾理和文選》

Zhong Lihe

EDITED AND TRANSLATED BY T. M. MCCLELLAN
FOREWORD BY ZHONG TIEJUN

COLUMBIA UNIVERSITY PRESS   NEW YORK

Columbia University Press
Publishers Since 1893
New York   Chichester, West Sussex
cup.columbia.edu
Copyright © 2014 Columbia University Press
All rights reserved

Columbia University Press wishes to express its appreciation for assistance given by the Chiang Ching-kuo Foundation for International Scholarly Exchange and Council for Cultural Affairs in the publication of this series.

Library of Congress Cataloging-in-Publication Data
Zhong, Lihe, 1915–1960.
[Works. Selections. English]
From the old country : stories and sketches of China and Taiwan / Zhong Lihe;
edited and translated by T. M. McClellan; foreword by Zhong Tiejun.
pages cm. — (Modern Chinese Literature from Taiwan)
Includes bibliographical references.
ISBN 978-0-231-16630-0 (cloth : acid-free paper) — ISBN 978-0-231-53649-3 (e-book)
1. Chinese literature—20th century—Translations into English. I. McClellan,
T. M. (Thomas Michael) translator. II. Title.
PL2757.L5A2   2014
895.1′351—dc23
2013022554
∞

Columbia University Press books are printed on permanent and durable acid-free paper.
This book is printed on paper with recycled content.
Printed in the United States of America
c 10 9 8 7 6 5 4 3 2 1

JACKET ART: ZHONG SYUNWEN

References to websites (URLs) were accurate at the time of writing. Neither the author nor Columbia University Press is responsible for URLs that may have expired or changed since the manuscript was prepared.

CONTENTS

Foreword by Zhong Tiejun   vii
Sources, Translations, and Acknowledgments   xiii
Translator's Introduction   xvii

Part 1: Formative Years   1

1. My Grandma from the Mountains 假黎婆   3
2. First Love 初戀   17
3. From the Old Country 原鄉人   31

Part 2: Stories from the Old Country   45

4. In the Willow Shade 柳陰   47
5. Oleander 夾竹桃   63
6. The Fourth Day 第四日   109

Part 3: *Homeland*   129

7. Zugteuzong 竹頭庄   131
8. Forest Fire 山火   145
9. Uncle A-Huang 阿煌叔   159
10. My "Out-Law" and the Hill Songs 親家與山歌   171

Part 4: Meinong Lyrics   181

11. My Study 我的書齋   183

12. The Grassy Bank 草坡上　189

13. The Plow and the Sky 做田　197

14. The Little Ridge 小岡　201

Part 5: Meinong Economics　205

15. Swimming and Sinking 浮沉　207

16. Rain 雨　221

FOREWORD

The movie *China: My Native Land* (1980) was a biopic of my father, Zhong Lihe. Without an iron will, nobody could have persevered in his ideals from start to finish, against poverty and illness, as thoroughly as he did, as seen in the movie. My father was a writer who stuck to his principles and never ceased to plow the literary field. His final, fatal, attack of tuberculosis came while he was in the act of revising his newest literary work, so that he has been dubbed "a writer who died, pen in hand, in a pool of his own blood." The volume of short fiction, *Oleander*, printed in Peking in 1945, was the only book Zhong Lihe saw published in his lifetime; his only completed full-length novel, Songs of Bamboo Hat Hill, won Taiwan's top prize for long fiction in 1956; his other works include the four-part novella *Homeland*. The year 2009 saw the publication of the eight-volume *New Complete Works of Zhong Lihe*.

A literary vocation is an extremely hard career. For Zhong Lihe it was all the more so because his golden age as a writer coincided with the period in postwar Taiwan when anti-communist imperatives held sway. The true-to-life descriptions of the land, the people, everyday life, and various intricate social phenomena that dominated Zhong Lihe's works were pigeonholed as "nativist literature." Naturally, most of his work never saw the light of day; even more naturally, there was no question of his being able to live by his pen. However, Zhong Lihe always believed that true worth would out; good literature could not be allowed to languish in obscurity. And so it has proved! Half a century has gone by, and at last my father's high place in literary history has been confirmed. Here in Meinong, where Zhong Lihe lived and wrote and fell in love, the Zhong Lihe Memorial Institute, Taiwan's first such institution to be funded in the community, was built in 1983; and before long, Taiwan's first "Zhong Lihe" literary eco-park will also start to take shape here at the foot of "Bamboo Hat Hill."

It may be said that Zhong Lihe gave his life for his literature, but it has also been said that "it was Zhong Pingmei (Taimei) who brought out the literature in him," and "without Zhong Pingmei there would have been no literature." Zhong Lihe's wife, my mother Zhong Taimei, was the epitome of the virtuous woman: she adored her family, loved her husband, and was devoted to us children. She was friendly, meek, and warm toward others. During her husband's long, recurrent illnesses she steadfastly bore the brunt of family duties and family economics on her own slender shoulders. She could do the work of any man—even the arduous and dangerous job of illegal logging.[1] "Pingmei" (the name my father usually used for fictional portrayals of her) never questioned her fate and was surely a heroine among Hakka women. And now, it is extremely fitting that the bridge that links the Zhong Lihe Memorial Institute to the rest of the world has been rebuilt and renamed as "Pingmei Bridge," because in life and death Zhong Lihe and Zhong Taimei could never be separated by the swiftest of torrents or the widest of rivers.

On August 4, 1960, Zhong Lihe was in the act of carrying out revisions to his newly completed novella "Rain" when tuberculosis struck again. Coughing up blood, he collapsed onto his manuscript and died at the age of forty-four. To have lived such a short time on earth, yet to achieve such a lofty posthumous reputation must be due not only to the author's own noble and steadfast character, but even more to the truth, goodness, and beauty of human nature that his literature expresses, and to the honesty, detail, and warmth of his writing. When we read his work we sense an elegant melancholy, but no plaintiveness; it conveys a profoundly tolerant attitude to Heaven, to Fate, and to the harshness of Time. Throughout his writings we find rationalism coupled with ardor

---

1. See Zhong Lihe's story "Pin-jian fuqi" 貧賤夫妻 (1957-1959), translated as "Together Through Thick and Thin" by Shiao-ling Yu, in Joseph S. M. Lau, ed., *The Unbroken Chain: An Anthology of Taiwan Fiction Since 1926* (Bloomington: Indiana University Press, 1983), 57-67. If we read the story as recorded fact, as people generally do with Zhong Lihe's autobiographical fiction, it seems that Zhong Taimei, in despair at her family's poverty, on one occasion joined a gang of local people to fell and steal timber from the state-owned forests around the Zhong home. Unluckily, Forest Patrol officers discovered the gang's activities that day. Taimei avoided capture, but dropped her log and sustained cuts and bruises in the chase. She never went logging again.

and a fervent love of life. Even though Zhong's typical subjects were the most ordinary and humble of rural people living the harshest, most basic of lives, he shows how tenaciously they struggle with themselves, with poverty. In their unrelenting struggle readers may clearly sense the nobility and dignity of human nature. Opportunists and waverers carry no weight in his literature: he felt a mixture of sadness, pity, and disgust for characters such as Li Xinchang in "Swimming and Sinking." Zhong believed that human beings should live their lives with dignity, should fight for life. He revered those who lived courageously and conscientiously, and part of his reason for writing was to eulogize them. As society grows ever more utilitarian, Zhong Lihe's works appear all the more pure and moving.

The faithfulness with which Zhong Lihe's works record the social conditions of his times offers us many historical glimpses. For example, "My Grandma from the Mountains," "First Love," and "From the Old Country"—three stories of childhood and coming of age set in Gaoshu—depict Taiwan aboriginals, Hakkas, and Mainlanders, showing their differing special characteristics and customs. From his period in Mainland China, Zhong's stories "In the Willow Shade," "Oleander," and "The Fourth Day" emphasize the contrasting outlook and behavior of Koreans, Japanese, North Chinese, and people from Taiwan (or "the South") like himself. Then again, when Zhong Lihe returned to Kaohsiung in 1946, he revisited the homeland he had been missing for so many years. Both his father and his "grandma from the mountains" had died in 1943, and his brothers had gone their separate ways amid the family's failing fortunes. The result was that Zhong's four *Homeland* stories—"Zugteuzong," "Forest Fire," "Uncle A-Huang," and "My 'Out-Law' and the Hill Songs"—chronicle the heartbreaking poverty and dereliction of postwar Meinong, in particular the economic and ecological devastation of the drought years of the time.

The next phase of my father's life, his last ten years, was spent in unemployment, poverty, failing health, and an oppressive environment; any one of these things was enough to threaten to destroy him and his family. During these years he wrote "My Study," "The Grassy Bank," "The Plow and the Sky," "The Little Ridge," "Rain," and other works that record his observation of life and work in the homeland, together with his own experiences and emotional reactions.

For a book of Zhong Lihe's works to be appearing in English translation, we have Dr. Tommy McClellan and my eldest brother, Zhong Tiemin, to thank. In spite of Dr. McClellan's proficiency in Chinese, he needed help with many aspects of Hakka language and culture that appear in my father's works. In preparing to do the translation, he visited Taiwan several times, took part three times in the Bamboo Hat Hill Literary Seminar in order to delve deeply into Zhong Lihe's literary world (in 2006 contributing a lecture of his own to the seminar), and even spent ten weeks of the summer of 2010 living and working in the Zhong Lihe Memorial Institute itself. Through several years he met many times with Zhong Tiemin to ask linguistic, cultural, and geographical questions on the texts, and to thoroughly discuss literary aspects of my father's work. Only after these preparations did Dr. McClellan begin work on the translation. Through McClellan's meticulous, sensitive work, Zhong Lihe's writing may at last find a place in world literature.

Zhong Lihe was a lonely intellectual, an isolated writer. Most of his life was lived among family and neighbors in remote rural Taiwan who did not share his passion for literature and the realm of ideas. Even his eight years in Mainland China were largely spent among philistines, and his beloved wife and soul mate, my mother Zhong Taimei, was actually illiterate. Only in the last three and a half years of his life did Zhong finally find a group of intellectual friends and equals to belong to. After his novel *Songs of Bamboo Hat Hill* won Taiwan's top prize for long fiction in 1956 he was invited by Zhong Zhaozheng (no relation) to participate in launching a literature circular entitled *Literary Friends Bulletin*. Although he never met most of the "Literary Friends" in person, not even Zhong Zhaozheng himself, the *Bulletin* and the extensive letter correspondence it generated were enormously important to Zhong. Finally he felt connected to a group of brother writers who validated his long, lonely years of literary struggle.

Zhong Lihe was physically isolated from his *Bulletin* friends, who were almost all resident in urban North Taiwan, but their appreciation and acceptance of him and his work gave him an enormous boost. Now Tommy McClellan, although separated from Zhong Lihe by very large distances in space and time and language, is another kind of "literary friend," of whom I feel my father would have been very glad.

Zhong Tiejun
Meinong, Taiwan

SOURCES, TRANSLATIONS, AND ACKNOWLEDGMENTS

All footnotes are the translator's notes unless otherwise indicated.

Zhong Lihe has the distinction of being the first Taiwan writer to have a "complete works" published, in 1976, and he now also has the most such collections. I have used all three "complete works of Zhong Lihe," listed below, as well as the transcriptions and manuscripts available in the Zhong Lihe Shuwei Bowuguan 鍾理和數位博物館 (Zhong Lihe Digital Museum, http://cls.hs.yzu.edu.tw/zhonglihe/home.asp—accessed Oct. 10, 2012). In the present volume I take the 2009 *New Complete Works* as my standard. In a very few places I have preferred details from the second *Complete Works* (II) or other versions, and I have noted significant discrepancies where they occur. The most significant deviations from *New Complete Works* concern "Oleander" and "My 'Out-Law' and the Hill Songs." Separate notes on these deviations appear in each of the respective translations.

Complete Works (I)	*Zhong Lihe quanji* 鍾理和全集 (Complete works of Zhong Lihe). Ed. Zhang Liangze 張良澤. 8 vols. Taibei: Yuanxing 遠行, 1976.
Complete Works (II)	*Zhong Lihe quanji* 鍾理和全集 (Complete works of Zhong Lihe). Ed. Zhong Tiemin 鍾鐵民. 6 vols. Gaoxiong/Meinong: Chunhui 春輝 / Caituanfaren Zhong Lihe wenjiao jijinhui 財團法人鍾理和文教基金會, 1997; repr. 2003.
New Complete Works	*Xin ban Zhong Lihe quanji* 新版鍾理和全集 (Complete works of Zhong Lihe: New edition). Ed. Zhong Yiyan 鍾怡彥. 8 vols. (Gaoxiong) Gangshan [高雄縣崗山鎮]: Gaoxiong xian zhengfu, 2009.

Of the stories included in the present volume, two have previously been published in my English translation. I am most grateful to the editors of *Edinburgh Review* for granting permission to republish "From the Old Country" here. The version that appeared in *Edinburgh Review* 124 (2008):53–68, under the title "Old Country Folk," was based on the *Complete Works* (II) "original" and has been substantially revised according to *New Complete Works* for inclusion in this volume. I am equally grateful for the same reason to the editors of *Renditions: A Chinese-English Translation Magazine*. The translation of "The Fourth Day" appearing here has required only trivial improvements on that printed in *Renditions* 72 (Autumn 2009): 71–93. My thanks also go to the editors and staff of both magazines for their work on the previously published versions.

Before I sent the manuscript of this volume to Columbia University Press I was honored to receive a promise from Zhong Tiemin, Zhong Lihe's eldest son and a distinguished writer of fiction and essays in his own right, to contribute a preface. Sadly, Zhong Tiemin died on August 22, 2011, at the age of seventy. On many occasions since I first met him in Meinong in 2004, Mr. Zhong provided me with an enormous amount of detailed information and a great deal of encouragement in my research on his father's life and work. He and his wife, his brother, and his sister-in-law (Mr. and Mrs. Zhong Tiejun), and his daughters have frequently been personally kind as well as practically helpful. (Here I must also express my gratitude to the staff of the Zhong Lihe Memorial Institute 鍾理和紀念館, particularly Ms. Huang Huiming, for similar kindness and assistance over the years.)

Meinong misses Zhong Tiemin. I like to think that my completion of these translations gave him some satisfaction; that the prospect of a first volume of Zhong Lihe's fiction published in English was for him another piece in the jigsaw preserving and promoting his father's literary legacy, which he took as a hugely important part of his own life's work.

I am delighted that Zhong Lihe's third and only surviving son, Zhong Tiejun, has stepped into the breach and provided a preface of as high a quality as I would have expected from his brother.

I am extremely glad to be able to include cover art and illustrations done by Zhong Tiemin's third daughter, Zhong Shunwen, a professional painter, illustrator, and photographer and also an outstanding blogger (see "小百合之印象盒子," http://blog.roodo.com/gjp4jp6). All of the illustrations were previously published in *New Complete Works*, except the cover art, which was done specially for this volume.

My thanks are due to Helen Parker of the University of Edinburgh and Yu-ling Chen for their help with the transliteration of Japanese terms. Yu-ling also read and commented on some of the draft translations. Bonnie S. McDougall provided me with meticulous and extremely helpful feedback on the entire second draft, of the type that she has most generously provided me many times over a number of years. I am also very grateful to the anonymous readers for their positive feedback and careful corrections and suggestions.

I list here all previously published English translations from Zhong Lihe of which I am aware. In selecting the stories and essays for this volume I have avoided these, except for "Bamboo-Root Village"/"Zugteuzong," where I felt a new translation was justified in order to present a unified English version of *Homeland*.

"Bamboo-Root Village" ("Zugteuzong" in the present volume). Trans. John Balcom. *Taiwan Literature: English Translation Series* 21 (July 2007): 21-34. [竹頭莊]

"Restored to Life." Trans. Timothy Ross. *The Chinese Pen* (Spring 1977): 54-70. [復活]

"Returning to My Home Village." Trans. John Balcom. *Taiwan Literature: English Translation Series* 21 (July 2007): 35-40. [還鄉記]

"The Tobacco Shed." Trans. Timothy Ross. *The Chinese Pen* (Spring 1978): 91-105. [煙樓]

"Together Through Thick and Thin." Trans. Shiao-ling Yu. In Joseph S. M. Lau, ed., *The Unbroken Chain: An Anthology of Taiwan Fiction Since 1926*, 57-67. Bloomington: Indiana University Press, 1983. [貧賤夫妻]

FURTHER READING

McClellan, T. M. "Home and the Land: The 'Native' Fiction of Zhong Lihe." *Journal of Modern Literature in Chinese* 9.2 (Dec. 2009): 154-182.

Ying, Fenghuang. "The Literary Development of Zhong Lihe and Postcolonial Discourse in Taiwan." In David Der-wei Wang and Carlos Rojas, eds., *Writing Taiwan: A New Literary History*, 140–155. Durham: Duke University Press, 2007.

Zhong Tiemin 鍾鐵民, ed. *Exploring a Literary Landscape: The Zhong Lihe Memorial Institute and Its Environs* 探訪鍾理和紀念館暨文學地景. Gaoxiong: Chunhui, 2010.

TRANSLATOR'S INTRODUCTION

Zhong Lihe (1915–1960) lived the first thirty years of his life as a citizen of the expanding Japanese Empire: mostly in his native South Taiwan, but also, for nearly eight years, in Manchukuo and Peking.[1] Zhong was the third of seven sons (by two concurrent wives) of a prominent local landowner and entrepreneur and grew up in comfort in a small village in his native Gaoshu township (Pingtung county), where he received a good Sino-Japanese education up to the age of sixteen. From 1932 he worked on his father's latest venture, a coffee and fruit estate at Jianshan 尖山,[2] Meinong district, Kaohsiung, where he fell in love with one of the day laborers, Zhong Taimei 鍾台妹. The ancient Chinese taboo against same-surname marriage was already much less prevalent elsewhere, but remained very strong in rural Hakka Taiwan, so that the couple's families, especially Zhong Lihe's father, vehemently opposed their wish to marry. Eventually they were obliged to elope to Manchukuo in 1940, Zhong Lihe having first gone there alone in 1938 to establish a livelihood. In 1941 they moved to Peking.

By the time the Zhongs returned to Taiwan in spring 1946, after years of struggle with poverty and the bare beginnings of Zhong's career as a writer, they had a five-year-old son, Tiemin 鐵民, born in Shenyang,[3] whose congenital good health seemed to vindicate Zhong Lihe's modern romantic and scientific principles. Although they had also had an infant death in Peking, they went on to have four more healthy children between 1946 and 1958. However, Zhong Lihe contracted pulmonary tuberculosis soon before or after returning to Taiwan, where they had received a one-seventh portion of the family's greatly diminished property.[4] Zhong spent three years in a Taipei sanatorium, returning home to Meinong in October 1950 after radical, life-threatening surgery as well as treatment with the new antibiotics. Earlier the same year nine-year-old Tiemin had contracted tuberculosis of the spine, which left him permanently disabled. The difficulties and sadnesses of the Zhongs' devoted marriage reached a tragic climax in 1954 with the death of their seven-year-old second son, Limin 立民, of a sudden, acute bronchitis, which had been denied effective and timely treatment by the family's unrelenting poverty and the inaccessibility of their home at Jianshan.

Zhong Lihe made great sacrifices to establish the basis for marriage to Taimei, and was the family breadwinner for a time in Mukden and Peking, working as a commercial driver and as a civil service interpreter. The latter job was even shorter-lived than the former, however, and from then (about 1941-1942) until his death Zhong increasingly depended on Taimei to support the family, while he devoted himself to literature. His few months as a temporary Mandarin teacher at a community middle school in Pingtung in 1946, cut short by the onset of TB, was the only time that he appeared to have prospects of forging a career in the intellectual field. During the fourteen years and four months of his life after returning to Taiwan, Zhong's only regular contributions to family monetary income were provided by that brief stint as a teacher plus two or three months of clerking at Meinong Town Hall in 1952 and another clerical job in a paralegal firm, which he managed to hold down from February 1957 to December 1958. He was forced to resign from both clerical jobs because of ill health. It appears almost needless to say that in his whole life he earned next to nothing from his literary work.

Zhong had begun writing fiction and other prose in earnest in 1938 and had financed the publication of a volume of fiction in Peking in 1945.[5] Apart from the contents of that book, before 1950 Zhong had completed only one further novella, four more short stories, and two essays, of which only two short stories and one essay had made it into print. After falling ill and being forced to quit the teaching job in Pingtung, Zhong wrote almost nothing, apart from a substantial diary, during the three whole years 1947-1949. However, during his last months in the Songshan Sanatorium, May to October 1950, he at last began to create some of his most important literary works.

Up to 1950, then, Zhong Lihe's literary output and record of publication had been very meager. Reasons for this may include the difficult conditions imposed by exile, poverty, and ill health. Another important factor was Zhong's linguistic background as a Hakka Chinese in Japanese Taiwan. His native Hakka has no standard written form of its own, and Zhong was formally educated to read and write Japanese and less formally taught to read a dead language: classical Chinese.

> At school I studied [in] Japanese, and during the period immediately after my school years I also encountered little but Japanese.... My Chinese (I should say my *baihua* 白話) was self-taught using Hakka pronunciation. These were the reasons for a great deal of unnecessary pain later on in my writing; they made my words stiff and disjointed on the page. In my first efforts at writing literature, even as I held my pen I would be mentally composing the first draft in Japanese, which I would translate into Chinese before transcribing. Japanese grammar and Chinese in Hakka pronunciation, these were my two great enemies.[6]

The Chinese of Taiwan (that is, the 95 percent and more of the population who were of Han Chinese extraction, including the Hakka) were largely excluded from the New Literature being created in mainland China from the mid to late 1910s in modernized *baihua* 白話 (vernacular Chinese based on Mandarin). Taiwan's own New Culture Movement of the 1920s emulated the developments on the Mainland, but was discouraged by the Japanese authorities, and there were few native examples for Zhong Lihe to learn from. He began teaching himself to read and write the older form of *baihua* from Chinese novels that predated the May Fourth Movement until he had the opportunity to encounter the latter in the 1930s:

> At the time, in the wake of the May Fourth Movement, the New Literature was surging forward like a mighty river, and collections of works by Lu Xun, Mao Dun, Ba Jin, Bingxin, and others were also available in Taiwan. I couldn't get enough of these books, and could hardly put them down.
>
> *(Letter to Liao Qingxiu* 廖清秀, *10/30/1957)*

Inevitably, Zhong Lihe's self-education in modern written Chinese, as well as in literary technique and style, was slow. His early work was painfully created, and it was not until 1950 that his literary voice appears to have fully matured. He finally became prolific in the last decade of his life, a decade he might not have seen without surgery at Songshan, and began to produce work of the highest quality. However, for most of the 1950s Zhong still had only rare success in submitting his work for publication, and only the last two or three years of his life saw a relatively large number of his short stories and essays published, including eighteen in *Lianhe bao fukan* 《聯合報》副刊 (United Daily News literary supplement), then one of the world's leading fora for literature in Chinese, in 1959 and 1960 (including one story that was being serialized at the time of his death). Zhong's only completed full-length novel, *Lishan nongchang* 笠山農場 (Bamboo hat hill farm), won the top Republic of China (Taiwan) prize for long fiction in 1956, but remained unpublished at his death. On August 4, 1960, Zhong Lihe was at home in Meinong working on revisions to a new novella, "Yu" 雨 (Rain), when he coughed up blood and died in its pool on the manuscript.

From the Old Country: Stories and Sketches of China and Taiwan is intended not only to present a selection of the best of Zhong Lihe's literary work but also to represent his life and times. The circumstances and events Zhong witnessed in his native Taiwan, in Manchuria, and in North China during and after Japanese rule invest his fiction with considerable documentary interest to anyone seeking insights into the turbulent and complex history of East Asia in the 1930s, 1940s, and 1950s. Therefore the selections have been arranged in chronological order according to their content's relevance to the author's life.[7]

Part I below begins with the story of early childhood "My Grandma from the Mountains" which, like "First Love" and "From the Old Country," is set in Zhong Lihe's native Pingtung. Unlike the second and third selections, however, "My Grandma" goes beyond the village and its immediate environs into the hills above it to the east. The importance of this landscape to Zhong Lihe may be seen in the record of his participation, at the age of twenty-one, in an expedition to the summit of North Mount Dawu (3,092 m.), the last 3,000-meter-plus peak at the southern end of Taiwan's Central Mountain Range. This travelogue begins:

I was born and brought up at the foot of Mount Dawu. From infancy to adulthood, the mountain was my constant companion. Its majesty and its legend wove themselves, lovely and exquisite like silken yarn, into the fabric of my childhood. I brimmed with longing and yearning for the mountain. It towered above the village; wherever you were you only had to look up or turn your head to see it gazing down on you. It was an eternal presence, and seemed to be watching us closely every moment, like a loving mother watching her grown child's business. It was our guardian angel.[8]

The importance of physical environment is quite evident in Zhong Lihe's literature, as we shall see, but in "My Grandma" the human element turns out to be even more important than the topographical. The story is about "A-He"'s personal relationship with his step-grandmother, and also about her special status as a member of the Paiwan "mountain people." The I-narrator A-He's childish perspective—Zhong Lihe's representation of his own innocence as a very young child[9]—shows the ignorance of Han Chinese toward aboriginal ways, lending them a mystic and slightly frightening quality. In particular, it is Grandma's singing of unfamiliar songs in her own language that spooks A-He. She sings apparently in celebration of the mountains of her people, as she and A-He walk further and further into them. When he bursts out crying at the strangeness of everything, she appears hurt and uncomprehending. In the end Grandma is just Grandma, and the bond of love between her and her little grandson is touchingly evoked, but there is also a sense that Grandma is obliged to deny her own culture in order to keep peace in her husband's family. "My Grandma from the Mountains" was one of the first of Zhong Lihe's works to appear in Taiwan school textbooks after 2000. No doubt it was selected not only for the central theme of grandparental love, but also as an expression of the multiculturalism that gained currency in Taiwan from the start of the first non-Kuomintang administration in that year.

On account of its frank, though innocent, description of the female form as seen by teenage boys, "First Love" would be less likely to feature in a schoolbook. Latent eroticism from the start of the story turns to more direct eroticism after A-He's "avowal," which amounts to no more than his saying "Chunmei's quite good-looking, I suppose?"

to his friends. The I-narrator appears utterly innocent of any smutty thought about the young woman he admires. His mild obsession with her begins with her appearance among the many human subjects for his sketches, and it is only a friend's teasing that alerts him to the possibility that her breasts may be somewhat out of the ordinary. Observing her again at the next opportunity, he is relieved to find that his favorite model is buxom, yes, but still proportioned within his acceptable aesthetic standards.

The action of this story mainly takes place in the author-narrator's native village, but like "My Grandma" it is made more vivid by a passage set amid distinctive scenery (just) outside the village: "the river flats, where maidengrass grew among the boulders." Like many rivers in Taiwan, the one that flows past Zhong Lihe's native village in Pingtung takes the form, outside of the rainy season, of a very wide, sandy, and stony flood channel with the river stream in the middle. In Zhong Lihe's stories young people come to the river flats to hang out together—swimming, paddling, catching frogs or crickets, or just lazing around on the boulders. It is a perfect arena for the teenage boys in "First Love" to gather and express their newfound sexuality in music, banter, and bragging.

It is no coincidence that singing features in the first two stories of this collection. Music plays a significant role in five of the sixteen pieces collected here, and a less significant role in a further two. Zhong Lihe was very interested in folk song: he collected the lyrics of two hundred and twenty-two of the local *shan'ge* 山歌 (hill songs), which appear in volume eight of *New Complete Works* along with a few tunes in his own notation. Zhong left no indication as to whether he simply recorded those two hundred and twenty-two songs, or whether he adapted any or all of them in any way. The songs that appear in "First Love" and elsewhere in his literature are not included in those two hundred and twenty-two and are assumed to be his own compositions, presented as extempore expressions of the singers' emotions.

Zhong appears to have adopted the *shan'ge* as a natural and genuine artform of the people. The narrator of "First Love" considers these "rustic folk songs" not to be "fine" or "remarkable." A character in another story is much more assertive of the cultural value of folk song:

"[Park] believed that in any country the best and most direct reflection of life—especially the moral life of the two sexes—was the folk song" (see "In the Willow Shade"). Perhaps the local flavor of the *shan'ge* particularly appealed to Zhong as suiting his literary project, because although *shan'ge* of various forms are widespread throughout rural China and Taiwan, Zhong's Hakka people, particularly in Meinong, consider their local form of *shan'ge*[10] to be among the most distinctive and attractive features of their culture, alongside *lanshan* 藍衫 dresses (see "Zugteuzong" and "Rain"), oilpaper umbrellas, and water buffalo.

"First Love" approaches its subject with lighthearted sexually suggestive humor and straightforward realism; the use of *shan'ge* allows Zhong to express with greatest pathos the emotional pain and yearning of the boys. At the same time, the everyday setting of the river flats, the homemade *huqin* fiddle, and the smutty talk prevent the story becoming sentimental.

The third and last story under the heading "Formative Years" begins with the I-narrator in early childhood, as in "My Grandma." By the end he is already a young adult, setting off to explore Mainland China. This I-narrator of "From the Old Country" appears to be the same autobiographical character as in the first two stories, although the name A-He does not appear here. In fact "Old Country" is even more strongly autobiographical than those two stories. Zhong Lihe blamed this for the story's failure with several journals to which he submitted it. "It can't be considered fiction," he wrote to fellow writer and friend Liao Qingxiu on October 2, 1959. "At most it's fictionalized autobiography, which is precisely why [*The United Daily News*] rejected it."

"From the Old Country" never did make it into print during the author's lifetime, but it has eventually become perhaps his most famous work of all. Oddly, it seems to owe that fame to certain manipulations and oversimplifications of what it actually contains.

The first part of "From the Old Country" (sections 1–2) is told from the perspective of the narrator in early childhood. The child's naïve questions and puzzlement at the answers are humorous, but also make the adult reader feel that no wonder the child is confused. Starting with "Who are Old Country people?" and "Where is the Old Country? Is it very far?", and touching on such burning issues as whether his family ever ate dog meat like "all Old Country people," in simple terms the child's central question is "Where do we come from?" But there seems to be nothing simple about the answers.

Moving from later childhood into adolescence, the narrator encounters first the hostile, contemptuous views of his Japanese teachers toward "Shina," second his father and other villagers' mixture of pride, shame, and disillusionment regarding "the Old Country," and third his favorite (half-)brother's ardent passion for "the Mainland, the fatherland."

With regard to autobiography, it is the characterization of the narrator's brother's attitude to China that is of the greatest interest here. In real life Zhong Heming 和鳴, who is clearly meant here, was indeed the most active Chinese patriot among the seven Zhong brothers. "Old Country"'s account of his leaving for the Mainland refers to Heming's risky 1940 adventure—he and his new bride, together with a cousin and another couple, took a route forbidden to them as Japanese citizens in order to join the anti-Japanese resistance in Canton province. On arrival the five young Taiwan Hakka intellectuals were suspected by the Kuomintang guerrillas of being Japanese spies and narrowly avoided execution. After months under arrest they were exonerated and then recruited, and spent the rest of the war doing paramedical, educational, propaganda, and other support work. Heming, who assumed the *nom de guerre* Haodong 浩東 while in China, became secretly associated with left-wing groups within the Resistance. After the war he was appointed headmaster of Keelung High School, and after the 228 Incident[11] he joined the (illegal) Chinese Communist Party and turned the school into one of the most important centers of Red organization in Taiwan. In October 1950, at the height of Taiwan's White Terror, Zhong Haodong/Heming was executed after more than a year in prison.[12]

Although Heming/Haodong appears in the Chinese original of "From the Old Country" only as "Third Elder Brother,"[13] it was courageous of Zhong Lihe to give him such a prominent role in the story, one based closely on the facts, during that period of suppression of communists. When "Third Elder Brother" returns from his first trip to the Mainland, the narrator's response is not a political or patriotic one, but a cultural reaction to the gramophone recordings and postcards Heming brings home with him: "these arias, together with those enchanting views of famous places, stimulated my imagination enormously and deepened my longing for the land across the Strait." Later, describing a political meeting apparently organized by Heming, the narrator lists a number of terms or slogans mentioned at the meeting, and comments: "I'd never been interested in these terms, and so I understood little of what I heard."

Zhong Lihe and Zhong Heming, half-brothers almost identical in age, were the firmest of friends. The fictional characterization of the latter in "From the Old Country" suggests a protective elder brother, although Lihe was in fact slightly older than Heming, and in his autobiographical writings Zhong Lihe mentions Heming as an important influence on his early development as a writer. Having succeeded where Lihe failed in advancing beyond (upper) elementary education, Heming encouraged his early efforts and sent him literature from high school in Kaohsiung city and from university in Japan during the mid-1930s. However, "From the Old Country" reveals fundamental differences between the brothers in their attitude to China: Heming's main concerns were political, while Lihe's were cultural. Both brothers went to the Mainland, in 1938 (Lihe, for the first time) and 1940 (Heming, for his only lengthy visit). Heming went to seek out Chinese forces engaging the Japanese in guerrilla warfare. Lihe went to Manchukuo and later Peking, far behind Japanese lines, seeking elements of Chinese culture that survived beneath the international conflict. In part 2 of this book we may see something of what he found.

We should not, however, expect some variation on *Patriot's Progress*, because "From the Old Country" has revealed great depths of ambiguity in Zhong Lihe's attitude to China. Through a child's eyes Zhong has exposed some of the absurdity for many Taiwan people of seeking identification with "the Old Country," but equally the impossibility of clearly distinguishing a Taiwan ethnicity from that (or those) of the Mainland; he also shows the conflicted attitudes of his father's generation—a mixture of reverence and disdain toward the land of their ancestors; and he even distances himself from his own dearly beloved brother's Chinese nationalist politics. He appears to remain a cultural patriot of sorts, and his longing for personal understanding of his Chinese roots remains alive at the end of the story, which announces his departure for the Mainland. Here, the words "I am not a patriot" may be a case of protesting too much, but they must not be ignored because those that follow appear to confirm a certain reluctance: "I am not a patriot, but Old Country blood must flow back to the Old Country before it can stop seething! So it was with my brother, and nor could[14] I be any exception." In context and quoted in full, these last two sentences of "From the Old Country" express cynicism about China and about patriotism, but they also acknowledge that because Zhong's Chinese blood still seethed with desire for knowledge of what China meant to him, he *could not but* go and see for himself, somehow reluctantly, and even though he was not a political nationalist like his brother.

Part 2 of this book is the "CJK" chapter of our selection from Zhong Lihe's fiction, each of its stories in turn dealing with life's difficulties for groups of Koreans, Chinese, and Japanese, respectively. The three stories, written between 1938 and 1945, are among Zhong's earliest works; that is to say, their earliest versions predate all the other selections in this volume. These translations, however, follow the author's revised versions, done at various known, unknown, or imprecisely known times between 1945 and 1959.[15]

"In the Willow Shade" is a simple story told by an I-narrator who does not have much involvement in the main plot and whose name (Zhong) and place of origin (Taiwan) are mentioned very much in passing. The story itself concerns two of "Zhong"'s Korean friends, classmates in the Manchuria Automobile School in Shenyang where all three are learning driving and motor maintenance in hope of finding lucrative employment in that rapidly developing industrial city. At the time of writing the first version of this story Zhong Lihe was enrolled in a driving school in Shenyang, and his ambition to find a livelihood as a driver was intimately connected with his plan to marry or elope with Zhong Taimei and start a new life with her on the Mainland. Remarkably, he keeps the anxiety and emotion that he must have been feeling almost completely out of this story, by telling instead two separate tales of trouble in love, marriage, and career. Park says of Kim: "He's a sacrificial victim of the [Korean] system of early marriage and arranged marriage." In reality this is true of both Park and Lim, but in different ways. Park is from a "comfortably-off family" and is a closer friend to Zhong because they share a similar educational background and interests, especially literature. But Zhong finds it difficult to understand why Park is so passive regarding his unhappy separation from his childhood sweetheart. When Park finally does act, quite suddenly, he puts his livelihood in jeopardy and the outcome appears very uncertain, because although he has graduated from driving school, he leaves without waiting for the issue of his license. The narrator appears on the one hand to approve of Park following his heart, but on the other to be very worried about his friend's prospects in a world where money is everything.

"Willow Shade" has a very strong theme, common to much of Zhong Lihe's work, of the ultimate importance of economic factors on individual and family life, which is most tellingly shown in the story of the other Korean. Kim is from a poorer background than Park, and is further burdened by an arranged marriage that made him a father by the age of fifteen. He is forced to quit driving school because he and his wife and daughter are almost starving to pay the fees. Ever optimistic and resourceful, he embarks on a new livelihood selling ice popsicles, but as autumn turns to winter he is unable to find new work and eventually leaves Shenyang, apparently to return to Korea. When he goes he has to give some bedding in lieu of the final rent to his Japanese landlady, a kindly old soul who has a very high opinion of Kim but whose own hand-to-mouth existence does not allow her to waive the rent.

Japanese people feature rarely in Zhong Lihe's work, in spite of so much of it being set within the broader Japanese Empire. The little cameo of the Japanese landlady at the very end of "Willow Shade" reinforces the story's theme of the extremely precarious economic situation of all sorts of ordinary people, be they from Taiwan, Korea, or even Japan herself. The result is that the compassion the story embodies toward people facing difficulties in their romantic and economic lives is extended universally, regardless of race or nationality.

No Japanese (or Koreans) appear in the novella "Oleander," even though the action is explicitly identified as taking place during the Sino-Japanese conflict, approximately between 1942 and 1944; all the characters are Chinese, and apart from the Zeng family, which is from South China, all are from Peking and its environs. Not only does "Oleander" confine itself to Chinese characters in the setting of the once and future Chinese capital, but the narrative actually focuses quite explicitly on problems of the Chinese race. Words like "race," "nation," and "people" occur several times in the novella, always in a negative or sarcastic sense. These negative utterances are usually put in the mouth of the southerner, Zeng Simian, and may be an expression of Zhong Lihe's own disillusionment at what he found when he came to live in what he had imagined as his own cultural heartland—"the Old Country." Perhaps what he found was not so different from the crude racist propaganda of his Japanese teachers, for it turns out that the "Shina jin" (Chinamen) of "Oleander" are indeed "opium addicts and a shameless, filthy race," among other unpleasant things. Then again, this novella dwells at great length on the crushing poverty that afflicts most of the families who inhabit the three courtyards of their typical Peking tenement dwelling. The moral shortcomings of these families are described mercilessly, but their almost impossible economic situation still invites compassion.

"The Fourth Day," written in late 1945, is very unusual in Zhong Lihe's opus. Not only is it not in the least autobiographical, but its single-viewpoint character is Japanese, as are all but one of the other characters. In the rest of Zhong Lihe's entire literary output none of the main characters are Japanese. Told from the perspective of Komatsu, a junior functionary, this longish story imagines the experiences of Japanese residents of North China immediately after the surrender of August 15, 1945. In spite of concerning itself almost exclusively with Japanese people, this work does share some of the representative themes and concerns of Zhong Lihe's literature. "The Fourth Day" deconstructs Japan's nationalist-militarist myth, demonizing it in the figure and actions of one central negative character. For the rest of the large group of Japanese characters, on the fourth day after their emperor's surrender, "war" and "nation" have suddenly become irrelevant. This is a huge relief to them, but also a source of great confusion and insecurity about the recent past and the immediate future:

> The people had lost interest in the war, and a general wish had crept silently into their consciousness: the hope that the war would soon end! ... now they should be allowed to think of their own personal affairs.

The positive characters, chiefly the central character, Komatsu, and his friends, are just ordinary folk, much like their Chinese and Taiwan counterparts in Zhong Lihe's other stories. Suzuki, for instance, is a big, strapping soldier whose army cap has been so constantly on his head that the forehead beneath is snowy white compared to his sunburned face. Surprisingly, it turns out he had been a violinist in a dance band before the war, but he announces near the end of the story that he has decided not to go back to that, but instead to seek factory work more suitable to his big hands. Suzuki embodies most of the Japanese whom Komatsu observes: drilled for years to think and talk of nothing but war and nation, and stunned by the abrupt reversion to the sole concern of "personal affairs."

Variations on phrases like *shanliang de renmen* 善良的人們, which I translate here as "good and honest folk," appear frequently enough in Zhong Lihe's works to suggest that a concept of "simple goodness" was important to the author's ideal of humanity. Although this conception is most closely associated with the Hakka peasantry of Zhong's native South Taiwan, "The Fourth Day" is another story that shows that this notion was applicable to other classes and even other nations, even though no such similar phrase actually appears in this story.

"The Fourth Day" also shows considerable compassion toward the Japanese in defeat. One might have expected a person from Taiwan to be more concerned with China's victory and the retrocession of Taiwan to Chiang Kai-shek's Kuomintang regime. Yet perhaps it is not so surprising that Zhong Lihe empathized with Komatsu and his friends. In some nonfiction writings of 1945-1946 he expresses indignation at the fact that Taiwan residents of the Mainland were treated in the same way as Japanese and Koreans by the victorious Chinese government: their assets to be confiscated, their persons to be repatriated. It is not at all certain that Zhong Lihe planned, in 1945, to return to Taiwan, as he still felt that he and his wife would not be accepted at home, for the same reason that they left in the first place.

Treated by his own fellow "Old Country people" as if he were part of the defeated occupying forces, Zhong Lihe decided, or was forced, to join the repatriation to Taiwan in March–April 1946. The family did not at first go back to Meinong, but stayed with one of Zhong's younger brothers, Zhong Lizhi 里志, not far away in Taiwan's second city,

Kaohsiung. Then came the job as a Mandarin teacher, cut short within a few months by the onset of Zhong's tuberculosis. His unfitness for work forced him to settle his family (now with a new baby boy, Limin) at Jianshan, and then to go to Taipei for extended treatment, from October 1947. Turbulent events (Zhong was undergoing assessment in Taiwan University Hospital, Taipei, in February–March 1947 and so witnessed part of the carnage of the 228 Incident), illness, and a gruelling treatment regime resulted in Zhong writing almost nothing in the years 1947–1949. When he began again in earnest in 1950 it was to work on a set of four short stories—*Homeland* (Guxiang 故鄉)—that arguably present the quintessential Zhong Lihe.

Three of the stories of *Homeland* were written in 1950, the first at Songshan while Zhong was being prepared for the surgical removal of six ribs and part of a lung. The success of the two operations, for which his doctors gave him only a fifty-fifty chance of survival, may have given Zhong an extra ten years of life. After five years of near-stagnation in his literary career, *Homeland* was a hugely significant relaunch. Although the four stories failed to find a publisher during the author's lifetime, this probably shows that they are among the most undeserved victims of Taiwan's postwar obsession with "conflict literature," that is, anti-Japanese and anti-Communist writing.[16] Their literary quality and importance is now widely acknowledged.

"Zugteuzong," the first of the *Homeland* stories, is strongly reminiscent of "Guxiang" 故鄉 ("My Old Home," 1921) by Lu Xun, whose strong influence on Zhong Lihe is clear in many of his works and explicit in some of his diaries and letters. The equally autobiographical narrators of the two stories are both returning to their native places after many years, and the pivotal idea in each story is the fond recollection of a friend in earlier life, followed by sadness at the discovery of his present benighted state and the gulf between him and the narrator in the present. Each story contains more than this common thread, but Lu Xun's professed custom of adding optimistic "innuendoes" (*qubi* 曲筆)[17]—in "My Old Home" the innocence of the younger generation represented by the narrator's nephew and his childhood friend Runtu's son—is absent in "Zugteuzong." In the latter the superstitious fatalism of the locals on the train is not brightened by any ray of hope. On the contrary, the devastation of drought is even surpassed in melancholy by the physical and spiritual decline of the narrator's friend Bingwen, a former "literary youth."

The fictional action of *Homeland* is supposed to take place over a short period after the autobiographical narrator A-He's return to Meinong in spring 1946. The main focus throughout is on various aspects of economic difficulty being suffered by the district and the individuals who inhabit it. Much of this economic difficulty is specific to time and place: Bingwen's unemployment is symptomatic of the changing times; the local people's complaints are based in the real-life successive floods and droughts in Taiwan in 1945–1946; poverty is everywhere, represented by the dietary reliance on sweet potatoes, and many families are actually starving.

A more general and ancient trend, superstition, compounds the problems, as people prefer to spend money, even in these hard times, on rededicating the Taoist temples prohibited under Japanese rule, and on extravagant worship. Worse than that, ignorance and superstition cause "these apparently simple, good, and honest folk ... [to set] their own hills on fire." Paradoxically, in "Forest Fire," the narrator's elder brother, representing a local gentry that is better educated and more modernized than the general peasantry, rages against the latter's ignorance and superstition one day, but takes pride in the lavishness of his temple sacrifice the next.

"Uncle A-Huang" and "My 'Out-Law' and the Hill Songs" also take perennial and general problems as their focus. The failure of the middle-aged A-Huang, once one of the most respected, hard-working young farmhands in the district, to provide for his family, or even to maintain a scrap of human dignity, suggests a fundamental problem in the economy: "If it is just as A-Huang said—'the more we work the poorer we get'—then what is to become of our world?"

Homeland's catalogue of deterioration and stultification is leavened with affectionate portrayals of "good and honest folk" and descriptions of rural beauty. These dominate in "My 'Out-Law' and the Hill Songs," the mildly melancholic conclusion of which is that even a rural idyll such as Meinong cannot escape change, but hope is still to be found in youth, friendship, family, and local culture. Approaching middle age, A-He, his wife, and their old friend Yuxiang realize that almost nothing remains of the youth they shared. Their old friends, especially the women, are physically changed out of all recognition by poverty, procreation, and domestic violence. Yet A-He and Yuxiang's own families appear relatively lucky in spite of their heterodox origins. The story does not refer to the same-surname marriage taboo, but here, plainly, are Zhong Lihe and Zhong Taimei in fictionalized form, apparently happy together and with a healthy five-year-old son. Yuxiang's family began with an affair with a widowed mother of one, who conceived a second child while Yuxiang was away with the Japanese army in the Philippines. From these unpromising beginnings Yuxiang seems to have established a stable family life. He has by now fathered two children of his own, but his greatest joy or comfort is his stepchild, a fine, sturdy boy already able to help him in his work as a carter.

The nostalgic mood of "Out-Law" is encapsulated in its eponymous hill songs: "Amid all the change and upheaval, perhaps this was the only unchanging thing I could find." But there is more than nostalgia here: in the story the songs are explicitly associated with the young people who sing them, young women in particular, and although the songs are old-fashioned and unchanging—representing hope for the preservation of local culture—they also suggest that youth, love, and sex must endure as forces for the future.

> When the time came, the decrepit, the ugly, and the sick would fall, so that the young, the strong, the healthy, and the well-formed could grow: like saplings under a rotten, fallen tree, they would supplant what had gone before.

As its title suggests, part 4 of this collection presents four lyrical evocations of Zhong Lihe's life at Jianshan in the 1950s. As such, these sketches largely speak for themselves. "My Study" is at once a lighthearted complaint about the author's impoverished situation and a rhapsody on the glories of nature and the mythic beauty of rural life that surrounded him. "The Grassy Bank," which appears in one of the short-fiction volumes of *New Complete Works*,[18] describes the death of a hen and its effect on her offspring as an allegory for the mother love of Zhong Taimei and her family's dependence on her. "The Plow and the Sky" is the most purely lyrical-pastoral of the four sketches. Its simplicity is deceptive, as its detailed reference to agricultural activity and repeated references to hill songs show how it is linked to Zhong Lihe's fiction's foregrounding of local economy and local culture.

Finally in this part, "The Little Ridge" is the most personal of the four pieces. After their elopement Zhong Lihe and Zhong Taimei endured unremitting poverty, an infant death, Zhong's life-threatening and debilitating illness, the crippling illness of their eldest son, and Zhong's long failure to gain recognition for his writing. But surely the biggest sadness in their life was the sudden death of their second son, Limin, at the age of seven in February 1954. The short story "Fuhuo" 復活 ("Restored to Life," 1960 [translated elsewhere]) dramatizes Limin's death so as to put the blame on his father's excessively strict discipline. According to Limin's elder brother, Tiemin, who died in 2011 at the age of seventy, this part of the story is entirely fictional.[19] Zhong Lihe was in reality a kind, perhaps even overindulgent father. It seems likely that he wrote "Restored to Life" in that way as a distillation of the guilt he felt at condemning his family to poverty and to an existence in the remoteness of Jianshan, both of which were true factors in the failure to get medical treatment in time to save Limin. Another sketch, "Ye mangmang" 野茫茫 (Wilderness, 1954), apparently written sooner after Limin's death, is a long, agonized lament, but it seems that by the time he wrote "Little Ridge," Zhong was calmer, and its quiet, straightforward tone, using the charming innocence of two-year-old Ying'er's (in)comprehension of her elder brother's absence to offset the terrible, literally unspeakable grief of her parents, makes for a subtler treatment of this most difficult of subject matter.

Economic realities are never far from most of Zhong Lihe's works. Mostly these concern the intimate day-to-day scraping by of ordinary folk. In "Swimming and Sinking," as in *Homeland*, Zhong Lihe attempts something more ambitious and more widely relevant. This story is a dryly observed yet bitterly impassioned social commentary on Taiwan in the first fourteen years of the Pax Sinica, 1945–1959. Here the autobiographical I-narrator, Old Zhong, presents in flashback the increasingly desperate and often disreputable efforts and failures of an old friend, Li Xinchang, to get rich in the unstable economy of postwar Taiwan. Meanwhile, Old Zhong himself declines into a kind of

Bingwen figure, albeit not as spiritually degraded. By the end of the story, presumably 1959, Old Zhong's erstwhile friend Li Xinchang has become a real big shot at last and does not even recognize Old Zhong.

In Zhong Lihe's swansong (and arguably his masterpiece), "Rain," Huang Jinde is one of the most memorable characters in Zhong Lihe's entire opus. As an ordinary tenant farmer in Meinong, as a family man, stern moralist, hard drinker, and gambler, as a returned war coolie, and most of all as a man with an obsessive concern with the rights and wrongs of land ownership and tenancy rights, Huang's words and actions throughout are invested with a strident, confident machismo. However, it is the ambivalences in his personal makeup that present the reader with the most engrossing and tragic cruces of the plot.

The chief motive for Huang's pursuit of justice against the power of local landlord Luo Dingrui lies in his sense of duty to his fallen comrade and blood brother Xu Longxiang. Thus he acts out of a traditional Chinese ethic of fraternal love. What is perhaps most significant, however, is that Huang's duty to Xu is a guilty one. Having had his own life saved by Xu while fighting for the Imperial Army of Japan, Huang failed to save Xu's and was forced to leave him to die during their attempt to flee from advancing American forces. Secondly, Huang, for all his machismo, is a compromised family head, having married-in to his shrewish wife's better-off family, a fact she never lets him forget.

Thus denied a confident sense of patriarchal superiority, Huang exerts himself all the more in his righteous pursuit of justice in the case of the rented land that he signed over to Xu's widow on his return from the war. He is disgusted at the latter's decision, condoned by her elder son, to sell the plot to the notorious and unscrupulous land grabber (and wartime collaborator) Luo Dingrui. The horror that occurs in the climax of "Rain" is partially due to Huang Jinde's all-consuming obsession with questions of land rights and ownership and to his loyalty to his fallen comrade and best friend. He is so taken up in these affairs that he fails to prevent heartbreaking calamity in his own family.

As so often in his fiction, Zhong Lihe shows that the people closest to his heart, the "good and honest farming folk" of Hakka South Taiwan, are bound to the soil and their homeland not by sentiment but by pressing economic necessity. Huang Jinde is a noble social figure in this context, but his obsession with land makes him a tragic failure as a father and as an individual. "Rain" is rare in Zhong Lihe's fiction in excluding any sentimental, nostalgic tone. No one, least of all Huang Jinde, appears likely to burst into a hill song at any point. In this story of rural economics, the only thing that sings is a hulling machine. We may speculate therefore that at the moment of his death Zhong Lihe may, with "Rain," have been moving toward a harder realism in his literature.

NOTES

1. Strictly speaking, only Taiwan was an integral part of the Japanese Empire (1895–1945). Manchukuo (the region commonly known in English as Manchuria, but usually referred to by the Chinese simply as "the Northeast") was a Japanese puppet state, 1932–1945; North China was occupied by Japan 1937–1945, with a puppet Chinese administration in Peking (Beijing).
2. Jianshan, 7 km northeast of the small town of Meinong, consists of a hamlet and a scattering of farms and cottages and is the hilliest, most remote townland in Meinong district. "Jianshan," meaning "pointed hill," refers to the small, almost perfectly conical hill that rises immediately to the north of Zhong Lihe's family home (from the early 1930s to his death in 1960; his surviving family still live on the site) and the Zhong Lihe Memorial Institute (Zhong Lihe Jinianguan 鍾理和紀念館), founded 1983. This little hill is now also—increasingly, it seems—known as Lishan 笠山 (Bamboo Hat Hill), the fictional name Zhong Lihe gave it in his novel *Bamboo Hat Hill Farm* (see below).
3. Shenyang 瀋陽 was known in Manchukuo as Fengtian 奉天 (pronounced "Hōten" in Japanese). Internationally, the city was long known mainly by its Manchu name, Mukden.
4. Zhong's father had died in 1943 at the age of about sixty-two. He had suffered business reversals before and during the war years, and the Jianshan coffee plantation, which was perhaps his career's boldest vision, had failed as the result of a rust infection.
5. Zhong Lihe, *Jiazhutao* 夾竹桃 (Oleander), Beijing: Ma Dezeng shudian, 1945. The volume comprises the title novella (translated here) and one other, plus two short stories. Both novellas and one of the short stories

were also separately published in the journal *Taiwan Wenhua* (Taiwan Culture) in September 1946.

6. "Zhong Lihe ziwo jieshao" 鍾理和自我介紹 (Zhong Lihe: Self-introduction, 1959), *Xin ban Zhong Lihe quanji* 新版鍾理和全集 (Complete works of Zhong Lihe: new edition, chief editor Zhong Yiyan 鍾怡彥), (Gaoxiong) Gangshan [高雄縣岡山鎮]: Gaoxiong xian zhengfu, 2009 (8 vols.) [hereafter *New Complete Works*], 8:277-278.

7. The selection is inevitably subjective to some degree, and difficult decisions have had to be made to exclude some novellas, stories, and essays from "the best." Two easier decisions were to exclude Zhong Lihe's only full-length novel and five short stories previously translated by other hands. (See "Sources, Translations, and Acknowledgments" in this volume.) The two aims "to present a selection of the best" and "to represent his life and times" came into conflict in one case. One of the pieces included in this volume (I will not say which!) was chosen because of its very great value to the second aim. If I had had only the first aim in mind there would have been several other works from "the best of Zhong Lihe's literary work" that I would have chosen ahead of it.

8. Zhong Lihe, "Deng Dawu shan ji" 登大武山記 (Record of an ascent of Mount Dawu, 1959), *New Complete Works* 2:81-100.

9. In several of his works of fiction, Zhong's autobiographical character is called A-He 阿和, which is instantly recognizable as a familiar or diminutive version of his real name, Lihe 理和, although in real life he was never known to anyone as A-He.

10. Zhong Lihe provides a quite specific definition of the Meinong hill song in *Bamboo Hat Hill Farm*: "This was a very special kind of hill song. Just like the cotton headscarves that trailed from the women's bamboo hats, it flourished only among the mountain villages on the north side of the upper reaches of the Xiadanshui River. The people called it the Meinong hill song, as opposed to the Pingtung hill song that could be heard on the other side of the river. Hakka people loved hill songs" (*New Complete Works* 4:50).

11. Kuomintang rule in Taiwan after 1945 was corrupt and viciously discriminatory against members of the native population, who were routinely treated as Japanese collaborators. A trivial incidence of police brutality in Taipei on Feb. 28 (= 2/28), 1947, provoked a backlash of mass

protest and violence against Mainlanders, which in turn provoked a very bloody military suppression. For many natives of Taiwan, 2/28 was the final straw, the end of any warmth toward the Kuomintang as compatriots and liberators.

12. Xingzheng Yuan Wenhua Jianshe Weiyuanhui 行政院文化建設委員會 (Council for Cultural Affairs, RoC [Taiwan]), *Taiwan lishi cidian* 臺灣歷史辭典 (Dictionary of Taiwan history), http://nrch.cca.gov.tw/ccahome/website/site20/contents/017/cca220003-li-wpkbhis-dict004463-1306-u.xml (accessed June 20, 2011).

   A very fine, very moving feature film based largely (but with postmodern elements) on Zhong Haodong's life, imprisonment, and death (1940–1950), entitled *Hao nan hao nü* 好男好女 (Good men, good women), directed by Hou Hsiao-hsien 侯孝賢, was released in 1995.

13. Heming was their father's third natural son, the eldest natural son of the principal wife. The latter had adopted a son who was eldest of all the brothers, so that Heming was the fourth son overall. Zhong Lihe, the second natural son, born to his father's secondary wife and older than half-brother Heming by about three to four weeks, was for some reason in the habit of addressing Heming in real life as "Second Elder Brother." In the two extant, undated manuscript versions of "From the Old Country," the one believed to be earlier refers to the brother as "Second Elder Brother"; in the later one (the basis for the version in *New Complete Works* used here) this has become "Third Elder Brother."

14. My translation of the last sentence of the story, using the word "could," is based on the new edition in *New Complete Works*, which in turn is based on the later of the two extant manuscript versions. (*New Complete Works* 2:47: San'ge ruci, wo yi wei *neng* liwai 三哥如此，我亦未能例外).

15. "In the Willow Shade": first version completed January in 1939, retitled and radically rewritten in 1954, minor revisions in 1959; "Oleander": April 1944, some corrections and revisions done by hand on the first print version (April 1945) by the author at a time or times unknown; "The Fourth Day": late 1945, revised (extent unknown) ca. 1958.

16. Zhong Lihe letter to Zhong Zhaozheng 鍾肇政, Nov. 19, 1958. See translator's introduction to Zhong Lihe, "Old Country folk" (From the Old Country), *Edinburgh Review* 124:53-54.

17. See Lu Hsun (Lu Xun), "Preface to the First Collection of Short Stories *Call to Arms*," in Lu Hsun, *Selected Stories of Lu Hsun* (Peking: Foreign Languages Press, 1972), 5.
18. In a few cases it is difficult to decide for certain whether some of Zhong Lihe's works are short stories or essays. *Homeland* was classified as a group of four essays in *Complete Works* (II) and "Record of an Expedition to the Summit of Mount Dawu" remains—erroneously, I would say—in one of the short-fiction volumes of *New Complete Works*. Overall, these ambiguities reflect the tendency of Zhong Lihe's autobiographical fiction to cling very closely to fact, and to have plots which are rather low on action.
19. The nonfactual basis of the story is also signaled by the fact that the second son who dies here is named Hong'er 宏兒, whereas Limin 立民 usually appears in Zhong Lihe's autobiographical fiction as Li'er 立兒.

From the Old Country

Part 1
Formative Years

Completed in December 1959 under the title "Wo yu Jiali po" 我與假黎婆 (The Gari woman and me). First published under the present title in January 1960.

1. My Grandma from the Mountains
假黎婆

I

One day my eldest brother, returning from the trip he made to our native village every year at the spring equinox, said he had run into our grandma's younger brother. He said this brother of Grandma's really missed us and hoped to come here for a visit sometime soon. This news excited me, and at the same time, for some reason I could not put a name to, it brought feelings of both sadness and nostalgia.

This grandma of ours was not the blood grandmother who gave birth to our father; she was our grandfather's second wife. Our blood grandmother died very young, leaving us no impressions of her at all. Whenever we mentioned "Grandma" we always meant this stepgrandmother of ours. In fact, this grandma had truly replaced the one we never knew, not only in terms of status and name, but also emotionally. She was fully worthy to be called "Grandma." She loved and looked after us, especially me, according to the ways of her race; the others were often jealous of her favoritism toward me.

She was a "Gari"—our Hakka word for aboriginal. When I talk about being loved and cared for "according to the ways of her race," I certainly don't want to imply that anything was lacking. She couldn't tell us the story of the Ox Herd and the Spinning Maid, nor could she teach us to chant "Moonlight so bright, plant ginger tonight." But she compensated with other things, and these other things were so beautiful, precious, and, for most people, difficult to come by.

As far as I know she never told lies to us children and she never lost patience with us. She was always even-tempered and her face was tranquil, sober, and calm; she always seemed to be smiling a profound, almost imperceptible smile. This expression of hers imparted a feeling of serenity and peace. I only once saw her lose her habitual calm. During the winter rice harvest one year, early one morning she went into the fields to hull rice. Suddenly the others saw her leaping about in the paddy, crying out loudly and waving her arms wildly in the air. Eventually she started howling and weeping. It was as if she were bewitched. When the other adults went over to her they found worms crawling all over the ground, so many that every footstep would trample seven or eight. Earthworms were what Grandma feared most all her life. Her elder daughter laughed so much that she had to squat down, but in the end she was the one who took Grandma on her back and carried her all the way home.

Grandma was very short, with a sharp chin, slender, and dark of complexion. She always braided her hair and coiled it all round her head Gari-style. Her wrists and the backs of her hands bore beautiful tattoos. It wasn't until I was a bit older that I learned that she was a Gari, and even then I found that it had no significance at all for me. Whether intellectually or emotionally, I simply couldn't accept this as a basis for looking at her, thinking about her, or evaluating her. It would have been too confusing for me. Even with her Gari hairstyle and tattooed hands, all I knew was that she was my grandma, nothing more. This was the only basis for me to know her, be close to her, remember her.

2

I don't know when or how I latched on to Grandma. I really wanted to know, so I often asked her to tell me. If she was in the mood she would smilingly but perfectly seriously agree to my request. This is how it went: she said that one morning she went to the river to do the washing and saw a Hoklo[1] woman abandoning a child under a stand of bamboo. She waited until the Hoklo woman had gone some distance

---

1. Apart from "Grandma," who belonged to the Paiwan 排灣 aboriginal people of south Taiwan, Zhong Lihe's family were Hakka Chinese. The Hoklo or Hokkien Chinese, otherwise known as Minnanren 閩南人 (South Fujianese), were, and still are, the large-majority ethno-linguistic group in Taiwan. At the time of the setting of this story the Hoklo accounted for over 75 percent of Taiwan's population; the Hakka were, and still are, the second-largest ethno-linguistic group, with nearly 20 percent. The Hakka of Taiwan, like their kin in Mainland China, are scattered across the islands in enclaves surrounded by Hoklo settlement. Often these Hakka townships occupy hillier terrain that is more remote from the larger cities. Meinong is a good example of this, as one of Kaohsiung's more remote districts, with Hakkas still today accounting for over 80 percent of the population.

away, then went and picked up the child, put it in her basket with the washing, and took it home. That baby grew up to be me.

Later, when I was bigger, I learned that every mother told her little darling this story about finding him abandoned and taking him home. However, in those other narratives the woman abandoning her baby was always a "Gari," whereas my grandma made her a Hoklo woman.

That was the only difference.

From what I heard I eventually figured out that it must have been during the year of my little brother's birth that I first latched on to Grandma. With this baby even littler than me at her breast, Ma couldn't look after me as well. And yet, I still had to drink milk, so what was to be done? This is how my grandma came to be responsible for feeding me condensed milk. In those days thermos flasks were still unknown to ordinary folk, and so for my every meal Grandma had to light the stove and boil water for the condensed milk. She really had quite a job of it back then, for two years of my life, until I was weaned around the age of three.

I know very little of this earliest period of my life. I should begin my narrative with my earliest memory, but that too is far from clear. I only remember a very dark room and patiently lying in bed pretending to sleep. Ma was humming tunelessly in a very nasal voice as she caressed my little brother. She hummed and hummed, then gradually fell silent, leaving only the sound of even, peaceful breathing. That was when I softly, quietly slipped down from my bed and tiptoed, feeling my way through the darkness, into my grandma's room. Grandma was clearly startled to see me, but she didn't scold me. I told her the smell of pee in Ma's room was very strong, and I couldn't get to sleep. Grandma sighed and let me lie down beside her.

Before long, Ma came looking for me.

"I knew he'd sneak into your room. He can't sleep soundly anywhere else." I heard her saying this to Grandma, then calling my name: "A-He, A-He."

I didn't answer, didn't move.

"He must be asleep." This was Grandma's voice.

"He's got to be kidding us! How could he fall asleep so quickly?" Ma spoke again, and then she called to me again, now shaking me at the same time: "A-He, A-He."

Still I didn't answer, and didn't move.

"Let him be!" said Grandma. "Just let him sleep here."

"But you haven't been all that well," said Ma guiltily. "He'll bother you with all his nonsense."

At this I felt I had to say something, so I said, "I won't bother Grandma."

I heard both Ma and Grandma laugh, and then in a little while Ma left the room.

So that's how I latched on to my grandma, and stayed attached to her right up until I grew up and left home to go a-wandering. In the story of my life she was the person I was closest to, clung to, ahead of my parents and siblings. I almost monopolized her love—even her two natural-born children, my two aunts, got a lesser share than me.

3

But back then I still didn't know Grandma was a Gari.

One day, Ma was chatting with a neighbor when suddenly something she said flew into my ear. Ma said, "Garis don't understand about years of age, all they know is that when the mangoes are in flower again another year has passed." This sentence particularly caught my attention because I had the feeling that it somehow had to do with my grandma. However, I wasn't at all sure that this was really the case, so when I saw Grandma I asked her if she was a Gari.

"You're not, are you?" I asked tentatively.

"How could you doubt it?" Grandma replied, smiling sweetly. Her warm, loving nature shone out from her face in a soft radiance. She stretched out her right hand toward me, asking, "Does your ma have tattoos like these?"

I had known those tattoos all my short life but didn't know they had any special meaning. Only now did I understand the meaning, but even so I still couldn't make out whether or not Grandma was a Gari. I looked at her face, and then I looked at her long gown. Her face was smiling; her gown was the same one she had always worn, as long as I could remember. I realized how muddleheaded I had been.

"Now that you know Grandma's a Gari," Grandma cupped my chin to make me look up at her, "do you still like Grandma?"

Clearly she had never troubled herself about the matter, which was a good thing for both of us.

I dived into her arms. "I like Grandma."

"That's right!" Grandma stroked my head. "That's Grandma's Little Puppydog!"

"Little Puppydog" was Grandma's pet name for me.

I knew that Grandma had two older brothers back home, one of whom had died, leaving a son. She also had a younger brother, who had spent a few years living with us, feeding our oxen, so he spoke good Hakka. Moreover, he had an honest, amiable face, lacking the mountain people's fierce warlike appearance. If not for the *guba*[2] at his waist and the turban on his head I wouldn't have known he was a Gari. He and I were really close; we really got on well together.

I noticed that when her brothers came to visit Grandma seemed very wary, keeping a watchful eye on everything they did: at meals she wouldn't let them drink too much; she wouldn't let them go wherever they liked; at night she spread straw on the floor of her room for them. It was plain to see how painstakingly Grandma dealt with her brothers' visits. Her aim was to manage things just so, neither showing favoritism toward her family nor lowering its dignity. Only when she'd achieved this state of irreproachability would she be wholly satisfied. Once, when one of her brothers was leaving, our family gave him a bag of salt and a peck of rice. Grandma let him take the salt but told him to leave the rice behind. Afterward, when I had an opportunity to ask her about this, she stared at me unhappily for a long moment, as if displeased at my question. So then I asked her, didn't my ma give presents to her brothers when they visited?

"We may be Gari," Grandma said, sounding not so much sad as indignant, "but we're not beggars!"

---

2. *Guba* 孤拔: this is presumably Zhong Lihe's transliteration of an aboriginal word for the machete-like large knives that Paiwan males traditionally carried as cultural and/or status symbols. Such knives, sometimes called "head-hunting" knives [guódāo 馘刀] (but in reality multipurpose), are usually curved, but some types are straight or curved only near the tip. In such various forms they are common among Taiwan's different aboriginal peoples (the so-called Nine Tribes). The *laraw* (Mandarin *lalao* 拉烙) of the Atayal people of north Taiwan is particularly famous.

Another time, Grandma's younger brother and his wife came to visit her, bringing the orphaned nephew. It happened to be a holiday—the Dragon Boat Festival, I think. That night, ignoring Grandma's instructions, my family encouraged the visitors to drink as much as they liked. The result was that the boy got roaring drunk; he wouldn't sit still but charged wildly about spouting nonsense. Somehow he managed to break a bowl. His uncle grabbed hold of him and dragged him into Grandma's room.

My grandma was weeping, speechless with rage. She picked up a net bag—her nephew's, I suppose—and flung it down in front of him. As she did so she said over and over, in a dull roar but clearly and distinctly, "You black donkey! You black donkey!"

"Auntie, Auntie," said my ma, who came in and did her best to placate Grandma. "It's our fault for plying him with drink. Today's a holiday, there's no harm in getting a bit tipsy! It's already dark, let him stay until morning."

It took quite some soothing before Grandma went quiet again. And still her tears fell silently.

Next morning I awoke to find the young man had disappeared. When Grandma was out of the room I softly asked her brother where he was.

"He's gone," he answered in a low voice, as though there were something asleep in the room and he was afraid to awaken it.

"When?" I asked.

"Last night."

I felt surprised. But actually I was more surprised about my grandma than about her nephew. I had never seen her so angry.

Grandma's brother gave me a nudge—I heard Grandma's footsteps approaching.

"Don't say anything." His voice was even lower than before, and he shook his head as he spoke.

4

One time I fell ill, probably with heatstroke, and was delirious for three days and nights. Everyone gave up hope for me. They wanted to move me from the bed onto the ground, but Grandma would not allow it. She insisted that I was going to get better, apparently perfectly convinced.

To this day it seems strange to me how accurate and reliable her judgment was, as though the line between life and death was visible to her eyes. I wonder whether this had anything to do with the experiences peculiar to her race.

Sure enough, under her day-and-night care, I finally came round on the afternoon of the fourth day. Later Grandma told me that another younger brother of hers—not the one my brother had run into, but another who is dead now—had once been bedridden for five days and nights without being able to eat or drink a single thing, but had got better in the end. She said it was the same with me as with that little brother of hers. She believed that if someone was still alive after days of illness like that, it was a sure sign that they would live. This seemed to be an article of faith with her.

It was toward evening that I began to feel as if I were floating in midair, levitating. Suddenly I heard a sound that seemed to come from the floor beneath me and at the same time from far, far away. Gradually the sound grew clearer and clearer, as I came closer to the floor. It was so familiar, and eventually I recognized it as my grandma's voice: she was singing, singing an aboriginal song.

By now I felt that I had come back down to earth, and was surrounded by solid things again; I no longer felt weightless but could feel my body, arms, and legs. My head felt so heavy and unwieldy, and even my eyelids were too heavy to open. Summoning up all my strength, I finally managed to open them, to find that I was lying in bed. The room was very dimly lit, and my eyes encountered only the gray-white of the mosquito net.

At that moment the singing came to an abrupt halt and Grandma entered my field of vision.

"A-He," Grandma's voice trembled with startled delight. "A-He, you're awake, oh!"

"Grandma!" I cried out feebly.

Slowly I turned my head, then my sight came to rest on her hand.

"Grandma, you . . . ," I said, after gazing for a while, but a wave of dizziness made me hurriedly close my eyes. But I was happy. I think I even cracked my mouth in a little smile.

"Look!" Grandma raised the thing in her hand to a place where I could see it more easily.

It was a chopstick wound round with homespun ramie thread, the kind I used for my kite. In the past I was always bugging Grandma to spin some for me, but she had many other things to do and could only spin a little at a time, sometimes only going through the motions to humor me. As a result, I could never fly my kite very high. But now she had spun a bulging coil around the chopstick. She must really have spun a lot this time.

"A-He, hurry and get better and I'll spin you some more," said Grandma, smiling all over her face. "Your kite's sure to fly very high this year."

My aunt came over from her bed to stand behind Grandma at the head of mine.

"Your grandma was spinning for three days and nights." Her bantering tone seemed very deliberate, but I could tell she was just as happy as Grandma. "She never left the foot of the bed while you lay there; she just spun away, really working hard." Then she turned to her mother, saying, "You should sleep now. I'll take over from you."

"I'm not tired," said Grandma.

"Oh, come on!" said Auntie. "If you don't get some rest you might get ill, and then who'll spin kite thread for your Little Puppydog!"

Grandma looked at her daughter and blinked a couple of times as she pondered, apparently still not sure whether she should rest or not, but in the end she went off to bed.

"Well then, A-He," she said to me with a smile. "Grandma's going to lie down for a bit." I saw that her eyes were bloodshot and ringed with dark circles.

"Your grandma hasn't slept for three nights," said Auntie after she had gone. "She wouldn't let anyone else watch over you!"

Then my ma came in from outside.

5

One time an ox belonging to Grandma's younger daughter went missing. The next day Grandma took me up the valley to help look for it. It was late summer or early autumn: the sky seemed big and bright and fresh; the trees harbored a profound tranquility and a soft warmth; and the mountains were lightly veiled in mauve mists. We crossed the

"Barbarian Line"[3] and went deep into the heart of the mountains. Now we would be penetrating deep into a densely forested valley; now we would be climbing high up toward the peaks. Although these are actually quite small hills, they looked tall enough to me. When I looked down from up there, the rivers and hills were spread out as if on the palm of my hand. It was the first time I had penetrated so deep or climbed so high in the mountains, and I was terribly happy. I kept flinging my arms in the air.

My grandma seemed very familiar with these places, as if she'd been here only yesterday. She seemed to see nothing special, nothing alarming in those valleys with their towering sides swathed in jungle, and the climbing was nothing to her. When we reached the top she asked me if I was happy, and then she pointed to a col off to the north and told me that was her home. One day she'd take me to visit the place where she grew up.

The col she had pointed to was dim and shady. I saw nothing apart from a cloud lightly floating above it.

Grandma kept singing aboriginal songs. The tunes were soft and mild, full of feeling, novel, and different from the songs the other grownups sang. As she sang she kept walking vigorously; her face bore a bewitching radiance, her eyes flickered animatedly in all directions, and her whole body gave off a brisk vivacity. She seemed much younger than usual.

She kept singing, louder and louder, although you still couldn't really call it loud. Her singing was full of her inner joy and passion, as if something that had been sleeping for a very long time, something jubilant, had suddenly been reawakened. Sometimes she would suddenly stop and fix me with her gaze, as if she wanted to know my

---

3. From early in the eighteenth century the (Manchu/Chinese) rulers of Taiwan designated districts, mostly above 300–400 meters in altitude, as "barbarian" areas that Han Chinese were forbidden to enter. This system, which arose out of concerns regarding the defense of settlers against the aboriginal tribes, was continued with modifications into the period of Japanese rule, including the time of this story. In the later Japanese period and after the return of Taiwan to Chinese rule in 1945 a revised system of "reservations" was promulgated, with a theoretical emphasis on preserving traditional aboriginal lands.

feelings. She smiled, but then the moment passed and she continued her singing.

Bewitching as this singing grandma was, my inner feelings were of confusion and fear; it was as if this grandma was no longer my own dearest, beloved grandma. This exhilaration of hers seemed to generate a pervasive atmosphere that belonged to her alone, an atmosphere that completely enveloped her and cast me alone and lonely on the outside. This consciousness made me sad and created a distance between us. Sometimes Grandma seemed to notice my dejection; several times when we stopped to rest she pulled me toward her and with surprise and concern in her voice asked me why I was unhappy. Was I not feeling well? At first I stayed silent, but in the end I could contain the feeling of loneliness in my heart no longer and I threw myself into Grandma's arms:

"Stop singing, Grandma! Stop singing, Grandma!" I cried, fervently, agitatedly.

Grandma was startled and completely thrown by my frenzied outburst, and just kept saying, "What's the matter? What's the matter?" Cupping my face with her hands, she made me look up into hers. Looking into my eyes in surprise, she said, "You're crying, A-He? What's the matter with you?"

"Don't sing, Grandma . . . ," I bawled again.

Grandma stared at me wonderingly, and then, forcing a smile, she said, "Did Grandma frighten her Little Puppydog with her singing?"

Grandma stopped singing. All the way home she silently trod the path ahead. Her face seemed sad. But as soon as we got home, all these strange feelings vanished. Grandma was Grandma again: serene, quiet and easy, sober and calm.

6

From the age of twelve when I left home for school, and later, after graduation, when I traveled around looking for my place in the world, many new things demanded my attention, and my devotion to Grandma imperceptibly diminished, especially as I wouldn't see her for months on end. But Grandma's feelings for me never changed. On the contrary, my absence may actually have deepened her love for me. Whenever I returned home after a lengthy absence she would sit down with me and have a good long look at me. Sometimes she would lift a hand and move it from the top of my head right down to my heels, as she murmured, "My Little Puppydog's all grown up! My Little Puppydog's all grown up!" From the tone of her voice and the look in her eyes I understood that she was trying to convince herself of this marvel: by some miracle her Little Puppydog had grown up.

Later still my travels took me far across the sea, and for years I never even wrote home. Grandma died at the height of the war, two years before Taiwan became part of China again. In her last illness she kept moaning my name, and on her deathbed she repeatedly asked if there had been any letter from me.

When I returned, guava trees and lush green grass had grown all over Grandma's grave. As I held the burning incense sticks I felt a cold, cold sorrow in my heart.

7

Not long after my brother had mentioned it, Grandma's younger brother came to visit. Had he not introduced himself, however, I almost would not have recognized him. This was not just because he had aged, but because his clothing and appearance had changed greatly. No longer did a *guba* hang at his waist; now he wore an old Japanese army uniform. He had cut his hair, so that he no longer wore a turban. His close-cropped hair was already white, and his cheeks were deeply sunken around his toothless gums. The only things that hadn't changed were the gentle, kindhearted look in his eyes and his fluency in Hakka.

I took him to Grandma's grave, where we burned incense and paid our respects. That night we talked until the small hours before going to bed. I noticed that every time he spoke he first shook his head, from which I gathered that things must be pretty tough for him in his old age.

"Hah!" he sighed when I enquired after that nephew of his. "He's no better than a beast."

He told me his nephew was a drunkard, a whoremonger, a layabout, and a good-for-nothing. Apparently these days there were "bad women" (by which he presumably meant prostitutes) in their mountain communities, which there had never been before.

He also said his eldest brother had only had the one son; who'd have known he'd turn out like this? He was all washed up now. As for his second elder brother, he was childless, and he himself had only a daughter, who was already married.

He shook his head again and said, "It's all because my grandpa took too many heads,[4] that's why we've ended up in this state!"

The next day when he was ready to leave we went to Grandma's grave again and burned a thick stick of incense. As he walked silently ahead of me I suddenly noticed that he was slightly hunchbacked. This discovery intensified my fond, cherished memories of Grandma. I truly felt that I had lost the most important and beloved person in my life.

---

4. The Paiwan people were, like most other Taiwan "mountain" aboriginal peoples, headhunters. The practice was eradicated during the period of Japanese rule (1895-1945).

Written and first published in 1959.

2. First Love
初戀

I

No sooner had I graduated from a Japanese upper elementary school than my father, saying I was still no good for anything, sent me to another school—an old-fashioned academy in our village with a traditional Chinese curriculum. He hoped that a classical education might "carve and polish" a "rough piece of jade" like me into something useful.[1] I was sixteen years old then, one of the academy's "big boys," so I had a great deal of freedom. The master hardly ever interfered with us.

Luckily I was able to maintain a calm heart and a cool head: while my classmates were busy pursuing the opposite sex, I alone was able to concentrate on my studies, so that I actually learned a thing or two in my first year.

Apart from studying, I passed my time on drawing and on sports such as running, skipping, wrestling, and kite flying. At sixteen, although considered one of the big boys, I was still a kid at heart, and when I was playing with others my age we really got pretty boisterous. The village elders would shake their heads and sigh, remarking that in previous times scholars had always behaved with absolute decorum and would never have been as wild as this lot.

Back then I had a sketchbook with a hessian cover for drawing. I had developed an artistic bent during my elementary school days, and it continued during my time at the academy. Whenever I had the time and the inclination I'd take out my pencil from the spine of the sketchbook and start scratching away at something or other. And so

---

[1]. The two famous lines (each of three Chinese characters) "If jade is not carved, no useful thing is formed" are to be found in the introductory section of *San zi jing* 三字經 (*The Three Character Classic*), which was a standard first primer for Chinese children from the late thirteenth century to the early twentieth.

the sketchbook was always with me, along with my ancient, thread-bound set books, as I went to and from school.

In Japanese school I had been passionately interested in the art classes, and it seemed I also had a certain talent: my drawings were always highly praised. For a while there had been plans to send me to art college—in Japan! Later, however, because of some regrettable tendencies among Taiwanese students in the "Mother Country" at the time, Father gave up this idea. Otherwise, it is clear that my career might have been very different from what it is today. It is at such little forks in the road that the vehicles of our fates take different paths.

One time, the master discovered my sketchbook, picked it up, and had a look inside.

"Oh, so it's a sketchbook," he said in surprise, turning over a few pages. "Hmm, nothing but pigs!"

"Look further on, sir," I said, embarrassed. "There are other things: oxen, chickens, and ... "

But the master had already closed the album and was handing it back to me.

"It seems you have a special interest in farm animals," he said with a laugh. "Well, you do draw them very well!"

I also drew people: farmers, children, women, too. However, almost without exception, the women in my sketches were composed of more straight lines than curved ones. They lacked the mysterious, elusive scent of Woman. Although they were among my favorite subjects, my interest in them was no greater than my interest in pigs and oxen. What a sin!

I was studying *The Book of Odes*. This book is now generally accepted as a record of the loves of our ancient male and female ancestors. From its opening poem it brims with the bitter longings and heartfelt avowals of lovelorn humans. But when I was studying it, I treated it no differently than the geography textbook. Burning with passion, surging with emotion as it was, it left me unmoved.

Obviously my physiological development had reached that most peculiar stage of sexual awakening that all boys must go through, when they appear to despise the entire female sex. My discovery of the existence of women came relatively later. I was still at what seemed a transitional stage, and a temporary one.

2

One day I was sitting at my desk looking out through the window; on the desk in front of me lay my sketchbook and a pencil.

Outside the window was a broad street, so my field of vision was about ten meters wide. On the other side of the road was a wall higher than a man, built in large, gray-green river boulders. This wall provided a superb backdrop, as if it were the work of a master scenographer: whenever a person's figure was "projected" onto this wall, his facial expressions and the contrasts of light and dark were made exceptionally vivid. As I watched, human shapes were constantly shuttling in great haste against this backdrop.

It was our village's turn for water again, you see. The water supply was channeled our way once every five days, so on that day the villagers had to carry enough drinking water to last the next five days. Every waterday the whole village assembled like an army going into battle. In every family, everyone capable of lifting a shoulder pole was mobilized: young, old, male, female—it didn't matter—even little girls. The sound of voices, water, footsteps, and buckets rose in a giant wave of noise that filled the streets and alleys. It was a strange, tense, lively scene, a grand spectacle that you would rarely see elsewhere.

I looked on, planning how to transfer the appearance of the water carriers onto my sketchpad.

But which one should I draw? I debated with myself. That man? Unfortunately, he's slightly lame. That woman then? Oh! The poor thing's bent double under the weight of two buckets of water. Well then, here comes a young man: just look at the rippling muscles along his gleaming tanned arms! They're like two iron bars: a marathon runner's arms in ancient Greece must have been something like his! And after the marathon runner yet another figure appears. Oh! It's only a little girl, but even she's got two water buckets made from gasoline cans bobbing on the ends of her carrying pole. How energetic she looks! But both marathon runner and little girl are past me in a flash! Next comes an old guy with a gloomy face, doddering unsteadily along. This is Uncle A-San who lives at the east end of Back Street. His son died last spring, so if he doesn't fetch his own drinking water, who will? No wonder he looks depressed. . . .

A whole parade of people had already gone past, but there I still sat, musing at the window, my mind a blank. My sketchbook lay open, but I hadn't made so much as a single line on the page. Just at that moment a young woman appeared at the far end of my backdrop. Her figure was stunning; her thighs looked sturdy and steady as she strode along. Suddenly struck by the realization that this girl was a real beauty, I grabbed my pencil. The action was almost unconscious; perhaps I was influenced by the good impression I already had of her.

My hand moved swiftly over the sketchpad; I only had the time it would take her to walk from one end of my backdrop to the other. When she left my field of vision I inspected my sketch. There were only a few simple lines on the paper, some dots and curves. However, I felt extremely satisfied. I would still have a second chance, and a third, indeed countless more chances. I could take my time and draw her at my leisure; I had no need to hurry, and she would never know.

I exhaled deeply and leaned back in my chair to rest and wait for her to reappear.

Chunmei lived with her parents, a younger brother, and two little sisters in the same street as Uncle A-San. Her brother had been in the year below me at elementary school. I guessed she must be nineteen or twenty. Her family owned an orchard of mangoes and longans. I would often go there when the fruit was ripe. However, she seldom involved herself in such matters. One time she was the only one home. She made me wait while she remained intent on her sewing. After I had waited for nearly half an hour she finally got up and went inside, returning almost immediately with a basket of mangoes. She put it down in front of me and told me to help myself.

"How many?" I asked her.

"Take as many as you like," she said, picking up her sewing again.

"What about the money?" I asked again.

"Put it on the table," she said, without even looking.

Now she had reappeared against my backdrop. I noticed that her buckets were made of steel. They were full of water and covered with bamboo leaves. They swayed to and fro with her steps. Strong, vigorous, lively: her figure really stirred me.

I picked up my pencil again.

Her eyes were long and slender, with very dark, expressive irises. Her nose was a bit flat, but otherwise all right. The taut flesh around her mouth could not have been more perfect, and her temples were extraordinarily tender and white. For the first time in my life I discovered the beauty of a woman's white neck!

She was walking past my window. Some more lines and dots, dots and curves appeared on my sketchpad.

I remembered one time when my cousin and I had gone to her house to buy mangoes. She and her mother were at home. Her mother brought out a basket of mangoes. They were all very small, and my cousin muttered incessantly as he picked through them.

"Ma!" she piped up. "Why don't you bring out that other basket?"

"What's wrong with these ones?" retorted her mother, displeased.

"These are left over from other people taking their pick. There aren't any big ones left."

"The ones inside are reserved!" Her mother was angry now. "What do you know about anything? All you know is how to eat!"

"Ma, really!" Chunmei found it funny. "Where's the harm in letting them choose a few? It's not as if they're going to take the whole basket!"

But no way would her mother bring out the other basket. The daughter looked at us in embarrassment but didn't say any more.

When we got out onto the street my cousin said he liked buying mangoes from her, because she sold them much cheaper than other members of her family. I agreed. She struck me as a good person.

The lines, dots, and curves on my sketchpad gradually multiplied with each time she reappeared. By her fifth or sixth trip, her whole figure had somehow been mysteriously transferred onto the paper. Toward evening when I stopped drawing I had sketches of her in several different poses. The sketches were all better than my usual work, more closely resembling a woman. I was very pleased. As I looked at the likenesses I had made, I involuntarily murmured her name: "Chunmei! Chunmei."

And with that I put away my sketchbook, ready for the next water-day.

3

At that time I was part of a small circle of friends, all about sixteen or seventeen years of age. We had known one another since early childhood and had gone to school together, so we were very close. And now the curiosity and adventurousness that came with the beginnings of sexual awakening heightened our instinctive need for companionship, bringing us even closer together. We were always on the lookout for opportunities to get together. Stormy days and moonlit nights were the best times for get-togethers, adding spice and interest to our conversations.

However, among these friends of mine, I was not only rather short, but also a late developer, so that I would often feel backward and left out because of my ignorance of the opposite sex. To me women had always been an unknowable concept. But my friends' conversations tended to revolve precisely around the subject of women, so that I was often left sitting dumbly on the edge of the group, almost like a real mute.

One beautiful, bright moonlit night our group came together again. Changfa had brought with him the *huqin* fiddle that rarely left his side—he had spent several lunch breaks making it himself, using a coconut shell for the body. Whenever there was a break in the conversation it would be filled by the music of this fiddle. Changfa was incapable of playing anything finer or more remarkable than rustic folk songs, but he himself was perfectly satisfied with this, and he was an enthusiastic player.

Passing through the dismal, lonely cemetery, we reached the river flats, where maiden grass grew among the boulders. It happened to be another waterday, so the river was flowing gently. The moon was sprinkling its pure radiance like a soft mist over the sprawling, desolate river flats. The north shore of the river was a precipitous cliff, with small clumps of trees all in a row, straight and unmoving, like sentries. On the dark riverbanks, insects were chirruping in the grasses.

As always, we sat on some rocks by the river.

Yi-yi O-o, Yi-o-yi-yi-o-o—

Changfa kept playing a folk air over and over.

His *huqin* was nothing less than a concrete manifestation of the sexual impulse, akin to the subtle, lithe, and graceful courtship songs of the birds and the beasts. He gripped it very tightly and as he worked the bow his arms seesawed fiercely. No! He wasn't merely working the bow: he was battling his frustration. His movements embodied a vehement desire to stop at nothing to destroy everything. At his fingertips the *huqin* gave out piercing cries of sadness, like that of a person suffering unbearable oppression.

Changfa was only a year older than me, but physically he was already well developed, and in particular there was no doubt that sexually he was close to boiling point. His ultimate interest and greatest concern were women, women, women. His blatant, blunt attitude amazed me; but more than that, the abundance of his knowledge of relations between the sexes raised him to the level of a god in my eyes. I could not imagine where he had acquired such expertise. Compared to him I was nothing more than an ignorant child.

"Come on, A-Qi, give us a song!"
Changfa's shoulders were rocking.

Yi-o-yi-yi-o-o—

The *huqin* began to play an introduction.
Placidly, A-Qi looked up at the bright moon in the sky, then his familiar, deep voice began to slide smoothly from his throat.

> Sixteen, seventeen, the perfect age,
> Flowers do blossom, better soon than late;
> Bamboo has segments, each older than the last,
> Now's the time for loving, why should we wait?

"Great! Bravo, A-Qi!" Changfa yelled hoarsely and crazily. "Let's have another!"

But instead of singing, A-Qi just kept gazing at the moon.

Like Changfa, A-Qi had reached sexual maturity, and like Changfa he already had a sweetheart, but he was more moderate, not always ranting like Changfa. At this moment he had his feet immersed in the river and was gently splashing them around. From time to time he sent up some spray—like fleeting will-o'-the-wisps, instantly extinguished. Copying him, I put my feet in the water and immediately felt a current of fresh coolness traveling from the tips of my toes right up to the crown of my head. It was extraordinarily refreshing.

Suddenly Changfa hung his bow on a tuning peg and asked a question of us all, in a tone of great seriousness: "Hey, who's the best woman in the village, eh? You go first, A-Qi."

In this context, Changfa's use of the word "best" had rather far-reaching significance, referring not only to prettiness and sweet nature, but also carrying connotations of "love."

A-Qi replied without having to think: "Baomei, of course!"

Baomei was the girl Changfa was pursuing at the time.

Changfa arched his eyebrows and glared at A-Qi, Then, after that moment of bemusement, he asked again, quite candidly: "And apart from Baomei?" He turned to me: "Hey, A-He, you're a sly one, always listening to the rest of us and never a peep out of you. It's about time you said something. So: who's the best, eh? Come on."

I was quite taken aback. I'd never expected to be put on the spot on such a subject. It was a tight corner, because I'd never given this question any thought before. I really didn't know which of the women was "best."

Changfa kept pushing for an answer: "Come on! Who's the best?"

Amid my embarrassment, suddenly the image of my model leaped from the pages of my sketchbook into my mind.

Stammering and stuttering, very unsure of myself, I found myself saying: "Chunmei's quite good-looking, I suppose?"

"Chunmei? Ah-hahaha!" Changfa guffawed. "Chunmei? Great! A-He, it's that huge rack of hers you've taken a fancy to, isn't it? You've a good eye! I'll guarantee each one weighs five pounds! Ah-hahahaha!"

I was so mortified that my whole body began to burn. The feeling of humiliation almost made me lose my temper, and I deeply regretted my candor.

A-Qi came to my defense.

"What's so funny? What a weirdo you are, Changfa!" he said. "Chunmei may not measure up to Baomei, but she's certainly one of the prettiest women in our village."

A-Qi had saved face for me and my Chunmei. I felt really happy and forgot the insult I had suffered only a moment before.

"No!" said Changfa, no longer laughing but explaining himself in all seriousness. "Don't get pissed off. I wasn't laughing at you. Of course Chunmei is a fine girl. I just meant her breasts are on the large side, that's all. It's no big deal, all women have breasts, and actually Chunmei's even prettier than Baomei."

"Come off it, Changfa!" A-Qi wasn't letting him off so lightly. "Chunmei doesn't measure up to your Baomei!"

But Changfa wouldn't get into an argument. After glaring at him again briefly, he sank into a dazed state, as if drunk.

"Oh, Baomei!" he murmured.

Obviously he had gone soaring off somewhere in his mind, leaving reality behind, searching among his memories for an old dream. He grabbed his *huqin* and began to sing. His voice was hoarse, like an old cracked gong; but the lyrics spoke from his innermost heart:

> Little sister's heart is true, brother reads it true,
> Grind down a steel rule for a needle to sew;
> Little sister is the needle, brother is the thread,
> Where the needle goes, the thread will surely follow.

It was very quiet. It seemed that everything in creation was holding its breath and bending its ear to listen to this youth's wild song to the moon. On the broad, empty river flats, especially so late at night, Changfa's singing seemed sad, rough, and shrill. It made a deep impression on me. One could almost feel the stubborn but forcibly repressed instinct roiling somewhere inside him, denied an outlet.

That night, we stayed sitting there until the moon descended beneath the horizon, before returning to our homes.

4

Most strangely, after that night's casual avowal, Chunmei's form began to linger in my mind. I didn't understand why this should be; perhaps it had already been there for some time. Before that night it had lurked in the folds of my subconscious, but now my avowal had freed it, allowing it to float to the surface. It really astonished me.

Was I in love with Chunmei? I couldn't help wondering.

I could not admit it, but neither could I deny it.

From that time on my interest in *The Book of Odes* changed: no longer did I see only the surface meaning of the words; I was now able to go further and appreciate the abiding human emotion behind them. What's more, I now seemed to understand and sympathize with the pain of King Wen's unrequited love. Besides, I was gradually coming to an understanding of what lay behind such lines as "My love hides from me, I scratch my head and hesitate" and "Her home is so near, but she is so far." Truly these were cries from the hearts of real people.

It was also from that time that I started often finding myself sitting in a daze at my desk, as if unaware where I was.

I eagerly awaited each waterday and couldn't understand why there had to be five days between each one. Why couldn't it be every day? How wonderful it would be if it were every day! Then I could see her every day. Above all, at the very next waterday I waited to see if her breasts were really as big as Changfa said. I would be hugely disappointed if he turned out to be right.

Alright then! Waterday again.

I stuck by the window and waited, swallowing again and again.

One, two, three—

After a bunch of people had walked past, here she came . . . here was Chunmei coming toward me, her gait and posture as sturdy and lively as ever. I felt a faint restlessness in my heart.

Her steps stirred up a breeze that sent the back of her smock wafting up. The critical moment was upon me, and I focused all my attention. I saw that where her breasts should be there were indeed two proud mounds, quivering in time with her steps. Certainly they were ample, but not necessarily in excess of the curvaceous ideal. This made me very happy. And because of this she seemed even more adorable than before. It was as if in facing our first trial, Chunmei had taken my side. Changfa had merely been shooting his mouth off. However, I had no intention of challenging him on it.

No matter how much I inwardly yearned for Chunmei, in real life I never had the chance to meet her even once. The more I thought of her the more depressed I became. I never stopped wondering how I might get to meet her and I longed to be able to tell her how I felt.

When mangoes came in season I went to her house three times on the pretext of buying some. I hoped she would be alone at home, but the first time I went she wasn't in, and the next two times I saw that her room's bamboo curtain was pulled right down: obviously she was at home, and only the curtain separated us, but how could I get to see her? I paced to and fro, keeping watch by her window, but in the end I could only walk away in dejection.

Since I wasn't fated to meet her face-to-face, I could only look at her lovely form from my window on waterdays and vent my unrequited passion on my sketchpad. In this way, portraits of her quickly multiplied in the sketchbook—over several months, almost all my drawings were of her. Her every pose and every aspect: frontal, profile; carrying buckets on her pole, empty-handed; wearing a bamboo hat, or with her hair in disarray; Chunmei tight-lipped, Chunmei smiling; and even upper-body studies, studies from the rear, studies of legs, hands, eyes, nose....

"Chunmei! Chunmei!" I cried, looking at my drawings.

"Chunmei! Chunmei!"

It really looked as if they were gazing back at me, smiling and beckoning.

And so I would hug the sketchbook to my chest, as if it were the real Chunmei.

It was bliss.

5

Before long, I learned that any chance of meeting Chunmei was about to disappear forever: she was engaged. It was A-Qi who told me.

"Do you know how old she is?" asked A-Qi, after breaking the news to me. "Twenty-two!"

What he meant was that Chunmei and I were too far apart in age, so I shouldn't feel bad about it. He meant well, of course. But I remained silent.

"Don't be upset!" he added.

That winter Chunmei was married.

On the day of the wedding, from first dawn there were several showers of chilly winter rain. Bursts of drum and pipe music from the wedding procession came through the rain to reach my ears in the academy. Perhaps because of the rain, the music sounded unusually desolate and awakened boundless melancholy in my breast.

As I sat there disconsolate, listening to the shushing, hissing rain with its fitful accompaniment of drum and pipe music, I suddenly felt that the universe had become infinitely lonely, vast, and empty. Sadness welled up in me and I could not hold back my tears.

Furtively I wiped away the tears with the back of my hand. I told the master I had a headache and asked to be excused for the rest of the day. I picked up my books and went home.

Two days later it was waterday again. I got out my sketchbook through force of habit but I didn't open it.

Outside the window it was as busy as ever. The slightly lame man was as incapable as ever of walking straight and true; the poor woman still had her two big buckets that one of these days were going to crush her flat. Then there were the marathon runner and the little girl, and Uncle A-San, whose face would forever be gloomy (unless the king of Hell should by some miracle take pity on him and let his son return to the land of the living).

All of this seemed vaguely familiar to me from the past, but I couldn't help feeling that something was missing, and it could no longer arouse my former excitement. I merely sat there idly, watching abstractedly. Eventually I put the sketchbook away. After that I didn't bother to get it out on waterdays.

I planned to leave it permanently stuffed in the corner of a drawer.

Completed on January 27, 1959, and first published, posthumously, in 1961. The *New Complete Works* version (used here) is based on a later manuscript previously published only via the Zhong Lihe Digital Museum (http://cls.hs.yzu.edu.tw/zhonglihe/home.asp).

3. From the Old Country
原鄉人

1

When I was a child my first lesson in ethnology was the Hoklo (Hokkien). This man was one of my father's business friends. By the time I was about three or four I was aware that he often came to our house and would have lunch before leaving, or sometimes stay the night and not leave until the next day. He was very tall and smiled a lot. If he stayed over, then in the morning before leaving he would be sure to give me and my brother ten or twenty cents; he seemed really nice. Only as I got older did I gradually learn that lots of Hoklo came to our village as traders. Ma often bought salted fish, cloth, or thread from them. By now I could even understand a little Hoklo language.

My second ethnology lesson concerned the Japanese race. They almost always wore a uniform from head to foot, with swords at their waists and trim little mustaches under their noses. They walked with great strides and heads held high. Awe-inspiring and impressive. Wherever they went you could hear a pin drop; people gave them a wide berth.

"The Japanese are coming! The Japanese are coming!"

Mothers would coax their crying children with these words.

The children would stop crying.

The Japanese went around hitting people! They might even carry off children who wouldn't stop crying!

2

One day just after I turned five, Grandma told me a teacher from the Old Country had arrived in the village, and Pa was sending me to school. This Old Country teacher was thin, sallow, and somewhat stooped, but otherwise I couldn't see any difference between him and us. This really surprised me. The Hoklo and Japanese were different from us. After school I went to Grandma and asked her about this. Grandma listened, then said with a smile: "We moved here from the Old Country."

This was a big surprise to me, and I was struck speechless.

"Was it my pa who moved here?" I asked Grandma after a pause.

"No! It was your grandpa's grandpa," replied Grandma.

"Why did he move here?" I pursued.

"I'm not really sure," said Grandma with regret. "I suppose they couldn't find a way to live over there any more."

"Grandma," I said again after thinking about this, "where is the Old Country? Is it very far?"

"It's to the west, very, very far, across a strip of ocean; they had to come by boat."

The Old Country, the ocean, and boats! This was a whole new field of knowledge. Once more I was dumbfounded—for a while I was stunned. Never before had Grandma taught me such a lot.

A year later we got a new teacher. We'd heard he was also from the Old Country, but he was completely different from the old teacher. He was slightly plump, with a ruddy face and eyes that gleamed; there was a great, big, black mole on his right cheek, and he had a big, booming voice. This new teacher had much more vim than the old one. Something else he had a lot of was phlegm, which he would hawk up any old where. And another thing: he liked to eat dog meat, especially suckling puppies. In those days almost every family in the village had dogs, so there was certainly no problem of supply. As a result, within two years our teacher had gotten even fatter and his complexion was even rosier, but his phlegm was more abundant than ever.

He was a real expert at slaughtering dogs. He would pinch the back of a dog's neck between his left thumb and forefinger, then with the knife in his right hand he made a quick cut across its throat; the wee dog would drag itself a few steps, yelping, before collapsing. He'd kill three at a time in this way. He also showed us how to use the dog's tail in gutting it: an amazingly good and convenient method.

He taught school in our village for three years, but then he developed a large sore on the back of his neck that just would not respond to treatment, so he got his things together and left. As we heard it, he died on shipboard and his body was tipped into the sea. Everyone in the village said he must've eaten too much dog meat and that's why he got the ulceration. Mind you, his teaching methods were good, and he was conscientious; he'd been a good teacher, so the villagers all felt it a great pity.

When I was seven I had to go to Japanese school, so that was the end of my old-style village education.[1]

The third Old Country person I met was also closely connected with dog meat. But he was a real puzzle to me because he wasn't from outside at all—he had always lived in our village. He had a wife and daughter and was getting on in age. His eyesight was poor and his limbs trembled slightly, but when it came to beating dogs he was both brutal and fearless. Whenever he was slaughtering a dog the villagers, young and old, would gather round in a circle. Outside his front door there was a silk-cotton tree, and he would tie the dog to the foot of the trunk, then begin swinging his huge thick wooden club with all his might, bringing it down on the dog's body. His eyesight prevented him from bringing any one blow down in a fatal place to end the dog's life quickly, and so its suffering was needlessly increased.

I remember one time the dog was dodging this way and that, as far as the rope allowed, staggering and struggling and yelping piteously, blood dripping from its mouth. All the other dogs in the village barked madly as though possessed by demons, while the people standing around held their breath, their expressions solemn. My brother told me not to dribble, and to keep both hands behind my back. I did as he told me, and watched even more timidly than before.

Red blood and the crazed howling of dogs only spurred on the dog beater's murderous intent. Down rained the blows: ba-*cha* ba-*cha*. Suddenly, the dog's head took a hit and it fell spread-eagled on the floor, blood coming from its nose and even its eyes. Its belly rose and fell violently, and its claws scrabbled wildly on the ground. As it struggled to get up, down came the merciless club yet again.

I kept as near as I could to my brother, my eyes closed. Encircling my head with one arm he kept urging me not to be afraid. After one

---

1. Zhong Lihe's "old-style village education" took its syllabus from the pre-1905 Chinese civil service examination system curriculum, which consisted primarily of Confucian texts in classical Chinese.

last heartbreaking yowl, I opened my eyes to see the poor animal lying flat out in a pool of blood, its flanks rising and falling more violently than ever, its limbs still twitching.

Finally my brother took me away.

Some grown-ups across the way in front of the village shop were discussing what had just happened.

"What a vicious man!" said somebody.

Another asked whose dog it was, apparently believing the dog's owner to be equally cruel.

"He paid them, though!" said someone else.

"How much did he give them?" retorted the other. "I'd never have agreed, no matter how much he offered me."

"All Old Country people love dog meat," said another grown-up with some feeling.

So he—the dog-killer—was from the Old Country. This was something I had never known before.

When I got home I went straight to Grandma: "Did Grandpa eat dog meat?"

"No!" she replied.

"What about Grandpa's grandpa?" I asked again.

Grandma looked at me in surprise and smiled: "I don't know. But I'm sure he didn't." Then she asked me why I asked.

I explained to her what I had seen, and told her: "Everybody says Old Country people all eat dog meat."

"Silly boy," Grandma's smile broadened even further. "We're not Old Country people!"

"But my grandpa's grandpa was from the Old Country," I insisted. "You told me so yourself."

"He was from the Old Country, but we're not," said Grandma. "We live in Taiwan now."

I was pleased to hear that my grandpa and my grandpa's grandpa didn't eat dog meat, but Grandma's explanation of "where we came from" still baffled me.

Later I saw many more Old Country people: drifting types who came and went like migratory birds. As far as I could see all of them were somewhat disreputable: itinerant doctors, plowsmiths, tinsmiths, locksmiths, umbrella repairers, fortune-tellers, geomancers, and so on.

And I found out that they came in all shapes and sizes: their speech, dress, and facial features were by no means all the same. According to the grown-ups, they came from Ningbo, Fuzhou, Wenzhou, and Jiangxi. This really was a strange thing: all from the Old Country, but so many differences! On this point Grandma could no longer give me much help. Meanwhile, I found them all to be mysterious, skilful, capable. Things that had gotten worn or broken through use only needed a few moments in the caress of their hands to be made as good as new. Seeing how satisfied the wives of the village were when they collected their things, I could see that the repairs must be pretty good.

It was the plowsmiths that most amazed and intrigued me. They didn't work by day like ordinary folk; theirs was a nocturnal trade. There were many of them, and they were big: every one of them a strapping fellow, carrying heavy loads on their shoulders, wearing big broad bamboo hats that doubled as fans to cool the red-hot plowshares just out of the mold. Whenever they arrived in the village they'd go around striking pieces of iron like chimes to collect broken plowshares from people's houses. When night fell they fired up the furnace and melted the iron; one man bent his back to work the bellows until the furnace glowed brightly, while another put the mold in position and used tongs to tip the furnace. The red-hot molten liquid poured from the mouth of the furnace into the mold, sparks flying everywhere. It was really scary, but the man showed no fear whatsoever. Bare-chested, with sweat pouring off his face, he was carrying out his task calmly and gravely, with all the resolve of those who bear heavy responsibility. The red-hot light produced a sculpturing effect, transforming his body into a gigantic column carved in relief. My thoughts were petrified by the scene. To me this man was a magnificent individual.

Early next morning when I got up they had already left. Where their furnace had been there was a pile of burned coal fragments. The coal had turned into all sorts of shapes and colors, a great bounty for our toy boxes.

3

As I gradually gained in years, I learned from my father's conversation that "the Old Country" meant China and that "Old Country people" were the Chinese; China had eighteen provinces, and we had come from Jiaying in Canton province. Later, I looked it up and found that Jiaying was the Qing dynasty name for the place now known as Meixian.

In the fifth grade of Japanese school I started geography lessons. Here I found that China had become "Shina"[2] and Chinese people had become "Shina jin." On the map, Taiwan and China were separated only by a narrow belt of water; across the strait China was like a half-moon curving out toward Taiwan, all the way from the southwest corner to the northeast tip. I had never expected it to be so big! It must be hundreds of times bigger than Taiwan! But Grandma had said my grandpa's grandpa had had to leave because over there he couldn't find a way to live any more. How ever could that be?

Our Japanese teacher often talked to us about "Shina," always with great relish and in unusually high spirits. For two years our ears rang with phrases such as "Shina," "Shina jin," and "Shina hei," and stories of them and other Shina phenomena besides.

All these phrases had specific implications: "Shina" meant "decrepit" and "broken-down"; "Shina jin" meant "opium addicts" and a "shameless, filthy race"; "Shina hei" represented craven cowardice, lack of discipline, and so on.

Among the teacher's Shina stories was the one about a foreigner who had arrived in China for the first time: when he dropped a few coins on the quay some Shina jin rushed over to pick up the fallen money, to his enormous gratitude. But he was mistaken: they pocketed every last coin.

Then there were the stories of the Shina hei. The teacher asked us: "What should we do if our troops are faced with an enemy force?"

"Shoot!" we replied.

"That's right! And Shina hei would also open fire. But in what direction?"

"At the enemy!" we replied again.

The teacher shook his head, slyly. "Wrong! They'd fire into the air."

This really baffled us. Why would they do that? So the teacher explained it to us: "They test the two sides, to see who will pay more.

---

2. In this section, the expressions given as "Shina *this*" and "Shina *that*" are transcribed from the Japanese. To Chinese people, these collocations are insulting—"Shina jin" is roughly equivalent to English "Chinaman."

Shina hei fight only for money, you see. They go over to whichever side offers more."

There were endless stories about Shina jin and Shina hei, and after telling us each one the teacher would always ask what we thought of it. Indeed, what to make of these stories? We weren't sure at all.

The teacher's stories were lively, appealing, and consistent; I couldn't decide whether to believe them.

I stared again at that beautiful curve on the map. The half-moon sure was huge, but otherwise it had nothing at all to tell me.

4

There were two people who simultaneously influenced me from different directions. One was my father, and the other was my brother.

At this time Father was doing business on the Mainland, and every year he made a trip to inspect his investments. His tours would cover all the maritime provinces, from Shandong in the north to Hainan in the south. His knowledge of China was vast, with some of it gained from his reading, and some from personal experience. The people of our village loved to hear him talk about the Old Country. "Old Country this", "Old Country that": they could never hear enough on the subject. But when Father talked about China it was in the tone of someone relating news of an uncle[3] who had formerly been a great man but had fallen on hard times: a mixture of scorn and lingering respect, but most of all regret. Similarly, his audience listened with disappointment, pride, and sadness. Many's the time I heard them sighing: "Ah, the Old Country! The Old Country!"

On one occasion Father undertook the arduous trek all the way to our ancestral village in Jiaying to sweep the graves of our forebears. When he returned he brought a youth along with him: my cousin. When the villagers heard of Father's return they flocked to hear news of "home." Father shook his head and then angrily told them how the place was just an outrageous mess: all the able-bodied men had gone

---

3. The original has *jiujiu* 舅舅 (mother's brother); in the popular Chinese imagination the *jiujiu* type of uncle is often seen as somehow lacking or disreputable. My thanks to Professor Ching-ming Ko of National Taiwan University for pointing out that this connotation appears to apply here.

overseas, leaving only the lazy and the weak at home. In this cousin's family, for instance, his father and two older brothers had all gone to the South Seas, and now he too had come to Taiwan; at home there remained only three women—an old lady and her two young daughters-in-law—and otherwise just a few little ones.

Once again everyone sighed deeply at what they heard.

Later Father became very interested in the island of Hainan and conceived the plan of forming a group within our extended family to move to Yulin and go into the trawler business. First he made two inspection trips there alone and was quite satisfied with what he saw. Then he invited four clansmen to go with him on a third trip. The idea was that if they were satisfied with this inspection they'd put their plans into action as soon as they got home. To their dismay, however, on the second day out from Haikou their automobile was ambushed by bandits. After nearly a fortnight stuck in a small town fearing for their very lives, they had no choice but to abandon the reconnoiter and return home in defeat. Father and his clansmen were cruelly disillusioned, and the dream ended there and then.

That same year, Father closed down his Shanghai subsidiary.

5

Secondly, we come to my brother.

It was mainly my brother who inspired my thoughts and feelings toward China. He had what you might call a strong congenital affinity—an adoration of the Mainland, the fatherland. At high school in Kaohsiung he had twice been formally reprimanded—for "dangerous tendencies" (rebelling against his Japanese teachers) and for reading "harmful books" (*The Three Principles of the People*). Worst of all, these misdemeanors resulted in Father being summoned to the school to receive a severe warning.

The year he graduated from high school, my brother finally received permission from Father to realize his long-held ambition to "take a look at China." He traveled widely for over a month, to Nanking, Shanghai, and other places. When he returned he brought back a gramophone and a great many photographs of the famous sites of Suzhou, the West Lake, and other places. That night our front courtyard was full of visitors. I carried the gramophone out into the center of the yard and wound it up, so that everyone could enjoy their fill of songs "from the Old Country." The records included Mei Lanfang singing from *Farewell to My Concubine*, Lian Jinfeng from *Yutangchun*, and a few arias by Ma Lianliang and Xun Huisheng.[4] There was also some Cantonese opera: *Little Red Peach Blossom* and *Zhaojun's Lament*, and a small number of popular songs besides.

The Cantonese opera bewitched me; its sentimental undulations, agitated surges, and heartbreaking melancholy intoxicated and stupefied me, making me completely forget where I was. These arias, together with the enchanting pictures of famous places, stimulated my imagination enormously and deepened my longing for the land across the Strait. I asked Father several times to allow me to go to high school on the Mainland, but he wouldn't permit it. I begged my brother to speak for me, but he said it was a hopeless cause, because Father was so disillusioned with China.

After the failure of his Mainland interests Father reconsolidated his business at home in Pingtung. My brother went further away than ever—to university in Japan. In the following year [1937] all-out war with China broke out; the whole Japanese Empire seethed with activity; and before long I was enrolled in the Defense Corps. My cousin from Meixian returned to the Mainland. We'd gotten along well during the years we'd spent under the same roof, so it was a hard parting.

As the war raged ever more fiercely, so the range of activities of the Defense Corps expanded: send-offs for new recruits to the army, victory lantern parades, air-raid drills, traffic control. Within four months, Peking, Tientsin, Taiyuan . . . one fell after the other. The Japanese in Pingtung went mad with jubilation: bright lanterns lit the streets by night and joyous voices rang out until dawn.

It was just at this time that my brother made a hurried trip home from Japan. He looked very tense and his eyes were bloodshot, as if he hadn't been sleeping properly. Nobody knew why he had returned to Taiwan, nor did he say. Every day he rushed all over the place, so busy

---

4. The details given suggest that these recordings were all scenes or arias from Peking opera.

that he almost had no time for eating and sleeping. Once he took me to a house out in the country where a dozen or more young men were gathered in a room as if by prior appointment. There was a big bed in the room, and everyone sat wherever they pleased. Apart from a cousin of ours, the rest were all strangers to me.

They debated with one another in fluent Japanese, frequently mentioning things like "colonialism," "the fatherland," "revolution," "the Cultural Society," and "the Sixty-Three Points." I'd never been interested in these terms, so I understood little of what I heard. The meeting dispersed after two hours, without any outcome. My brother seemed very disappointed.

That same evening my brother and our father were talking in Father's bedroom, which was next to mine. At first their conversation sounded friendly, but the more they talked the louder their voices grew until finally it was obvious that they were arguing. I could hear the agitation in my brother's voice. Then suddenly the argument was over. When my brother came out he was in low spirits; his eyes were like two firebrands. When I woke during the night I saw him sitting alone at the desk, writing away at something.

A few days later my brother went back to Japan. Before he went, Father earnestly urged him: "You're a student, so concentrate on your studies. Keep well away from politics." Father's tone was both apologetic and soothing. But my brother remained silent, his ears stoppered against Father's words.

When he next came back from Japan he was calmer and more at peace. By now the [Chinese] national government had retreated to Chungking and the battle lines were moving toward deadlock. My brother said the Japanese were now planning long term, and China too seemed resolved to fight to the bitter end, so the war was set to drag on. He had already decided to go to the Mainland. To my great surprise Father no longer dug in his heels, though neither did he show any pleasure.

On the day of my brother's departure, a cousin and I went as far as Kaohsiung with him; he had arranged to meet up with his traveling companions in Taipei. At every stop on the way to Kaohsiung we encountered new recruits being sent off to the war. They wore red sashes over their shoulders and kept nodding and smiling, while those sending them off craned their necks and belted out the "Infantry March."

> To pacify the unrighteous, to do Heaven's will,
> Our Combined Services are brave and loyal beyond compare,
> . . .

Inside our compartment my brother buried himself deep in his seat, solemn and silent. I had always admired him, and on this occasion I was more impressed than ever by his personal nobility. I told him I too wanted to go to the Mainland. He only smiled and said very quietly: "Good! Good! You'll be welcome."

Not long after my brother left, the military police and secret service started coming to our home asking about him. Again and again they pressed us on his whereabouts and activities. We always answered that we did not know. And in fact we hadn't heard a thing about him since he left; we didn't even know whether he had reached the Mainland.

6

Exasperatingly, it proved impossible to quit the Defense Corps or get out of it in any way. I did once try to resign, citing a long-standing gallstone condition, but my request was denied. The corps commander was an affable middle-aged doctor from Japan. He lifted his singlet to show me a postoperative scar, then patted me on the shoulder and said soothingly that gallstones were extremely easy to remove surgically, and if I so wished he would be happy to oblige me on the spot.

Once during an air-raid drill, half the corps was directing traffic while the other half monitored the blackout neighborhood by neighborhood. It was past midnight when we spotted a sliver of light in the area my group was patrolling. We quickly pinpointed the source of the light. It was a pastry shop, and the owner came to the door to greet us. He told us that the reason for the breach of blackout was that an invalid in the house had gone out to the toilet and failed to draw the blackout curtain back properly.

Considering this to be pardonable in the circumstances, we issued an admonishment to the owner and were about to leave. But just then a Japanese policeman with ratlike eyes came into the house from behind us. First he started roaring like a wild beast, fit to bring the place down, and then, brushing aside all attempts to explain, he took down the pastry cook's name.

We trooped outside in silence, feeling very bad at the turn of events.

"That pastry cook's a Mainlander," said a fellow corpsman when we were back at the lookout tower. His family had been in Pingtung for generations. When he said "Mainlander" he used the Hoklo term *Tangshan ren*, the equivalent of our Hakka "Old Country people" (*yuanxiang ren*).

"He's Tangshan?" I asked him. "Then why didn't he go back to the Mainland? Doesn't he know there's a war on?"

"Couldn't bring himself to leave, could he?" said the Pingtung man. "His wife's from here, and then there's his shop!"

He went on to tell us that a little while ago, during a fund-raising drive for the war, the pastry cook hadn't donated as much as the Japanese had expected from him. They had been greatly dissatisfied with him, so now he might be in for real trouble.

The conversation turned from the pastry cook to the Sino-Japanese War now being fought. My Pingtung friend felt that China's chances of winning were very slim.

"To fight a war you need unity," he said. "But the Chinese are too selfish; every man loves only his own wife and children."

From our vantage point up on the lookout tower, the city of Pingtung was a sheet of pitch black. With no sounds and no lights, it was like a dead city. Only from a few places, where our traffic patrol was carrying out its duties, did the sound of challenges and barked orders carry faintly to our ears. The crescent moon had already set. Stars twinkled in the sky. The Three Stars had passed diagonally across the middle sky and were now sinking toward the west.

Where was the war?

I thought of my brother, now disappeared without a trace. I suddenly missed him very much. I didn't know if he had made it to Chungking, or what he was doing now. Since I lost him it was as if my life had been emptied of substance: everything had become vacuous and meaningless. Somehow I felt that I should follow him, that he was waiting for me somewhere all this time.

"You'll be welcome! You'll be welcome!"
My brother's voice kept echoing in my ears.

7

I left not long afterward—for the Mainland.

At the time I had no passport, but I had discovered a route I could take: first by ship to Japan, then from Japan to Dalian; if you could only get there, you could then go south or north as you pleased.

And so I just went!

I set myself no plan of what I would do—I just wanted to get away from Taiwan; and I didn't go to Chungking to look for my brother.

I am not a patriot, but Old Country blood must flow back to the Old Country before it can stop seething!

So it was with my brother, and neither could I be any exception.

Part 2

Stories from the Old Country

The first version was completed on January 10, 1939, in Shenyang under the title "Dushi de huanghun" 都市的黃昏 (The city at dusk). It was first published in 2009 in *New Complete Works* 8:9-40. It was completely rewritten and completed on August 21, 1954, in Meinong under the present title. This version was first published in 1959 in *Lianhe Bao Fukan* 聯合報副刊 [United Daily News: supplement] with further minor revisions.

4. In the Willow Shade
柳陰

It was in Shenyang that I met Park Shin-jun, a young man from Korea, born and brought up beside the Taedong River.

He was the type of man whom one encounters but rarely in the wilderness that is life: a person worthy of one's most cherished memories who would long have a place in a corner of one's heart. Rather dark of complexion, Park had a broad but elegant forehead and feet that seemed out of proportion to the rest of his body. With his quietly gleaming eyes, he had the intelligence and slight tendency to melancholy common to literary youth. In his tight-fitting oil-stained khaki working gear, with narrow sleeves and underlength trousers, he looked even taller and slimmer than he was—like a bamboo pole. In reality, what lay beneath that sackcloth attire was a soul that matched any bamboo pole for goodness, simplicity, and straightforwardness.

Among my many classmates, and especially among the Koreans, Park was the first one that I got to know—on account of his love for art and literature, as well as his quiet but straightforward nature—and we became the best of friends.

At the time, we were enrolled at the Manchuria Automobile School. In the mornings we practiced driving, and in the afternoons we received training in auto mechanics from Lieutenant Hirotsu, a retired officer who, with his big "Jintan" mustache, looked just like the "mustachioed man" on the billboards.[1] There were two practice grounds:

---

1. Jintan 仁丹 pills were an extremely popular throat medicine and cure-all throughout the Japanese Empire of this period. The distinctive advertisements, featuring a cocked-hatted and epauletted military officer with a fine mustache, were widely known. The brand remains popular in Japan today as a breath-freshener. In Chinese, *rendan hu* (*xu*) 仁丹鬍(鬚) (Jintan whiskers) became synonymous with the indigenous term *bazihu* 八字鬍 (八-shaped whiskers, i.e., mustache).

the first was the school quadrangle, where first-term students practiced the basics—going forward and in reverse in a straight line. From second term more complex driving skills were taught for which the quadrangle was rather too restricted, so we moved on to the second circuit.

Number 2 Practice Ground was where the main road swept out, about one kilometer past the southern suburbs. It was surrounded by wire fencing. To the west it faced Military Camp A across a motor road. Hidden in the shadows of the round concrete blockhouses' gun-slits, the soldiers' steely gaze was constantly fixed on our practice circuit. For all the world like the most dutiful of sentries, a triangular wooden sign naming our school and stating the purpose of the site stood proudly on empty ground by the entrance, where some grass was growing. Two awnings had been set up on the north side of the circuit, looking like a pair of white clouds. Almost all of the students whose turn to drive had not yet come were sitting or lying or huddling in groups under the awnings, chatting, resting, waiting. This is where Park and I first met, but later the two of us spent more of our time in the shade of a row of leafy willows above the road, to the east of the awnings.

In North China, willows like these are everywhere. Their branches formed green curtains trailing down to the ground, shutting out both the burning sun and the noise. When the odd gust of breeze coursed through the trees, the twigs and the leaves would lightly, dreamily pitch and toss, gathering delicious coolness in their embrace.

Behind the willows was a vineyard, where great bunches of grapes grew, their skins covered with white bloom.

Through the willow fronds we could see the much bigger, blue curtain of the sky above. And we could see the yellow-earth spaces of the practice circuit lying exposed under the burning heat and ferocious glare. Over to the north we could also see the city of Shenyang, wreathed in billows of smoke and dust that resembled a silent prairie fire.

In the shade of those willows Park and I whiled away the sweltering hours, in conversation, in silences, and in brooding.

He spoke Japanese with exceptional fluency and accuracy. Through Japanese he had read widely in world literature. He had a habit of stripping off one willow leaf after another and putting them in his mouth as he talked. With his mouselike small sharp teeth he gnawed each one to fine shreds, folding it in as if between the cogs of a machine. Fold it in, mince it with his teeth, then spit it out. And then it began again as he plucked the next leaf. . . . Chewing willow leaves became almost an addiction with him.

Amid his gnawing, folding, spitting, and plucking, our conversations and our friendship were quietly woven. One day, after we had been discussing the relationship between literary works and the lives of their authors, we began talking about the traditions of early marriage and arranged marriage in Korea. Park's ardent words and bitter tone and his intense personal engagement with the topic were very convincing: in Korea, the land he loved so fervently, the younger generation's most precious asset was being neglected, devalued, and wasted in the name of something utterly irrational. But what made an even bigger impression on me was the way the fiery darts from his burning eyes targeted the unconscionable silence and empty sighs of other people.

Then he changed the subject to Korean folk songs. Park believed that in any country the best and most direct reflection of life—especially the moral life of the two sexes—was the folk song. He sang for me an extremely moving folk song that brimmed with the suffering and recriminations of a strange love affair: "Arirang."[2]

We lay on our backs in the willow shade, our hands behind our heads, letting the smaller curtain of the willows and the big curtain of the sky take us in their soft, serene embrace.

> Arirang,
> Arirang,
> Arariyo,
> Arirang,
> . . .

---

2. Believed to be very ancient in origin (perhaps as early as the fourteenth century CE), "Arirang" is Korea's best-known song, a kind of unofficial national anthem. In this song of lovers' parting Arirang is the name of a mountain pass, but has not been identified with any actual place.

Park didn't really have much of a singing voice, but the beautiful musical phrases and rhythm of the song took me away to that sad, far-off country described by its lyrics.

When he finished singing he suddenly propped himself up on one elbow, looked at me, and asked: "Have you read *Resurrection*?"

When I said I hadn't, he sat up and said, "That's a shame! It's a really good book. In it Tolstoy teaches us ... why a man must cherish the love in his heart!"

A few years later I had the opportunity of reading *Resurrection*, but I couldn't find what Park felt to be so good about it. I reckoned the reason the book had moved him so much must lie in a remarkable coincidence between its content and his own life. But then again, what if it was actually the book that had inspired him to imitate the religious redemptive motivation of its protagonist, Nekhlyudov?

But these thoughts came later....

One day the weather was very hot, so that the might of the sun could be felt all around.

A boxy 1934 Ford, old and battered beyond recognition, juddering despairingly, was slowly staggering and crawling round the practice circuit like an unruly old mare carrying the weight of its great age on its back. Boiling water foamed out from the radiator, which had never had a cap, hissing as though the engine were a winded monster gasping for breath. The steam and the blue smoke of overheated engine oil enveloped the hood in heat and mist. Every twenty minutes, from the dusty shadows of this pitiful automobile there would come a broad, somewhat impatient yelling. Directed at the cotton awnings and all around, the shouts came from our practical driving instructor, a Korean with a Japanese name: Mr. Yamada was calling the next student to the car....

"Next! Park—Byung—yung...."

On one side the clamorous city of Shenyang lay sprawled in the windblown dust like a nouveau riche caught with his trousers down and no time to make himself decent. To our west, in Tiexi, which means "west of the tracks," factory chimneys were opening wide a thousand mouths, belching filthy, sticky smoke, blackening half the sky.

One had to raise his eyes above this dark satanic miasma to see, far to the east, how the sky displayed a continental vastness and profundity, and how in its infinite immensity it gathered the entire expanse of the Liaodong Plain to its bosom.

Park Shin-jun was gnawing his umpteenth willow leaf, staring fixedly, levelly, and silently north to the grimy city of Shenyang with his intense, limpid eyes. On an area of grass bathed in the torrential rays of dazzling sunshine, several white and yellow dots, like flowers—stray dogs—were tearing around, frolicking, rolling around like footballs.

"Just look at those coal fumes, and all that dust!" said Park, pulling a face as though some sand had just blown into his mouth. "This city will never be clean!"

And so, as he stripped the willow leaves with his teeth, he told me how this "uncleanable city," buried in coal fumes, clouds, and dust, was nevertheless expanding at an unbelievable rate. It was like a warehouse: once the door was opened, anything could go inside—hooligans and gentlefolk, dross and gold, ideals and depravity. The record for population growth stood at ten thousand new residents in a single day.

"How do you know?" I asked, my eyes wide.

"The South Manchurian Railway keeps statistics!" answered Park.

"That's an amazing figure! But I don't like this city at all. One day I will definitely leave."

A few minutes of silence followed before the conversation turned to our respective reasons for coming to Manchuria.

"Let me guess," I said, half jokingly. "You came here to realize all your hopes and dreams. Am I right?" As I spoke I was thinking of all the people who at that time were surging like a ferocious tide—almost blindly, rabidly—into the New Found Land that was Manchuria.

Park had been born and brought up in a comfortably-off family in the countryside by the Taedong River. He had scarcely been weaned from his mother's breast when his father arranged for him to marry a local girl when they both grew up. But when Park did grow up and formed his own ideas about the future, it was another female he chose: a childhood playmate. Eventually he and his sweetheart reached and passed through that make-or-break moment in their relationship, that point of no return that society allows only married couples to pass. But just at this time, Park's parents and those of that poor other girl put pressure on them to marry. And so my friend Park decided to show a clean pair of heels, taking off for Manchuria.

That was in September of year 12 of the Showa period, the twenty-sixth year of the Republic of China....[3]

When I heard this part of the story I became very interested, and so when Park paused slightly in his relation I couldn't help interjecting a question: "So did you and your sweetheart have an agreement that you would come here first, and when you had got things ready you would go and bring her to join you here?"

"No!" he replied, shaking his head. "That would have been good thinking, but at the time she and I never thought of that."

"You should have thought of it," I said.

"You're right, I should have."

"And so, what became of her?"

Park sighed, and a shadow of worry and depression fell over his shining eyes. After some hesitation he said, "Her family found out about our relationship and her father was very angry. He wanted to force her to marry ... "

"Oh, so she married someone else?"

"She ran away."

"Where to?"

"Nampho."[4]

"Nampho?"

"That's right, Nampho."

"What did she do there?"

"At first she was a waitress in a coffeehouse."

"And now?"

Park sighed again, and looked at me as he hesitated. Then he shifted his darkened gaze toward the driving circuit....

"She's a prostitute!"

I was stunned. The conversation came to a halt.

And so, we ... kept silent.

I looked at him. He sat with both knees drawn up; his body was turned toward me, but his face pointed in the other direction, and he seemed to be gazing into the far distance.

3. 1937.
4. Nampho is a port city at the mouth of the Taedong River, about 50 km downriver from Pyongyang.

As a fresh breeze came blowing, the willows' skirts gracefully flounced and began to dance as trippingly as young girls.

Our classmates' merry laughter rose up from under the white sun canopies. They sounded so boisterous, so utterly uninhibited.

Suddenly, Mr. Yamada's sonorous voice called out from the practice ground: "Next! Park—Shin-jun..."

After Park had left I lay down again, looking up at the sky. Quite naturally, my thoughts turned on the unhappy fate of my friend and the girl now reduced to prostitution. What melodrama, what unexpected twists in the plot, what a miserable denouement... I had never expected such a remarkable story. Personally I was disappointed by my friend's reaction to his problem. I couldn't understand why he meekly allowed himself to be manipulated by Fate. Nor did I understand how he could tell his own story as if it was someone else's and nothing to do with him, shaking his head and sighing, but not taking any action.

I truly felt like weeping for that woman.

The sunlight flowed down, as heavy as water. The baking sky was flickering like cicadas' wings.

I closed my eyes.

Somewhere a peddler was crying his wares, and from even further off the breeze brought the faint, crisp sound of a horse's bridle bells—di-ling, di-ling, di-ling...

Suddenly, a sharp voice that I knew very well rose up in the direction I was facing. It was a metallic sound, with the quality of a hysterical woman's voice.

"Sheesh!"—the voice was yelling—"Damn! This is just too much..."

I opened my eyes.

An extremely short man was in the act of stooping to part the swaying willow curtain and enter the area of shade. This was my second Korean friend, whom I had got to know through Park Shin-jun. He was nicknamed "Mr. Misfortune," but his real name was Kim Tae-ki. Apparently there were two reasons for the nickname: one, he had a wife six years older than him (it seemed the age difference was not the point here, but the fact that theirs was an arranged marriage); two, at the age of fifteen he had become the father of a daughter.

"He's a sacrificial victim of the system of early marriage and arranged marriage," Park told me, fuming. "An absolute masterpiece of the type. Just think about it, what can a young man in his situation ever hope to achieve?"

Even so, although he had been forced at such an early age to shoulder the burden of the trivial intricacies of family life; although he had been cruelly tossed into the dizzying, rapidly swirling whirlpool of life, Kim had somehow lost none of his bright and cheerful, youthful outlook. And there was another side to him that attracted me: his ardent and innocent curiosity about the meaning of all things, his refusal to rest until he got to the bottom of every last obscure secret of life. Indeed, when I looked at how, faced with a mountain of ugly and chaotic mundanity, he still managed to preserve and maintain a childlike purity, this resolute personal struggle of his aroused in me the kind of compassion one might feel for a small bird caught in a thunderstorm.

At any rate, it seemed to me to be a virtue in itself that in spite of forever being either in the frying pan or in the fire he still adhered so closely to what he believed to be important in life.

With all the innocence and self-confidence of a child he would ask me: Was Taiwan so hot that people needed to take cold showers? Did bananas grow wild everywhere, even on hillsides and in the wastelands? As wonderful as Taiwan was, wasn't Korea even better?

I told him about the cultivation and management of bananas, their actual distribution, and the different habitats to which they were suited.

He listened intently, his head slightly tilted, thought for a moment, and said: "That's not how I imagined it. I thought they grew all by themselves, all over the hills and filling the valleys, and you only had to reach out a hand to pick one."

What a poetic imagination.

Regarding the grasping principal of our school, Kim said: "Why on earth does anyone have to be like that?"

Now, as he spoke, his pale, malnourished face—which soot, heat, dust, sweat, and fatigue had turned the gray-green color of yesterday's *mantou*[5]—constantly emitted steam. His yellowish eyes stared wide in

---

5. *Mantou* 饅頭: steamed buns, typical of the wheat-based traditional staple food of north China, as opposed to rice in the south.

surprise. His yellowing double-breasted cotton jacket, apparently unwashed for quite some time, gave off the uniquely human sour smell of sweat and natural body odor combined. On his feet was a pair of rubber-soled shoes covered in patches.

He was slight as well as short, with a long slender neck; among his tall, strapping compatriots Kim looked like a mutation. He gave the impression of being a creature whose physiological development has suddenly been arrested due to some biochemical change in its body—a premature degeneration.

Wiping the sweat from his face and taking off his misshapen, discolored hunting cap, Kim breathed loudly through his wide-open mouth.

"Are you done?" I asked him.

"Yep!" He spoke Japanese with a very heavy Korean accent.

"Goddammit . . . !" He let loose a stream of curses at the unbearable heat.

"Hey, Kim, are you and Park from the same part of Korea?" I asked him, after a pause to let him catch his breath.

"No, he's from Hwanghae province; I'm from North Cholla. We met here in Manchuria."

"Did you know he had a sweetheart? And that she's now . . ."

Kim stopped fanning himself for a moment and gave me an inscrutable look.

"Didn't he mention it to you before?" he asked. "Well, he doesn't like others to know about it."

"Is it true she's become a prostitute?"

"Probably."

"Where?"

"Pyongyang. Park only learned about it recently. He's very upset."

"Is there no way he can go and get her out of it?"

"I don't know. . . . Apparently not."

Holding the hunting cap in his hand, Kim watched the practice circuit.

In the raw hands of an inexperienced driver, the Ford—or rather, the old mare—was howling bitterly and helplessly on her knees, as though goaded by a brutal, pitiless rider. In the car, although I could not make him out through the swirling dust, steam, and smoke, was our friend Park Shin-jun.

All of a sudden, I had the saddest feeling.

It seemed incredible that that simple, straightforward guy, stitched into those sacklike clothes of his, could be carrying such an unspeakable wound—a wound he lived with every day and carried with him wherever he went, even now as he tried to learn to drive.

And on the other hand, there was she, that poor young woman!

Having watched the circuit for some time in silence, Kim finally shifted his gaze from it to my face.

"Zhong, are you taking the test this term?"

"It's almost upon us already. When is it again?"

"At the end of the month."

"What about you?" I turned his question back at him.

"I'm not taking it!"

"Me neither," I said. "This is only our second term. Taking the test would just be a waste of eight yuan."

"That doesn't matter so much. What I mean is . . . " Kim stopped and thought, but did not say what it was he meant.

With his brows knotted in a frown, he seemed lost in his own thoughts. All the while he kept fanning his face. His hair was very fine, like that of a newborn babe; it was light in color, more brown than black, and the ends curled up all around his head. His hands were very thin and wrinkled—like those of an old person.

"I'm going to pack it in," he said, after fanning a while longer. He spoke calmly, his head bowed. . . .

"What?" I stared wide-eyed in surprise.

Now he looked up. In his eyes there burned a resolute will: a way of thinking carefully and painstakingly arrived at.

"I'm going to withdraw from the school. Shorties like me can't drive automobiles. When I sit down in the cab it's like falling into an ocean. I can't see a thing. When a shorty's driving he feels like he's hanging from the gallows; it's a living hell. There's no way I'll pass the test. Anyway, my circumstances won't allow me to go on. From enrollment to taking the test and finding a job takes at least six months. Starting from next month my family won't have enough to eat. This morning I put in a request for the school to refund my remaining fees, but the principal refused.

"Enrolling here was a mistake," he continued, after a pause. "Even if the principal won't let me withdraw, I'm still quitting. I need to find another way. . . . It's different for you guys!"

From the next day Kim no longer came to classes. When I realized this a few days later I asked Park Shin-jun about it, but he didn't know what Kim was doing either.

On the day of the test, although Park and I had not registered, we went along to watch, not only because we intended to take the test next term, but because of our intimate involvement in the process.

The test ground was just north of our Number 2 Practice Ground and separated from it only by a wire fence. Test candidates and spectators formed a dense crowd, almost completely filling the test ground, which was half an acre or more in area. In several places the crowd pressed the rope barrier out in a curve over the track. The stewards kept shouting angrily at the crowd to keep back.

It was the most beautiful day. To the south the endless blue sky, like a kindly old grandmother, cradled a few floating clouds in its arms. The little clouds looked like flowers embroidered on a bed-curtain. Through the dry, clear air, the sun—the unimpeded sun—was scattering great quantities of light and heat down to the ground.

The shape of the test circuit was an Arabic numeral 5. The car was one of the newest streamlined Buicks. One by one a hundred or more candidates took their turn for the prescribed three minutes each. As if on a great sieve, each one struggled, sank or swam, playing his role in the tautest, most thrilling of tragicomedies . . . the smiles of those who passed, the sighs of those who fell through the sieve.

Park and I mingled with the overflowing waves of people, sweating, irritated, red in the face . . . until finally we escaped the test ground.

Outside the main gate peddlers swarmed like flies, selling cooling food and drink, glutinous rice cake, and candied haws.[6] The sound of wares being cried, the grating of ice being scooped, and other con-

---

6. Chinese hawberries are a popular snack in north China. Typically, about six or seven of the fruits, which resemble tiny apples, are skewered kebablike on thin sticks and coated with a kind of toffee.

fused noises of the marketplace formed a countermelody to the surging clamor of the test ground.

Just as we went out through the gate, we heard someone calling us by name. Stopping to look, we saw a peddler pushing his bicycle toward us.

Good heavens! What a surprise. Wasn't this Kim Tae-ki?

Sure enough, here came Kim, wreathed in pleasant, honest smiles—looking for all the world as if he'd been in business for a decade.

"Are you here for the test? Or just to watch?" he asked.

The same smiling face, the same guileless, ever-cheery Kim Tae-ki! He put his bike on its stand and opened the green-painted box on the back, each side of which bore the legend "Hygienic and Tasty—Chilled Fruit Ices." He chose four ice popsicles, two cream flavor and two red bean.

"Have a popsicle!"

I stared stupidly at this smiling, happy little man for a while before coming to myself.

"So you really packed it in?" I asked him.

"Why wouldn't I?" And he smiled his happy smile some more.

I felt strangely depressed.

"So how's business?" asked Park.

"Not bad!"

After we'd left Kim and were walking home, Park said to me: "You see! See how much we are forced to suffer, just for the sake of a woman, for the sake of a bad marriage!"

In late autumn we took the graduation test, and Park and I both passed. We only awaited the arrival of our driving licenses—then we would be drivers.

While waiting for the licenses to be issued I was away from Shenyang for a few days, seeing a friend in Changchun. The day I returned, Kim Tae-ki came to my lodgings and handed me a letter.

"Park has left," he said.

"Left? Where to?" I was stunned.

"Zhangjiakou."[7]

---

7. Zhangjiakou 张家口, in Hebei province on the Great Wall facing Inner Mongolia, has sometimes been better known by its Mongol name, Kalgan.

"What for?"

"I think the letter will explain it."

I read the letter with disbelieving eyes.

"I expect you'll remember the prostitute," said Kim, who had remained silent while I read. "That poor woman. Recently she had an offer of work from a hotel in Zhangjiakou. Park didn't tell me this until the day it happened. He had had a letter from her saying she would be passing through Shenyang. He met her train, and then they went off together...."

I thought about this in silence, but it was beyond my powers of imagination. I just couldn't comprehend what lay behind it all.

Then Kim piped up again: "He seemed very worked up. I think he made up his mind on the spot."

I looked at the letter again. It was in a hasty scrawl, betraying a turbulent mind.

Two aspects of this event threw me into a state of bewilderment and vexation for a long time: first, the loss of a friend; second, the hidden significance and drama of the affair itself. Although the letter asked me not to bother myself about it, I couldn't help being disturbed by such thoughts as: Was it she who asked him to go with her? Or was it his idea? And why?

Having lost Park, Kim and I also gradually lost touch with each other, all the more so as before long I started work as a driver for the Shenyang Transport Company. After almost ten hours of driving each day, I was so tired I felt like a lump of wood, so I rarely felt in sufficient spirits to hook up with Kim. From autumn into early winter we didn't see each other at all. I don't know how he lived during that period: with winter coming he wouldn't be able to sell ices; might he have turned to some other trade?

One cold winter's day, a biting north wind was blowing the thick snow from the branches and gusting into my face as I walked. I needed a new place to stay and was going to see a room at No. x, Liujing Road. Recognizing the address, I hoped to see Kim Tae-ki while I was there.

I was in luck with the room, but I didn't find Kim. It turned out he had moved out a fortnight before and had left Shenyang. The room for rent was the very one his family had vacated.

"Where did they go?" I asked the landlady, an old Japanese woman.

"Probably back to Korea," she replied.

"Back to Korea?"

"Of course, he didn't want to go back. He had no option. His popsicles wouldn't sell and he couldn't find other work; his family was going hungry half the time...."

I moved into the room that same day. That evening the old Japanese woman, kneeling on the tatami, smiled apologetically and, showing warm concern, told me the story of that unlucky man. She praised him lavishly as an upright and honest person, for his sincere attitude toward life and toward his fellow man, and for his straightforward and cheerful nature. Eventually I learned from her that Kim had had to give her a quilt in lieu of his last two months' rent.

"What could I do? These few rooms are my only livelihood!" A sad smile crept onto her face, like a child who has just been forgiven for doing something a bit naughty.

That night in bed, listening to the wind howling like a wolf, I tossed and turned and could not sleep. I was thinking about my friends—Kim Tae-ki back in Korea and Park Shin-jun in Zhangjiakou.

I remembered Park's words:

"See how much we are forced to suffer, just for the sake of a woman, for the sake of a bad marriage!"

Completed on July 7, 1944, and first published in 1945 in *Jiazhutao* (Oleander), Beijing: Ma Dezeng. This translation incorporates corrections made by hand by the author on his copy of the first edition, and selectively includes other revisions shown in *Complete Works* II (reprinted in *New Complete Works* 3:315-371).

5. Oleander
夾竹桃

I

"Canopy, fish basin, pomegranate." The tenement yard corroborated various studies that had been written on the living landscape of Peking people. In other words, this compound was a typical representative of all the courtyard dwellings of the city of Peking.

When the season of lilac blossom arrived it was the habit of Mrs. Shao—the wife of the sub-landlord—to bring out her fish basin and all kinds of flowerpots from the corners of her bedroom, even from under the bed, and set them out in the courtyard. She brushed away the cobwebs and thick, thick layers of dust covering them, mounted the fish basin on a high pile of bricks, and then surrounded it with the various potted flowers: pomegranate, oleander, dwarf lilyturf, hydrangea, crab apple, jasmine, Indian azalea, and so on. It was a pity that she only rarely kept goldfish in her fish basin, which was usually stocked with a glossy green profusion of sweet flag instead. Although the mood sometimes took her to buy one or two goldfish from a passing peddler, generally before the day was out, or within only four or five days at most, her daughter or some other naughty child in the compound would have scooped them out. By the time she discovered them, the poor creatures would either be caught in the flag fronds, high above the water, or else they'd be lying on the ground by the basin where they had been flung, their lovely golden bellies bathing in the sun.

"Impossible children!" she'd say, as she looked pityingly at the desiccated fish.

Summer had arrived. People were removing their lined gowns and changing into unlined cotton ones. The foliage in Mrs. Shao's pots was already abundantly green, and the oleanders were beginning to put out their pretty little red or white flowers.

This was also the time when the sub-landlord, Shao Chengquan, would get the canopy company to erect a simple canopy in the rear courtyard as shelter from the burning sun.

However, there was another regrettable thing, namely, Mrs. Shao's one and only Peking pomegranate, which looked half-dead with its sparse leaves of what could only be called gray-green and its two or three small flowers. Seemingly finding it unpresentable, Mrs. Shao shoved it in a corner, while her pots of luxuriant oleander replaced it in the position of honor. So there was nothing for it but to revise the three great ideals of the Peking courtyard to "Canopy, sweet flag, oleander." Luckily, as far as the reality was concerned, there was no great conflict here. Firstly: as long as there was a fish basin, there was no real need to be overly persnickety as to what was kept in it, goldfish or sweet flag. Secondly: oleander was not necessarily any less beautiful than pomegranate. Moreover, the Pekingese are a smooth, slick race of people, vastly experienced and resourceful—they would never allow pedantry to get in the way of the true meaning of things. Although there were certain other matters, such as the fact that the new phrase didn't trip off the tongue with as much resonance as the old, nobody bothered about them all that much.

It is human nature to assume that any place where flowers are in bloom must also possess the brightness of spring, healthy lives, human dignity, and human warmth. But goodness knows what this compound possessed! It was overflowing with all the evil and misery of human society that can be expressed in the vocabulary of ugliness and sorrow.

The first thing that must be mentioned is that, as with other Peking courtyard dwellings, very few people knew—or, more precisely, very few people could be sure—how many rooms there really were in this compound. According to the local way of counting, anything that had a covering—these coverings were many and varied: tiles, plaster, mud, reeds, sheet iron, even a sack of straw or a rush mat, and one could extend the list; anything that had something to hold it up—the "something" may be divided into three categories: three and a half posts, two and a half walls, or a few bricks—then no matter whether it were a garbage dump, a kennel, or a toilet, and no matter whether it were inhabited by those lords of creation—human beings—or by some other kind of animal, then each was counted as a room. . . . Thus, according to the sub-landlord's report there were altogether sixteen rooms in the compound. But . . . the devil knows. Luckily all the occupants were members of the world's most superior race, blessed above all others in possessing all possible human virtues: they were forbearing, satisfied with their lot, reticent. Like wild pigs they had the ability to live in their dark, filthy, damp nests, comfortably and contentedly. And so they felt very pleased with their situation. They even had a nice way of putting things: they had "the tenacious vitality of animals! the yielding but tough adaptability of wild grass!" Outsiders, however, would open their wide eyes in amazement, shake their heads, and exclaim: Good gracious! What a people! What an extraordinary people!

The compound was composed of three courtyards: front, middle, and back. The middle courtyard was small and narrow and was nicknamed "the passage"; at either end there was a wooden door, but these doors were never closed.

All kinds of people lived here. At the top there was Zeng Simian, a civil servant who lived with his family in the three-room apartment—the only rooms worthy of the name—on the north side of the middle courtyard. At the bottom was the family—heaven knows what they did for a living—who had the two rooms on the south side of the back courtyard.

Rather than say they "lived," one might just as well say they "crouched like bats in caves," muddling along, muddling through, muddling aimlessly through. And yet on the surface they lived very amiably, they got along very well together, and they even occasionally showed one another consideration (although most of the time no one paid anyone else any attention). They were like people who had come together by chance, like strangers on a stricken vessel. Since they could not fight the destiny that they bore, there was no other way for them to get through their storm of the century, the journey of their lives. As Mrs. Shao said: behind the compound door they were all one big family!

And now, summer was here again.

The oleander was growing vigorously, putting out its first flower; the sweet flag in the basin was also sprouting lovely thick stems and leaves. The sun canopy had been put up in the back courtyard, so that most of the cramped, stifling hot yard was now covered with refreshing, pleasant shade.

On such roasting summer days, the shade of the canopy became a natural meeting place. As a lush green pasture lures a herd of deer, the cool shade drew these neighbors under the canopy. After the midday meal and in the evenings they would gather here to enjoy the cool and indulge in conversation.

One early afternoon, looking over at the deserted south apartment, Mrs. Shao reported to the two ladies enjoying the cool alongside her, Mrs. Zhuang, who lived in the east wing, and Mrs. Zeng: "The day before yesterday I saw Old Mrs. Yan's daughter. She told me the old lady will be moving back in in a couple of days."

"Is she better?" asked Mrs. Zeng.

"They say she's better, but she's not really herself. Miss Yan says she can't put up with her any longer, so she has no choice but to send her back here and let her brother's family look after her."

"Why didn't she just go and live with them then?" said Mrs. Zhuang.

"Them? Hasn't Laosan's wife got enough mouths to feed? And now he's unemployed, he might be needing to go out and beg before long! Miss Yan says that in order to persuade her sister-in-law to come and look after the old lady she had to give her a pair of trousers, for she'd none to wear!"

The three women fell silent, turning in tacit agreement to look at the south apartment, which had been empty for half a year. Long-legged spiders hung from the eaves and the windows were long since sealed with dust.

2

This rectangular compound, its street-side roof all covered in jet-black sludge, its wall corners and plinths speckled with moss—probably nobody knew how many alternating times of prosperity and decline it had seen, what great changes in the world it had witnessed. Its decrepit, gray, and faded exterior not only made it clear that it was approaching its last years of decline and decay, but also shed light on the undulating worldly road it had traveled. Yes! It was already as weary and haggard as the tenants who roosted in its cramped and dirty quarters, more like pigeonholes than so-called human dwellings.

A dozen or more years ago the proprietor of a barbershop had bought the compound as a gift for old Mrs. Yan, the elderly woman Mrs. Shao had been talking about to Mrs. Zhuang and Mrs. Zeng. He had wanted to take her only daughter as a concubine, and the gift was a token of his sincerity. However, within two years the old lady's sons began secret discussions about selling the property and splitting the proceeds. When he learned about this the barbershop boss bought the compound back again. This time, however, he put his own name on the title deeds instead of his mother-in-law's, and he still remained the owner. Thus the old woman fell abruptly from the position of landlady to that of a resident cloistered in the two south rooms of the back courtyard. Mind you, she didn't pay rent.

Among the oldest residents of this compound, after the old lady the next in line were Shao Chengquan and his family, who had lived here for over eight years. Mr. Shao had moved in after getting a job in a large hotel. He was an amiable man, approaching forty years of age, short in stature. He always smiled broadly at you, appearing kind and friendly—although at any hour of day or night one might see him, face and neck flushed, eyes popping out of his head, and a voice like thunder, shouting at his wife or his six-year-old daughter. The cause of these outbursts was usually that his wife had used sesame oil making pancakes, or his daughter had bought twenty cents' worth of roast sweet potatoes between meals, that kind of thing. So apart from this minor blemish—and it has to be said that not giving proper consideration to the hour of the day when scolding one's wife in a voice that is audible several lanes away is an extreme lapse in good taste—this sublandlord of ours was really a fine, good-hearted man.

He had worked in that large hotel for eight years now, and the precision of his timekeeping was like that of an American-made clock. Every week he worked one night shift, and unless something absolutely prevented it, he went to work every day, rain, hail, or snow. So Lu Qizhong, for example, who lived in the south apartment of the middle courtyard, would ask his wife: "What time is it?" Clever Mrs. Lu wouldn't need to turn and look at the desk clock they'd had for at least ten years, and tell him: "Half past eight!" Instead she would answer: "Mr. Shao just got back from work!" The time Shao Chengquan got home from a night shift happened to be precisely the time Lu Qizhong had to leave for work.

Toward the tenants of the compound he, Shao Chengquan, could be said, to a certain extent, to be very polite, and even affectionate. Although his home was rent-free (because he spread his rent over that of all the other tenants) he still would often wear worry and distress all over his face, and his voice would be full of sighs and lamentation as he said: "Ai! What's to be done. I'm so poor, the paltry amounts I get for my labors at the hotel aren't even enough to keep my wife and daughter in gruel, so how can I keep subsidizing others every month! On one hand there's the landlord: if he says the rent's to go up then the rent must go up; but on the other hand, aren't we all good neighbors? You've all been very good to me, so how can I ask you for more? Isn't that right, Mr. Zeng? Ai, what can I do?"

At times like these everybody in the yard knew perfectly well what he was up to: instinctively they knew that the sub-landlord was about to raise the rent again. And so they were extremely unhappy, and couldn't help grumbling about the landlord's insatiable greed. But after grumbling for a while they would end up dutifully acceding to the demand.

Almost invariably, every few months the sub-landlord would repeat his performance of sighs and lamentation, and afterward, sure enough, within at most a month Mrs. Shao would go from household to household telling them that from next month the rent would increase by three yuan per room. They would be most aggrieved at this, unable to understand why the rent should keep endlessly rising.

Mrs. Zhuang in particular, the sub-landlord's next-door neighbor in the back courtyard, who often chatted and had a laugh with Mrs. Shao and seemed to get on with her very well, acted as if nothing less than a lump of her flesh were being carved out, and would be deeply wounded for months on end. At the start of every month she'd be grumbling even as she handed the rent money over.

Mrs. Zhuang was short and fat while her husband Zhuang Jingfu was tall and thin, so that they looked just like the comedy film star Tang Jie and his wife. Mr. Zhuang was a traveling agent for a warehouse-inn, so he was rarely at home during the day, and not often at night either. But strange to say, Mrs. Zhuang's fecundity was in no way inferior to that of a sow: her children came one a year, hot on each other's heels. Although she was still in her early thirties, her children were already like a swarming brood of ducklings.

Whether for good or for bad I don't know, but the fact is that China has more women like Mrs. Zhuang than any other kind. They are everywhere. Miserly, selfish, abject, petty, nosy, interfering, quarrelsome, sharp-tongued . . . and so on and so forth: these are the stamps of their character. Schadenfreude—sniffing around to see if some family or other is harboring a juicy calamity—is one of their biggest daily concerns. As for their children, these women resemble machines: all they know is how to manufacture them. Moreover, they're congenitally blessed with mouths that they can open like a bellowing ox, awe-inspiring in sound and power, capable of frightening their produce into behaving as meekly as lambs.

"You dare?!" they roar. And with one swift lunge they're upon the child, lashing out with hand or foot to its head, its back, its stomach, bang bang bang . . . as if beating a big drum. That'll learn 'em! In this way they mold children who will sit nice and obediently on the stone section beneath the house plinth, staring vacantly at the sky like lumps of wood. This is what makes these mothers happy and content.

Above all, miserliness and pettiness are the special secret heirlooms of these women. Just take a look at the scene as they buy vegetables at the street door, for example. I guarantee you'll be shocked and amazed, and gasp at their ingenuity and the agility of their handiwork. Somehow they can manage to spirit four or five sticks of celery or a handful of beans from the vendor's barrow into their baskets, without anyone seeing how they do it, as if by magic!

The front courtyard was shared by two one-room households. In the south wing was the Western-style tailor Lin Dashun; the north apartment was inhabited by a widow with thickly swollen eyelids.

The story went that because the Lins had once stolen a few briquettes of the widow's coal—or perhaps it was the widow who stole the Lins'—the accusations had never stopped flying since, and each side blamed the other. Anyway, on one side were thieves and on the other were victims, or it might actually have been that both were thieves and both victims. Even the parties involved didn't seem sure, so naturally no outsider was in a position to pass judgment. To this day the two households were irreconcilable in their indignation.

The widow had one son and one daughter. The son had no reputable employment. He slept during the day, and his bluish complexion was to be seen only at night, as he flitted in and out like a ghost. The daughter was a waitress at Restaurant X at Dongdan. She was twenty years old, but at first sight you'd mistake her for a child of eleven or twelve. Her complexion was a pallid yellow, she had her mother's thick eyelids, and her face was covered with acne. Her brownish hair was permed to three times the height of her head in curls. She looked more demon than human. Before a shift she would spend more than an hour on dressing and making herself up. Most of that time was spent on artificial means of compensating for the deficiencies of her underdeveloped body, such as trying somehow or other to attach two balls of cotton wool to her chest in order for that part of her to achieve its proper charm.

At such times you can be sure that Lin Dashun's wife from the south wing opposite would once more be venting the old enmity, her ten-year-old stepdaughter becoming the false target of the scorn and loathing written all over her face: "Can't you ever stay put, you little tart? Some stray dog of a man waiting for you again, is there?"

And thus the two women, if not contenting themselves with filthy looks, would set about pulling hair and trading slaps in the middle of the tiny yard they shared, like two insane hens.

Put simply, such were the living conditions of the people in this courtyard dwelling. These weeds grew up from seeds that fell on this barren patch of stony, shady ground. They had been deprived of nurturing sunlight and thirst-quenching rain and dew. In order to maintain their half-dead existence they were always waiting for any fated opportunity to put all they had on a single throw of the dice—and to hell with everything else.

All this was very perplexing to Li Jirong, the rather sentimental and susceptible philosophy student who was Zeng Simian's neighbor in the middle courtyard. Basing his observations on the laws of biology, and taking into account other requirements of human life, he found it very hard to understand how his neighbors were able to go on living as well as they did.

Take Lu Qizhong, who worked as a driver for the Y Company. His standard of living was relatively high for this compound, but his monthly salary was a mere thirty-three yuan, out of which fully twenty yuan went on rent. Was the little that was left sufficient for their monthly living expenses? No matter how Li Jirong scratched his head, he couldn't understand. Surely they couldn't be like cicadas, which can fill themselves up on dew alone? Seeing how perfectly smug and satisfied they looked, he couldn't help feeling mystified.

However, our poor humanitarian, like so many other people, had forgotten an utterly commonplace but extremely important law of the universe. When it comes to the necessities of human life, whatever is necessary to A will also be necessary to B, and such necessity can lend A or B enormous strength to attempt certain efforts to obtain these necessities of life. How laughable it is to apply morality and law to these people, whose very existence cannot be assured. On this point it would seem that those wretched beggars on the streets, who cry out for pity in hopes of getting a little handout from their fellow humans and who might need to run half a mile behind a rickshaw to get it, actually understand the situation better than our young Mr. Li.

One day toward evening Lu Qizhong arrived home with yet another can of what looked like gasoline. Zeng Simian, standing at his doorway, eyeballed the steel can. Without pausing for thought, but with a knowing smile lighting up his face, Zeng said: "Ah, gasoline?"

Lu forced an awkward smile in return, and explained: "Mm, yes. A friend asked me to buy some for him."

That night Zeng Simian and Li Jirong had another debate—they often had such disputations on one thing or another.

"How about it, Mr. Li?" said Zeng Simian sarcastically. "Do you still find it impossible for anyone to understand how they survive? Don't mistake yourself, sir: there really isn't any amazing mystery to it! You would only need to go hungry for three days to learn, quite naturally and ingeniously, how to find the two nest buns[1] that you need. It's quite simple; there are lots of things your stomach can teach you."

---

1. Nest buns (*wotou* 窩頭) are a nest-shaped form of steamed bread made from mixed flour (*zaliang* 雜糧), mainly maize. They are traditionally despised as the poorest of fare.

3

Zeng Simian felt a great deal of sympathy for the people of the compound, but also disgust. At the same time, these feelings of disgust also caused him much vexation. Sometimes he was even assailed by serious doubts about himself and his relationship with his neighbors. He often had misgivings about whether they truly were all descended from the people of the Wei river basin[2]—whether the same blood could really be running in their veins as in his own. Were he and they really members of the same race, with the same customs, cultural traditions, history, and destiny?

Since his discovery that they had radically different ways of thinking and concepts of living from his, that they had basically lost all power of moral judgment and all human sense of beauty and brightness, his former beliefs suddenly changed. Now he loathed and detested them.

First of all, what did he see? He saw an accumulation of all the evils in the universe, a group of human beings scrabbling around at a level of animal subsistence.

They were like pigs huddled together in a pestilent sty: short of a miracle, the only possible outcome for them was extinction of their kind from this world.

Let us try opening one of the books on philosophy bequeathed to us by our ancient sages as sacred manuals for social conduct. There we will find a line that is a marvelous remedy uniquely inherited from our ancestors: "Sweep clean the snow from your own doorstep; mind not the frost on anyone else's roof." This maxim appears to embody selfishness, lack of public spirit, absence of neighborly love, fear of getting into trouble, and much besides.

Thus, if the house of our neighbor to the east should catch fire this morning, what our sagacious ancestors tell us to do is not to go immediately to help extinguish the blaze and save lives. No! They tell us to stand at a good distance—the further, the better—and, as leisurely

---

2. The Wei river basin, where the modern city of Xi'an is situated in northwest China proper (south Shaanxi province), is traditionally regarded as the "cradle" of earliest Han Chinese culture.

and elegantly as if we were admiring the goldfish in Central Park,[3] to watch the distant flames as they shoot up into the heavens (at this point, the flames had better be "shooting up into the heavens," otherwise they're not really much in the way of flames, and the spectators will not be well satisfied) and cry out loudly: "What a great blaze!"

At a time like this, if there's a fly in the ointment it's hearing a neighbor say that in the confusion he picked up an Yixing teapot that was still more-or-less intact. At this you experience the uncomfortable feeling that that teapot should by rights have been yours, but somebody else got hold of it just because you didn't go to the scene. Ai! What a pity!

In the same way, the person in a public park who sees someone willfully breaking off branches and picking flowers and goes to prevent it and to lecture the perpetrator on public morality.... Well, he is quite the silliest of fellows, and I guarantee he will get himself nothing but grief. The other person is sure to look him up and down for five minutes before asking contemptuously: "What's it to you? Huh!"

Yes! What is it to him? Greatly dejected and put out, the fellow will go home and think about what happened for fully three days and nights. The more he thinks, the more he'll regret his actions and the more he'll reproach himself for interfering. Eventually he slaps his own face fifty times as hard as he can. When the slapping's finished he strokes his stinging cheeks and begins to feel happy again in his mind. He feels he has learned something, grown cleverer and wiser. In future if he sees someone picking flowers he'll go up to the person and say generously: "Would you like me to help you? These ones are very good, much nicer than you'll see at the flower market!"

Zeng Simian saw how such attitudes were absorbed, whole and unresolved, and then dissolved in his neighbors' physical tissue and in their outlook on life. Heaven only knew how much sympathy or assistance might be expected of them if some disaster were to occur.

When Zeng Simian first came to Peking from his home in the south and moved into this compound, the first things he sensed about the emotional life of his new neighbors were their dejection and apathy.

---

3. This refers to a public park adjacent to the Forbidden City and Tiananmen Square that is now known as Zhongshan (Sun Yat-sen) Park.

Each household formed a unit, and none of them paid any of the others any heed, existing in loneliness and isolation. They did not socialize; each door closed on its own. Several times Zeng had seen the attitude and demeanor of others when one or other of the families had a brush with the law or suffered illness or bereavement. It was not only that they did not come forward to offer sympathy or assistance; instead, if passing by the door of the afflicted family they would actually avert their eyes and hurry gingerly past, afraid that the misfortune might fall from that house onto theirs. Fear and revulsion would be written all over their faces, and they might even curse those neighbors for disturbing the peace.

Zeng Simian, who was passionate about society and who had, moreover, been born and brought up in the environment of simple kindliness and affection among neighbors that is typical in the south, found it very difficult to get used to such attitudes. It pained him and caused him no end of vexation. Even now such things still upset him.

However, it seemed that, as Mrs. Shao said, nothing in this world was as it should be. Take the following instance (to this day when it is mentioned Mrs. Shao curses the wickedness of it), which caused quite some displeasure in the compound, lasting several days.

For some reason that nobody knew, the old man whose job it was to carry away the night soil didn't come for over a week (this was quite a frequent occurrence), and so there was nothing for it but for the neighbors to steal out at night and empty their buckets in the lane. However, they didn't empty the stuff by the entrance to their own compound but by the doorway next door. They didn't bother about whether or not it was right to do this. After all, even the police officer in charge of this beat didn't bother about it. Mrs. Lu had once asked him: "Well, where are we supposed to dump the night soil?" He just came right out and said he didn't care. He told her to ask at City Hall. And so they just had to go on dumping the stuff in the lane; not by their own doorway, however (according to Mrs. Shao, "surely that would be too unhygienic!") but next door. Anyhow... the hell with you, just dump the stuff!

But next day they kept smelling waft after waft of acrid, smelly stench coming right in through the main door. When they opened it to take a look, they found a puddle by the entrance that turned out to be the source of the stink.

"It's piss, goddammit! What a liberty!" exclaimed Mrs. Shao in horror.

Next we come to a very clear trait: their contentment with their lot. They neither blamed Heaven nor accused their fellow man, but just kept working away diligently like oxen, indefatigable. Like their ignorance, dirtiness, and poverty, this almost praiseworthy spiritual state was capable of flabbergasting any foreign traveler or sociologist who might witness it.

Lin Dashun in the front courtyard was an example. Often he sat on a low stool under the eaves, staring at the gray-black wall, with no expression whatsoever on his face, not moving a muscle for almost half the day, as if he were a shadow. Although one might equally say that the reason for this was his loss of capacity for thought, it probably wouldn't be too far wide of the mark to class Lin among those contented with their lot.

And then there was Lu Qizhong of the middle courtyard, an even clearer manifestation of the type. When he came home from work he'd put his little son—one year old and just learning to talk—in the baby cart, and go off for a wander somewhere without too much traffic, perhaps to the Imperial Ancestral Temple or somewhere like that. Whenever he met anyone he'd say: "The weather's good today, it'll be lovely in Beihai Park, you should go." And he'd say to his son: "Little Fatty: say 'Hello, Mister!'" . . . Then at night, as soon as his head hit the pillow, Lu would sleep as sound as a pig until dawn.

Only on one occasion did Zeng Simian witness what he took to be an indication of dissatisfaction with reality, one that affected him in a very special way. The person concerned was Shao Chengquan, and at first it wasn't clear whether he was expressing satisfaction or dissatisfaction.

"Whaddaya think, Mr. Zeng: eight years!" The sub-landlord spoke with great feeling, thrusting his right hand up to Zeng's face, thumb and index finger spread in the sign for "eight." "I've worked in that hotel for eight years now! Whaddaya reckon—fed up, or what? Eight years? But what can I do? What else could I do, Mr. Zeng?"

At the time, Zeng Simian sighed to himself on Shao's behalf, but when he thought it over later it seemed there was actually more to it. Afterward, each time Shao waved the "eight" sign in his face again and started to complain, it was already clear to Zeng that this was really just another way of expressing satisfaction.

As for indolence, vanity, pride, the tendency to make a great hue and cry over nothing ... many such phenomena were everywhere you looked, in every street and alleyway, as common as anything. They were like the beggars of Peking: our human society was bursting at the seams with them.

If other examples are needed, no problem: just go to any wedding or funeral—of any family that still has something worth forty or fifty cents at the pawnshop—and you will see vanity, that source of unfounded human satisfaction. And from that sub-landlord of ours you may learn the emptiness of face: at the same time as he is putting up the rent, he tries to give and keep face with the neighbors. Or come and spend a couple of minutes or so in our compound and you may have your eyes opened by the gratuitous quarrelling and commotion among the women.

Laziness is another thing that was rife in this compound. Lin Dashun's father was like a chain around his son's neck. The widow's son did nothing but eat, sleep, and shit, except when he got hold of some money—then he wouldn't come home at night while his mother, demented, looked everywhere for him; and when he did come back the only difference would be that the money was all gone and the boy's face was greener than ever. When Lu Qizhong got home at midday for lunch he'd find his wife still asleep; in the morning before going to work he had got a good fire going in the stove, but now it was just as if he'd never lit it. ... These are just a few examples.

4

Old Mrs. Yan moved back to the yard four days after Mrs. Shao mentioned her in conversation with Mrs. Zhuang and Mrs. Zeng.

But the old lady was a different person compared to a few months before. She had lost normal consciousness and now resembled an old crazy woman. Her skin was dry and shriveled, cracked like the bark of an old cypress tree and purplish in color. Her senses were dulled and her faculty of thought greatly slowed. Her powers of sight and hearing were especially weakened. Wearing the purple satin, short, lined jacket with the longevity pattern that hadn't been off her back for ten years, leaning on a wooden walking stick and looking like a person with rickets, she hobbled all through the compound, in and out of the courtyards. She would chase after anyone she happened to meet, crying and complaining like a child: "Why are you ignoring me? Aren't we all the best of neighbors?"

Everyone in the compound would dodge or hide or shut themselves in as soon as they saw her, as if she were a terrifying god of plague.

Several months earlier—that's to say, on a day in late winter when the morning was already getting old—Mrs. Shao had noticed that there was no sign of movement from the old lady in the south apartment opposite hers. Wondering if there might be something the matter, she went over to see if she could see anything. The moment she opened the door she was assailed by a stench fit to make you spew, so that she was forced to cover her nostrils and rush back out again. When the smell had subsided somewhat she advanced once more, fearing an unhappy discovery. And what should she see but old Mrs. Yan sitting on the bed clutching wildly in the air, like a person drowning. She could not talk but was making a rasping sound in her throat like a duck being held by the neck. Seeing someone come in, like a frightened child whose instinct is to fly to its mother's bosom, she made a grab for Mrs. Shao. The latter, frightened out of her wits, ran straight off to find the old lady's daughter.

Half an hour later the daughter came and took her away.

When Mrs. Shao was locking up the south apartment she found a briquette-burning stove in a corner. The stove was cold. She wiped down the tightly sealed windows, and locked the door as she came out. She said to the neighbors: "Well, she's lucky she didn't kill herself with the fumes!"

Now, several months later, although she had escaped with her life, nothing could restore the old lady's mental state to what it had been before.

Not only was she weak-minded and unable to exercise moral judgment, but there was another special phenomenon: she suffered continually from a form of anxiety.

"Sister-in-law," she would call to Mrs. Shao. "Tell me, please, what time is it now?"

"Three o'clock!" Mrs. Shao would reply impatiently.

So the old woman would walk another two paces and say to Mrs. Zhuang: "Sister, can you tell me what time it is now, sister?"

As usual Mrs. Zhuang ignored her. Bang! She closed the door in her face. So the old woman went to the middle courtyard, then the front courtyard, asking the same thing over and over.

And so, whether they paid her any attention or not, she'd often find a way of butting in. This wasn't simply out of loneliness and depression, it was her anxiety that wouldn't give her any rest, and compelled her toward groups of people.

As a rule, however, people like this are lacking in self-criticism, in contrast to their very strong sense of self. Old Mrs. Yan was unable to appreciate other people's feelings, and at the same time she had lost the concept of social decorum that required her to take care of her appearance. When she was speaking to someone, her failing powers of sight and hearing meant that she had to go right up to the person, eyeball to eyeball. This was extremely unpleasant and odious to her interlocutors, because of her bad breath and filthy body. Grease, grime, dust, fleas—things that should only be found on animals—covered her clothes and her hair.

Starting from the time when Mrs. Shao had seen a shower of fleas fall to the ground from the old woman's clothes, everyone would run a mile as soon as they saw her. That day Mrs. Shao, seeing the old woman chasing people round the yard yet again, tried to tell her for her own good: "You've got fleas. They're afraid of you!"

"I haven't!" the old woman replied indignantly. And to prove it, she brushed herself down all over with her hands. Wherever her hands touched, clouds of dust rose up and fleas fell to the ground like rain, crawling and leaping around.

"You haven't, huh? Just look!" cried Mrs. Shao in righteous vindication.

Meanwhile, everyone else had already fled.

However, it was not her dirtiness alone that made the old lady so unpopular. As far as the possessions of people in the compound were concerned, she seemed no longer to recognize the distinction between "yours" and "mine." If she needed something, no matter what, she'd just go right ahead and take it, without a word to anyone. If there was something she couldn't get hold of, so that she needed to ask the owner, from her tone of voice you'd think she was talking to one of her own sons, brazenly and without any restraint. Firewood, coal, salt, pickles—these were the things she needed.

"How can you go taking my coal!" they protested.

"I am *not*!" she said, and carried right on taking it.

"I suppose you're going to say somebody owed you that coal!" they said, angry now.

"I'll tell Laoliu to buy you some more later, alright?" she retorted calmly. "I wouldn't just take what's yours without paying it back!"

And so they began shutting all their things indoors, as if afraid of burglars. If it was Mrs. Zhuang, she'd be quickly hiding things away with one hand while her other hand would be pointing the old woman in the direction of the Zengs' apartment, meaning that she should go there looking for what she needed. But the half-blind old lady wouldn't take the hint; she just kept on and on: "Don't worry, I'll tell Laoliu to buy you some more later; I wouldn't just take what's yours."

By now Mrs. Zhuang would be hopping mad, shrieking: "I don't want your son to return it to me. It's mine and you're not having any!" And so saying, she'd reach out and seize back anything and everything the old lady was clutching in her arms.

"As if I would!" she whined. "They're all ignoring me, every one of them." She turned and went off to look for her daughter, leaning on her grandson's shoulder.

Her grandson, the son of her third son, Yan Laosan, had come with her when she moved back in and stayed as her helper. He was twelve or thirteen, with dull, vacant eyes. He wore an unlined long gown, probably his father's, that was too big for him in every dimension, so that he was forced to tie it round his middle with a hempen rope, making him look like a little Buddhist monk.

The old lady's "they" referred not only to her neighbors in the compound; when she was hungry it also often included her daughter and sons. And "ignoring me" referred specifically to the fact that she hadn't seen any of her children for several days.

You see, the old lady's daily food and other expenses were provided by her only daughter (the landlord's concubine) and her sixth son, Yan

Laoliu. The latter worked as a waiter in a pancake eatery at Tianqiao. Every three to five days one of them would bring over some money or nest buns for her.

But she hadn't seen them for several days now. Since early morning the old woman had been so hungry that she kept walking in and out of the courtyard, wondering what had happened to her children.

And so it was that she went off to look for her daughter, leaning on her grandson's shoulder.

"As if I would!" she whined. "They're all ignoring me, every one of them."

5

Only a few days later, Yan Laosan's wife and their four-year-old daughter came to stay. From one point of view, they had come to look after the old lady; from another, she was actually nothing short of their savior, a rare prospect. Because this way the daughter-in-law no longer needed to live the monotonous life of a sidewalk seamstress, but could sit comfortably at home every day and never go short of nest buns.

Moreover, although this woman brought only her daughter, somehow her husband, Laosan (a bald guy with a purple face and a pot belly who had a smarmy smile for everyone he met) now also took to coming round. Whenever the clatter of bowls and chopsticks began to sound—that's to say, whenever meals were being got ready—this third son of the old lady would appear as if by invitation. When he'd finished eating he would wipe his face with the backs of his hands, like a contented cat, then take a tattered rush mat to any convenient shady spot under the eaves and lie down with a great display of satisfaction. Five minutes later the thunderous sound of his comfortable snores would strike up.

When he'd had a sufficiently long siesta, he'd get up, give a lazy stretch, and leave. Come the evening, just before meal time, he would appear again, neither a moment too soon nor a moment too late.

Once he started coming round, Laosan put considerable terror in the hearts of the people of the compound. First among them was Mrs. Shao, who was beside herself with fear as she hid everything of any value at all away in her cupboards, not saying a word to anyone. When

Zhuang Jingfu came home at night, he gave special instructions to Mrs. Zhuang to keep an eye on the windows and doors at all times.

But the most worried of all were Laosan's own brother and sister, because he added enormously to their burden. Finally the day came when this state of affairs brought about conflict among them.

That evening there were hardly any nest buns. As soon as they were out of the steamer, Laosan, like the wind whisking away fallen leaves, swept away enough of them to eat his own fill. Old Mrs. Yan was sitting woodenly by the bed, but though she waited for ages, still no one brought her any nest buns.

"What about my buns?" she started to wail, like a child.

"What buns? The last of the nest buns were finished at midday!" replied her daughter-in-law, bringing her a bowl of spinach soup. "Quiet now, drink this!"

Coming back into the outer room, she lowered her voice and urged her sons: "Come on, quick, eat up."

The little monk and his brother, who was an apprentice, were munching away at their nest buns.

"That can't be right." In the inner room the old lady raised her voice again. "I remember there were some nest buns left! How could they be finished so quickly?"

"If we had nest buns, wouldn't I give you yours?" said her daughter-in-law.

Next day, when her sixth son came, the old lady complained: "Laoliu, I'm hungry. They won't give me any nest buns!"

These words were the spark that ignited a quarrel between the brothers. Laoliu's opinion was that the nest buns bought with his wages were for Mother to eat, not for Laosan and his family. After all, his means were not so great that he could feed such a crowd of people. Laosan's response was that he could take his family back home straightaway and Laoliu could find someone else to come and look after the old lady.

"We can go right away!" he said, sticking out his belly, steam rising from his bald pate. "I'm telling you, we'll just leave Ma to her own devices! Come on, let's go!" He turned to hurry up his wife. "Let's go! Get your things together, we're leaving!"

And in order to emphasize the strength of his resolve he berated his younger son, who was just standing there gawking: "Can't you bear to leave? Is this your home?" And he slapped him across the head for good measure.

Laosan was a clever one. He knew there was no need to "get your things together," because apart from the dirt and fleas they had brought with them and would take away with them, there was nothing else whatsoever. There was a reason for this pretense: he believed that it would surely put the wind up Laoliu. So they put on a show, went inside, tramped around a bit, and then waited a little before coming back out. Laoliu, however, behaved unusually: he merely looked coldly on, which made his brother feel very awkward, and rather panicky. Observing Laoliu's resolute air from the corner of his eye, Laosan didn't know what to do. Naturally he had no wish to take his family back to their own home, where nothing but hunger awaited them. So, should they stay? Um, er . . .

He stood dumbly in the middle of the courtyard, utterly at a loss.

Just then, his sister arrived. This Miss Yan, as Mrs. Shao called her, was a shrewd woman. The moment she entered the courtyard she saw this incident for what it really was. Without saying a word, she came and stood between her brothers and, completely ignoring them, said to the old lady: "Get yourself ready, I've got all the paperwork in order with the old people's home, they'll be sending someone later on to take you there. I've made up my mind it's for the best, the neatest arrangement. It'll save everybody getting so upset and give us all some peace. Come on, get ready, let's get it over with!"

The old lady stamped her feet and wailed and begged: "I won't go! You're my only daughter, I won't go . . . !"

"You can't just say you won't go," replied Miss Yan, all seriousness. "It's all arranged. This will save a lot of strife!"

"I'm not making trouble, dear! They're the ones making trouble," whimpered the old lady. "They're the ones who ate all my nest buns and wouldn't give me any!"

The brothers were speechless in the face of this sudden turn of events. Not knowing what to do, they just stood where they were in a daze.

Just then, everyone's eyes were drawn toward the entrance by the sound of heavy, jumbled footsteps approaching. A moment later three or four men in uniform charged inside. Everyone thought this must be the men sent by the old people's home; they couldn't help feeling worried about the old lady. Only the daughter was thrown into confusion; instinctively she felt that this squad of men must be harbingers of some ill fortune.

Seeing these men in uniform arrive, the old lady was so frightened that she began howling at her daughter: "Darling! I won't go . . ." And begging: "I won't go! Darling! Tell them I won't make trouble anymore . . ." At the same time she was entreating the uniformed men themselves, almost going down on her knees: "Don't take me away, I beg of you, sir, I won't go!"

The men spared only an uncomprehending glance at this peculiar behavior.

"They're not here to take you away," Miss Yan explained to her mother. "Stop making such a scene. Stop it now!"

The man who seemed to be the squad leader put a question to the people in the courtyard:

"Is Yan Yongtai here?"

Everybody's gaze focused on the elder brother. His bald pate shone out amid the crowd.

"That's me!" replied Laosan in great alarm, turning slightly pale. "Sir! And you are . . . ?"

Two minutes later, Yan Laosan was taken away by the men in uniform and the crowd dispersed, everyone talking at once. However, feeling as if everyone in the compound was somehow implicated, the neighbors were plunged into disquiet, and for a long time no one dared speak loudly.

That night, when the moon was rising slowly above the sun canopy, Mrs. Shao spoke quietly, as if mentioning something that was taboo: "You know why they took Laosan away? He stole money from a shop!"

"So, will he get out again?" asked Mrs. Zeng.

"Who knows?" replied Mrs. Shao.

As if wishing to take their time savoring this juicy incident, the women fell silent. No one spoke for a while.

Then Mrs. Lu, her eyes on the oleander swaying dreamily in the breeze, said with a sigh: "What a lively place we live in!"

"There's liveliness yet to come!" said Mrs. Shao. "Just wait till Laoliu brings his new wife here to live. Hah! Then you'll see 'lively.'"

"Laoliu got married?" said Mrs. Zhuang. "How come we never heard?"

"Well, he didn't send you an invitation to the wedding, did he? So how would you know? He picked up this bride down Tianqiao, you know!"

"Picked her up?" asked Mrs. Lu, making a big deal of it.

"You find that strange? It's the commonest thing in the world! These days you can pick up anything you want. If you like, you can even pick up a very fine fellow for yourself!" Mrs. Shao lowered her voice again and put on her most serious expression. "But you'll never guess," she went on. "This woman slept with three men at a time in the brothel. Three men!" And now she spoke loudly again: "What do you think of a piece like that! So there you go, he picked her up down Tianqiao, didn't I say?"

Imagining the kind of things that might be about to happen, Mrs. Zeng murmured to herself: "Really, who knows what kind of things our compound may be in for!"

6

The bride that Laoliu had picked up at Tianqiao was bushy browed, big nosed, and big boned—more like a strapping man than a woman. But Laoliu, a bachelor of nearly forty, was delighted with her.

"Come on!" he called to his new wife, beaming and grinning all over his face. "Come on! This is Mother, come and meet Mother!"

The woman went over and greeted her mother-in-law respectfully and submissively, just like a country girl.

"And this lady is Mrs. Shao!" Laoliu introduced her to them all one by one. "This is Mrs. Zeng. . . . From now on we're all like one big family. If there's anything you're unsure of, don't be shy, just ask Mrs. Shao, Mrs. Zeng, Mrs. Lu, or one of the other ladies whatever you like. They're all such good neighbors, always willing to help." Laoliu was playing the parts of good husband (earnestly instructing his wife) and good neighbor (deferentially addressing everyone else): "From now on, please don't be hard on her, she's newly come from the country and there's a lot she has to learn."

That night the newlyweds slept with the old lady on her six-foot-square brick bed platform.[4]

For his first week of married life Laoliu's boss had granted him leave to come home to sleep, but after that he could only sleep at home once every three or four nights. Occasionally he managed to find the time to pop home during the day.

A few days after the marriage, when Laoliu wanted to go and register it, he discovered that his bride had no residence permit.

"So where is it then?" he asked her.

"At home in the village. I forgot to bring it with me."

"How could you forget something like that?" he pressed her. But he immediately resumed a milder tone. "Never mind, we'll get you a residence permit when we go to the police station for the marriage certificate."

She remained silent, fiddling with her clothes. She didn't seem all that willing.

"We can't not register, you know!" Laoliu explained.

"Can't you at least get me a pair of leather shoes and some material to make some clothes?" She spoke like a spoiled child. "I haven't got a thing to wear, how can I even go out in public?"

Next day Laoliu left work early and on the way home he bought two pairs of woven stockings, drip-dry material for two blue shirts, and two pairs of black woolen trousers. These purchases used up two-thirds of the five hundred–odd yuan he'd saved since he began his apprenticeship at the age of eleven. Parting with the money was really very painful for him. But soon his pain began to turn to joy. As he walked he inwardly imagined his wife's happiness. How lovely that would be!

---

4. Brick bed platform (*kang* 炕): in traditional houses in north China sleeping quarters (often also living quarters) are usually equipped with a built-in hollow brick platform about two foot high, for sitting and sleeping. Heated by an integral stove, the *kang* usually stretches the entire length of one of the walls and often occupies more than half the total area of the room. In "Oleander" every "bed" mentioned is a *kang*, except for Mrs. Shao's movable one (*chuang* 床) in the second paragraph.

However, he had completely miscalculated. His wife still wouldn't agree to go and register. She hummed and hawed and made him agree to drop the subject until her clothes had been made up.

"What's the hurry?" she grumbled, flirtatiously. "I'm yours now anyway, who cares if the registration's a little late?"

Laoliu listened happily. Sure, what did it matter? And wasn't she so womanly and sincere, so much like a housewife?

He was completely content.

After that Laoliu could only come home once every few days, and every time he asked her about the registration she put him off one way or another and humored him this way or that, until he himself began to forget about it. Meanwhile, just as Laoliu had imagined, his wife was extremely pleasant and solicitous, tending to his mother with great tenderness and obedience. Sometimes, it's true, he saw an expression of annoyance come over her face, but she exerted herself to repress it, never allowing her inner feelings of disgust to reveal themselves in her actions.

"Dear!" said the old lady, addressing her as her own daughter. "Help me outside for a bit of a walk. I feel so suffocated."

"Go for a walk?" her daughter-in-law said, frowning impatiently. "On one of the hottest days of the year?"

But she acceded to the old lady's wishes and took her outside. With contempt etched deep in her face, looking anywhere but at her mother-in-law, avoiding her smelly breath, she looked for all the world like a coolie roughly tugging a poor, clumsy old beast of burden along by the nose. Meanwhile, the neighbors could hear the old lady's plaintive cries: "Don't pull me so fast . . . !"

Soundlessly but ceaselessly the days rolled by, and now it was the season where summer and autumn overlapped.

One day, when Yan Laoliu returned home at dusk, Mrs. Shao called him into her house and said: "You'd better check your wife's stuff, and see if anything of yours has gone missing. Today at noon when I saw her go out she seemed to be wearing far too many layers of clothing, and she looked suspicious. I wouldn't be surprised if that piece turns out to be a con-woman who's been out to rob you all along! Go home and take a careful look!"

Laoliu went home, and sure enough, the things he'd bought her recently had disappeared.

It was very late when she finally got home.

"What've you done with all that gear I bought you?" Laoliu began the interrogation the moment she came through the door. At first she seemed flustered, but she composed herself and then, appearing almost on the verge of tears, she began to complain in a most piteous tone.

"I pawned it!" she said. "You don't come home for days on end, leaving me not a single penny. Ma goes about asking here and there for pickles and kindling, but I'm too embarrassed to do that!"

"Where's the pawn ticket, then?" asked Laoliu.

"I've put it away," she said, darting a nervous eye at him. "Surely you don't think I'm lying?"

"That's not what I mean," said her husband. "I want to go and redeem those things tomorrow. I bought them for you to wear, how could you go and pawn them?"

"Well, it doesn't make any difference if I hold on to the ticket then, does it?" she replied. "Just bring me the money and I'll go redeem them right away."

Next day as Laoliu was going out, Mrs. Shao again stealthily called him aside. "You'd better come back and stay at home again tonight," she told him. "I reckon that piece of yours is going to run out on you. And I wouldn't put it past her to make off with some of your stuff while you're out; after all, the old lady's eyesight isn't up to much!"

Laoliu thought about this, then went back into his house and told his wife: "It's very busy in the shop recently, I'm afraid I won't be able to come home for two or three days, so you take extra care of Ma!"

That day his wife went out very early and didn't come back until after nightfall. When she came in and saw Laoliu sitting there large as life, having said he wouldn't be back for two or three days, she turned pale and began to scowl. The three of them passed the night without talking.

Next day Laoliu didn't come home for the night. At dusk, his wife went out empty-handed, reluctantly and resentfully.

First thing next morning the old lady set up a cry, sounding like a dog that was being beaten: "She's taken the quilt! She's taken the quilt!"

At almost the same time (actually a little earlier) a quarrel started up in the front courtyard.

"That fine son of yours stealing people's quilts, and you still deny it? A shameless thing like you was bound to raise a shameless thing like him..."

This was the metallic shrieking of Lin Dashun's woman.

"Did you see him? Did you see him? Did you see him...?"

This was the voice of her opponent, the widow.

"I saw him steal it with my own eyes. With my own eyes I saw him bring it through that door in the middle of the night! You still dare to deny it, but tell me this: what was your son doing going out at that hour, huh?"

"Where he goes is none of your business; what he does is none of your business either, none of your business!"

Before long the people who crowded into the front courtyard to watch the fun were nearly bursting down the walls. With gratified expressions on their faces these ladies and gentlemen of the audience pointed out the finer points to one another: which of the performers' voices was the more sonorous, which voice was crisper; which of the antagonists had the greater mastery of the art of cursing; whose curses hit home just where it hurt the other most. The only thing they felt far from satisfied about was that the two women traded only abuse; no blows were exchanged. Otherwise it would have been a really fine civil-military variety performance, and admission was free!

But they were not disappointed after all, because the very next instant the two women started leading with their fists and feet, producing a truly spectacular performance.

Seeing Mrs. Shao and the old lady arrive, Lin Dashun's wife went toward them, saying: "Old Mrs. Yan, I can tell you, your quilt was taken by..."

Before she could finish her sentence she suddenly felt a vicious blow to her face which almost sent her flying. The pain made her see stars, but as she turned, out of the corner of her eye she saw the widow launching her whole self at her again. Dodging, the Lin woman then pounced in her turn and grabbed the widow by the hair. But in the same instant she felt her own hair grabbed hold of.

The two women scratched and mauled and rolled together this way and that, like a pair of lionesses. Only after Mrs. Shao, Mrs. Lu, and Mrs. Zeng had tried for some time to separate them were they finally pried apart.

"Inside that door we're all one big family!" said Mrs. Shao. "Why are you causing such a commotion at this hour of the morning? You're neither of you youngsters anymore; aren't you ashamed of yourselves?"

The two combatants retreated through the crowd, rubbing the places where blood flowed through the scratches and cuts on their faces. But from inside their houses each continued to shout abuse at the other: "Mark my words, next time it'll be your old smelly cunt that's bleeding, or I'm a mongrel bastard! You dirty shameless bitch!"

7

Lin Dashun was from Tongxian, the county to the east of Peking, where his family were farmers. However, no matter how hard they worked and no matter how much hardship they were prepared to endure, their mere half-acre of land could hardly support a family of ten. Moreover, Lin's first wife had died in 1936, leaving one son and a daughter. At the time, he had already been considering leaving home to seek a livelihood elsewhere. After full-scale war broke out and the Japanese invaded the following year, life in the countryside became even harder, and Lin decided to strike out for another place. Luckily he had trained as a tailor, which meant he shouldn't go hungry unless his luck was bad. So he bade farewell to his parents, elder brother, and sister-in-law, and one bitter cold winter's day he came with his children to Peking. As to whether city life turned out as he expected, he alone knows.

During his third year away from home he remarried, and from that year, whether because of Fate or because his economic burden was too great (actually he had never had much to spare), life got more and more difficult. Eventually he was like a man with a heavy load on his back climbing a precipitous mountain path, gasping for every breath. What's more, in 1938 his elder brother went missing and the family sold their little bit of land; when his father had come to live with him two years ago life grew even harder. Under this excessive burden Lin's back became bent and a vacant expression fixed itself on his pale, slightly greenish face, which resembled a puny weed forever hidden from the sun. At work he sat silently at his table in a dark basement room where electric light burned day and night; at home he either sat on the edge of the bed and daydreamed or sat outside on the edge of the plinth and stared at the gray wall thinking heaven only knew what. He took no interest whatsoever in his own family, seeming like a sponger in his own home. Toward his wife he was as tame and meek as a family pet.

Seeing him just endlessly sitting there dumbly, like a piece of wood, his acutely anemic wife would often become hysterical: "That's right, you just sit there daydreaming!" she'd cry with a contemptuous snort. "You think the god of wealth's gonna bring you a present of silver dollars if you sit there long enough, do you? Damn my rotten luck to marry a useless deadbeat like you!"

Terrified, Lin would shift further over toward the corner of the wall or the bed, keeping a fearful eye on his wife's expression.

This woman was another of the leading lights of the compound. Whenever she looked at her own two children and saw how weak they were, and then looked at the two left behind by Lin's first wife, she got angry and upset in a way that seemed both natural and inexplicable. Try as she might she just could not understand how those two little so-and-sos managed to thrive. Whenever she thought of her failure to get rid of them quickly and efficiently she got angry with herself and would blame it on being too good-hearted. And then she would suddenly leap up and start screaming accusations at her stepson, an eight-year-old with a complaint against hunger perpetually in his timid eyes: "Don't we give you enough to eat? Or is that damn dog-belly of yours bottomless? Let me tell you, your pa isn't so rich that he can keep throwing money into that bottomless hole of yours!"

She did all she could think of to overwork and ill-treat these two thorns in her side. She made them go two or three hundred yards to fetch water from an old well in another lane. She made them go all over the place scavenging for the family's daily fuel: scraps of coal, branches, and twigs. She made the boy work the stove bellows, and sent the eleven-year-old girl in the middle of the night to stand in line at the nearby grain shop for the next morning's ration of mixed-grain flour.

The Lins lived in a small one-room apartment in the south wing of the front courtyard. At night they all slept together on the six-foot-square platform bed. The room was cramped and dark; in summer it was like a steamer, and in winter like an icehouse. The walls were spattered all over with sad, comet-shaped, dark red stains—these were the remains of bedbugs, which is to say that this was their own poor, thin blood spattered on the walls. Separately, out on the plinth under the eaves, they had put up a crude shelter using two thin bamboo poles and two tattered reed mats, with a few thin wooden planks on the ground. This was where the old man slept.

Filling the room and overflowing into the courtyard were all kinds of worn, bent, and broken furniture, chipped and cracked pots and vats, bits of wood that the children had scavenged, piles of straw, scraps of wood, and so on. It always looked as filthy as a cattle pen, as if it had never been clean for a single day. At the corner of the outside wall there was a rough stove; at midday and in the evening the first wife's boy would be crouched there working hard at the bellows, his skeletal little body almost buried in the straw. Thick smoke billowed up from the stove, roiled around the plinth and into the room, and floated into every corner of the courtyard. The smoke permeated every cooking vessel and item of clothing and left an acrid smell permanently hanging in the room; it irritated the nose and eyes of the boy at the bellows, making him sneeze and weep and feel suffocated.

And so they lived—amid smoke and dust, filth and anemia, scarcity and bedbugs, poor light and forbearance. No matter how hard they worked, no matter how small and how low—unhealthily low—their hopes for security and material comfort, their lives never improved. On the contrary, life's menace and cruelty toward them only grew. They were like a man at the end of a rope: the more he struggles, the tighter the noose grows.

When Lin Dashun's father came from the village to live with them his daughter-in-law was far from happy. It aggravated her hysteria and intensified her cruelty toward her unfortunate stepchildren. Again and again, like a summer thunderstorm, she would burst into bouts of fierce cursing against the family she had married into. These would be accompanied by ill-treatment of the stepchildren, scolding of her "useless" husband, and the throwing around of objects. When the storm died down she would start wailing like a pig being slaughtered, and a wave of uncontrollable anger with herself would sweep over her. She would noisily grind her teeth, and even lose consciousness, falling to the floor foaming at the mouth.

Later, she began to notice that some things in the house, including recently bought sorghum, millet, and maize flour, were going unaccountably missing, in part or in whole. This discovery—that somehow or other her father-in-law had fallen into that dreadful habit—sent her almost completely mad, unleashing one of her worst outbursts.

When this latest storm finally subsided it was already late at night. Soon the whole compound was sunk deep in sleep, but the Lin woman alone was still tossing and turning. Her mind kept dwelling on things, bringing her bitter regret, depression, and despair. After the evening's bout of burning fury, her body felt extremely tired and limp; wave after wave of restlessness flowed through her, a most uncomfortable feeling.

Just at this point she heard the sound of the widow's door across the yard. Abruptly alert, she immediately recalled that the widow's waitress daughter had often been seen stealthily welcoming or seeing off young men in the middle of the night.

She quickly moved over to the window, in time to dimly see a tall, thin figure squeezing through a crack in the door before going toward the inner courtyards. The figure was male right enough, but she recognized it as the widow's son. Disappointed, she went back to bed. She didn't know how much time had passed before she heard footsteps coming out from the inner courtyards. It seemed to her that the footsteps did not go to the widow's apartment but were heading for the main door of the compound. Sure enough, the next thing she heard was the sound of the main door's bolt being very quietly shot. In her surprise she went to the window again: she saw the same tall, thin figure as before, but this time there was something very large under its arm. Looking more carefully, she made the object out as a quilt. Then in a flash the figure, walking on tiptoe but moving very quickly, disappeared through the street door.

Staring at the big lonely door, now closed but not bolted, the Lin woman was delighted.

"This time I've got you right where I want you!" she thought.

8

The day before, the two elder Lin children had gone scavenging for coal along the railway tracks outside Peace Gate.[5] The boy, Xiaofu, was feeling unwell and also hungry; cold sweat was pouring from his brow and he kept stretching and yawning, as if just out of bed. He strained himself to keep going until each of them had collected almost half a basketful. At last the children turned for home. As they were passing a shop Xiaofu saw two or three bits of coal on the ground and unthinkingly picked them up. Only when he looked up did he see the pile of coal in front of him, no doubt just recently unloaded there.

Suddenly a middle-aged man came roaring out of the shop. Without waiting for any explanation, he took aim and walloped Xiaofu across the face, seized his basket, and poured its entire contents onto the coal pile. Xiaofu, stunned and dizzy from the blow, reeled and almost fell. He staggered some way before his head cleared enough to realize that his sister had been helping him along as they fled. Coming to the end of a very long lane, Xiaofu could walk no further. He felt waves of nausea surging up from his stomach, sparks were swimming before his eyes, and his legs seemed unable to bend, like two pieces of wood.

"Sis!" he said weakly. "I can't walk any further."

Coming to a patch of shade under a tree by the road they sat down for a rest. Xiaofu lay down on the ground, his breath dry and bitter. He felt faint and soon fell asleep. He didn't know how long he slept, but when he awoke the sun was almost setting. Somehow or other his empty basket was half-full again, not with coal this time but with little bits of wood. Beside him, his sister was calling: "Xiaofu, quick, get up. It'll be dark soon. Ma will be angry again when we get home."

It was very late by the time they finally got home. No sooner had they entered the compound than their grim-faced stepmother began bellowing at them: "Oh, that's just fine! Seems like you've been having a really lovely time. Why don't you just not bother coming home? Off

---

5. Peace Gate (Hepingmen 和平門) was a modern gate (opened 1926) in the south side of Beijing's former Inner Wall, between Zhengyangmen 正陽門 (Qianmen 前門) and Xuanwumen 宣武門.

you go and play some more! Just come back whenever you've finished your little games; free nest buns will be waiting for you!"

Though their tummies were rumbling they didn't dare say they were hungry. They shrank shivering into themselves and didn't dare move a muscle, like little demons facing the king of hell. Their father cast a melancholy look in their direction, but said not a word.

That night the Lin girl went with another girl from a neighboring compound to the nearby grain store to wait for the next day's rations.

The next day was the day their stepmother quarreled with the widow from across the yard.

The whole of that day the Lin woman was in a bad mood, her face tripping her. The fury in her heart needed only to light on a suitable target for it to burst out as fiercely as gunpowder.

Turning, she saw the girl working the bellows and snapped: "Has your brother died or something? What are you doing working the bellows?"

"He . . . Xiaofu isn't feeling very well today," the girl stammered.

Looking up, the woman saw Xiaofu sitting on the ground by the street door, his face flushed with fever. She flew into a rage.

"Not very well? Oh that's great, it's all very well for some, this is a fine time to go and be ill! Just you keep on lying there, and I can tell you, that's real comfort for you!"

Like an old nag startled by the crack of the whip, the boy fearfully rose to his feet, moving quickly but as if sapped of all his strength, and walked over to his bellows. The smoke billowed out from the top of the stove, which had no flue, casting a veil over most of the wall behind it. From within the thick acrid smoke the child's helpless, irritated coughing was heard over and over.

That evening, feeling very tired and unwell, Xiaofu went to bed and fell asleep before the evening meal. When he awoke it was already late night. At some point autumn rain had begun falling outside, pitter-patter, pitter-patter. All around was bleak and lonely. The sound of the rest of the family in deep sleep filled the room, closing in all around him. On the inner part of the platform bed, his father, stepmother, half-brother, and half-sister were breathing evenly and deeply through their noses, not moving at all.

Xiaofu's whole body felt as hot as charcoal that was ready to explode; the heat caused unbearable pain, which made him groan. It was very difficult to breathe and his throat made a dry rasping sound like the bellows he worked. His eyes were dry and irritated, and it felt as though someone were pushing down hard on his eyelids. With difficulty he forced open his eyes, but what was there to see apart from the low, pitch-black ceiling and the dark night that crowded into the room?

Hardest to bear were the thirst in his mouth and the hunger in his belly. Oh, how he longed to eat or drink something. Since the day before yesterday, when he began to feel unwell, it was over forty-eight hours since he'd had a proper meal.

He gave his sister sleeping beside him a couple of pushes and whispered her name. Having spent all the previous night squatting sleepless in a queue for grain, she didn't wake up. Sitting up on the bed, all the boy saw in the dark was the indistinct outline of one body-shaped hump after another where all the others were sleeping soundly. Raising his head he looked out the window and was startled to see a human shape moving about out there. His heart began beating fast and would not stop. The shape was cowering right up against the window. It seemed to be sitting with both arms around its knees and rocking, now to the left, now to the right, as if trying to dodge something. Xiaofu had to think for a while before it came to him that this was his grandfather. But why would his grandfather not be asleep at this time of night?

Empty-headedly, he watched his grandfather's silhouette and listened to the melancholy sound of the rain. Just then his sister, still asleep, turned over to face him. As she did so she spoke in her dreams: "Xiaofu, Xiaofu, nest buns!"

In return, Xiaofu whispered again: "Sis! Sis!"

But she did not speak again, and the room returned to silence.

"Sis! Sis!"

As before, there was no answer. Moments later the boy himself was carried away by a wave of exhaustion to a hazy country ruled by fever, moaning, and delirium.

When he awoke it was already late in the morning of the following day. Who should he see but his grandmother at the side of the bed with concern and kindness in her eyes. When had she come up from the countryside? And there too was his sister standing beside the old woman. Otherwise, the room was quiet, no one else seemed to be around. He wondered where his stepmother, half-brother, and half-sister had gone.

"Feeling a little better, Xiaofu?" asked his grandmother anxiously.

"Granny!" This one word cost him such an effort.

"Where is it sore, where are you uncomfortable?" she asked.

He looked at her with lifeless eyes; and wearily closed them without answering her. His face was as red as an iron in the smith's fire, his little nostrils flared feebly, and his breath was hurried and burning hot. By the time his grandmother asked him again he had already fallen back into an unhealthy sleep.

Glancing round the empty, quiet room, the old woman asked her granddaughter: "Where has your ma gone?"

"Home to her ma!"

"And your grandpa?"

"I don't know. I saw him just a moment ago!"

The old woman had come to Peking only that morning (she came to the city about once a month or two to see them, and to get a little money from her son while she was there) and had found the place still as the grave. There was no sign of her daughter-in-law and her children, nor of her husband—her son, she knew, would be at work.

When she pushed open the door she saw only her older granddaughter sitting alone by the bed looking anxiously at the boy who lay there, her older grandson. Suddenly seeing her grandmother, the girl acted as if a savior had come in her hour of need, and launched herself into the dear old lady's arms. Stroking the girl's hair, the old woman felt as if something had caught in her throat, and at first she said nothing.

An hour later the old man came back. Seeing his wife, he seemed startled at first, but a moment later he crawled like a ghost into his little hovel.

"Look how ill Xiaofu is, and not a soul at home!" It wasn't clear whether the old woman was complaining to her husband, or just muttering to herself.

"How was I to know he was ill?" retorted the old man coolly. "He was right as rain yesterday, wasn't he?"

As he spoke he looked nervously all around him, then ever so carefully removed one third of the tobacco from the end of a cigarette, got out a little bag from his pocket and put some white stuff from it into the cigarette, and finally replaced the tobacco he had taken out. Then he lit up and began to smoke slowly.

Inside, the boy woke up again, opened his eyes a crack, and said weakly: "I'm hungry, Granny!"

"Didn't anyone make breakfast this morning?" the old woman asked her granddaughter.

"No."

The old woman searched all round the room but found nothing.

"Don't you know where it's kept, the maize flour or whatever?" she asked her husband.

"How should I know where it's kept?"

The old woman looked round again carefully, but there was nothing at all that could be eaten.

"That woman surely has a poisonous heart," grumbled the old woman. "To leave nothing at all—what were they to eat?"

"Are you telling me you eat nothing at all?" she turned again to her husband.

But there was no reply from the old man. When she went out to look, she found him snoring soundly—he'd had a sleepless night with the rain coming into his lean-to, and just now he had smoked a good fix. Angry, his wife stared at him for a while, but there was nothing she could do.

Supporting her grandson and leading her granddaughter by the hand, she walked into the middle courtyard, put on a smiling face, and implored Mrs. Zeng: "How do you do, Mrs. Zeng? I'm sorry, Mrs. Zeng, can you give a nest bun or two to these children? The boy's taken real bad, but his stepmother has gone off to her mother's, not leaving so much as half a bun for them to eat. The poor children haven't had a thing to eat for two days now!"

"Ah, how do you do, Mrs. Lin?" said Mrs. Zeng. "Please come in and sit down. We have freshly steamed *mantou*!"[6]

---

6. *Mantou* 饅頭: steamed wheat-flour buns. Greatly preferred to nest buns, *mantou* are the traditional staple food of north China, as opposed to rice in the south.

The old woman sat Xiaofu down in a chair. His eyelids were drooping, and he was too tired to try to keep them open.

Mrs. Zeng bustled around, selecting a few hot *mantou* from the steamer and putting them on plates in front of the two children. Hearing the word *mantou*, Xiaofu smartly opened his eyes and grew lively again. Like a ravenous eagle, he grabbed a *mantou* in clawlike fingers and began greedily eating. But after only one bite, his brows creased into a frown and a pained look came across his face. Bringing the *mantou* close to his eyes, he looked again and again at it, as if trying to see if what he was eating was really a *mantou* and not a stone.

He looked, nibbled a bit more, looked again, and then, after forcing himself to eat a few more mouthfuls, he shook his head and put the *mantou* down and ate no more.

"I can't get it down, Granny!" he said, and dejectedly closed his lifeless eyes once more.

That night neither the children's stepmother nor their father returned home. They knew that their father would have gone to his mother-in-law's straight from work, as he had done before.

Xiaofu went on sleeping all evening, dead to the world. Next day he awoke only a couple of times, and even then his eyes stayed firmly shut and he did not respond when spoken to. Sitting on the edge of the bed, his grandmother thought he looked close to death. She wrung her hands and her eyes filled up with tears.

The boy's father and stepmother came home together toward evening.

The grandmother complained to her son: "See how sick the boy is, how could you just go off without a care? If you had to go, how could you not leave so much as a single nest bun? Anyone would think you wanted the boy to die!"

Lin Dashun stayed silent, not replying, but his wife began to roar: "Heaven is my witness, if I didn't leave some maize flour for them let it strike me and my children barren and let me die a bad death!"

"What good are such oaths in this day and age?" the old woman spat back, not letting her off so easily. "Why would I falsely accuse you! Just go and ask Mrs. Zeng. If there had been any maize flour would I have asked Mrs. Zeng to give them some *mantou*?"

"That's nothing to do with me. All I know is I left maize flour for them. Some swine, some mongrel bastard must have sold it." By now she was shouting loudly. "It was some swine, some mongrel bastard son of a whore that sold it!"

She knew who it was who had taken the flour. From outside, the children's grandfather could be heard muttering: "I don't know anything about any maize flour!"

Like people who have lost all human sense of goodness, like wild beasts, they snarled and fought around a little boy's deathbed, shouting fit to raise the roof, implacable and unstoppable. And thus it was amid such venomous sounds of cursing and accusation that an unfortunate boy slipped unnoticed from an unhappy world.

9

Two minutes later, a mixture of tragic weeping and shrill howling rose up from the front courtyard. The weeping came from the deceased's grandmother and from the sister he had left behind in this lonely world. The howling was another of his stepmother's hysterical fits.

"Aiya!—oh my God—and they say I deliberately caused his death!—as heaven is my witness—oh my God!"

Even while the wailing and weeping was going on, Li Jirong and Zeng Simian began debating the problem.

"What a vicious woman that is!" Once again our young humanitarian took up the cudgels on behalf of humanity. "To treat a living, breathing child like that; why, she as good as tortured him to death!"

Listening to Li's long and profound sighs, Zeng Simian looked coolly at him but said nothing. The corners of his unspeaking mouth held a cold smile that was akin to fury.

"Oh my God . . . !" Another shrill cry came from the front courtyard.

Listening to this shrieking of a woman who had lost all sense of human goodness, Li Jirong frowned, depression and dejection showing in his face. "The stepmothers of China!" he muttered, as though talking in his sleep. "The stepmothers of China!" he repeated. "I just don't understand why tragedies like this seem to be inevitable in human society, especially in China!"

At his side, Zeng Simian couldn't help wanting to laugh at the sight of his sorrowful expression, like that of an actor in a Western-style play.

"It seems your humanitarianism and your grumbling have been provoked yet again—this time by that woman in the front courtyard!" Zeng sneered. "But you'd better put away that humanitarianism of yours, it's not worth a dime! Let me tell you: that stuff can't be applied to China, it's just too far from the reality!"

"Here we go again! I only have to open my mouth for you to accuse me of humanitarianism," said Li Jirong, crossly. "So I suppose in your view that child deserved to die!"

"How should I know? Look at you, you look as if you want to take a bite out of me! Hey, hey, Jirong, don't get me wrong, I'm not out to pick a quarrel with you!"

Zeng very nearly laughed out loud at the childish manner of Li's outburst. After a little pause, he continued what he had been saying, but in a more serious tone.

"However, there is a very obvious truth to be observed here, which is worthy of our careful consideration: there's a two-thirds probability that that child was destined to die anyway. It's mere chance that the agency of his dying fell into his stepmother's hands."

"Mere chance or not, there's no getting away from the fact of that woman's responsibility for the boy's death!" Li made his point forcefully.

"From what you say," said Zeng, deliberately provoking his young friend, "if you were a judge that woman would certainly receive a heavy punishment. And if you handed down such a punishment, then I would call you a truly excellent judge. But looking at it from another angle, you would be a truly dreadful so-and-so, a machine for the implementation of the law. If you . . . Well, how about we broaden the question out a bit?" Zeng dropped his mocking tone. "Because in this way you will immediately see how negative your methods are, and how unsuitable they are to China. . . ."

"Words of wisdom, words of wisdom!" Li Jirong was quickly learning a mocking tone from Zeng; far from backing down, he now went on the counterattack. "Summing up everything you've said, we can conclude that China has no use for morality, isn't that right? In other words the Chinese are neither more nor less than savages. Well, in that case you are very welcome to go and live abroad!"

"Oh no!" said Zeng Simian gravely. "I think you misunderstood me! I was only saying that morality is something to be studied and put into practice by a nation of people where there is health and freedom in life, and where normal faculties of thought and judgment are maintained. But the problem these people here face is how to stay alive, and how to overcome all the obstacles that threaten their lives. They are toiling to escape with their lives from a dead-end street. They are constantly faced with hunger and death! They are puppets in the hands of Fate...."

"Puppets in the hands of Fate?" echoed Li. It was unclear whether he sought clarification or was just mocking Zeng.

"Yes, puppets in the hands of Fate!" Zeng Simian repeated himself impatiently. Then he resumed his cold, mocking tone: "It's the stage of Fate that they tread, but they don't even know it: they're fumbling in the darkness. Sometimes, whether consciously or unconsciously reacting to something, they do try to flee the stage. Indeed, their efforts to escape began a very long time ago. There are records of this from ancient times. More recently, we've seen the National Revolution of 1911, the May Fourth Movement, literacy movements, concern for the woman question, rural emancipation, labor security, reforms to the family system ... and so on and so forth. But long ages of history have made China's stage of Fate as invulnerable as a prison. The way things are today shows us just how puny the effects and achievements of all their struggles have been. And the clearest evidence of all is that they are still hungry.

"This is the heavy historical burden they bear. They're like fish swimming around at the bottom of a net. Here they live and die, laugh or weep: stepmothers mistreat stepchildren; they pour their sewage out at their neighbors' doors; mothers and children, brothers and sisters fall out over a couple of nest buns; theft, drunkenness, drugs, crime, idleness.... Both abusers and abused (in other words, those who live and those who die) are puppets of Fate. And what is Fate? When you come down to it, it is poverty, ignorance, conformism, illness, disorder, homelessness, poor hygiene, lack of safe and reliable medical facilities, substandard education, official and commercial corruption, opium and gambling addiction, suspicion toward new systems and new things.... All of these, the iron hooves that trample them day after day, are the heritage of their ancestors!"

With a look Zeng signaled to his wife—who had just come in from the yard to say something to them—not to interrupt. After a pause he continued.

"You know very well how the families of this tenement are getting poorer and poorer, one step at a time, don't you? And you know how they go from poverty to annihilation? If ever they fall just once into the grip of poverty, it's so hard to break out again. Poverty is a calamity in life; it brings about a vicious cycle, which is to say it induces every adverse circumstance, and soon there is no telling where lies cause and where effect. A deep abyss of death is created, in which poverty's captives thrash about, trying to keep their heads above water, with no hope of escape.

"Their wages are too low: what the father earns in a day is usually enough only to maintain his own animal needs, and the material needs of his family have to be found by each individual member. For this reason, not only the father but even their little ones' opportunities for betterment and advancement are all mercilessly cut out. And so their children—their posterity, and China's second and third generations—have no choice but to accept the same status and the same conditions as their fathers, and struggle on like them. This is just their fate, their present situation."

"Oh, I see," said Li Jirong disdainfully. "There I was, thinking you had some fresh new idea, but you go on and on and it turns out that all you have is a snare for your own neck. You're the one who's the real humanitarian. Well then, according to you, what should they do for the best?"

"Do for the best?" Zeng echoed scornfully. "How should I know what they should do for the best?"

"Well, that's strange. You prattle on and on with your grand discourse, and in the end all you have is 'How should I know?' What a lot of words for so little substance!"

"No substance? Fine! I admit there's no substance. My aim was merely to set out the facts. As to the question of what they should do for the best, we can only leave that up to them. Luckily they are a clever race, it seems to me that what they lack is actually not the means but the willpower. That's right, it's probably something like willpower that they lack—or, to put it another way, they lack practicality!"

With this Zeng fell silent. Judging by how extremely fed up he looked, one would say that he must be thoroughly sick of discussing such pointless and nauseating affairs.

"So there you go again, talking and talking and then . . . suddenly you break off without rhyme or reason! Utterly lacking in rhetorical organization, and just silly!" It was not clear whether Li Jirong's dissatisfied grumbles were addressed to himself or to Mrs. Zeng.

"The widow's son just came back," reported Mrs. Zeng, after a pause in which she judged that the two men had finished talking, "but the old lady's quilt is gone and the money is all spent. Yan Laoliu wouldn't let it rest; he said he'd get the police. The widow took fright at that and gave him twenty yuan to put an end to it."

Mrs. Zeng stopped talking when she saw that the two men seemed to be neither listening nor not listening. They remained silent.

By now the hysterical shrieking in the front yard had stopped and only the sound of desolate weeping continued to reverberate through the hushed compound.

At dusk the next day a small coffin was silently carried out through Hatamen Gate.[7]

Toward evening, when Li Jirong saw the lonely figure of the dead boy's sister secretly shedding tears while working the bellows her brother had worked before her, he remembered what Zeng Simian had said the night before. Here he was now getting a clear glimpse of how it was the fate of a nation of people to get poorer and poorer, one step at a time, and to go from poverty to annihilation, one step at a time.

10

The seasons turned, and now it was late autumn of the following year. Soughing gusts of autumn wind were blowing the yellow leaves down

---

7. Hatamen/Hadamen 哈達門: popular name of Chongwenmen 崇文門, one of the great ancient gates in the south side of Beijing's former Inner Wall.

from the roadside trees, and in the tenement yard the last flower had faded and fallen from the oleander.

Mrs. Shao was beginning once again to move her flowerpots indoors. Standing by one of the pots, she looked at the mess of yellow leaves on the ground and the half-naked branches shivering in the cool wind, and said with real feeling: "How quickly the time passes. Before we know it winter will be upon us again!"

As she spoke she pruned the branches of one withering plant after another.

"This summer when I brought the plants out, Old Mrs. Yan was still living across the yard. Who'd have thought that only a couple of months later she would have moved away. Her family scattered, Yan Laosan dead, how our compound has changed! Who knows what other changes there may be by this time next year!"

"Yes!" chimed in Mrs. Zhuang. "Only a few months ago my husband was saying we should find somewhere else and move, but now the compound's already much less unruly, so I told him there's no need!"

Yes, just as Mrs. Shao said, this compound had changed. And top of the list of changes was the change in ownership.

During the summer the authorities had discovered drugs, including opium and heroin, at the owner's barbershop. The shop was closed and sealed and its employees took to their heels. Sentence came down one month later: three years in prison. Two months later, according to the wishes of the owner's first wife, the compound was sold to a member of that new class that is so adaptable to prevailing conditions and so adept at taking advantage of opportunities, that class which is most capable of bringing its strengths into full play precisely when social conditions are at their most unstable.

Among the changes rippling out from this sudden disturbance of the previous calm were, naturally, changes affecting the inhabitants of the compound. First of all, old Mrs. Yan's security of tenure suffered a shock. Secondly, at the suggestion of the new landlord, the two families in the front courtyard had to find somewhere else and move.

This affable middle-aged man had taken one look at the battered furniture, piles of coal, kindling, and so on stuffed into every available space of the front courtyard, wrinkled his brows in a frown, and said: "Filthy! Just filthy!"

And so, two months previously, one by one the old lady, the Lins, and the widow and her children had moved out.

"Will the old lady be going back to live with her daughter?" Mrs. Zeng asked Mrs. Shao one day.

"Her daughter? Huh!" Mrs. Shao snorted dismissively. "Who knows where the daughter herself is even going to find a place to live now! Think about it: a concubine, and one who hasn't even produced any children; now she doesn't have her husband with her anymore, do you think she'll be able to challenge the legal wife? I wouldn't be surprised if she doesn't even have a place to stay herself, so how do you think she's going to take the old lady in?"

"Well then, surely the old lady can't go back to live with Laosan's family?"

"Where else can she go? Laoliu doesn't have a home of his own, he eats and sleeps at the shop, so where would he put the old lady if she went to him?"

"But Laosan's dead, isn't he?"

"Even so!"

Sure enough, the old lady had gone back to live with Laosan's family. Unfortunately it was just then that Laosan died in the outbreak of bubonic plague that was terrorizing Peking, so who was going to look after his mother and the rest of his family?

As for Laoliu, since the debacle of his marriage he had been very depressed and full of regret. In particular, he could not get out of his head the heartbreaking thought that the five hundred yuan he had struggled so hard to save for over twenty years was now spent. So he resolved to put aside all other things and concentrate single-mindedly on doing his job in the pancake bar to try to put together a bit of money again.

"With a bit of money I can get a new wife!" was what he thought.

And finally, it seems just a few more words are required regarding the recent circumstances of this courtyard dwelling. Shao Chengquan had now sunk to the status of an ordinary resident, and whenever it was time to pay the rent—he too now had to pay rent—he would feel an inner discomfort that might last up to half of the following month. Mrs. Zhuang's children had by now been educated by her into the most well-behaved and obedient of children, while her husband had enjoyed great good fortune in his finances. He had earned quite a bit of money this spring, and Mrs. Zhuang, in turn, had very quickly learned how to cherish her own possessions. For example, when Mrs. Lu would ask to borrow a stovepipe for a while she would turn her down absolutely flat. Mrs. Lu herself meanwhile was very busy plaguing her husband because he wouldn't hire a maid for her. That warm-hearted humanitarian of ours had for some unknown reason changed overnight into a melancholy, gloomy person. The people who had moved into the front courtyard were altogether two persons more numerous than the two previous families ... and various other similar minor circumstances.... That's all.

After about one more month, winter gradually descended on the ancient city of Peking. On the day that the last yellow leaf was blown down from the treetops, while he was out walking on West Chang'an Street, Zeng Simian saw a youth with a hempen rope tied round his middle, making him look like a little Buddhist monk, on whose arm an old woman was stumbling along, finding it very hard to walk. Zeng recognized these beggars as the old lady who had been his neighbor in the compound until a few months ago and her grandson, the son of the deceased Yan Laosan. The youth stared coldly at Zeng, then without any expression on his face, as if toward a stranger, held out his right hand. At the same time the old lady, who now seemed almost totally blind, began pleading in the most piteous of tones: "Kind sir, please do a good deed today, oh please take pity on us who have nothing to eat. May heaven reward your kindness, sir...."

Zeng Simian looked at them with deep sorrow in his heart, took out a little money, and stuffed it in the boy's hand just as he would for any beggar. Then he walked on without looking back. As he did so, his feelings were akin to loathing and contempt.

First written in late 1945 and revised in 1958–1959. First published, posthumously, in *Complete Works* I (1976).

6. The Fourth Day
第四日

I

Komatsu took the cigarette end from his lips and flung it into the air with some force. It flew up in a straight line; when it struck the wall a shower of sparks and tobacco shreds cascaded down, and then it flipped over and fell to the ground.

With curiosity he watched the butt's aerial stunt as he stretched his limbs to get the blood flowing freely around his body again. Leisurely he closed his eyes. He could hear the life harmoniously and rhythmically pulsing, singing in his veins.

The feeling of having no work to do—the sense of liberation from the sundry intricate tasks of his job—was inutterably comfortable, pleasant to the point of giddiness. He couldn't remember experiencing a time like this in oh-so-many years.

Outside the sun was glaring down brilliantly, but this room had only one small window, making it cool and dim, while constant waves of sound came in from the courtyard. Sometimes the waves were of laughter or debate, shouting or whispering; rarely, they turned into repressed quarreling. Sometimes among the sounds came the piercing laughter of women, as shrill as a file sharpening a saw, enough to set the hairs on end of anyone listening. Occasionally the sound of a motor vehicle could be heard from the front yard, as a peaceful day began to writhe back into life. Obviously another batch of "resident compatriots" (Japanese expatriates) had arrived, coming from a distant county or having been delayed for some reason or other.

Komatsu turned to look at his colleague, a short man named Yokoyama of the Economics section, who remained lying motionless, curled up on his side facing the wall; for a long time now he had been lying in the same position in the same obstinate silence. Komatsu knew that he wasn't really sleeping; it was just that he had things on his mind. Almost the whole afternoon the two of them had each lain stretched out on his bed, ignoring one another, allowing the time to slide away past their tightly sealed lips. It was as if they had already said everything there was to be said; there was nothing left worth talking about.

And in fact in the last few days, apart from taking their turns on watch, they'd had no end of idle time, idle minds, and idle tongues. Cigarettes alight, they had talked about everything. Through the eddies of blue smoke that crawled in the air like caterpillars they perspicaciously viewed the world. Every matter appearing or potentially appearing on the surface of the earth, both large and small, underwent their ardent and exacting analysis: the Potsdam Declaration, the atomic bombs, concentration camps, refugees, food supply and birth control, democracy and public order....

The topic that most commanded their consideration and fervor was the future of Japan in defeat. Yokoyama would immediately fall into Malthusian despair. Quite clearly, the four cramped little islands of Nippon were about to face enormous population pressures, and neither of them could think of any effective way of solving the problem. Perhaps Japan should take Britain's path. But Japan lacked the territories Britain had relied on for the establishment and development of her light industry. Japan had the same difficulties as the UK but not her advantages. Poor Japan, where would she go now?

Those problems that could be settled were mostly solved satisfactorily on their lips, the insoluble ones stuck like fish bones in their throats. Now, their argumentative, hysterical enthusiasm was past and each of them preferred to sink into thought, undisturbed. They needed to have a really good think. There were so many things they had to think about, so many that it made them feel completely adrift and at a loss. It was just as if they had suddenly been taken from a brightly lit place into a dark room, where they needed some time before they could get their bearings.

For so long now they had given no thought to their parents or their wives, left at home in the mother country. Now it seemed they should take advantage of their present leisure to think carefully about all that. Previously everything was so simple, undisputed; everything was managed for them without the need for individual thought. Nation, family, and life were a continuum, all roped together in a line. Now, things were different. The rope had been cut, and what had formerly been linked together had become separate, independent events that had to be dealt with one by one.

On his cot Yokoyama still lay silent, motionless. Komatsu glanced at him, perplexed, and then got up and walked to the window. His broad shoulders covered it like a curtain.

—Just let the poor guy go on trying to think of a way forward for Japan!

2

The department occupied two adjoining private houses. They had blocked one of the entrances, making the other one the front and only entrance; they knocked through the two-meter-high wall between the two yards to form a single compound. In one day they had selected all the furniture and fittings from the two houses that they wanted to keep and destroyed the rest, and then cleared and swept out the dozen or more rooms and spread rush mats on the floor to make a temporary collection center for the "resident compatriots."

For four days the "resident compatriots," scattered like stars across the vast yellow plain, had been converging here. At irregular intervals the army trucks carrying them roared up and in through the open gates, bringing with them billows of yellow dust before stopping in the front courtyard with its tall elm. The people were startled and disorientated; having stared blankly into the distance for so long, their eyes suddenly widened as they looked in surprise at the surroundings and at the people on the ground. With great difficulty, taking all the time they needed, they negotiated the chaotic piles of luggage and climbed down, the women in the arms of the men, one by one, like so many sacks being unloaded. These were bags of flesh fattened by filth and debauchery. Heaven knows what they were doing here. Each surrendered her entire bulk to the man who received her, kicking her heels in the air, laughing contentedly in his embrace, and squealing in feigned distress. The men's faces were without exception thin and wasted from worry and hardship, covered all over with dust except for just three holes, two above and one below. From the upper round holes radiated two beams of nervous insecurity. The impression of defeat was further deepened by their piteous demeanor of utter witlessness, like men in a trance.

Now the rooms around the courtyard were stuffed right up to the thresholds with these "resident compatriots" and their luggage and assorted belongings: suitcases, backpacks, bedrolls, and what have you. At first the people were talking and laughing or humming songs, but now the humming had stopped, as had the talk of "Japan this" and "Japan that," and they simply sprawled on the floor in sleep.

Over in one of the corner rooms a woman lay fully clothed, apparently asleep, her head pillowed on a pale green bundle. Her Western-style white floral-print dress had two buttons undone at the neck, shamelessly revealing her snowy upper chest and the swell of her left breast. Her sleeping face was contorted painfully as if with neuralgia. This face was sunk on her chest as if admiring its beauty.

In another room a skinny man with wild hair sat by the door, forever reaching in through his shirt to scratch at a place below his waist. Each time, he soon pulled out something between finger and thumb, placed it in his palm and held it up to the light for a thorough inspection, then reached through the doorway and tipped it out. In every almost oblivious move there lurked a deep primitive instinct, reminiscent of monkeys.

Komatsu turned his back and reached for a cigarette on the table by the window. These people, who seemed to live by sense of touch alone, made him feel queasy.

At some point Yokoyama had turned over in bed to face this way and was now staring vacantly at Komatsu with his childlike, round, and innocent eyes. Apparently he had been paying attention to Komatsu's movements for some time now.

"Gimme a cigarette." Yokoyama sat up lazily.

"Do you think they'll all really make it here today?"

"Who cares!" Komatsu replied, not beating about the bush. "We're packing them off tomorrow anyhow."

Because of the blocked-up windows the room was extremely dark and gloomy, casting dim gray shadows on Yokoyama's face, body, and all around him, so that the man himself, sitting cross-legged in the gloom, looked like a portrait. Those round, round eyes of his were fixed on some place beyond the circle of grayness in which he sat.

"They're a burden," said Yokoyama, slowly blowing out a mouthful of smoke. "In normal times they know how to look after themselves, but now somebody else has to ship them out like a load of bricks."

As he spoke he spread his right hand and flicked nervously at his brow as if shedding the burden just like that.

"Why did they come here anyway?" Yokoyama went on. "The men came to make their fortune, that's alright, but the women, that's hard to understand. This was the front line!"

From the front courtyard the sounds of voices and motors rose up again. Obviously another batch of "resident compatriots" had arrived.

The two men smoked in silence.

Suddenly a tall, powerfully built man charged in like a whirlwind, a canvas military backpack in one hand.

"Hah! Goddammit, I'm done in," the big guy shouted. "That yellow dust alone is more than anyone can bear."

He took off his army cap and threw it and the backpack together onto one of the beds. In the same movement he snatched the handkerchief out from his belt and began dabbing away at his face and brow, like a woman applying powder.

"Eh? Suzuki—so here you are too!" said Yokoyama, smiling at their guest. "How embarrassing, running for your lives like women!"

"Embarrassing? Well, I was the last to run!"

Suzuki gave a great laugh. Due to long years wearing his army cap, the area above his brow was white as a *mantou*, in marked contrast to his grimy, sunburned face.

"Mentally prepared, are you, Suzuki?" asked Yokoyama.

"For what?" Suzuki pressed his handkerchief to his forehead and stared blankly at Yokoyama.

"What else? The concentration camp! Internment till who knows when? Your days of sincere repentance, as required by the United Nations!"

Yokoyama was deliberately aiming to scare, but his voice was rather at odds with his intention. Within it was a sound that came from the depths of the soul, the sound of a wolf howling at the moon in the dark night. Komatsu couldn't help glancing at Yokoyama.

"Ai, let's not even talk about it. Losers in war, don't you know how..."

"I do know!" The corners of Yokoyama's lips twitched slightly. "Some hunters trap the hind legs of the wild boar and let it die slowly. That's the cruelest death, and that's just how Japan was defeated!"

"All right, all right! I look forward to hearing your grumbling another time, right now I need a wash."

Suzuki opened his pack, took out his soap box and safety razor, and went out. With his pendulumlike, swaying gait, from behind he looked as if he were drunk.

3

Just after Suzuki left, Hirotsu appeared at the door. He was the oldest man in the General Affairs section, and as he said himself, if his daughter hadn't turned her nose up at all the young men who sniffed at her skirts he'd surely have been a grandfather several times over by now. But among all his colleagues he was the most positive and cheerful: free from care and worry, when he laid his head down at night he slept like a great hog. He was very tall, but not slim like Suzuki; he had a good layer of flesh on him and a ruddy complexion. His big, round head, always shaven so close that it shone blue, plump body, and pink cheeks almost gave people the impression that he was younger than any one of them.

"Come on, Yokoyama, let's have a game." As soon as he came in, Hirotsu's booming, cheerful voice drove out the heavy atmosphere in the room.

"What, you're not still brooding about Japan, are you?" Then he turned to Komatsu and said, "The Head wants you."

Hirotsu walked over to the head of the bed and took out a wooden board and two small cloth bags: a go board and pieces. He opened one of the bags, and with a rattle and clatter tipped out a great pile of black pieces.

"One of the compatriot couples just now: guess how much luggage they had between them!" Hirotsu made one hand into a funnel, filled it with go pieces and poured them back into the other hand. "Eight pieces, big and small! Plus a boiler, a galvanized bucket, crockery, everything but the kitchen sink! To them it's just a house removal! To people like that Japan herself is worth less than one of their vases."

"Come on! Don't be a woman, taking it to heart so."

Komatsu walked out of the room. When he reached the room on the corner, he couldn't help taking a look in through the door. The place where the woman had been sleeping just now was empty, and there was no sign of her. There were a few other men and women in the room at the moment; if not rummaging in the piles of luggage, they were all either sitting dull and subdued or just lying lazily on their sides. Two women sitting close together and talking in low voices in the far corner now stopped and stared rudely at Komatsu.

A large truck stood in the front courtyard, unloading its last batch of cargo; on the ground a man and woman were moving luggage.

Komatsu thought to himself: could that be the foolish couple Hirotsu mentioned?

The office and quarters of the Head of Department were upstairs in the main building of the front court. As he stepped in on the ground floor Komatsu happened to glance at the adjutant's billet on the left. The Head's adjutant, the Special Advisor, and a businessman named Akuzawa were sitting on the tatami with *sake* cups, plates, chopsticks, and so on spread out before them. The three of them looked somewhat uneasy, as if their secret had been discovered.

"Komatsu," said the adjutant, smiling shiftily. "The Head sent for you."

The SA beckoned to him: "Come and join us!"

Komatsu declined and went on upstairs.

These three characters were known behind their backs as the Big Three. They often got together on the sly for drinking and womanizing, and it seemed that the Head of Department was aware of this. Of the three only the SA was not universally disliked. The adjutant had a big head, a big nose, a pencil mustache, and a fat belly; his face exuded all the guile and treachery of the merchant class. Because of his habitual arrogance, his fawning on superiors, his bullying, and other despicable behavior, he was roundly loathed by all in the department.

Akuzawa was the local manager of a Mitsui subsidiary. His dealings in the field were an endless, shameless string of swindling, intimidation, and extortion. He referred to all Chinese as swine. His usual form of address for them—"Hey you!"—embodied sentiments of the most utter contempt and venom. His malicious attitude and conduct had undermined the department's political propaganda work more than anyone could have foreseen. A few years ago the military police had laid simultaneous charges against many large companies in every district and arrested many of the bosses, agents, and the like. It shook them up a bit for a while, and resulted in a great boost to civilian and military morale. The Head was among the majority in favor of capital punishment for this gang of unscrupulous profiteers. One time, from the next room, Komatsu had heard him roaring, "Take the heads from their shoulders! Take the heads from their shoulders! Take the heads from their shoulders!"

The Head of Department, Mr. Saito, was alone, wearing slippers and sitting quietly smoking a cigarette in a big rattan chair, the back of which was much higher than his head. He handed Komatsu an official letter and told him to take it to the garrison. He spoke sparingly, his head somewhat bowed. When Komatsu took the letter he looked up at Saito for a moment. He saw a pair of bloodshot eyes and the highly complex expression of a man who, the greater the misery in his heart, the more he puts on a calm front. He even thought he detected a slight tremble in Saito's lips as he spoke.

On the way over, Komatsu thought of Yokoyama's comparison of Japan to a trapped boar. Whether it was Japan at war or Japan in defeat, he thought differently from Yokoyama. He felt that Yokoyama's sighs were real enough, but his words and his simile were lacking in realism. It wasn't Japan's hind legs but her heart, her very heart that had been struck. This led him back to Mr. Saito. If there was anyone here who truly and sincerely took grief for the nation's defeat on his own shoulders, it would be the Head. Komatsu found himself strangely saddened by Saito's terrifying expression, which seemed to suggest that he was just looking for someone or something to bite a piece out of.

In between Yokoyama and the Head of Department there was another kind of person. Perhaps those "resident compatriots" belonged to this category. When these folk met, they too started talking about "Japan this," "Japan that." But in the torrent of their chaotic and entangled conversations, Japan frequently disappeared like soap bubbles, leaving only their own affairs hanging emptily between them.

As for Akuzawa and his ilk, they were un-Japanese, saboteurs of the war effort who should be cast out by the entire nation.

The army was garrisoned in town; Komatsu knew a lot of folk there, some of whom were fellow provincials. But they merely happened to come from the same place as him, that was all.

Having carried out his official task, Komatsu met a fellow provincial and had a chat with him. This man told him how a contingent of troops had been withdrawing from the front yesterday and on the way a soldier had fallen in his sleep from the train. The train had rolled over his head; it exploded like a hand grenade.

"Just think," said the man. "He'd marched and fought all over the combat zone and survived; then to die so senselessly just when he was happy to be on his way home—it's a bit ridiculous, don't you think? What if his parents and his wife learn how he died, imagine how they'd feel!"

He went on: when the fatherland told them to go and kill the enemy, they went—every one of them was loyal to the fatherland and hoped to win the war for the fatherland. But now, having given their all for the fatherland only for the war to be lost, now they should be allowed to think of their own personal affairs.

Later, Komatsu ran into some other friends, and no matter what they talked about, they never strayed far from the lesser hopes that they shared: for home, property, a certain way of life, their wives, children. In a word: time to go home!

Komatsu was taken aback and deeply moved by the openness and warmth of feeling in his friends' personal testimonies. In the past, even just a few days ago, not one of them would have dared to speak like this. They might have harbored such thoughts, but the fatherland did not allow them to be spoken; if someone did dare to voice such ideas, they would immediately be branded un-Japanese, a fearsome accusation that could cripple a person for life. So they had fought on the front line, closed with the enemy, and faced death again and again; some had spilled their last blood on the battlefield, now to rest in a corner of this foreign land.

Every one of them believed this to have been right; they did their duty, that which the fatherland required of them. But now they had cast off such thinking and such attitudes like a pair of worn-out shoes, and without the least reluctance. So rapid had been this change, so clear-cut and so complete, that it seemed like they had just awakened from a long dream. This now seemed to be the general way of thinking in the minds of all Japanese, whether at home or in the war zone.

Two or three months ago Komatsu had received a letter from his mother that mentioned a neighbor named Toyota. Between the lines were traces of something resembling envy. Toyota had been in the Pacific Fleet with Komatsu's younger brother; Komatsu's brother had died at sea in the battle for Guam, but Toyota had only lost a leg and subsequently been sent home. Now, the letter said, he had opened a small eatery, which was doing very well; he and his wife worked from dawn till late at night. Often in the middle of the night Komatsu's mother heard them coming home talking and laughing; they had a really nice life.

Obviously, long years of war had diluted the zealous feelings of the nation at the start and cast them into somber shadows; the people had lost interest in the war, and a general wish had crept silently into their consciousness: the hope that the war would soon end! All of this could be encapsulated in those words of Komatsu's fellow provincial: now they should be allowed to think of their own personal affairs.

4

On the way back Komatsu avoided the commercial streets and took a detour via the suburbs. After a while he came to an earthen embankment and irrigation ditch that doubled as rampart and trench. The department headquarters were on a street near this embankment.

On one side were fields and orchards; on the other side, between the embankment and the city wall, were vegetable plots and more orchards. Dotted among the vegetable plots were small thatched huts. Willow trees hung their pendulous branches right down to the ground, shading each hut and its tiny front yard.

Climbing to the top of the embankment, Komatsu saw a figure standing motionless and alone on its far end near the department.

"That guy!" Komatsu flashed a pitying and contemptuous glance at the figure. It was Yokoyama.

"Listen," said Yokoyama, when Komatsu came near him, "that's field artillery, isn't it?"

Komatsu listened in silence. Yes, there was the heavy boom of artillery fire coming from somewhere or other, in irregular bursts with lulls in between, but it didn't seem to be very near.

"Well, there were reports of instability," said Komatsu. Just now at the garrison he'd been told of intelligence that Chinese forces would be advancing to positions in the city tonight.

The sun was already low in the sky. Two long clouds were converging from either side, like a pair of gathering hands just waiting for the sun to come down into their clasp, as if it were a watermelon. The sky behind the clouds presented the turbid pallor of late summer. From the horizon the western sky was already gradually drawing up the sallow and pallid red colors of sunset. This was the backdrop for the scattering of villages that cowered on the land, bleak and hushed, as though dead. Only the sporadic cannon fire occasionally broke the overwhelming sense of desolation all around, and reminded one that living people were still active on this great open plain.

"How awful this endless flat country is!" Yokoyama exclaimed. "Komatsu, do you think Japan had the wrong idea here?"

"Do you think so?"

"I'm asking you!"

"I don't know!"

The sun safely parted the two convergent clouds as it came down between them. The clouds dispersed to either side and became a pair of dark gray curtains covering half the sky. The brilliant red fringes of the last golden rays ignited a shimmering sea on the horizon.

A twilight mist began to flow and spread unchecked all over the plain.

The plain was deep, broad, endless. It seemed to stretch from some unknown place in the remote distance right to their feet, and then past them to some other place far, far away in the distance. Before it everything seemed tiny, commonplace, puny.

Perhaps it was as some people said: it was a bottomless swamp and Japan had unfortunately allowed both her legs to stick in it. Was this not a tragedy?

5

The department had bought a fat pig locally, and four or five Chinese cooks had prepared a fairly modest banquet for a dozen or so tables. This was a sending-off for the "resident compatriots." First thing tomorrow they were off on their way to internment, so this was a last gathering, and the department wanted to give everyone a happy time; after all, they had been through quite some times together in the war zone.

The top table was occupied by the Head and other high officials in the department plus some prominent local figures. For the occasion a few of the prettiest young "resident compatriot" women were chosen to wait on table, to ply the men with drink, and to add to the atmosphere of merriment. By now the feast was already into its third round of *sake*. Drop by drop the yellow liquid was dissolving people's concepts of decorum and rank, encouraging them to drink even more uninhibitedly.

Some of the women had long since left the feast, but the men were by now pretty drunk and sinking into maudlin lamentation. Their emotions were tending toward the heavy and serious. The *sake* may have been cheering, but it was also bitter. Not for a moment did they forget that their fatherland was defeated in war, though only the moon that hung bright in the sky could glimpse the red hearts in their breasts.

Clink! Another toast. But can you be sure that what they drank was not tears!

Come on! Another cup, let's have another cup!

The pretty waitresses poured them yet another brimming round.

Drink!

Give us a dance!

Clink!

The Head drank one cup after another, but spoke very little. Perhaps precisely because he spoke so little, he drank all the more. He kept his mouth shut, burying himself deep in his rattan chair with his arms crossed over his chest. His eyes shone with a hot light; like an eagle he watched the men's excited, tragic-heroic faces. No one noticed his face, as taut as sheet metal, as cold and stern as sheet metal.

Since nightfall the cannon fire of the day had become more persistent, and seemed to be nearer. The boom of each quickening salvo gripped hold of the people by their ears. At lamp-lighting time they had received news that the situation had grown even more volatile, so the garrison had posted sentries outside the city and the department had added to the guard at every post.

The Special Advisor cocked an ear. The pure, bright moonlight bathed his face in a dismal wash of white. He listened carefully for a while before saying, slowly and quietly, "It seems even nearer now; are they really moving in?"

"Surely not!" said the square-faced consultant Sakamoto coolly. "We still have a strong military capability here; they're not likely to take the risk."

"If they come we'll do 'em, teach 'em not to mess with the Imperial Army." Akuzawa, seated to the left of the Head of Department, spoke indignantly, excitedly. He was already a bit drunk. Both his fists were very tightly clenched. "So they think Japan was defeated, do they? That's a joke! Japan didn't lose the war! Japan had the Pacific and the Chinese mainland at her feet. Japan accepted the Potsdam Declaration because she didn't have an atom bomb; we didn't invent the atom bomb in time. Japan lost at science!"

"That's dead right!" The SA slapped the table as he chimed in.

Akuzawa was deeply moved by his own words; his face was twitching in paroxysm, and his head slightly tilted to one side. He waited until his emotion had abated before continuing.

"We must develop scientific enterprise in Japan, make it robust! We only need ten years, just ten years for Japan to rise again. You have to make Japan strong and rich. Ten years! Just ten years! Let's go for it!"

Akuzawa concluded his oration in the atmosphere of vehemence it had whipped up. Arrogantly he stretched out a hand. Face contorted and eyes blazing, he looked a stern and valiant figure, reminiscent of those ancient warrior heroes whose swords clashed in the moonlight.

"That's right, ten years: let's go for it!"

The SA stretched out a hairy hand to meet Akuzawa's. And so across that table a fervent and sincere handshake took place, a sacred ten-year vow!

Clink! *Kampai*!

Komatsu was sitting at a neighboring table, so he saw all of this as clearly as could be, but all it produced in him were a frown and a feeling of nausea. Underneath the highly melodramatic gestures he perceived their basis in a pathetic and capricious patriotism.

He put down his cup and left the table.

At the other tables, among the "resident compatriots," the effects of the *sake* were already coming into full play: the men were showing themselves in their ugliest colors. Several were flirting with the women, some insisting on kisses, and others making them sit in their laps and spouting: "You are my heart and soul, my very flesh!" The women struggled and squealed like monkeys. One of them had begun to play on a samisen. The strings strummed thickly and monotonously like an old woman coughing, sounding very strange.

As Komatsu passed the top table Sakamoto reached out to grab his arm:

"Komatsu, have a cup with us!"

Komatsu told him that the next guard watch was his.

"There's plenty of time yet!" said the consultant, turning to a waitress: "Miss Tomiko, pour us some *sake*."

Komatsu raised his cup. The Head had not changed his posture but was silently surveying all the excited faces from on high, as though distancing them from himself. Akuzawa held his hand over his cup; with his head slightly inclined and a moist sparkle in his eyes, he affected a statuesque splendor. Oh! Those were tears!

Komatsu frowned again, then drained his cup in one and returned it to Sakamoto.

Tomiko refilled the cups to the brim. Sakamoto never took his eyes from her. She was young, beautiful, and always smiling.

"Miss Tomiko, you are very beautiful! I offer you a toast."

Tomiko smiled radiantly. "I don't drink."

"No excuses! You've attended on us very well tonight. I'm in a good mood, and I want to drink to you."

"I said no! I don't drink."

"I won't take no for an answer!"

Sakamoto made to grab Tomiko. She immediately recoiled. Just then one of the cooks came out carrying a large bowl of piping hot stew for the top table; seeing Tomiko step back he hurriedly dodged to one side. Sakamoto saw what was happening and cried out urgently: "Tomiko! Tomiko..." But Tomiko had already bumped into the cook, and the stew spilled. It splashed onto the cook's hand: he frowned, but the worst was that some of it flew onto Akuzawa and the Special Advisor.

The cook was petrified: he just stood there aghast, with the half-empty bowl of stew still in his hands, not knowing what to do next. What he never expected was that Akuzawa leapt up and walloped him on his right cheek.

"You bastard! Are you blind or what?"

Akuzawa's angry eyes were popping, and his curses venomous.

The cook, unable to keep his feet, staggered back and fell over beside a table, almost tipping it over. The bowl of stew flew out of his hands, splashing scalding sauce and meat everywhere. The people at the nearest tables jumped up, crying out in alarm.

Sakamoto got up and tried to help the cook to his feet, explaining as he did so in his broken Chinese: "He drunk! He drunk!"

The cook clambered to his feet, brushed himself down, and made off without a word.

Going back to his seat, Sakamoto protested to Akuzawa: "What do you think you're doing! He didn't do it on purpose, you know, why on earth did you hit him?"

"Didn't do it on purpose?" Akuzawa's ire was unabated. "Hasn't he got eyes? These swine, you can't be lenient with them. Best of all to just behead the lot of 'em!"

Before his voice had died away the Head finally broke his long silence. Sternly he demanded answers from Akuzawa in a voice that was severe and imperious: "Why did you hit him? What cause do you have to hit a man?"

He leapt to his feet and strode toward Akuzawa.

All at once the whole assembly went dead silent; no one dared utter a word or move a muscle. They all held their breath, and swallowed back the saliva that rose in their mouths.

The bright moon shone down. The wind soughed, rustling the leaves in the trees. It was so silent all around that it seemed a falling needle could have been heard. The atmosphere was raw, cold, and grim. Komatsu sensed that something big was about to happen. "Here it is; it's coming at last," he thought.

Saito grabbed hold of Akuzawa's lapels and dragged him away from the table.

"What cause do you have to hit a man? Huh? Talk!"

As he spoke he brandished his fist in Akuzawa's face, then bang! Akuzawa reeled but did not fall. Then came another blow. He reeled again. The Head leaped at him and grasped him round the neck, stuck a foot between his legs, and tried to throw him to the floor.

Akuzawa didn't struggle, nor did he resist or ask for mercy. But although he was short he was stockily built, and it wasn't easy for Saito to wrestle him down. The Head summoned up his strength for another try. The two men staggered some distance, collided with a table, and came crashing down together with the table and chairs. Cups, plates, bowls, and dishes clattered to the floor in a chaotic mess of fragments.

All the women were shrieking, their faces pale with fear and alarm. The more timid among them couldn't bear to watch any more and ran indoors, their hands over their faces.

Akuzawa got up very quickly, but Saito lunged at him again. This time they smashed into another table: crockery and cutlery clattered and showered down again.

Still Akuzawa did not defend himself; still he uttered no sound.

After their third tumble to the ground Saito immediately leaped up and began stamping furiously on the body still sprawled on the ground. He'd gone crazy. He was a carnivorous beast that had smelled blood.

"Why'd you hit him?" he roared. "What cause do you have to hit a man? Huh? Talk!"

Kazuki of the Intelligence section was standing to Komatsu's left, looking like a general with his head held high and his hand on his left hip, where his sword hung. This guy's mysterious, inexplicable behavior was an infuriating, daily riddle to his colleagues. Now his face was solemn as he yelled bizarre imprecations into the middle of the ring. "Think you can get away with that? Son of a bitch! Think you can get away with that?" Nobody could figure out who his words were aimed at or what they meant.

Saito stamped down on Akuzawa, raised his foot again, stamped a second time, and then a third. By the third kick Akuzawa could bear it no longer. This stamping expunged all his dignity, reserve, pride.... All that remained were the survival instinct and the basic senses.

"Aiya! Mr. Saito! Sir! Aiya!"

There was utter anguish in Akuzawa's wails. Saito paid no heed, but just kept kicking: four, five, six, seven . . .

"Aiya! Mr. Saito! Aiya! I lost my temper, I—aiya! Aiya!"

"Lost your temper? Not likely! You think too highly of yourself. You're a member of the superior Japanese race! You despise others, the 'inferior' races. But oh, the shame! The superior have lost the war, and somehow the inferior are victorious. What are you going to make of that then? What have you got to be so cocky about?"

Mr. Saito was positively murderous now, as he struggled for breath.

"Pah! You reckon Japan can rise again in ten years? You want to develop science in Japan? You blowhard! Japan was defeated not because she doesn't have the atom bomb but because she has a shower of dirty swindlers like you for merchants; our boys at the front put their lives on the line while you lot made an easy killing in the rear. If anyone should lose their heads it should be the likes of you, not anyone else. Understand? Think you can help Japan back to the top in ten years? Hah! Quit dreaming! Even in a hundred years Japan will never rise again! Understand? You son of a bitch!"

"Aiya! Mr. Saito! Have mercy on me, please! Aiya! Mr. Saito! Sir! Aiya!"

Akuzawa kept on wailing, but he was now stretched out stiff and motionless.

At this point Sakamoto stepped forward and whispered something in Mr. Saito's ear, as if entreating him. Saito stopped stamping on Akuzawa.

"All right!" he said, lifting up his head. "Mercy? No problem—but on one condition: ask him if he's willing to go to the cook and beg his pardon. If the cook pardons him then I will too."

Straightaway two men helped Akuzawa up from the ground. He was covered all over in mud, and his face was bleeding in several places. He was badly weakened, unable to stand steadily, and his arms hung loose by his sides. The men took him by his armpits and dragged him toward the kitchen. Nobody asked him if he was willing to go or not.

"Son of a bitch! Think you can get away with that?"

The mysterious Kazuki began yelling again. His eyes stared straight ahead, the moonlight reflected in them reinforcing his enigmatic role.

6

Komatsu went to his room and dressed for duty, then took his Type 38 rifle from the rack on the wall, and went out.

His post was at the rear wall of the compound. A section of the wall here had collapsed, leaving a large gap, which had become a regular shortcut for anyone who wanted to save a few paces when entering or leaving the department. His watch companion, Suzuki, had arrived before him and was sitting on a bench, head bowed, deep in his own thoughts. A light machine gun was already set up on its stand on the ground at the gap in the wall, its muzzle trained on the deep darkness fused with the peach grove beyond the broken wall.

Komatsu propped his rifle against the end of the bench and fished in his pocket for his cigarettes.

Suzuki silently accepted a cigarette, lit it, and began smoking. After a while had passed he spoke: "Did you see that? The scene back there? How hideous!"

Then, with an air of reminiscence, he told Komatsu what had happened yesterday as he made his way back from the front among the ranks of the retreating army. It made Suzuki shudder inside to recall it. Local Chinese had dogged their heels the whole way, flitting like ghosts, relentless, and always shouting: "Lay down your weapons, leave your rifles—"

Their cries seemed to come from underground, and at the same time they seemed to come from all sides, all together; they sounded shrill with grief, grim, savage, and insistent.

Eventually this corps of the once-invincible Imperial Japanese Army just had to start running.

"In a word," said Suzuki, bringing his narrative to an end with unspeakable bitterness, "it's all just wretched. It's all so heartbreaking!"

Komatsu said nothing.

In the sky a disordered mass of white clouds was building, like a pile of white ceramic tiles waiting to be fixed, with larger and smaller wells of darkness in between.

The sky in those wells was deep, remote, and the not-quite-full moon lightly floated through them. At this moment, it showed half its face from the umpteenth well.

Suzuki looked up at the sky, apparently pondering for a long while, and then suddenly sighed with feeling: "Autumn is here!"

Still Komatsu said nothing.

"Komatsu," said Suzuki after a short while.

Komatsu looked up at him from under his eyelids: "What?"

"Komatsu, when we get home, what do you plan to do?"

"Oh, I haven't got as far as thinking about that," said Komatsu. "What about you, Suzuki? Will you go back to your band?"

Before the war Suzuki had played violin in a dance hall in Tokyo.

"No!" Suzuki shook his head. "When I shipped out I gave my violin to another guy in the band."

"You can buy another."

"Of course I can buy another; but that's not what I'm thinking. I'm thinking that I'll give up that game."

"Why?"

"Look at me, Komatsu." Suzuki straightened up on the bench. "Do I fit with all that?"

Mechanically, Komatsu turned his face toward him and quizzically and inspectorially sized him up from head to toe, as if they were meeting for the first time. Suzuki's shoulders were broad and strong; seated next to him, he was almost a head taller than Komatsu. Komatsu could see that for a strapping big guy like this to play a small delicate instrument like the violin was like a plowman trying to hold a pen. Not too fitting, right enough.

"I plan to go and work in a factory," said Suzuki, his gleamingly close-shaven face smiling sadly, mysteriously. "For me, I think a hammer will fit my hands much better."

Another long, long silence.

So still, so still. From somewhere outside the city a few rifle shots were heard. The peach trees quivered as though alarmed, making a rustling sound, a dim incomprehensible murmuring, like sleep talk.

Komatsu's gaze passed over the tops of the peach trees, to a much farther space. There, the clouds were very few and an expansive pure blue sky opened up. It was high and far and fresh.

"Autumn is here indeed!" thought Komatsu, and once again he wondered when they would be allowed to return home.

Part 3

Homeland

Written in spring 1950, and revised in 1952 and 1958. First published, posthumously, in *Complete Works* I (1976).

7. Zugteuzong
竹頭莊

One day in April 1946 . . .

Toward noon I took the Taisuco half-gauge train[1] home to Zugteuzong,[2] after fifteen years away. The train was really battered and shabby, and the wooden carriage, with its joints all loose, screeched and squealed as it rocked and juddered wildly, so that passengers' knees bumped off the knees of the person opposite and their elbows jabbed into the ribs of the person beside them. Each time this happened, the passengers would smile at one another in mutual understanding, without saying anything.

There weren't many passengers, but all of them were strange to me. When I looked more closely, it did seem that a few faces were familiar, but I couldn't remember any of their names. They were all good farming folk: simple, honest, frugal, and hard-working, devoting their whole lives to their land and their crops. As in the past, they wore bamboo hats and went barefoot; some of them had pipes in their mouths, and some

---

1. Between the 1920s and the 1960s the "half-gauge" train (*wu fen che* 五分車, aka *xiao huoche* 小火車 [little train]) was the most important means of modern transport from relatively isolated Meinong to the port of Kaohsiung, Taiwan's second city, and the world beyond. Taisuco is the Taiwan Sugar Corporation 台灣糖業股份有限公司, founded 1946. The sugar railways were established for the transportation of sugar cane during the Japanese occupation by Taisuco's predecessor companies, including the Great Japan Sugar Co., Ltd. 大日本製糖株式會社, which ran passenger services as well as sugar cane wagon trains on the 2′ 6″ tracks (Standard Gauge is 4′ 8½″, hence the approximate term *wu fen*—literally "five-tenths").

2. I use the Hakka transliteration of the fictional place-name 竹頭莊 (Bamboo Village) instead of the Mandarin (Zhutouzhuang). Read in Mandarin, the name seems to mean "Bamboo Head Village," but the Hakka noun-suffix *teu* 頭 is meaningless (similar to -*r* 兒 in Mandarin). The name of the real-life village, the home of Zhong Lihe's wife, Zhong Taimei (Pingmei), has always been Zugteupoi 竹頭背 to its almost exclusively Hakka inhabitants. It was officially named Taketōkaku 竹頭角 during the Japanese period and officially renamed Guangxing 廣興 after the return of Chinese rule in 1945.

held bamboo shoulder poles, their loads between their knees. It seemed to me that something was missing here. Only after a while did I realize: none of them were chewing betel nut; this was different from before. I particularly noticed those with blackened and recessed gums: these had been betel-nut chewers in the past. Another thing was that most of the women did not wear the traditional smocks that had been kept to by our Hakka women since immigration.[3] Partly because of strict Japanese prohibitions, partly for economy, the younger women in particular had switched to simpler, pretty tunics worn over trousers.

They sat on the hard wooden benches. Some tucked one foot up on the bench, while others sat with legs crossed, letting the train shake them to and fro like grain being riddled. Some talked to their neighbors about farming; some only sat, staring idly at the scenery outside the windows; and some made no sound at all, unless to clear their throats.

The train left the sugar refinery terminus and headed into the countryside. Formerly, the only crops in the fields round here had been sugar and bananas. Now, as far as you looked there was nothing but paddy fields planted with nothing but rice. But the fields were dry, at this season when water was so absolutely essential. The rice stalks, now over a foot tall, were gasping, anemic; the leaves hung numbly, not just yellowing but with a white color that showed that the plants were suffering. The tips of the leaves were a gray-brown color, some even burned dark brown; they were all curled up like tea leaves. As the dry wind swished over the paddy they presented a sea of parched yellow as far as the eye could see. To the onlooker it was like an endless field of fire. Dazzling sunlight flickered and shimmered over the paddy fields. The sky was like a sheet of red-hot iron with a ball of cruel fire hanging in the middle, darkly smoldering as it beamed out maximum radiation to burn up the land.

Amid the paddy's roots the earth was white and cracked like a tortoiseshell; the edges of the cracks were gaping toward the heavens, like lips opening thirstily for a drink.

---

[3]. The distinctive traditional smock denoted here is most commonly known as the *lanshan* 藍衫 (blue shirt). Royal blue or cobalt blue is the default color, but the smocks are also made in a wide range of hues, including various shades of red. Essential to every *lanshan* smock are the intricate multicolored bands embroidered around each sleeve and diagonally across the breast.

Children were grazing cattle in every field. They were laughing, whooping and yelling, racing, wrestling, turning somersaults—every one of them brimming with high spirits. Alongside, a great herd of water buffalo were freely and happily eating the paddy. As they munched, from time to time they swished their tails, a picture of ease and leisure. This was a feast of rare opulence such as they had never known. Apparently, the desperately hard work of the people who planted the rice had all been for the sake of these animals.

—No two ways about it, this season's rice crop was beyond hope!

Like people watching at the bedside of a dying relative, the train passengers stared out through the carriage windows at the fields stretching in all directions.

Across the carriage and to my left two farmers were chatting idly. One of them was puffing away on his pipe. The other, one leg crossed loosely over the other, prattled away as he watched his companion's pipe bowl glow and dim by turns: "In our village the Kings[4] always used to heed every prayer, but now for some reason the prayers don't work; we've held three days of ceremonies and we've made vows: a whole pig and a whole goat, promised in thanks for the autumn harvest! But what do you know? A fortnight has passed now and the sun is as white-hot as ever, from rising in the east to setting in the west!"

His companion's answer was a loud spit, a spout of brown liquid: "P-tuh . . . ! Goddamn! Your luck's in all right! Just wait till the skinner gets you . . . !"

At the foot of the embankment an old ox with large horns was chewing to its heart's content, shaking its head and swishing its tail, all the while watching the train with an air of unconcern.

"—The Kings? The Kings long since . . . the gods are all holed up in heaven, what's the use of prayers? Stuffed into sacks and kept hanging for years[5] . . . it'd be a wonder if they still answered prayers!"

---

4. In the real-life Zugteuzong (Guangxing) the most important Taoist temple is that dedicated to the Three Mountain Kings (*San shan guowang* 三山國王), who are among the most popular deities in Hakka Taiwan.

5. *Author's note*: "In 1940 the Japanese, for political reasons, tried to destroy all Taiwan's Taoist temples. In many cases the people hid the effigies of their deities in secret places in hopes of preserving them."

A man with a square, unshaven face, sitting on my right, turned and joined in the conversation: "That's . . . Brother A-Yuan, that was the Japanese, we had nothing to do with . . ."

"The Japanese did it—but it's you that'll pay the price!" The man called A-Yuan spoke with conviction: "There's your retribution staring you right in the face. It's so dry a single match would set the stones on fire!"

"Well, they said so, didn't they?" said the one with one leg crossed over the other, as if to remind A-Yuan. "The Celestial Fire is coming down."

"The Celestial Fire?" said the unshaven man. "Uh-huh, that'll be in the seventh month! On the wall at home we've pasted up a piece of paper we got from the Pushantang Temple: 'Virtuous Families, Two in Three Be Spared; Wicked Families, Root and Branch Shall Burn.' Yup, they're gonna burn!"

In the fields, a farmer was cutting whole paddy plants with a sickle. Everyone just stared, dumbfounded.

"Ai! All that hard labor to plant out the seedlings, and now with a flick of the wrist the sickle cuts it for cattle fodder. I've never seen anything like it in all my long years."

As he spoke, A-Yuan brought out a twist of tobacco from his Ohta's Antacid tin and refilled his pipe.

"Who knows how many families in town haven't any rice!" he said. "When the pot comes to the table you can count the grains of rice; the children scoop away the layer of shredded sweet potato and dig down to the bottom with the rice paddle, not worrying that they might scrape a hole in the bottom."

"Hey, Brother A-Yuan, they're the lucky ones!" said the unshaven man after a few dry coughs. "A-Xiu and his wife have had nothing but sweet potato leaves to eat for two weeks now. They keep the sweet potatoes for the children. . . . Oh, Uncle Dechang! Been visiting your daughter?"

The train had stopped at a small way station. A bareheaded old man clambered unsteadily into the carriage with a cloth bundle on the end of a bamboo pole over one shoulder. He grunted a reply and went over to sit opposite the unshaven man. He wiped the seat down and dusted it off before carefully sitting down, putting his bundle on his knees.

"Didn't your son-in-law ask you to stay to lunch, Uncle Dechang?" asked the unshaven man.

"What?" the old man gave his chin a rub; his hand trembled slightly, clumsily. "Oh, A-Tian? No! Um, he isn't home. Longmei's just had a baby..."

Now it was the turn of the people on my left to turn and look across to my right; Brother A-Yuan was still holding his pipe.

"A baby? A boy?" said A-Yuan. "So you're a grandfather again, eh?"

"Uh-huh, a boy; just a scrap of a thing; a cat could give birth to a bigger kitten! Well, poor folks like us, the grown ones can't eat properly, so the children go hungry too, and they're weak—there's no help for it! A great brood of children and a field no bigger than the palm of your hand; they work all year for a paltry few grains of rice: that won't fill their bellies, not even in the thinnest gruel. Longmei should be 'sitting out the month,'[6] but she hasn't had so much as a whiff of chicken, and after only a few days she had to go and work in the fields. You should see how hard she works: such a pile of washing and starching, and she even has to carry the water herself. No sesame oil chicken in rice wine[7] for the daughters of the likes of us, eh?"

Just then the train crossed a metal bridge with a great rock and roll and a clattering, deafening din. The old man frowned as if he had a migraine.

I stuck my head out the window to look at the bridge: the riverbed beneath it was dry. The stones that used to be yellow from the salt water now presented a dark, green color. Both yellow earthen banks were thickly entangled with great bamboo trunks, like a mesh wire fence.

"Uncle Dechang, Brother A-Tian is clever and capable. He goes off on his bicycle and does whatever work he can find. He soon turns a profit, and his life is tripping along very nicely. You needn't worry."

"What's the use of me worrying? I'm just an old bag of bones waiting for someone to put the lid on my coffin.... But these days, just be-

---

6. *Author's note*: "Zuoyue, ji fenmian 坐月, 即分娩." ("Sitting out the month" refers to confinement.) [*Translator's note*: Traditionally, Chinese women were expected to remain confined to their room with the new baby for a month after birth, and to observe restrictions in their diet, hygiene, and behavior.]

7. *Author's note*: "According to the old customs of Taiwan, after giving birth women should always eat chicken in sesame oil and rice wine."

ing capable isn't good enough! To catch a chicken you need a handful of rice; you'll get nowhere empty-handed. Whatever way you look at it, having your own land is the surest way, ain't it?"

"Your own land . . . Uncle Dechang, look . . . " A-Yuan pointed out the window with his chin as he spoke: " . . . just one more thing to worry about!"

Everybody looked out. The sunlight shimmered like a torch, so bright that the old man's eyes blinked and blinked until a few tears squeezed out. With lips slightly parted, he put a trembling right hand up to shade his eyes. He looked out for quite a while, and then cried out in surprise: "Eh? So many oxen!"

In his line of sight there were two children, one running, the other hot on his heels, chasing in and out among the oxen. A bit further off was another gang of kids, utterly intent on their play. One water buffalo, its four stout legs planted firmly on the ground, stretched its neck up toward the distant northern sky and bellowed: "Moo . . ."

The three farmers stared in a trance, completely silent, the old man quite forgotten. After a while, the unshaven one said: "Surely we're not already done for, just like that?"

With a long blast on its whistle, the train arrived at another station. This was a big town; more than half the passengers alighted and a fairly large number straggled on to take their places. The old man shouldered his bundle and hurried off behind the three farmers.

The next stop was the end of the line: my home village, Zugteuzong.

As soon as the train pulled out of the town I looked up: off to the northeast lay a village completely encircled by a thick dark-green belt of bamboo. A light gray mist hung over it, as if it were on fire. Earnestly, ardently I fixed my gaze, and the hot blood surged in my veins.

Finally the train pulled into the terminus. I mingled with the crowd of locals, as silent and solemn as a funeral procession, and made my way to my wife's childhood home. My excitement communicated itself to my feet as they went erratically up and down, almost staggering, as if I were walking in an utterly unknown place. Houses covered in layers of dust squatted on both sides of the street; they all looked so low, so shabby and cramped. People scuttled silently in and out of them, like mice or rats. All along the street at regular intervals were great big stone basins. In the past these cisterns were always overflowing with clear water, so that their sides were thickly covered with bright-green moss and the ground around them was wet. But now the cisterns were dry to the very bottom, and a poster had been put up above each one: "Strictly no laundering. Strictly no watering of animals."

Was there anyplace that did not show the desolate signs of the drought?

"So this is my homeland!" I thought to myself.

My wife's family home was at the other end of the village. My leather shoes clip-clopped on the stone pavement, producing a hollow, distant sound. At the mouth of the lane I met a woman carrying a bamboo basket. It was the wife of a friend of mine.

"Well, well! A-He, you're back! Bingwen's just inside, come on in!"

Bingwen was one of my wife's relatives, and he also used to be one of my best friends. He was a quick-witted, lively, hardworking young man of great prospects who had worked in the post office in Kaohsiung before the war. At the time I often went to Kaohsiung on errands for the family business in Pingtung and I would always be sure to look him up. We used to get up to all sorts of fun and games; as soon as we got together we'd start mouthing off, setting the world to rights. Sometimes we'd go to a tavern, drinking and messing around with the bar girls. . . . We'd get up to all sorts of mischief until deep into the night before weaving our drunken way home. The thing I prized most was that at that time he was also one of the very few of my friends who could read and discuss Chinese literature with me. This added a special layer of feeling to our friendship that took it beyond the ordinary.

I stepped into the room I knew so well. Inside it was very dark and quiet. A very, very small person was sitting askew in a bamboo chair over by the wall. My eyes had to grow accustomed to the dimness before I could make out his face. But when I did, I almost cried out in surprise. Involuntarily I recoiled a few steps. Could this man I saw before me, who had lost all appearance of being a man, really be my old friend Bingwen? Bingwen the snappy dresser, my companion of so many hours spent in teahouses and taverns? I couldn't believe my eyes, far less connect the man of my memories with what I saw now.

Ever so slowly, the man's thin lips parted: "Just got here? Have a seat!"

The voice was as thin as a mosquito's whine, and there was no emotion in it.

I mumbled a reply, put my case down on the bench diagonally opposite him, and sat down. I didn't know what to do with myself. My feelings of excitement and tension had disappeared in an instant.

Summoning my composure and observing more carefully, I was astonished at the change in my friend. On his pointy head there remained only a very few pale hairs, which stood up on end like those of a chronic malaria sufferer. His eyes were very pale brown, almost yellow, staring feebly out of their sunken sockets. His neck was terribly thin and his wrists terribly long; you could count all his bones.... He held, rolled up in his hand, an old-fashioned thread-bound book that I knew very well: *The Three Kingdoms*.[8] His bamboo chair was so worn-out that its back and armrests were held together by string. He only had to move slightly to set the whole thing creaking.

"Like shriveled up pieces of dried turnip!" I thought.

Our conversation was a disjointed series of question and answer; moreover, it was businesslike and bereft of emotion. Though long awaited, our reunion proved unable to conjure up a poetic, moving scene. It was as if there had never been any such things between us as friendship, parting, the war, or Taiwan's retrocession to China. His cold—one might almost say impatient—gaze and his twisted, mocking mouth were extremely upsetting.

"Don't you work at the P.O. any more?" I essayed.

"No," he simply replied.

"So . . ." I tried to think of something else.

"Huh?"

---

8. It seems clear that the book is the early Ming novel *Romance of the Three Kingdoms* by Luo Guanzhong, not the third-century authoritative history *Records of the Three Kingdoms*. Nevertheless, in the context of A-He's idea of modern "literary youth," Bingwen clutching this ancient book seems to be a symbol of his regression. Moreover, given that Zhong Lihe was profoundly influenced by Lu Xun as a kind of godfather of modern Chinese literature, it is likely that the mention of this book here draws an intentional parallel with a reactionary character associated with *The Three Kingdoms*, Zhao Qiye 趙七爺 (Seventh Master Zhao) in Lu Xun's 1920 short story "Fengbo" (A storm in a teacup). See "Translator's Introduction" at the beginning of this volume for more parallels with Lu Xun's fiction.

After a while I thought of something else to say. I was beginning to feel depressed: "I'm living in Kaohsiung!"

"Hmm, Kaohsiung? Oh!"

Bingwen suddenly perked up, and he propelled his upper body nimbly toward me. Apparently he hadn't yet been able to forget Kaohsiung.

"Kaohsiung," he said, his eyes and voice both showing signs of life again. "Do you know if the Relief Commission fertilizer has arrived yet? Oh, there's money to be made there! What if we were to transport some of it here? And what about cement?"

I watched him in surprise. I found his sudden enthusiasm inexplicable. Even his pallid, translucent face was now slightly flushed, and I could read in it something of his former lively intelligence.

"I haven't heard anything about that," I said. I knew nothing about that kind of thing, nor had I ever had any interest in it, but I did my best to humor him. "But if you want, I can try to find out. Cement? There's bound to be cement—I've seen the factory chimneys smoking. I'll ask around, no problem!"

"There's bound to be, there's bound to be!"

Bingwen's eyes shot out hot sparks, and the corners of his mouth curled in a crafty smile.

"... I've done it a few times already, you can double your money! I'm planning to give it another go. You don't need a shop, oh no—just turn the goods over, and that's it! Hah! It's great! It doesn't matter how much or how little capital you have, as long as you have something, then ..."

Just then, the sound of voices from outside interrupted him in midflow. The voices were warm and happy and familiar: I recognized one of them as my mother-in-law's. And sure enough, following her voice, she appeared in the doorway.

"Were you on the train that just got in?" My mother-in-law was beaming at me. "Are you all on your own? What about Pingmei and Tie'er?[9] I reckoned you must be due to come.... Let's go through!"

I nodded goodbye to my host. In the same instant Bingwen shot a look of hatred at my mother-in-law and looked back at me in disap-

---

9. In Zhong Lihe's autobiographical stories, if the narrator's wife is named it is always as Pingmei 平妹, not her actual name Taimei 台妹. "Tie'er" 鐵兒 refers to Tiemin 鐵民, the real name of the Zhongs' eldest son (1941–2011).

pointment, his mouth slightly open. But the next moment, with a blink of his eyes, he assumed an expression of great indifference.

"I'll stop by again after we've eaten."

So saying, I picked up my case and followed my mother-in-law out of the room.

A few rooms further in was my mother-in-law's home. As we entered the hall[10] she poked her head into the kitchen to give instructions: "Your brother-in-law's here. He can eat sweet potato rice same as the rest of us, but add a couple of eggs."

Then she turned to me and smiled: "For lunch I'm going to give you something new. All these years you've been gone, do you know what us folks back home have been eating? Shredded sweet potato! The rice is just for show; dig for it in the pot and you'll only get a few grains."

One by one, those who'd been out at work were also returning home. First of all came two of Pingmei's younger brothers. Both had married and had children since we left. From different parts of the room the children all stared at me with the same curiosity and timidity. A girl sitting on the threshold was digging in her nostril with a finger the whole time.

Before long, lunch had been set on the dining table and clamoring children surrounded it, each with a bowl in one hand as they fought over the rice paddle with the other.

"Hey! Aren't you ashamed to let your uncle see you behave like this? Give me the rice paddle; stop grabbing at it, all of you!"

The children turned as one to look at me, licking their lips.

My second sister-in-law snatched the rice paddle from a boy's hand, swept the top layer aside, and dug down into the pot to fill a bowl, which she put in front of me. Then she filled another bowl for our mother-in-law. These bowls were full of small orange and green strips lying this way and that, with a few grains of rice in between. When I looked at the other bowls, I saw that they had nothing but shredded sweet potato.

---

10. "Hall": this is the *langwu* 廊屋, originally a kind of corridor linking the main building of a traditional Hakka clan compound (*huofang* 夥房) to the bedroom wings on either side of the courtyard. The main building is usually reserved for religious observances, so the *langwu* becomes the main space for ordinary daily life.

The dishes on the table were one bowl of fermented soybeans and three big bowls of sweet potato leaves, plus some diced dried turnip. In front of me was placed an eye-catching large bowl of duck egg soup with red yeast. The children knelt by the table looking greedily at the bright-red soup.

"These children, no manners at all!" my mother-in-law scolded good-naturedly, as she added two or three ladlefuls of egg soup to every child's bowl.

"Get off now; your uncle is watching you!"

The children retreated to sit on the stone stools or the threshold, where they slurped and sucked up their food happily, with great relish.

"If you want to know the truth," my mother-in-law said, half-indignantly, half-proudly, "there's plenty of families in the village that are getting by on sweet potatoes alone. These days, who's in any position to mock anyone else? The Japanese taxes and levies were heavy, and even heaven refused to help us: the year before last it rained all through the autumn so that the paddy rotted in the field and we harvested only a few grains. Since last June there hasn't been a drop of rain. It's so dry even the stones are splitting. Unless you've accumulated good luck in your last life, you needn't even think about eating sweet potatoes . . ."

"Why didn't Pingmei come back with you?" My eldest brother-in-law interrupted his mother, impatient with the old woman's prattling.

"She'll be back in a few days," I said. "They're still in Kaohsiung."

"I saw your names in the paper on one of the refugee lists!" Now my third brother-in-law joined in the conversation. "You sailed from Shanghai, didn't you?"

"Uh-huh!"

After a pause my mother-in-law spoke up again, fixing me earnestly with her eyes and showing great concern: "A-He, did Bingwen mention selling cement or fertilizer just now?"

"Eh?"

I looked at her in puzzlement. I wondered if she had overheard my conversation with Bingwen. But that was impossible.

"He didn't ask you for a loan, did he? Saying he was going in for cement or fertilizer?" my mother-in-law persisted.

"A loan? Cement or fertilizer?" Flustered, I repeated her words.

"You see... who asked you to interfere?" My eldest brother-in-law frowned.

My mother-in-law glanced at her son, and then turned back to me and smiled mysteriously.

"Well, that's alright then," she said.

Obviously there was more to this than met the eye. I made a mental note, and after lunch, when the men and their wives had gone out to work again, I asked my mother-in-law to explain everything to me in detail.

"Hai!" she sighed. "It has to be said that Bingwen has had a terrible time of it these past few years. He lost his job in Kaohsiung, and when he came home he had to rely on his own two hands for a living. But just think, the way things are these days, even those who own rock-solid property are living from one day to the next, aren't they? As for those without so much as a strip of land, they'll be lucky to scrape by even for a few days! It's been several years now, and Bingwen can't stick it out any longer. Since last year he's been telling everyone he meets that he's going into cement and fertilizer, tricking money out of people left, right, and center. The devil only knows what he's selling! Strip off a man's mask of decency and he's capable of anything. Their child's so hungry she's like a little chick, cheep-cheeping round the yard. Who wouldn't feel pity? But what can anyone do? Now that I've explained the whole thing, don't you go falling for his scam. These days we can hardly fill our own stomachs."

I felt like I was listening to a story. I found it quite hard to believe it was true. What? Could Bingwen have fallen so low? It was a truly terrifying thought. If it were true, I was even willing to "fall for his scam," although my pockets contained a pitiful sum of money. His swindling evoked more sorrow in me than disgust!

Leaving my mother-in-law's house, I went back to that room to find Bingwen still sitting askew in his ratty bamboo chair, the *Three Kingdoms* between the fingers of his left hand. It looked as though the whole scene had remained unchanged for centuries, and as if it might yet stay the same for centuries to come.

His wife was clearing things away from the table. A malnourished girl of about four was sitting on the threshold of the back door, holding a bowl of sweet potatoes in her hand, one chopstick skewering a piece.

"A-He, have a seat," said the woman, and then turned to her daughter and barked, "A-Hong, go inside!" and dragged her into an inner room.

"Sorry!" As I spoke, I sat down on the bench as before and put down my case.

I was sure that Bingwen would have something more to say to me, so I waited in silence for several minutes, but he said nothing. The expression on his face had now reverted to the lifeless state I had seen when I first arrived. He looked like a simpleton. His eyes were unfocused and dull, the corners of his mouth were slack and somewhat crooked, his whole mouth was deeply sunken, and there were just a few brown hairs on his head, like a newborn baby . . .

Now that he had reverted to his natural state, the change in Bingwen was even more dramatically emphasized. This wasn't just decrepitude—it was annihilation.

"Done for!" I thought to myself, but at the same time my mind was summoning up a friend of yore: another Bingwen, the image of a radiantly handsome, elegantly dressed young man. I felt that this image in my mind seemed clearer, truer, closer to me than the one in front of my eyes.

A sadness swelled inside me, as at a difficult parting.

After a pause, it was again I who spoke first: "Would you like me to ask around for you, for news of cement or fertilizer, for example?"

I had my right hand stuck in my pocket, grasping a few tattered notes, ready to pull them out as necessary.

But Bingwen was now very impatient.

"No need!" he said gruffly.

That stumped me. Eventually I managed: "But aren't you planning to go into business?"

"Not anymore!"

"You don't want . . ."

"Nothing!"

He waved me away angrily.

I understood that it was all over between us, and what was even clearer was that my friend was gone forever. So I picked up my case and walked distractedly from that frightful room. Feeling a depression that was just the opposite of my feelings on arrival, I walked eastward toward the hills and my own home in the valley. . . .

Written in 1950, and revised in 1952 and 1958. First published, posthumously, in *Complete Works* I (1976).

8. Forest Fire
山火

I came to where two small rivers flowed together. The spur of hills between them was clad in swaths of towering bamboo. The valley to the west of the hills was very narrow. On the west side of the valley there was an almost perfectly conical hill; a few brick and thatch buildings were visible at its foot. The buildings were low and crude, and as the abundant sun of this southern land shone brilliantly down on them it drew up a barely perceptible pale blue haze.

Home—just as I had left it!

But just to its right a sad and shocking scene stopped me short. I saw now that the hills of my own home had not been spared, but had suffered unprecedented disaster by fire!

I had lost count of the number of such burn trails left by out-of-control forest fires that I'd seen all along my journey. Such an extraordinary event had scarcely ever been known during the Japanese period.

When I arrived home, no sooner had I put down my things than my older brother Lihu[1] was telling me all about it, pointing to the hills that were now blackened, reduced to ashes. Summoning up the most venomous epithets he could muster to describe the unidentified arsonists, he cursed them down to the eighteenth circle of hell, never to be reborn, and then he somehow lumped in all the other unfortunate villagers and farmers living in a three-mile radius. The light of hatred that shone in his eyes and the tight, bulging muscles in his face forcefully demonstrated the fury in his heart.

"Do you know why they're setting forest fires?" he asked me. "If I tell you you'll never believe it: they're scared stiff that come autumn a Celestial Fire will come down, so they're setting preemptive fires

---

1. I supply the name of Zhong Lihe's brother Lihu (里虎), upon whom this character is based, although the original text refers to him as *gege* 哥哥 (elder brother) throughout.

in the hope of heading off the Celestial Fire. You hear? What kind of thinking is that? Sonofabitch! Celestial Fire, my ass! Catch me believing in that, this autumn or any autumn!"

Lihu's thick, black brows were bunched up; below them his eyes formed a pair of clearly defined triangles. His right hand gripped the edge of the table. His whole body, down to the tip of every toe, was fused solid by the heat of his rage.

"It's superstition! There's nothing in it!"

In an agitated tone of voice he pronounced his conclusion: "—This has got nothing to do with the gods' wishes; it's all whipped up by men!"

This certainly was something new to me, that such unprecedentedly damaging forest fires should turn out to be the result of mere ignorant, absurd superstition. In the past, accidents arising from random carelessness, or during slash-and-burn or hunting, had occasionally caused small-scale fires. I knew about these things, and although they could not be condoned, they were understandable.

Now I remembered the "song to encourage virtue" I'd seen in my mother-in-law's house, pasted on the wall, which was no doubt printed and distributed by one of the local Taoist temples. I remembered the following lines from it:

> When the seventh moon comes, just wait and see,
> Heaven's Fire will pour down, no mercy shall there be;
> Good folks may yet be saved, two in every three,
> Wicked folks shall perish: root, branch, and tree.

At the time I had read this casually in passing, taking it for the usual type of virtue-encouraging rhyme urging people to do more good deeds, but now I understood that its latent power to incite or terrify might be enough to cause some people to do almost anything.

I felt that our home had become gloomy and depressing, and its inhabitants irascible. Their tempers were extremely frayed and they wore terribly long faces, as if punishing themselves for something. Realizing that all of this must be connected with the forest fires, I understood their emotions and sympathized with them.

I knew only too well how much blood, sweat, and tears my father and my own generation had shed opening up the virgin forest and making a go of this farm. I could still remember how Father would have a few cups of White Chrysanthemum *sake* of an evening, saying over and over to my brothers and me: "Ten more years of hard work; ten more years of hard work!"

His intention was to encourage us and comfort himself with a promise that the time would come when we'd be able to sit back and enjoy the fruits of our labors. And in fact such visions of future rewards are precisely the driving force behind the single-minded determination that some people show in struggling ever onward.

But now, this inexplicable conflagration had burned it all to nothing and our hopes had burst like bubbles, all in the blink of an eye!

We walked among dead, shriveled fruit trees, no longer useful for anything but firewood. Black ash lay in an even carpet on the ground. Tender *guan* grass[2] shoots were already spreading over valley and hill, as if seizing this rare opportunity—ash was a superb fertilizer for it. Apparently this place would soon be taken over by life-forms hardier and greedier than what had been burned, but not so welcome to man.

Climbing halfway up the side of the conical hill brought us to the outside edge of the fire's extent. Standing here, we could see to the furthest limits of our father's 125-hectare[3] farm, which covered almost the whole of this range of hills. The hills were burned completely bare; almost nothing remained, like a bowl that had been licked clean by a dog. Hardly anything was left of the timber bamboo plantation behind the house and the lovingly selected and tended orchard. Leafless, twigless, unrecognizable acacia, teak, large bamboo,[4] and many other

---

2. *Guan* grass (*guan* is the Hakka pronunciation; the Mandarin is *jian cao* 菅[草]): villous themeda, one of the most common wild grasses on these South Taiwan hills; tall, tenacious, and invasive, it is harvested as kindling and fuel for household fires.

3. The original has "our father's farm of about one or two hundred *jia*." According to my interview with Zhong Tiemin (August 16, 2010), the actual approximate size of Zhong Lihe's father's farm at Jianshan was one hundred and forty *jia* 甲. One *jia* equals 0.97 hectare.

4. "Large bamboo" (*taizug* 大竹): this is the Hakka name for *Bambusa blumeana*. The Mandarin is *cizhu* 刺竹 (spiky bamboo, so named because its budding twigs are viciously pointed).

trees stood stark and bare, wordlessly appealing to heaven. At their feet stretched the scorched and charred gray-black corpse of the hill.

In low-lying places, in gullies, and on the shaded side of slopes, white and black ash lay in thick drifts, lifeless and empty, and yet this was the very stuff of the lush green forest that had covered the whole hill and valley. It seemed quite fantastical!

The bamboos and trees beyond the edge of the fire stood whole and unharmed. It was as though they had stood shoulder to shoulder to defy the pitiless destructiveness of Fate, erecting a solid green fortress to encircle the path of the fire. One side was green and bursting with life, and the other side was gray-black and naked; the contrast was stark.

Some stands of tall bamboo had been damaged but not consumed; a few sprays of grayish yellow foliage near the tops resembled mourning flags at a new grave site, waving sadly in the air. If anyone had been able to understand their language, these bamboo survivors of the carnage could have told them of the cruel, savage burning that had taken place at their feet a few weeks before.

Lihu was fondling a blackened fruit tree. Looking upward, he said with regret: "Small-kerneled lichees . . . nothing but the best seed!"

Among the branches hung a few dry, brown, elongated leaves. When you took one and rolled it in your hand it broke into little pieces with a crackle.

These trees had been planted thirteen or fourteen years ago. By now each one had a trunk as thick as a saucer and should have been capable of producing a considerable crop. Even now I could clearly remember the individual history of each tree: how it had come to us from the Farmers' Union, or from the nurseries at Xinpu or Yuanlin, the endless paperwork and to-ings and fro-ings, until finally it could be transplanted to this place.

During this whole inspection of the fire scene Lihu and I scarcely spoke; like the ground at our feet, the bottoms of our hearts were carpeted with bleak, silent ash.

That evening we brought our chairs outside and sat in the courtyard.

There was no moon nor any stars. The stain-dark, primordial night was like a thick viscous liquid lying congealed over the long thin valley.

The ranges of low hills to left and right were like a pair of outstretched arms, silently thrusting into the endless darkness of the night.

"Surely the fruit trees can bud again, can't they?" I asked Lihu.

"Burned to charcoal, how can they still bud!"

Lihu's voice was somewhat hoarse, but it was his calm and sober tone, like that of an uninvolved observer, that really shocked me.

"If we can get some rain before too long, then there just might be hope for the bamboo."

I told Lihu about the forest fires I had seen on my way home; it was a terrible disaster, and so preposterous in origin.

Lihu listened quietly, and then said with feeling, "It's as if people have gone insane; they can't tell right from wrong anymore.

"The township is planning to build a middle school. They've budgeted for 700,000 yuan to be raised by public subscription, but it's been months now and they've only just managed to scrape together half the amount. Meanwhile, over there, at Sheshanwei . . ."

As he spoke he pointed with his chin into the distance straight ahead of us. I did my best to try to look through the darkness in the direction he indicated, but it was absolutely useless: I could see nothing but the sallow lights of a few rural homes.

"At Sheshanwei," Lihu went on, "toward the end of last year they were building a new Guanyin Temple, and the subscriptions actually exceeded the building budget, so they extended the original plans. It's as if people no longer believe in themselves and only the gods are considered reliable. That's all very well: if the gods can guarantee good harvests, then the benefits are immediate; but what about education for our children? Where's the benefit there? You can't see it, you can't touch it; people won't put their money into such a dead loss. If the rain continues to stay away this summer, the hills will suffer even worse fires. People believe this is the only way to escape the Celestial Fire in the autumn."

Lihu's words provided me with the material for a fantastical picture of chaos, in which people had become detached from their center and were blindly spinning around it, getting more and more confused as they spun, until they melded into the surrounding primordial darkness.

The sky was bigger than ever, higher than ever. . . .

Deep in thought, Lihu stared straight ahead, sunk down in his chair, his dim, silent figure as profound and solemn as a statue. The solemnity of the moment seemed to harbor a mystical, fateful sadness.

After a period of silence, the dark shadow that was all I could see of my brother gave a strange spasm and he spoke in quite a different, businesslike tone of voice: "Tomorrow the Grand Dharma Master is returning to his altar, and the Temple is combining the celebration with the spring thanksgiving mass. It's our *jia*'s[5] turn to lead the rite. Come along and see the show!"

Next day Lihu killed a goose. There was also pork, tofu, and so on—altogether a highly passable sacrifice. My sister-in-law carried it to the temple on a shoulder pole. This was Lihu's personal offering. On the public side our *jia* also contributed a full Five Meat sacrifice.

The Temple of the Grand Dharma Master stood at the foot of a precipitous, imposing peak; a small stream flowed in front of it, and on the other three sides it was surrounded by lush dark-green trees and bamboos: a place of murky numinosity. The temple was old-fashioned and crudely built; cobwebs hung everywhere in the darkness among its beams and rafters. Pasted on the columns of the doorway was a brand-new couplet:

> Lost land returned, the Celestial Master back upon his throne,
> Old liberty restored, gents and commons praise the gods anew.

The content was fresh and unconventional for a door couplet. It certainly was eye-catching. It included two extremely different sentiments: disrespect and profanity toward the gods came together in a turbid mixture with human elation and the fervor of universal rejoicing. I couldn't help being amused by it all. The mysterious drama of history had become a comedy, with the gods as clowns.

A dozen or more sacrifices were already set out in orderly fashion on the offering tables, each uniformly presented on its own red-

---

[5]. The Chinese *bao-jia* 保甲 system of defense, local government, and communal accountability was implemented, with modifications and occasionally falling into disuse, from the Song dynasty (960-1279 CE) into the mid-twentieth century. Each *jia* comprised approximately ten households, and each *bao* was ten *jia*. The headmen of the *jia* and *bao* were elected and rotated.

lacquered wooden tray. Flames and thick, black smoke belched up above the warm, harmonious glow of the lanterns and candles; more clouds rose from the great incense-rods and sandalwood incense sticks in the tripod censer, filling the whole temple with their thick, choking fragrance.

All the idols, blackened by long years of smoke, sat in their niches completely bathed in the sea of incense smoke, their eyes squinted half-shut, showing not the slightest interest as their devout believers scurried in and out. Along the main altar stood five faded war banners: red, yellow, green, white, and black, each embroidered with a dragon, its head rearing upward, and the legend: "The Celestial Master of the House of Zhang." The banners were covered in a thick, thick layer of dust, which would fly up in misty clouds at the slightest touch.

"Is it Celestial Master Zhang Daoling?" I asked a farmer, a member of our *jia* who was standing beside me; his face was stained with sweat and he had both sleeves and trouser legs rolled up high, as if he had just been planting out rice seedlings.

"Celestial Master Zhang Daoling?" The man looked me up and down in surprise, before going on with a face creased into smiles, "—I suppose that's him. I'm not really sure."

He immediately turned his attention back to an appreciative appraisal of the three tables of sacrificial offerings, and couldn't help gasping in admiration when he saw Lihu's Five Meat feast for the gods. Not only was it ample, but it was also quite special. The goose, so large and plump, stretched its neck back peacefully in a curve, and its skin was glistening bright yellow all over, the fat oozing out like drops of gold.

"That's a devil of a fat goose!" said the farmer. Lihu smiled, very pleased with himself, but replied modestly, "Oh no, it's nothing really! No chickens left, you see, so we just had to kill a goose."

As leader of today's rite Lihu had applied hair cream to his thinning locks until they shone. Over his traditional long gown he had draped a Western-style serge jacket. His shirt collar was open, his feet bare, and his smile dazzling.

I left the courtyard and went to sit at one of the tables outside. Two young farmers there were arguing heatedly, spittle flying everywhere. One of them was a tall, skinny guy; the other had thick, stiff hair like a brush, and eyes that glowed with expression.

"—A-Rong told me. It must be true!" said this latter one, citing his ultimate authority.

"But there's nothing wrong with it!" the other one argued.

"That's because the whole statue's been redone in gold leaf! He should've been brought back to the temple last year. That's why they couldn't do it till this year. If you don't believe me, you can ask the caretaker—of course he might not tell you! A-Rong's pa gave him instructions: he said it wouldn't be right to tell people about it!"

At this point the brush-haired youth snorted cockily like a puppy.

"A long time ago A-Rong's pa had guaranteed that the Dharma Master would be safe if they hid Him at his place. So after the Japanese surrendered, the temple caretaker went to A-Rong's pa and asked when they could bid the Master to return to the temple. Then A-Rong's pa invited Him out of the cupboard, but as soon as they looked they saw that His nose was gone!"

I seemed to sense a certain falsity and pretense in the youth's tone.

"You can never trust what A-Rong says!" The skinny guy was equally stubborn.

In the tiny yard in front of the temple a dozen or more tables had been set, with a filthy gray cloth awning stretched over them. A band was playing ancient tunes by the table nearest the temple eaves. The blind *suona* player puffed his cheeks out like balloons, big droplets of sweat oozing out from his big, flat nose and his chest heaving like great waves, as if his lungs had unlimited capacity. The *suona*, responding to the springlike movements of the young player's fingers, sounded one minute like a woman's scream, the next minute like a child's laughter, and the next again like mournful cries. An invisible iron claw, it gripped the heart of everyone within earshot.

The air was full of all kinds of sounds and smells: sweat, smoke fumes, and sour human breath. The people were immersed in the celebration, giving themselves over to talk, laughter, and boisterous noise, going off this way and that like fireworks. The sun burned like a torch above their heads, its searing heat turning their faces and ears crimson. Yet this only excited them further and made them even more agitated and fervid.

And then—the ceremony.

An altar had already been set up at the foot of the steps, with a rush mat spread out in front, on top of which was a bloodred pleated rug. The Master of Ceremonies, the head of our *li*,⁶ stood reverently beside the altar table, overseeing the rituals and offerings. He wore a cotton garment that wasn't short enough to be a jacket but wasn't quite a long gown either; his arms hung straight down, his eyes stared straight ahead, and his voice trembled: it ululated most unnaturally as he read out the ritual protocol. He drew out each word as he intoned: "Sound the drums—three times—"

The drummer responded immediately by raising his sticks:

Doong, Doong, Doong, doong doong doong doong . . .

Locals as well as worshipers from further afield were arriving in a constant stream. A congregation of female worshipers of all ages had formed on the bumpy lane beside the stream. The hot sun sent up a thick, overpowering smell of *tung* oil from the paper umbrellas they shaded themselves with. The ushers piled on clowns' smiles as they greeted them and guided them in, then in crisp voices reported to the accountant who sat on the east veranda:

"Received from Liu Qingmei, fifty yuan for incense oil; from Yang Juxiang, thirty yuan for incense oil . . ."

Inside the temple, under the eaves, in the yard—people crowded everywhere in great confusion and excited bustle. Amid all this clamor, observation of the rites continued without letup.

"Let the leader of the rite take his place—let the assistant leader also take his place—"

The *li* head's whole face was flushed bright red, and his mouth was strangely contorted.

Lihu and a fair-skinned man of about thirty stepped up to the altar and stood shoulder to shoulder. At the Master of Ceremonies's "Kneel!" they knelt together on the red rug. Their eyes stared straight ahead, unblinking, as if mounted in their sockets by human hand;

---

6. The *li* 里 (locality/village) is the smallest unit of formal, elected local government in Taiwan. In a town or city it may form a small urban district of a few blocks. In the case of Zhong Lihe's home district the *li* is the small village of Guanglin and its surrounding area of scattered farms and hamlets, including Jianshan. Rural *li* may also be known as *cun* 村 (village).

their arms swung limply and abnormally long from their shoulders, as if dislocated.

"Bow—bow the second time—bow the third time ... "

In everything there was an atmosphere of discord; everything was contradictory and comical. Blasphemy and piety, willfulness and absolute sincerity, solemnity and offhandedness—it all blended so naturally together. They personalized the gods. Here there was none of the veneration for the gods that ordinary people would imagine. However, it was from another angle and in another sense that they astonished me—they approached the gods with the same intimacy and warmth as they would their friends and relations!

Their innate ability to invest anything, anything at all that they touched, with the nature of a child's game seemed so laughable. But they patiently and earnestly played the game through to the end with all the innocent enthusiasm of children. There was something more here, something more solemn than mere amusement. These apparently simple, good, and honest folk were the very same people who were setting their own hills on fire, for some unfathomable reason adopting the stance of bare-knuckled pugilists.

How absurd! How hateful! And how very sad!

Suddenly I remembered Lihu's agitated tone and stance yesterday as he lambasted superstition. Imagine: if we separated my brother from our forest farm, would he still attack the people's stubborn ignorance? Or would he turn around and join in on the side of the forest arsonists?

The answer seemed very much in doubt.

That night Lihu and I, as on the previous night, moved our chairs out into the yard. Our old neighbor Uncle Chuanfu and his eldest son, who lived at the foot of the hill to our right, came to sit with us on their way back from burning incense at the temple. In the darkness Uncle Chuanfu's pipe bowl shone red from time to time, like a glowworm.

There was still no moon, but many stars were twinkling above. The night sky was much clearer than last night. The two miniature mountain ranges stretched out like a pair of arms into the far distance at either side.

The hot, oppressive air carried the bland fragrance of grass, while the sporadic sound of dogs barking further downhill created an air of restlessness.

Near the end of the eastern arm flames were rising up, turning a large quadrant of the sky a fanciful red. Black smoke churned high into the air. The hills nearer us were dimly lit as if by a feeble soybean oil lamp shining through a fanlight.

This forest fire was silent. With the silent forbearance of the sages, the forest accepted the suffering imposed on it by ignorant people.

"Sheshanwei?" asked Lihu calmly.

"It doesn't look like Sheshanwei; I'd say it's the other side of the hills—over by Xinzhuang." Uncle Chuanfu took another draw on his pipe. "If they keep on burning the forest like this, won't they burn it all away? The forest is like a child, it needs constant care: ten years of planting can't withstand a single burning match! Isn't that right? If your pa was still alive to see them burning the hills like this, it would kill him, surely? Bless him, he gave his sweat and blood, everything, for this place."

Then he turned to me and asked: "A-He, where were you when your pa passed away? Didn't you get word?"

I told him where I'd been at the time, and how wartime obstacles to shipping had meant I never got the letter from home.

"So far away?" said the old man thoughtfully. "That would've been two years before the Jap surrender, when the big man passed away..."

In the murk of the night the old man appeared unusually big and powerful; he gave the impression not of sitting on his chair, but of floating or swimming above it. From time to time his glowing pipe flared up in a streak of light, and in those moments one could see the deeply wrinkled, coffee-colored hand that held it.

The extent of the distant hill fire kept growing; billow upon billow of tarry black smoke stained half the sky darker and grimier than ever. Red tongues of flame blazed and climbed, spreading and extending in a broad curtain of fire.

"It's a lot bigger now!" The old man spoke with concern. We all looked silently in that direction. After a while, he spoke again: "Before we even know where their Celestial Fire is at, the whole mountain will have gone up in smoke. Your gods, you see—if you worship 'em and leave 'em alone you'll have clement weather, timely rain, and peace and harmony in the land. But if you go and ask 'em, well then it all comes down: if it ain't war in the east it'll be demons in the west!

That's the gods for you! That's their territory! But who knows for sure about Celestial Fire coming down in the seventh moon! That's just folks making a rod for their own backs, ain't it?"

"Let 'em burn their mothers' assholes in the seventh moon! Celestial farts!" Strangely, there was an element of melancholy mixed in with the profanity of Lihu's indignation.

"Still no signs of life in the fruit trees and timber bamboo?" asked the old man. "If only we could get a fall of rain, perhaps some of them might still be saved, don't you reckon?—All it needs is a fall of rain!"

"Easier said than done!" Lihu shook his head in despair.

Suddenly the old man turned to his son and asked: "It was you who told me, wasn't it, that the Grand Dharma Master Temple received much more incense money today than any year before?" Then he turned back to my brother: "Is it really so? Oh, *twice* as much! Hai! Where's the reason in that?!"

The dogs had gone silent, but now something startled them into renewed frenzy. The old man peered into the distance, cocking an ear to the dogs' barking. His pipe flared again.

"It's really about time heaven sent down some rain; the earth's so dry even the sweet potatoes won't root. If it goes on without rain . . . Ai!"

Uncle Chuanfu raised his eyes to the sky.

In the sky a rash of stars still twinkled. Silently they peeped down on a suffering world. . . .

Written in 1952 and revised in 1958. First published, posthumously, in *Complete Works* I (1976).

9. Uncle A-Huang
阿煌叔

Since I lacked a kitchen, my elder brother Lihu had rigged up something for me on the veranda. Six poles of stiff bamboo had already been sunk in the ground, and the frame and rafters, made of long-stem bamboo, had been strapped to them. All we were waiting for now was for it to be thatched. But Uncle A-Huang had thatched only the two ends of the veranda, leaving the major part in the middle uncovered, before putting down his tools and staying away. So my kitchen was like a child wearing one of those crownless ceremonial hats; for days now it had brazenly bared its head to the skies, open to the wind and exposed to the sun.

Which was all very well, but not for my poor wife, Pingmei, who had to cook three meals a day there. Her bamboo hat had to do the job of the missing roof, and whenever things went somewhat against her liking she'd start to complain. Moreover, at the least excuse she'd include me in her complaint, as if her unwanted sunbathing was all my fault. The injustice of this goes without saying, but I never defended myself. After all, I couldn't help feeling some remorse as I looked on at Pingmei's suffering: wearing her coolie hat as she slaved over our meals, burned by a fierce sun above and a hot stove below, blackened like the charcoal, and flushed like its glow.

Even that would have been all very well, but since yesterday at lunchtime the weather had started to look pretty bad. A gray blanket of cloud had engulfed a great chunk of sky in the northwest, so it looked like rain was on its way in the next couple of days. As she came in and out of the house, Pingmei kept looking up to inspect the weather signs, her brows knitted together in a frown. Her complaints grew in quantity and frequency, and it began to seem that I could no longer keep myself aloof: what would become of us if it really did rain!

"It's going to rain any time now," said Pingmei unhappily. "Can't you go and see Uncle A-Huang?"

Well, there was an idea! It seemed my anxiety had made me stupid, so that I hadn't even thought of this. And so, having asked my brother the way, I determined to set out on this mission.

Come to think of it, twenty-odd years ago I had actually known Uncle A-Huang well. In our village, when it came to the winter sowing of rice in the paddies, three or four of the best young laborers would organize weeding gangs and tender for contracts with the local farmers. These gangs were semi-cooperative units; the members were all young people. A-Huang was the foreman of one of the gangs, and his was the gang most in demand in the whole village for its work ethic, its skill, and its speed. Most of the young people, boys and girls alike, wanted to join A-Huang's crew. The farmers also hoped to get A-Huang's gang for their fields.

One day, when the rice sprouts were already standing in the fields, it was our family's turn to welcome Uncle A-Huang's gang. This was no ordinary day. The farmer always had to prepare a slap-up lunch for the gang. As if it were New Year or some other feast day we had to kill a chicken or a duck and buy liquor and good things to eat. It was quite a to-do.

I was only a young boy, so the festive atmosphere soon had me in a state of high excitement. My eldest brother's wife killed a large capon, while my older sister (who has since passed on) and I excitedly looked on. Xiumei, who was ten, wore a short jacket, white with blue flowers, and hanging from above her ears was a pair of pigtails, tied with bows of bright red wool. She had shining black eyes, and her rosy cheeks, set off by a plump, white face, were like the "red turtle" buns that people set out at gravesites during the Qingming festival. Opening those big round eyes to their fullest extent, she fixed them unblinkingly on the capon's half-closed eyes. She was famous for her weakness for poultry heads. Whenever a chicken or a duck was killed in our family, the head was always hers. Whatever it took—tears or tantrums—she had to have that head.

"Xiumei, you really can't have the chicken head today. It's for Uncle A-Huang—he's the gang foreman!" Our sister-in-law spoke kindly as she turned to Xiumei from her work gutting the capon.

The chicken head had to be presented to the gang foreman. No one knew when this rule had become fixed as a folk tradition. Its symbolic meaning seemed to have as much force as the ancient Confucian rules about respect for elders and reverence for ancestors. Although unwritten, it had been respected for as long as anyone could remember. If anyone were careless enough to break the rule, it would be considered an unforgivable crime.

But Xiumei just stared at our sister-in-law, dumbfounded. Her eyes were opened bigger than ever, and in them were mixed equal parts of mistrust, incredulity, and puzzlement.

"The chicken's head is reserved for the gang leader; nobody else can claim it." Sister-in-law was putting on all her smiles for Xiumei, half-explaining, half-cajoling.

When everything was ready for this special lunch, Sister-in-law packed it all into two baskets and carried them by shoulder pole down to the fields. Full of excitement, Xiumei and I followed her, skipping along happily, laughing, chatting, and playing.

Our paddy-fields, four hectares or more, lay to the north of the village, bordering the wide river flats to the north and east. Apart from a few plots of bananas, almost everything was under paddy. The seedlings were already as tall as chopsticks.

The weeding gang was made up of a dozen or more young men and women, all bursting with vibrant life and strong as oxen. They were lined out across the field, each with a row of paddy between their knees, kneeling to turn the mud and pull out the weeds around the rice-sprout roots. Every single trouser leg was rolled way up high, and their lower legs were now superfluous extremities trailing behind, swishing from side to side with the movement of their bodies. The males of the team were stripped to the waist, their backs bared to the sun and looking just like the mud: dark brown and shining. Meanwhile the girls had used their blue headscarves to hitch the fronts and backs of their skirts securely up around their waists. Their well-rounded thighs, normally so white, had been turned red by the blazing sun overhead and the hot brown mud underfoot.

They never stopped talking, laughing, whistling, or calling out cheerfully to one another; and of course from time to time one of them would break into a hill song. And all the while they were deftly and skillfully digging and scraping at the skin of the land. Where they had passed, the water in the field was turbid and the black earth was shiny and smooth as if laced with sesame oil. The rice sprouts looked like the trees in the forest after a typhoon, tossed this way and that and all in disarray, as if their benefit in all this were the least of anyone's concern.

As the gang finished weeding another plot, one of them suddenly called out loudly and authoritatively: "Stop work, everyone: here's lunch!"

This was Uncle A-Huang. He was the first to weed as far as the bank and the first to straighten up. He was a strapping, tall guy with broad shoulders, built like a wall. His every gesture and movement was as keen as a sharp knife and as cool as a steel hammer. His hands, his legs, his torso, and even his face were smeared all over with mud splashed up during the weeding and dried by his body heat. Somehow this lent his remarkable face a certain swashbuckling, heroic quality, an expression of boldness and power that perfectly suited his imposing physique. Even the mere shadow of his every action made a clear and compelling impression on me—in a word: strength!

In the banana grove next to the paddy-field Sister-in-law cut a few leaves, spread them on the ground, and then transferred the meal onto them from the pole baskets. The gang all went to the irrigation ditch, washed off the black mud that covered them from head to toe, and nimbly gathered round. Immediately the banana grove and the air above it were filled with the chatter and laughter of these cheerful young people.

The women adjusted their clothing and fixed their hair; each of them put on a new face and became a different person.

A sparkling light shone from the young people's eyes; happy smiles parted their lips.

A-Huang stood in the shade of the banana trees, his left hand on his hip and his broad torso swaying as he surveyed the sun-bathed paddy-fields with satisfaction. His face still dripped sweat, which he kept wiping away with his right hand, which he then wiped on his waistband. Soft, bushy hair grew on his big broad chest: like the hair of his head it was thick, black, and shiny. The lines and angles of his face were chiseled, his mouth was large, and his gaze was calm and assured. He exuded the unaffected heartiness common to people who pay no attention to anything other than the drama of real life itself.

After looking out for a while, he turned to the others: "Is everyone here?" he asked. "Well then, let's eat."

Then he noticed Xiumei in the crowd, seemed to remember something, and said in surprise: "Oh, Xiumei! Come here!"

A-Huang strode over to the picnic spread and bent down. He took the chicken head out of one of the biggest bowls with his fingers and held it out to Xiumei.

"Here you are! For you. Go on—it's yours! I know you like 'em." And he roared with laughter.

My sister was shy; blinking, she looked around at everyone out of the corners of her eyes.

"What's to be shy about? It's yours!" Another burst of bright, happy laughter.

Finally Xiumei accepted the chicken head, and then turned and went off into a deep part of the banana patch to eat it.

Watching her go, with her two bright-red bows bobbing behind her, Uncle A-Huang laughed again and called after her: "Xiumei, what a good girl you are!"

Watching all of this through eyes wide with astonishment, almost wonder, I was as baffled and confused as if I had gotten hold of a new toy but didn't know how it worked.

And that is how the impression of this extraordinary man was left indelibly on my childish mind.

But the Uncle A-Huang I had known was the youthful A-Huang of more than twenty years ago. Since that time the paths we had taken had allowed a dark, unknowable ocean to intervene between us. Now, when our worlds overlapped once more, he was no longer the A-Huang of old.

I had heard that in the second year of the war he, like my own family several years before, had left our native village twenty-five kilometers to the southeast (our home since immigration generations before) to move here. He had married into a family in the village below the hills that we could now see from the front of our house. As for his family back in Pingtung, all my brother could tell me was that everyone had died and everything they owned had been sold. As to how they had all died and how everything had come to be sold, it seemed Lihu hadn't been able to get all the details.

"That guy's all washed up; lazy to the bone!" Lihu spoke angrily.

According to him, Uncle A-Huang's being "all washed up" was entirely due to laziness! He was too lazy to work, too lazy even to move! If ever he did manage a day's work he would have to rest for three or four days afterward. Precisely because of this laziness, his father-in-law had thrown him out, along with his wife and children.

"Go and take a look if you like," said Lihu. "He's bound to be at home in bed as usual! He's even too lazy to cook for himself. He'll end up sleeping himself to death!"

As I walked along the narrow path I tried to make a connection between the "strong" Uncle A-Huang of my childhood memory and the "lazy" Uncle A-Huang of the present. I hoped to make full use of the cement of my imagination and deductive powers to build a bridge over the gap between the two in order to rationalize these extremes of industriousness and indolence. But soon, after giving it my best effort, I gave up this attempt at synthesis. Like a child's game, the only way to make it possible would be to employ the strangest of weird logic.

The narrow path wound this way and that through the dense, shady forest of sky-scraping bamboos. As I walked alone my feelings were of gloom and oppressiveness. At the other end of the tunnel of bamboo I came to some small, terraced fields going down to the banks of the broad, dried-up bed of the Shuangxi River. From here one could just see, among a tangle of shrubs and trees beyond the fields, the eaves of a small, thatched house.

This must be A-Huang's home.

As I got near to the house I was assailed by the stench of sun-baked shit and piss. A swarm of blowflies flew up like a buzzing cloud. Looking down, I saw a pile of excrement. But it was when I looked around that the real shock came: all over the ground was one black pile after another. As I walked forward, swarm after black swarm of blowflies flew up to reveal the brown piles underneath. All of them were piles of shit! Many of them had been baking in the sun so long that they had crumbled. Countless dung beetles, armored like ancient soldiers, were enthusiastically but awkwardly using both front and back legs to roll balls of excrement bigger than themselves off somewhere or other.

Two children were playing under an Indian cherry tree beside the house. The older one, a girl who held a piece of hemp thread attached to a dung beetle, stared at me with eyes wide in surprise. Above her upper lip hung two trails of thick, yellow snot. The dung beetle, clad so imposingly in military garb and in a bid to avoid extinction, was scrabbling uselessly at the earth. The girl's little brother was sitting bare-bottomed on the ground beside a pile of excrement. Flustered by this impediment, the blowflies buzzed up and down, this way and that, round and round the boy, steadfastly refusing to leave altogether.

I had to be most assiduous about where I placed by my feet; the slightest lack of care might result in stepping in any one of the piles of excrement. At the door to the house a black dog was feigning sleep in the dappled sunlight and shade. When it saw me it clambered unsteadily to its feet. It was shriveled and gaunt, not much more than skin and bones. You could count every one of its ribs. It fixed its melancholy eyes on me for a moment, and then turned up its tail and slunk indoors, swaying like a drunkard.

I went through the low doorway. Inside it was very quiet, not the slightest sound to be heard. In this narrow, dark space, two joyless, luminous bodies glimmered in my direction. These were human eyes, and in the next instant I saw that they belonged to a woman. She seemed to be sitting on the floor, leaning sideways against a smoke-blackened bamboo pillar, until I realized she was on a squatting-stool so low and small that it was completely hidden under her rear end. Her face was like a pig's; her eyes were the narrowest of slits, also like a pig's; her thick lips and eyelids were even more like a pig's; she appeared unthinking, her mind blank, again like a pig.

With great difficulty the woman moved the lower half of her body but remained sitting. Then I heard an age-worn, thin, but dignified voice coming from the bed at one side of the room.

"Who is it? What does he want?"

The bed, which was very low, was woven of mountain palm stems. On it lay a man carelessly enfolded in a filthy quilt. The sallow light that emanated from the two holes in his face signaled no greater interest in my unsolicited visit than had his questions. I recognized that look only too well, the kind of look that gathers every single thing that you value and includes it in its derision.

I had a terrible feeling about all of this. Naturally I no longer had any doubt as to the identity of the man on the bed—it was Uncle A-Huang. And yet I looked him over as though I had chanced upon something incomprehensible. His posture and his tone had utterly confounded me. Perhaps trying to straighten out my own thoughts, I explained to him in a businesslike manner my particulars and the reason for my visit.

Uncle A-Huang listened coldly. I could not tell if my explanation had produced any reaction or not. He went on lying there for a while before listlessly raising himself up to a sitting position. As he did so, he grabbed a tobacco pipe, no longer than a chopstick, from beside his pillow.

With infuriatingly slow gestures he filled the pipe with tobacco from his tin. Then, with head slightly bowed and eyes staring vacantly at the floor, he smoked several pipefuls without making any sound other than the suck-suck-sucking of the pipe itself. That sound gave me such a strange feeling. In a world that was about to sink and perish forever, that sound, together with the flaring and fading glow in the pipe bowl, seemed to be the only sign of life!

A-Huang had grown extremely bloated, the skin stretched weakly over his body. Who on earth could believe that that skin had once been as taut as sheet iron? Under his eyes were great purple bags, as if two lumps of meat had been stuck there. Decadence and indolence had eaten deep into his flesh, like maggots.

For the first time I realized the futility of language. It would be useless to try to express an idea to a person who no longer hoped for anything at all from this world. This visit had turned out to be an impossible obligation.

"Uncle A-Huang," I said, already lacking all conviction, "my kitchen still isn't finished, you know!"

Only after a long, long time did A-Huang look up.

"I know," he said languidly.

Still leaning against the bamboo pillar, the woman's eyes were closed; now it was her mouth that was agape. She looked so very comfortable. Lying in the shadow of the wall, the black dog timidly raised its head to look up at me. Behind the woman the wok, burner, bowls, chopsticks, and other utensils lay in disorder where they had been tossed—desolate, cold, and still. Waft after waft of sour air brought the smells of mold and putrefaction to my nose, so that I almost suspected I was standing beside a midden.

I turned toward the door. The terraced fields lay before me like a simple diagram. And now the fields reminded me again of the Uncle A-Huang of my childhood, the young embodiment of "strength" who always got the chicken head. But the present A-Huang immediately negated the possibility of an equation between the two. Perhaps you could say it turned out to be an insoluble problem.

I glanced at him again. He still held the same pose, gripping his pipe with his head slightly bowed. But now I noticed a large, dark mole in the middle of his right eyebrow. The two or three hairs growing from the mole were very long and stretched down over his eye. Unbelievably, these hairs were trembling.

"Is it you that farms those fields, Uncle A-Huang?" I asked.

He shook his head.

"Farm? What for?"

He got angry. He whacked his pipe bowl on the edge of the bed with a great bang.

"Haven't I done enough? The more we work the poorer we get! I ain't as big a fool as all that!"

He paused, then added: "Back in the day, everybody knew I was the one who ate the chicken head! But all that's just useless! I won't be no fool no more."

As he spoke, his eyes lingered dazedly on the field ridges.

I stood by the bed for a while longer, but there seemed nothing more to say, so I said goodbye and went out. Only as I was going out through the door did I hear him add the words for which I had waited so long: "I'll be there tomorrow!"

Outside, brother and sister each led a dung beetle along the ground in a race. Thrusting through cloud after cloud of blowflies, I didn't stop until I reached the fields. I thought to myself that I might never have another opportunity to come here, nor did I have any intention of coming to this place a second time. Uncle A-Huang's words, saturated as they were with frighteningly twisted sentiments, stuck uncomfortably in my mind, like a mass of indigestible food lying in my stomach. Everything about the place terrified me: the gloom, mess, and moldiness; the sour smell and putrefaction; the dung beetles; and the piles of shit everywhere. If a person lives for a long time among things that are regarded as unhealthy, might it not produce an abnormal psychology, just as bacteria can cause abnormalities in a person's cell tissue? Was A-Huang not a perfect example?

Generally, no matter where we go in life, what we see and hear and read all combines to make us believe in the essential connectedness of hard work and riches on the one hand, and of indolence and poverty on the other. Linked to that is the contrast between the idleness and comfort of the rich and the hard work and harsh lives of the poor. This is how things must be, for everything to be right and proper and for people's lives to be worth living.

But A-Huang, not only by the unequivocal curse he had uttered but even more so by his way of living—no! by his very life itself—had stood up courageously to deny this universal truth.

If it is just as A-Huang said—"the more we work the poorer we get"—then what is to become of our world?

I couldn't help remembering the intense hatred carved into Uncle A-Huang's bloated, ugly face!

I only hope that the curse he uttered was a prejudice, a vicious prejudice resulting from his abnormal psychology.... Let us all hope so!

Written in autumn 1950, and revised in 1952 and 1958. First published, posthumously, in *Complete Works* I (1976).

Translator's note: As with the other selections in the present volume, this translation of "My 'Out-Law' and the Hill Songs" is primarily based on the version of the story printed in *New Complete Works* (1:157-172), which in turn is based on the later of the two extant manuscripts. However, in this translation I have included all the hill songs that appear in the earlier manuscript, on which the *Complete Works* II version was based (3:69-82). The second manuscript cut the total number of lines of hill song from twenty to nine. The reinclusion here of the original songs in toto—while otherwise following the revisions to the first manuscript—gives the reader of this volume a fuller showcase for folk song, which plays an important part in Zhong Lihe's oeuvre.

10. My "Out-Law" and the Hill Songs
親家與山歌

The whole morning I sat alone on the veranda, gazing ahead into the distance and listening to the hill songs from across the river. Down on the plain the people, the fields and villages, mist and haze, bamboos and trees, and hills and rivers presented themselves in their ancient, amiable guise; at this distance, the landscape seemed unchanged. In the past I myself had sung its hill songs, shared its heartbeat, and felt its feelings. But now I knew how impossible it would be to try to rediscover the emotions of yesteryear among these people and things. Everything had changed so much; it was all a long way from what I had known so intimately.

Overhead, from deep within the blanket of gray, misty clouds, the sun set the land alight with its pitiless fire. The roasted crops were shriveled and haggard. The soil looked like new-fired lime: gray, desiccated, thirsty, crumbly. One gust of wind and the earth flew up; the acrid smell of the scorched soil irritated the lungs, making it difficult to breathe. Ahead of me, at the foot of the low hills, the village stretched itself out lazily, apparently lifeless. Its betel-nut trees and the fortress formed by its encirclement of bamboo were more gray than green, terribly pale and wan. They swayed feebly, as if they no longer possessed the strength or the will to carry on.

And yet, behind this scene, human life was seething, churning, swarming, and buzzing like the beehive my son poked with a stick. The clouds, steaming hot and shining with dazzling white light, draped over the land like ash covering an iron in the forge. Underneath, the people were frantically writhing around—on edge, restless.

Kicking at the sun-bleached soil in their fields, these good and honest folk mournfully knitted their brows. Often they complained to me that their beans weren't podding, the sweet potatoes were no bigger than hen's eggs, and the sesame stood gaping in the field, waiting for rain to drink. It was not the first time their fields had teetered on the brink of reversion to wilderness. In fearful tones, each tiller cursed the cruelty of Heaven; in more strident tones he cursed the hard times, or the human race, or his sallow-faced, slatternly wife and her brood of insatiable little monkeys.

"Ai! Ai!" one farmer neighbor had sighed as he spoke to me. "A bad year—even Heaven's gone all contrary."

I remembered his eyes, darting fearfully in all directions as he spoke; in them one could plainly see the uneasiness of a soul stripped of all confidence.

Somehow I felt the people had changed beyond all comprehension; they hadn't been at all like this in the past.

And so, gazing into the distance, I felt depressed.

—Perhaps he's right!—Afterward I had attempted to construct an explanation, to seek some sort of logical thread: perhaps there's nothing else they can do!

In the past, their lives were their own; they embraced this existence and devoted themselves to it, as naturally as a bird sleeping in its own nest. Everything appeared harmonious and smooth. But now it was different. Above all, they no longer understood their lives. Like a vicious, treacherous hooligan, Life had far eluded their grasp and was swaggering alone across the expanses of this world, wherever it liked. The people had lost all sense of connection with it. Life was changing from minute to minute, changing most strangely, weaving absurd stories otherwise seen only in a magic lantern show. But the stories somehow always turned out to be closely related to their lives.

—Perhaps he's right! For thousands of years the land had provided their every need; it matched their portion of toil, blood, and sweat with the corresponding rewards, and never disappointed them. But if this land were suddenly to stop giving ... then what?

Now, they were betrayed by everything around them!

—Perhaps he's right!

But then, what was it all about?—Naturally I began to think of the things I'd seen and heard in the last few days: A-Tian's troubles, Uncle

Dechang's sadness, Bingwen's deception, my mother-in-law's grumbling, the arsonists' folly, my brother's curses, A-Huang's decline....[1]

Perhaps it was all a mistake, an utterly random mistake. When the time came, everything would be put aright again and life would reassume its splendor, harmony, and reason—just as when we wake from a nightmare: opening our eyes, we see that the world is still as beautiful as ever!

Let us hope it is so!

Another hill song reached my ears—

> Once for the lad that's in my heart, up I get and go;
> Long the road, high the hill, deep the river flow;
> Up here on the mountain, the birds sing all around;
> But in the forest deep and dim, oh where's my laddie-oh!

The singing was sinuous, mellow, and delightful; the lingering melody was achingly sad, but the song retained the simplicity and unaffectedness of the pastoral. This was an extremely moving example of a hill song. In the past, whenever I heard a good hill song the most wonderful feelings would arise in me. Now I listened in silence, allowing myself to melt into those feelings once again.

"Listen, someone's singing!" My wife, who was tidying up a neglected plot beside the house, looked up with a smile. Pingmei had never been much of a singer herself but had always loved to listen. "I haven't heard a good hill song for years. How lovely!"

I looked east, where the teak trees grew lush and green on the steep hillside. I saw human figures dressed in blue flitting in and out of sight among the trees. Female figures. Blue headscarves were tied

---

1. The names are all of characters from the first three parts of *Homeland*. The collective time span of these four linked stories is nebulous, but clearly extends over more than just a "few days." The action began, at the start of part I ("Zugteuzong'), "one day in April 1946," but in this story Yuxiang tells A-He he has four children, two of whom must have been born no earlier than 1946, given that Yuxiang could not likely have been repatriated much before the end of 1945.

round their bamboo hats, the corners trailing behind and flapping in the breeze like tails.

That's where the hill songs were coming from.

> Twice for the lad of my heart I go, down to the land god's shrine,
> Kneeling here, O! Uncle Earth, pray hear this plea of mine:
> Truly if you have the power, take these words to my lad,
> And do be sure and tell to him, I miss him all the time!

The notes of the song quivered in the atmosphere, dissipating in every direction. Off in another direction, the crisp pure sound of tree felling seemed to chime in with its rhythm: ding, ding, ding, ding ...

It was very strange: the calm, warmth, and longing in the tone of the hill song, and the vacillation, unease, and coldness of its real-life surroundings were so out of balance. Through the profound emotions of romantic love the song expressed an insistent love for life. You could imagine those young, tender lives being nurtured and maturing in the bright sun. Amid all the change and upheaval, perhaps this was the only unchanging thing I could find. Back then the girls worked just like this, and sang; the hill was the same, the tails, the blue headscarves. And from then till now the same stories of youth continued to be sung and celebrated over and over again.

That's right! When the time came, the decrepit, the ugly, and the sick would fall, so that the young, the strong, the healthy, and the well-formed could grow: like saplings under a rotten, fallen tree, they would supplant what had gone before.

These thoughts heartened me somewhat.

My sister-in-law came in. Taking off her bamboo hat and rearranging her messed-up hair with her fingers, she cheerfully reported: "Your 'out-law' will be here in a minute!"

"My out-law? Oh, you mean Yuxiang? Where is he?"

I quickly realized who she meant.

"Just over there; he's with his son—they're doing a job moving timber."

"What? Has he got a son big enough to help him to move timber?"

"It's not his own son!"

So my sister-in-law told me my "out-law"'s ordinary and yet extraordinary story.

—Tu Yuxiang was one of the ablest workers on my father's farm, and a good friend of mine, just a couple of years older than me. For two or three years he and I worked together almost every day: planting coffee and bamboo, harvesting silk-cotton, breaking new ground. He was a superb singer; perhaps his teeth were too big for him to be an attractive man, but he had a fine, deep, and mellow voice; he knew how to modulate his singing to make the phrases just perfect. Moreover, he had somehow learned many strange and wonderful songs that nobody else knew. All the workers loved to hear him sing, especially the girls.

He'd throw his arms around a silk-cotton tree and climb up, spry as a monkey, to the very top, stand and survey the surrounding hills beneath him, and then crane his neck to sing out loud and clear, yet tenderly.

> An orange falls into the wellspring,
> Half is floating, half is sinking,
> If you sink, then sink right down,
> Don't float up to pluck my heart-strings.

His singing would resound among the clustered peaks and valleys. He struck a handsome, stirring pose, and there was something mysterious about it, suggesting the image of a mountain sprite.

Such were the circumstances in which one day he and I, out of the harmless banter of innocent youth, began to address one another as "in-laws," even though not only was neither of us father to a child old enough to marry, but we were both still unmarried ourselves. Hearing us address one another so intimately, one of the older women teased us:

"Unmarried in-laws? More like out-laws, I'd say!"

A few years after I went to the Mainland, Yuxiang had an affair with a widow who already had a child. Then he was conscripted into the Japanese army as a porter and sent to Southeast Asia. Two years later, when he was demobilized and repatriated, the widow came to see him. In her arms was a child that had just passed its first birthday.

"Your child!" she said simply. While Yuxiang was in the army she had been cast out of her late husband's house and forced to go out to work to support herself and the two children.

Looking at the woman and her two children, Yuxiang had been stumped for quite a while. But just as rice that's already been boiled can't be put back in the jar, he had to accept the fait accompli, and so he left home and went away with the woman and her children to make a new life together.

"It wasn't such a bad thing," said my sister-in-law in conclusion. "He got himself a well-grown son into the bargain, a handy help in all kinds of work, heavy or light. Father and son, they drive their cart, moving whatever people need moved; they've got work every day of the year, they're never idle—they work even harder than the ox itself!"

No sooner had my sister-in-law finished speaking and left than my "out-law" and his "into the bargain" son arrived. The boy was about fourteen; his face was anemic, but his dark shining eyes suggested a keen intelligence. He was leading the two water buffalo. Yuxiang and he looked more like brothers than father and son.

"Drive them over there, into the orchard . . ." My "out-law" pointed as he instructed his son. "—Just watch them while they graze."

I left the veranda and went to meet him. "Brother Yuxiang!"

"Brother A-He!" he replied, then turned to Pingmei in the kitchen doorway, and, after a slight hesitation, called to her: "Sister-in-law!"

His tone sounded unnatural. In the old days he had always called her "Sister Pingmei."

"I thought you were supposed to be in-laws!" She reminded us with a laugh. Back then, the three of us had all worked together.

Yuxiang scratched the back of his head, a bashful smile spreading from the corners of his mouth.

"Moving timber, eh?" I said.

"That's right. For the brick kilns . . ."

We sat down on the veranda. Pingmei busied herself getting tea.

"You've hardly changed at all," said Yuxiang, accepting a cup of tea from Pingmei. "Except Sister-in-law's a bit thinner!"

"Not thinner, just older!" she corrected him.

"But you've had a dozen or more years of eating since we last met!"

We looked at one another with knowing smiles.

Yuxiang was no longer the youth of a dozen years ago, still wet behind the ears and not knowing the meaning of the word "worry," but a strapping man, thoroughly mature in both mind and body. Long years of life's tribulations seemed only to have tempered the vitality that lay beneath his dark-brown skin, and made it firmer and more resilient. Perhaps this was the kind of man who could weather any storm, withstand any frost, rain, or snow.

Through the window on my right I could see his son in the orchard and the two oxen moving in and out of sight among the trees. The boy was sitting in the shade with his back to us, invisible from the shoulders down.

Turning my gaze away from the orchard, I asked, "How many kids?"

"Four! The oldest helps me out a bit, but the others are either too sickly or too small to be much use."

As he spoke Yuxiang was looking at our eldest son, nestling at Pingmei's knees.

"So this is your . . . ?"

"Our first-born!" said Pingmei, caressing Tie'er's head. "He's five."

"How time flies. It's only been a dozen or so years, and here we all are with whole broods of children!"

As he spoke Yuxiang took matches from his pocket, together with a "Bowelove" Bowel Salts tin. He opened the tin, which contained tobacco and a sheaf of snow-white cigarette papers. Taking a paper, he pinched up some tobacco and spread it evenly, then began rolling with skilled, experienced fingers. Once it was rolled tight, he brought the cigarette up to his mouth and gave it a lick, and there was his hand-rolled smoke at the ready.

I thought this was great fun; people never used to roll their own.

"You probably both remember Rongmei . . ."

He inspected his cigarette with some satisfaction, stuck it between his lips and lit a match.

" . . . You might say Fate has been pretty kind to her; she has five kids now. A few days ago I bumped into her on the road and she had one on her back, one by the hand, and what looked like another in her belly. Her hair was like a bird's nest and she looked ugly and old. You'll both remember how fastidious she used to be about her appearance. There was that time I accidentally got some mud on her headscarf . . .

she was angry with me the whole day, her face almost purple with rage. Unbelievable!"

He spoke pensively. His Japanese was much more fluent than before, to judge from what he mixed in with our native Hakka. Apparently his two years of military service had allowed him to reach a level of Japanese hardly imaginable for someone who hadn't got any further than primary school.

"What about the other girls?" Pingmei piped up. "Lanying got married before we left; and what about . . . ?"

"How could any of them be any different? In a nutshell: they got married, had children, and one by one fell on hard times, as simple as that. But the amazing thing is how fertile they all are, each of them has a great litter of kids, and because they have so many, they all end up looking like fat sows straight from the sty. But if you go back a decade or more, all of them were good-looking, neatly turned out lassies. It sure beats me!"

"Is Lianmei married too?" persisted Pingmei. "She had an older sister whose husband wasn't poor, right enough, but he turned out to have a violent temper and would give her terrible beatings twice a week or more. One time he busted her forehead open and she ran straight home to her family the same night and didn't go back for ages. That was the sister who tried to make a match for Lianmei. She said to her, 'Haven't you taken enough beatings yourself? Do you need me to make up the numbers?' She was determined not to get married; she often said that when a woman married, if she didn't get beaten up she'd be reduced to poverty; if she wasn't reduced to poverty she'd get beaten up—either way it was a sorry state to be in."

As Pingmei spoke she bowed her head and stared at the floor, sunk in her memories.

"I'd like to see them," she said after a while, looking up. "Could I?"

"That's difficult! Apart from you, it's not easy to see any of the girls from our old crew!"

So saying, Yuxiang nipped out the ember of his cigarette with his fingers, and then flung the butt forcefully to the ground.

"And then there's Xiudi: after her husband died she started living with a man . . . "

"Oh!" Pingmei sighed. "And now?"

"What do you think? She was disowned by her family..."

At this point Yuxiang suddenly pricked up his ears and said enigmatically, "Listen, a hill song!"

> Thrice for the lad of my heart I go, down to the river strand,
> The water, it runs winding there, twisting through the land,

We all listened intently, exchanging smiles...

> My laddie's heart is fickle-oh, switching like the stream,
> I cannot stop it trickling-oh, like water through my hand.

"That's really good hill-singing!" Yuxiang was well satisfied. "A beautiful voice!"

"They still can't get away from the 'laddies' and 'lassies,' can they?" I said, then smiled and added: "Do you still sing? You used to sing really a lot, and really well!"

"Me? Oh, I'm no use anymore! The mood doesn't take me, and my voice just isn't what it was. When I was young I didn't know a damn thing, but I was really happy when I sang; once you know a thing or two, it's not so easy to sing. Only the youngsters—especially the girls—and the hill songs never change; the singing goes on forever, no matter how good life is, or how hard!"

He set about rolling a second cigarette and lit it. White smoke climbed out from his mouth, curled into his nostrils, up the bridge of his nose, and over his forehead. It rose up very slowly, like a little caterpillar. He watched it dissipate in the air as he switched to a cooler tone of voice: "And times really are hard, you know. All the folk just shake their heads; it's the same wherever you go. I just can't figure it out."

Yuxiang's gaze was fixed on the farmland down on the flat, as if that's where the hard times lay for anyone to see. The sunlight glared and shimmered there, where a gray human figure could be seen on one of the ridges between the fields. The figure looked small, insignificant, antlike.

"The sun has just burned everybody crazy," Yuxiang went on. "But it's so strange; it's as if people are fated from birth to suffer like this, and it's the same all over. Once, when my unit was scattered by an

American attack in the Philippines, everyone was fleeing for his life, and four or five of us found ourselves in the middle of a mountainous jungle. We climbed mountain after mountain for a full day and night without a bite to eat. Then we came to a valley, where we found a house. We were overjoyed and walked toward it, only to find not even the shadow of a ghost—the local people were so scared of the Japs. We searched the whole house but could find nothing better to eat than sweet potatoes; and there was not so much as a single pig or chicken. Think about it—this was a farmer's home!

"One of my friends shook his head and said: 'It beats me why the Japanese want to fight a war like this!'

"'Why?' I asked him.

"'It's just the same here . . . poor!' he said.

"He sure wasn't wrong: the people there were really poor. It just didn't make any sense."

"I'd better be going." Yuxiang flung down his cigarette end and stretched lazily.

"I sure am bushed! I haven't had a day off in over a month. A-Hui! Where are the oxen? Let's go!" He yelled in the direction of the orchard.

Then he picked up where he had left off speaking: "In the past our bellies were full, so we sang hill songs of lads and lasses and never bothered about where our next meal was coming from. But now, we've all become parents of children, haven't we?"

The boy drove the oxen out from the orchard. Yuxiang got up and said warmly, "I'll drop by again another day. I often pass this way!"

Outside he stopped again and turned back to us.

"Listen," he smiled. "She's singing again; she's good, really good! See you again!"

> Fourth for the laddie of my heart, high in the hills I go,
> Where the crooked path as long's the brook, meanders to and fro,
> Whoever I meet along the way, I ask as I go by,
> Which of these hills must I climb for the laddie I love so?

Part 4
Meinong Lyrics

Written in 1957. First published, posthumously, in *Complete Works* I (1976).

11. My Study
我的書齋

Most people would agree that just as a general has his headquarters, an engineer his design room, and a carpenter his workshop, so should a man of letters have his study. The interior arrangement and décor will be adjusted to the man's individuality, taste, and aesthetic feeling. Everything will be harmoniously disposed to perfection, so that whether he is working, resting, or just sitting deep in thought, he will always feel free, at ease, and serene. A scholar without a study is like a lady without her boudoir—even in everyday situations he will constantly feel awkward, and the tranquility he seeks will elude him.

My present residence was originally a banana-curing shed. It is not small in area, but apart from two spaces in the middle that could just about qualify as rooms the rest is just a single encircling veranda under the eaves. Even our kitchen had to be built by enclosing a section of the veranda, so there was no question of a separate study for me. As for building an extension, decades of adverse circumstances had already forced my extended family to economize in many ways, so where would I have been able to find the resources?

What's worse, it pains me to admit that I didn't even have a desk. The only tables we had were a small coffee table and a solitary dining table—the latter having been a loyal servant to four generations of my family. There were two holes in the surface, each almost big enough for a bowl to fall through, and two of the legs were so rotten that sticks had had to be strapped to them. This table was where I did my writing when we first moved here. Among all its various inconveniences I need only mention the way it swayed and shook like a rickety cradle. It was quite heartbreaking. I had to take care at all times, or the slightest wrong move, such as putting down my pen a little too forcefully, would cause the table to pitch and creak in a most alarming fashion.

Sometimes this would cause my inspiration to take flight altogether. Nothing could be more dreadful.

I once made a vow that I simply must get a little money to buy a new table. "Heaven fails not the adamant heart": eventually my prayers were answered, and at last I could write without constant fear of lurches and wobbles. But it was not a new dining table that I got, but a study of my own!

My study! Oh, nothing could beat it! I believe no one ever had a better, more agreeable study than mine.

But please don't imagine that I had struck gold and become a great tycoon with the means to build a fine, stylish study. No! I was still just as infuriatingly poor as ever. But finally I did have my own study. This study was not built, nor could it be made with money: I had discovered it.

My study was the earth and the sky that we inhabit!

My house has a big, wide concrete front yard originally designed for laying out bananas during the curing and drying process. Several years ago I had planted some Mexican papayas along the edge of the yard where the concrete dropped off to the soil. After two or three years the papayas were over ten feet tall and stretched out lush clusters of hand-shaped leaves. On sunny days a patch of cool shade appeared under each of the trees, and every year, in the six months from the autumn solstice to the spring solstice, the shade lay right across the yard.

One winter's day, when the long shadows of the papaya trees were falling across the yard, those cool, dark patches gave me an idea. I brought a rattan chair outside, plus a small round stool on which to place paper, ink, and so on. And so I began to write. My writing desk was a wooden board less than a foot long and about seven inches wide. I would support one end with my hand and rest the other end on the arm of the chair. Because the shade from the papayas was constantly shifting I had to keep moving to stay in shade. This would happen about once every half-hour.

I was enormously pleased with my discovery. It was just so beautiful. Doing my writing there, I could be both comfortable and content. That dingy house and its rotten, wobbly table couldn't begin to compare with this. Why, even the most exquisite architectural gem of a study was no whit better than this!

Perhaps you have a pristine, well-lit study, ornately furnished, maybe a bonsai plum tree on the desk and pictures and calligraphy by famous artists on the walls.... But compared with the grandeur of the landscape before my eyes—the profound blue of the broad sky and the great patchwork expanse of farmland—your study seems paltry and shabby, unspeakably vulgar....

Your study may be opulent, whereas mine is plain and rustic. But I don't love your opulence—I love my simple rusticity. Because my study is open to the sky it has abundant light; because it is on the hillside it has a commanding view of the hills, the streams, the fields, the villages, clouds and mists, bamboos and trees, and the people.... This whole vista lies before me, leading my eye to distant prospects.

Your study confines you within a limited space and cuts you off from the outside world; but since my study has neither roof nor walls and is situated amid the great vastness of sky and earth, it is free to breathe the spirits and humors of the universe and to be at one with Nature itself.

Sometimes when I grow tired from writing I put aside my pen and paper and look up. White clouds are slowly spreading and changing shape in the sky. They silently move en masse toward the northwest, their shadows racing and chasing each other across the hills and fields below, so that light and shade go dancing across the land. The weather brings infinite variety to my view.

The land is like a green ocean. If it happens to be a busy time on the farms it is dotted all over with busily wriggling figures. They are digging away at the land in search of human sustenance. It is a scene of tense activity, but a peaceful one; a scene of industry but also of joy.

And then, behind the gradually dispersing smoke rising from kitchen chimneys, the distant hills are as black as mascara.

Mother Nature has framed for me a grand, immense picture that could never find room on the wall of a manmade study. It is a poem of the universe!

From *lichun*[1] the shadows gradually retreat, and then after the spring solstice they shrink until they are too small to shade me. But

---

1. *Lichun*: the "Beginning of Spring," according to the Chinese solar calendar, falls on the third, fourth, or fifth of February each year. Below, *lidong* is the "Beginning of Winter," falling in the first week of November.

the idea I first got from the papaya shade now takes me to the shade of other trees. Luckily there is no shortage of shade trees in my surroundings: on the hillside, in the orchard, or halfway up the hill at the back of our house—they are everywhere.

Wherever there is a patch of shade, plus a rattan chair and a wooden board, there I'll have my study, where I can sit down and write with no need to fret about any dingy room or wobbly table.

During last year's typhoons all my papaya trees were either toppled or damaged. Not one was unscathed. However, I immediately replanted a few saplings. This time I planted them nearer to the edge of the yard, and now they are already over three feet tall. Perhaps soon after *lidong* they will be able to give me a few patches of deep, cool shade. Then I will once again be in possession of my incomparable study!

First version completed on March 12, 1950, under the title "Caopo bian" 草坡邊 (By the grassy bank). First published on May 1, 1959, in *Lianhe Bao Fukan* 聯合報副刊 (United Daily News: Supplement) under the present title, literally "On the Grassy Bank."

12. The Grassy Bank
草坡上

Finally the gray-brown hen can't walk anymore!

It is early dawn, and the other chickens have left the henhouse and walked onto the grassy bank or into the wood, but that hen's chicks are circling round and round her, cheep-cheep-cheeping.

Apparently the rheumatism that began to affect her leg a few days ago has developed to the extent that her knee can't work properly at all. She crouches on the ground, using her wings to prop herself up on either side. Now and then she groans in pain.

"Pa! Our hen can't walk anymore!" My elder son strides up and helps her to stand. But as soon as he lets go she is paralyzed again, flopping back down like a ball of cotton wool.

"Aiya, she can't even stand anymore!" Tie'er is filled with pity.

The chicks are in the middle of molting: their soft, yellow down is gradually dropping off and being replaced by untidy patches of gray, black, brown, or other colors—as dirty and ragged as housewives' cleaning rags. One of them is completely bald, bright red all over like an octopus; others have grown new feathers only on a little patch around their rumps, as though they have decided to start from that point in putting on their new finery. They seem to have a new swagger in their walk, which makes them look really funny.

The chicks stare wide-eyed, looking all around in panic and milling around the hen. Six little beaks cry out as one, as if to ask why Mother isn't taking them out to play as usual. From time to time she makes an effort to flap her wings and lurch forward, but she can only move a very little before falling heavily back down again. You can see the pain in her eyes as she shakes her head in despair.

The hen's attempts to move seem to throw the chicks into an even greater panic. They cry shrilly and keep cocking their heads to peer into her eyes, as if hoping to discover there what on earth is going on. Once more the hen struggles to get to her feet, and again she moves forward just a little before falling down as before. She and the chicks keep nuzzling one another, looking into each other's eyes, helplessly sticking together. The hen's throat trembles and she makes a gloomy sound, as if weeping.

This is the doorway of our house, a disused banana-curing shed; on one side there is a short slope where some little shrubs and plenty of lush, green grass grow. Wildflowers of red, yellow, white, and purple grow among the grass, all the way up to the door of the shed. The grass and flowers are dainty and lovable as a child's eyes. The early morning sun sprinkles a soft yellow radiance that makes the grass, shrubs, and flowers appear fresh and lovely. Dewdrops sparkle on the blades of grass, whose clear fragrance floats in the air. Butterflies and white moths chase and play among the thickets; their tiny wings shimmer where the sunlight touches them, like tiny stars in an autumn sky.

The insects trace amazing circles and curves in the air, now rising, now dipping, as they dance from flower to flower. Suddenly a pair of little wings darts right at the eyeballs of one of the chicks. The chick gives a start and hops back a few steps. It glares, then launches itself at the insect! The moth dodges, and flies leisurely off. The chick boldly pounces again, but not only does it not catch the moth, it finds itself turning head over heels instead. Feeling sorry for itself, it clambers to its feet again and flaps its little wings. It watches the moth fly far away, and then turns and runs back to its mother's side.

The white moth makes a loop and flies back again. This time the chick doesn't hesitate. It pounces! The moth slips away under the chick's neck. Another chick who has been watching intently pounces from another direction. The insect shimmies to one side and escapes with great poise. Caught off balance, the chick staggers into a thicket of grass and tumbles over and over like a ball.

The white moth flutters here and there among the chicks, enjoying itself enormously, as though this were the most wonderful game. The two chicks stick close to one another as they blunder among the shrubs and grasses in hot pursuit. Little by little they get further and further away from Mother.

Another insect comes flying up; two more chicks vie with one another to chase it, and so they too leave their mother's side. Another insect comes flying up . . .

Gradually, all six chicks are lured onto the grassy bank.

The hen still crouches where she was, all alone.

Gradually it has grown quieter by the banana shed door. . . .

"Pa! Our chicks have all run off onto the grassy bank!" cries Tie'er in high delight.

Toward noon, my wife says she's afraid the hen will be scrawny from hunger in another couple of days and we'd better kill her while there's still some meat on her.

I don't know whether it would be better to kill her or not to kill her, so I just say "Ah" by way of response.

Late in the afternoon when my wife is feeding the chickens, I notice that the gray-brown hen isn't there anymore and I remember what she said.

"Did you kill the hen?" I ask her.

"Choo—choo-choo—choo." She is calling to the chickens on the grassy bank.

"Yes!" she says, as she goes on calling. "I told you: it would be a waste to let her starve and get skinny. Choo-choo . . . "

Hearing her calls, the chickens gather together from various directions. All different sizes, all different mottled colors, they jostle and peck each other in great confusion. The old hen's six chicks also return from the grassy bank. Ever so timidly, they go to and fro on the edge of the flock, now and then pecking up a few grains that have fallen a long way from the center. Quite unexpectedly, one of the hens makes a lunge at a chick, lifts it up high in her beak, and dashes it down. The chick comes to earth at quite some distance, its feathers scattering.

Cheep cheep cheep . . .

The six chicks cry out in sharp distress. Now they are more timid than ever.

My wife gets a chicken cage out of the shed so the six chicks can eat alone. The mesh of the cage is just wide enough for them to get in and out.

"Poor little things . . . " My wife stays by the cage and mournfully watches the chicks peck at the grain.

The sun finally gathers up the last veil of radiance from the hilltops and takes it away west over the mountains. Dark clouds spread across the sky in all directions, swallowing up one rosy cloud after another like fierce animals. The curtain of the night now covers the earth; all the chickens have returned to the henhouse.

After a whole day out and about, the six chicks return to the shed doorway but can't find their mother. Where is Mother Hen? They wander back and forth at the place where the hen was squatting when they left this morning. They stretch out their necks and cheep shrilly and mournfully. And so, amid this sorrow and lamentation, deprived of the rock on which they depended, they begin their lives as orphans.

My wife is anxiously fidgeting, going in and out of the house, not knowing what to do. Finally she goes over to the chicks, intending to catch them and put them in the chicken cage, but they all dart off into the grass thickets. Tie'er and I come down from the steps to help catch them, but we only make things worse: the poor little things just get further and further away. In silence we stand by the door of the shed rubbing our hands together, helplessly watching the swaying shadows of grasses and shrubs. We hold our breaths and listen carefully for the cheeping of the chicks. Invisible in the darkness, their little cries sound quite desolate.

By now I am feeling a keen sense of loss for the mother hen, but I force myself to say something comforting: "The chicks will get used to it."

My wife keeps silent, turns, walks up the steps, and sits down, silently nursing our one-year-old, Li'er.

On the dinner table, the head of the sacrificial hen floats on the surface of the soup in a large bowl. Her eyes are half-closed, as if she is listening to know if her children are all right: are they sleeping soundly?

My wife breaks the silence. "I shouldn't have killed the hen. If we'd kept her, even if she couldn't look after her chicks, she still could've cuddled them at night."

Behind her words lies a deep sense of regret, and as she speaks she draws Tie'er to her bosom, even as she holds Li'er more tightly than ever. The boys meekly snuggle into their mother's embrace. They don't move a muscle, as if their little souls fear that something may separate them.

Seeing the tears trickling down her cheeks, I also feel sad.

That evening we all eat exceptionally quietly, and exceptionally little, especially my wife. No one so much as touches the bowl with the chicken in it, not even six-year-old Tie'er. Clearly this child shares his parents' feelings.

The six chicks spend that night in the former banana-curing stove.

Those unfortunate chicks become the center of our lives from then on. Each of us seems to carry a certain responsibility for them. When feeding the chickens my wife singles them out for special treatment. She cleans out the stove and spreads sacking in it, so that they won't feel the damp. As for Tie'er, almost every day he goes into the fields and brings back lots and lots of baby frogs, worms, tadpoles, and so on to feed to them.

Seeming to realize their situation, the chicks themselves, brothers and sisters, stick lovingly together, going everywhere as a group, never leaving anyone behind. As soon as day breaks they call to one another, and then go together onto the grassy bank to look for seeds, insects, and grasshoppers. When their bellies are full they flop down together in a heap somewhere in the shade, kicking their little legs in happiness.

I don't know how many days pass like this, until one day my wife and I are putting up a wattle fence at the edge of our yard above the grassy bank while Tie'er and Li'er play nearby. The autumn sun is already sinking, and the grasses and trees are bathing in the soft sunlight; all is warm and tranquil. A few white clouds hang in the blue sky, moving slowly and quietly and changing shape. Beautiful and varied, they seem like living animals, like our chickens.

On the grassy bank the six chicks are lying resting in the sun, stretching their legs, and preening their feathers. These are the habitual actions of adult chickens. Their plumage is already full and well rounded. And under that sleek, beautiful plumage, mature life forces are throbbing, possessed of the strength and will to break through however many obstacles may stand in their way.

It is a beautiful thing, a solemn sight.

"Look, how beautiful they are!" says my wife with a smile. "They've got all their feathers now!"

She smiles an exquisite smile, the goodness and purity in her eyes revealing the sacred beauty of the human soul.

I smile happily too.

Turning, I suddenly realize that our children have also grown without our having noticed.

My wife and I look at one another and smile, feeling relief and happiness, as if a great load has been lifted from our shoulders....

First version completed on July 8, 1954. First published on April 18, 1959, in *Lianhe Bao Fukan* 聯合報副刊 (United Daily News: Supplement).

13. The Plow and the Sky
做田

Like a hidden paradise on earth, the plain at Jianshan has hills on all four sides. On one side is the Taiwan Central Range; the other three sides are mere hillocks. Mostly they are covered in rocky soil on which nothing but wild grasses grows.

The Central Range extends in many peaks and ridges, the nearest of which are covered all over with teak forest, the pride of the Forestry Bureau. The teak forest is a tender, translucent green, reminiscent of a fresh watercolor. Further into the mountains the forest is painted a dark, even green. In the deepest parts of the range the high peaks are swathed in a mauve haze, like immortals wearing Taoists' robes. The highest summits are wrapped in layer upon layer of mist and clouds, giving an appearance of solemnity, delicacy, and grace.

The sky is a pure wash of blue, like a bolt of indanthrene cotton before its first wash. The sun has risen to the mere height of a bamboo pole, with a white cloud flitting to and fro before it. In the far southeast another column of gray cloud is gathering.

Sky, clouds, and hills lie quietly upside down in the brimming paddyfields. The plowman plows them up along with the clods and water. Together with rampant tendrils of sesban weed, they become entangled on the plowshare, like a scarf. Every two or three paces a great bundle of weeds, sky, clouds, and hills twines itself round the plow. It's as if the whole field is draping itself over the plow: the ox stumbles, staggers, and comes to a halt.

The plow has run aground!

"Yah!" The plowman scolds, lifting his whip and flourishing it. "Yah! Dammit, I'll beat you to death!"

Startled, the ox lunges forward with all its might, stretching the hitch-ropes as tight as steel cables, but it can't budge an inch, as if it has taken root. Well, no wonder: those are the sky and the hills caught on the plow; how could the ox ever lift them?

Looking very hard done-to the plowman bends to clear the tangled mess that clogs the plow. And so the plow moves freely again, the ox pulls with renewed vigor, and the plowman's in the mood for whistling once more.

When the plowing is done it's the turn of the thirteen-toothed harrow to break the clods. Then they harness the "ironing plank" to "iron" the field flat. By this point the field looks like a gray woolen blanket spread out on the ground, smooth and even.

Now the rice seedlings can be planted out.

The planters bend their waists, backs to the clear blue sky, like so many insects. But these insects do not crawl forward; instead they inch backward.[1] The men's dark-red backs are bare, giving off a dull, dark, steely sheen in the sunlight, like the carapaces of beetles. Luckily, the morning breeze comes blowing—sweeping away at the steadily growing summer heat.

The young women are repairing the banks and paths, or else cutting the weeds growing there and on the banks of the ditches. They wear colorfully patterned cotton smocks tied at the waist with multicolored cords. The tails of the blue squares of cloth folded and tied round their bamboo hats flutter in the breeze like sails. As they work, their hill songs and laughter adorn their youthful vivacity. Each of them is a fresh bloom, and these flowers are blossoming all over Jianshan's little patch of pastoral heaven, embellishing it with fresh and lovely life.

High above the people's heads, a crested serpent eagle spreads its mighty wings and traces circles as big as cartwheels, uttering short, high calls as it seeks what the land tries to conceal: perhaps a snake or a dead field mouse. At such a time there is no shortage: the raptor need only look on the banks, in the grass thickets, or on the little slopes. High in the sky it soars, searching, its small head alert as it focuses on the ground, now to the left, now to the right. Then suddenly it gathers itself and plummets with all the force of a thunderbolt. When it flies

---

[1]. It is a well-known curiosity in Taiwan that when planting out seedlings, Hakka farm workers move backward instead of forward.

up again its claws are grasping something long and thin. It's a snake, and the eagle flies off with it toward some cliff or forest corner.

From east to west, from south to north, the whole Jianshan plain is full of human shapes, bright laughter, hill songs, children's squeals, birdsong, and the wordless murmuring of water. The rank smell of the earth, the sweet fragrance of grass and seedlings, the stench of sweat and sesban and dead creatures rotting in the field: mingled together, these smells float on the air. The sun climbs ever higher.

Everything is concentrated in a joyful, harmonious rhythm, rolling on toward a solemn common goal.

A member of one of the planting gangs starts to sing a Hengchun song:

> Yearning; longing . . .

First version completed in November 1954. First published on October 3, 1959, in *Lianhe Bao Fukan* 聯合報副刊 (United Daily News: Supplement).

14. The Little Ridge
小冈

I picked a few rambling roses, a few stems of bachelor's buttons, and one of goldencup[1] to make a bouquet. These are all flowers that fade quickly, but they would just have to do: there was nothing better in the garden. I added a spray of pine. It seemed only yesterday that Li'er had helped me plant these flowers; I never thought that one day—today—I would be using them to garland his grave.

Li'er was our second son. Our eldest was weak and sickly from birth; Li'er was the strong and bright one, bursting with life and energy like a lion cub, always itching to bound out onto the savanna of life. My wife and I both placed our greatest hopes on him. His death brought home to us the cruelty of the universe and the hopelessness of life. Even now we had not yet recovered from the blow: the physical and mental wounds, the shock and enfeeblement. At the time my wife had fainted with grief and needed first aid treatment before she came round again.

Afterward we avoided mentioning Li'er and anything to do with him. We didn't touch any of the drawers that held things of his. We wanted the painful memories to go to sleep in the deepest parts of our consciousness, never to be woken. Sometimes in the middle of the night both of us would wake from dreams: my wife would stuff the quilt in her mouth and softly sob; on the other side of the bed, I too would be silently weeping. Each of us knew why the other was crying, but neither tried to comfort the other. I was afraid that any words of comfort might stir the name and the things that we both tabooed. That would only make the pain worse, and that was what we most feared.

---

1. Goldencup: *Jiandaohua* 剪刀花 (Scissor flower, also known as *Jinsimei* 金絲梅), *Hypericum patulum*, Goldencup St. Johns Wort.

Side by side, we wordlessly shed tears, and when we had cried enough, wordlessly we each sank back into deep sleep.

Today was the Hundredth Day since our son's death; since his burial we had not been back to the grave except on the Seventh Day. Now I wanted to go and take a look. I wanted to know if the grave was all right. The whole of spring had passed, so was the grave all covered in grasses? I didn't say anything to my wife, nor did I know if she realized what day it was. This morning all I told her was that I was going to take Ying'er to the village for a haircut.

Having cut the flowers, I tied them in a bunch, got Ying'er's clothes changed, picked up the spirit money and incense, locked up the house, and led Ying'er off in the direction of the village.

It was late spring, early summer; the wind was warm and the sun shone beautifully. Wildflowers were growing all along the path: yellow ones, white ones, red, purple . . . ; butterflies and bees were flying all around, while skylarks sang in the sky.

We walked at Ying'er's toddler's pace. She had been very happy to hear I was taking her to see her big brother, and that the flowers were for him. All along the way she pestered me with questions I had no way of answering, and kept asking to be allowed to hold the bouquet. Although she couldn't understand what I meant by "going to see Li'er" she cocked her head and looked up at me through her eyelashes as she pondered the words, seeking to establish a concrete image of where her brother might be found. She was really still too small to try to understand such mysterious matters, but that didn't stand in the way of her enthusiasm. She kept saying to herself, "I'm going to see Li'er, I'm going to see Li'er."

Ying'er was not yet three years old. Li'er had always been the one to play with her or to carry her places on his back. One might almost say it was Li'er who brought her up, because apart from breastfeeding, their mother hardly had to bother with her. When Li'er died it fell to me to take charge of Ying'er, but it was clear that I fell short of Li'er's standards of care: nowadays she seemed to spend most of the time crying. This was yet another thing that kept cropping up, suddenly reminding us of Li'er with a stab of pain to the heart.

The cemetery was about a hundred meters off the road to the village, on a little ridge coming down from the hills. Even more wildflowers were growing here, while the guavas had already formed fruits as big as fingertips and the wild strawberries were as big as thumbs and already ripe. Both kinds of fruit were growing everywhere amid the tombs that were dotted high and low all over the ridge. Along the path I picked lots of wild strawberries for Ying'er. She was so happy she kept waving her arms in the air.

Li'er's grave lay low on the ridge beside a thorny hedge. Behind the hedge was a garden; the path led along the edge of the ridge all the way to the house beyond the garden. As we walked up to the hedge suddenly a large dog came through it with something in its mouth. I instantly recognized the thing as a human bone; it seemed like a piece of shoulder blade. I immediately felt my legs turn to jelly and cold sweat break out on my brow. I hurried over to my dead son's grave. Oh, thank heavens! The grave was intact and unharmed, covered all over with grass. I have no way of expressing in writing how glad and comforted I felt to see this. But how strange! In front of the grave was a spent incense stick and a pile of black paper ashes. I could see that both incense and paper had only just been burned. I could also see that the grass and shrubs around the grave seemed to have been tidied up. Silently observing all this, I realized what it meant.

I placed my bouquet on top of the grave mound, got out the incense, and lit it. Then I told Ying'er to pay her respects to her brother—to bow to the grave. I told her that this was where her brother was. Once more she looked up at me from under her eyelashes, and then she stared hard at the grave, but the upshot was that her face only seemed to show more confusion. Holding the incense stick, she solemnly bowed several times, then performed a kowtow. I stuck the incense sticks in the earth, then opened the packs of spirit money and burned them. No other person could be seen anywhere on the ridge; there was only the sough of the wind, the cries of birds, and the chirruping of insects, only the bleak scattered grave mounds and the burgeoning grasses, and the sun shining coldly from above. Bleak desolation shrouded the cemetery, and deep sorrow overwhelmed my heart.

I told Ying'er to perform another kowtow as a goodbye to her brother, and then I led her out of the cemetery to the village for her haircut. When we got home it was already past eleven. My wife was back, and was sitting alone thinking. As I entered she looked up; her face was solemn, and her eyes confused. I could see that her heart was still troubled by what she had been thinking about.

"Ma!" Ying'er dived into her mother's open arms. "Me and Pa went to see Li'er," she reported. "I had lots of strawzers."

My wife glanced up at me again; silently, wordlessly, we looked at one another. She appeared somewhat uneasy. Each of us realized that we had discovered the other's secret worries, and each of us realized that the other knew that we knew it all, but we said nothing. All of this took only a moment; in the next instant a dark cloud of regret and sorrow swept over that lean face of hers. She gathered Ying'er to her bosom, pressing her own cheek to the top of the child's head, and large teardrops began to fall onto Ying'er's hair.

"There's lots of strawzers at Li'er's place," Ying'er was saying proudly. "The strawzers there are really big. Pa picked lots for me; they're lovely."

More tears fell from my wife's eyes.

I turned and went into the bedroom. I felt more listless and empty than I had ever felt.

Neither of us tried to comfort the other. For years afterward we would be wary of our mouths or ears coming in contact with that dreaded name and everything associated with it. These things should be buried forever alongside that poor, unlucky son of ours.

Part 5
Meinong Economics

Written in 1959. First published, posthumously, in *Complete Works* I (1976).

15. Swimming and Sinking
浮沉

As I put down the receiver I couldn't help wondering at what I'd just heard: "Li Xinchang, from Tainan"?

I turned to one of my colleagues: "Do you know a Li Xinchang?"

"Yes; who was that on the phone?"

"The boss. He said when Mr. Li Xinchang arrives, see him upstairs and make him comfortable. Tell him the boss will be back just as soon as he's finished what he's doing."

"Is Li Xinchang from Tainan?" I added.

"Oh no! He's originally from Pingtung county."

Then I really pricked up my ears: "Li Xinchang from Neipu? Now running a chemical plant in Tainan?"

"That's him! The very one!" Lin's face lit up. "Do you know him then?"

"Me? Oh no," I replied evasively. "I've heard the name, that's all."

"Plenty of people in this town do know him, you know!" He sounded quite bitter at not being one of them. "The chemical works is making a packet."

"Does he often come here?"

"At least once or twice a year. He's very thick with the boss and some other people in the town hall. Whenever he comes they get together and drink till dawn."

"Oh."

I sighed ruefully. Lin could not have known the reason for my sigh. He looked up at me before going on: "I hear he went through some real hard times in the past. Years ago he went in for bamboo on a hill farm in the township, but he ended up not only losing money but even getting beaten up by his own workers. Luckily for him Mr. Yuan and a few others in the town hall helped him out. That's how they became friends. He often comes here, partly for business, partly to go drinking with his pals. Obviously there's an element of gratitude on his part. You wait and see, they'll surely be up all night again tonight."

"Do you know why the workers turned on him?" I asked.

"No." Lin shook his head. "I only know what I've heard."

"Oh." I gave another rueful sigh.

I was lying when I told Lin I didn't know Li Xinchang. Not only that, but there were other things I knew, such as Li's origins, his character, and why he'd been beaten up by his own hired hands.

It's a long story....

Li Xinchang was a friend of ours. I say "ours" because my friendship with him arose within a circle of friends and was multilateral by nature.

Every person has his own private circles of acquaintance, aside from those associated with place of study, politics, and family. In such private circles it is not necessary for every member to get along with every other, or to share the same interests. X and Y may not necessarily be well matched as friends, but within a certain small circle they interact exceedingly well, just perfectly. To a great extent their friendship is collective or communal.

As a youth I was part of just such a circle. All of us were in the vigorous prime of our lives, and on some basic points we were in complete accord: we had all received some education and came from good, solid family backgrounds; we had high ideals and great ambitions, and loved to debate, to rail against the mundane world. Our hearts were pure....

It was in such circumstances that I became acquainted with Li Xinchang. He was in the same class as my half-brother in high school, so he had received a fairly good education. He was clever, bright, and lively. His appearances in our little circle were normally made in the company of my brother. Eventually we became very good friends independently. During the years that I spent in mainland China, Xinchang was conscripted into the Japanese army as a translator and sent to the South Seas. In spring 1946, when I returned from the Mainland, my brother put me up in his home in central Kaohsiung, and that's how I ran into Xinchang again. He said he too had just been sent back from overseas and was also living in Qianjin, only a block away. It was as if Fate had brought us back together. He and my brother saw a great deal of each other, and he came to our place almost every day. And when he came we'd always end up talking, talking ... about all sorts of things, setting the world to rights.

During this immediate postwar period of demobilization and restoration, the old order had collapsed but a new order had yet to be established. Society was pretty chaotic: the old Taiwan dollar was depreciating by the day, and public morale was in a state of flux. The lives of public employees were very hard, as their fixed salaries were unable to keep up with the crazy inflation. At the county level and below, salaries were being sat on for several months on end, so that when employees were finally paid, the value of their remittances was a fraction of what they should have been.

Li Xinchang had had a Japanese education and had known a stable and privileged existence. Like most natives of Taiwan, he was somewhat disconnected from mainland Chinese society and customs, so he felt very dissatisfied with the current state of affairs. He often showed this in his pessimistic and indignant conversation. Whenever I asked him about his future activities and goals he would always shake his head and sigh, before concluding: "Let's wait and see!"

But my circumstances were not the same as his; I couldn't just sit and wait like him. At the time I had already done the rounds a few times to Taipei and elsewhere, before getting myself fixed up through an acquaintance with a teaching job of sorts in Pingtung city.

"You really want to work in the public sector?" he asked me rather doubtfully at our gathering that evening.

"Would I lie to you?" I laughed.

"You realize your salary won't even be enough for you alone?" He seemed genuinely concerned for me. "So how will you support your wife and children?"

"I know," I said, still smiling but now less naturally, because what he said was indeed true. "But at least one of us will be taken care of."

"I don't think so!" He shook his head again.

Later I asked him again about his future plans. He said a few friends wanted him to go in with them in a trading venture.

At that time trade was a red-hot area, with ships constantly plying among Japan, Shanghai, Hong Kong, the Philippines; officially it was trade, but in reality it was flagrant piracy. Adventurers and profiteers were attracted to this trade like ducks to water, as if trade were the only path to riches.

A few days later I moved with my family to Pingtung. Xinchang and my brother saw us off at the train station. After several happy months together in Kaohsiung, naturally we shared a sense of impending loneliness now that we had to part. As the train prepared to leave we shook hands and wished one another well.

"To success in your adventure!" I said to Xinchang as I shook his hand. He just smiled.

I settled down in Pingtung and went to work on time every morning and home again at night: a clockwork existence. After a few months I received a letter from my brother from which I learned that Li Xinchang had gone into the construction business with an architect friend. There was not a word in the letter about trade. I was quite surprised by this. Only later did I hear that Xinchang's father had strenuously opposed his going into trade. His father was an old-fashioned sort who believed in knowing one's own place in society; old-fashioned people are afraid of taking risks.

Mind you, in those days the construction business certainly was a promising field of endeavor. During the war Kaohsiung had been badly bombed by the Allies and turned into a pulverized waste, its system of streets and buildings destroyed. Everything had to be begun again from scratch, so you could imagine what a prosperous business construction was. Unfortunately inflation was rampant and construction projects almost always went over budget as a result. Again and again this month's perfectly sound estimate for building materials would buy only a fraction of what was necessary come the following month. When the building was finished and payment was made by the client, profit on paper would turn out to be loss in real terms. After a year or more of this Xinchang was battered and bruised, and even his health was affected.

Unable to carry on in construction, Xinchang went into fishmongery. It was now already late 1947 and from what I heard his fishmonger's did rather well at first. I visited his shop once when I happened to be in Kaohsiung. It wasn't that big but looked pretty good. The shop assistants were young and spirited, polite and attentive, and its distinctive smell of fresh seafood and salt fish blended with the prosperous air of a thriving shop. The result was that just stepping inside made you feel invigorated and cheerful.

That evening Xinchang invited me and my brother to a small tavern for a couple of drinks. He'd always had a good capacity for liquor, and now, with two of his best friends, he seemed even happier than usual and drank accordingly. He got through almost three of the four bottles, and his conversation poured as freely as the *sake*, as he denounced social corruption and bemoaned the inflationary economy. His eyes gleamed, his nostrils snorted like a bull's, and he seemed much more energetic than usual. As the third bottle grew emptier his head was already rocking wildly on his shoulders as he gesticulated and babbled like a madman. He grabbed the hand of the waitress and placed it on his own chest, mumbling thickly: "C'n ya feel whass inside here? Huh?"

"I know what's inside," the girl said, smiling merrily. "There's roast chicken, sushi, and *sake*."

"*Baka!*" He used Japanese to call her a blockhead. "*Baka!* Wrong! Thissn't my stomach. Izh-ish my shtomach?"

He glared at her and took her hand again.

"Feell't again."

"Oh, ah! I can feel it." She smiled even wider. "It's your chest, and inside it lies your true love!"

"*Baka! Baka!*" He flung her hand away violently. "Inshide 't sitsh a bomb, you know? Sh'about t' shplode!"

There were tears in his eyes, his nostrils were flaring, and his face grew alarmingly red.

"Ah! Ah!" He raised a fist and hammered it down on the table, sending cups and plates and all jumping several inches in the air and clattering back down. "'Sh unbearable, and's gonna xshplode any minute!"

The waitress grabbed his hand and spoke soothingly, pleading with him.

"Mr. Li, don't bang the table. You've had too much to drink."

"'m not dzrunk, don' talk nonshenshe!" The tears were now flowing from his eyes. He didn't bother to wipe them away but allowed them to flow down his gaunt cheeks. "D'ya shink I haven' made money? In c'nshtruction n zh' fish chrade, I've alwayzh made profitsh. Bu' 'nflation'z eaten zh' lot; zhat demon'zh eaten my whole life, eaten everyshing."

He raised his fist again. The waitress hurriedly grabbed it.

"Mr. Li," she kept smiling sweetly, hoping to soften him with her charms, "don't bang the table, please calm down."

"Ge' zh' hell outta here, you foksh-fairy!"[1] He shook off her hand. "Whadda you know?" He sank into the sofa. "Ah! Ah! 'Sh unbearable!"

He was completely inebriated.

When we got home my brother and I talked about Xinchang's fish shop, and I told him what I'd seen earlier in the day.

"No!" said my brother. "It seems things are not looking too good. The shareholders are grumbling. I don't think it can go on much longer like this."

The next day Xinchang was completely sober. When sober he was calm, mild, and polite. Naturally he didn't remember what he'd said and done the night before.

"Old Zhong," he said to me quietly, "perhaps you're right."

Not knowing what he meant, I asked, "What about?"

"I think I should sit down and wait, like you."

"Mm."

"Our past education isn't suited to today's society. If we hope to get back on our feet, we have to start again from scratch—we have to remold ourselves, don't you think?"

Before long Li Xinchang got out of the fish business. Later he moved back to his native place. But I only learned of these things the next time I went back to Kaohsiung. That would have been in early autumn 1948, as I recall. I'd been prepared for his retreat from fishmongering, but his removal back home came as something of a surprise.

"I did ask him what he planned to do after going back to his village," said my brother. "He said he wasn't going to do anything, and that he just didn't want to go on trying to get by in the city. I think he's very disillusioned. But perhaps there are even more practical reasons for his decision—his daily rice, for example!"

---

1. Fox-fairy (*hulijing* 狐狸精): in Chinese mythology there are many tales of beautiful and oversexed vixens in human form seducing men and sometimes causing their deaths. There are similar stories from Japan and Korea.

"Surely he's not so hard up?" I said.

"I'm not really sure. But it's true that it's easier to get by in the countryside. With no job here, going home was another way forward. What's more, he and his brothers have now divided up the family assets. They couldn't keep the whole clan together any longer."

One day not long afterward Li Xinchang came to visit me in my Pingtung lodgings.

He was as pessimistic and discontented in his conversation as ever, but the difference was that he seemed to be seeking some harmony in it all. There's no use in wallowing in depression and dismay, a man has to seek a way out in order to go on living, in order not to die of frustration. This much is understandable, but precisely for this reason Xinchang's painful inward struggle made me feel even more sympathy toward him.

That same year I fell into ill health and gave up my position and city life to return to a quiet existence in the Kaohsiung countryside. I had hardly any contact with the outside world and could hear of Li Xinchang only from my brother's infrequent letters. He wrote that Xinchang had finally gone into trade as he had always wanted. Less than a year later another letter reported that his trading venture had collapsed disastrously, swallowing almost every penny he had. My brother wrote that if Xinchang had been allowed to go into trade before, he might have been in the right place at the right time, but now everything was gradually settling into established patterns and the economy was getting increasingly stable. It was getting very difficult to succeed in irregular profiteering. And with his family now divided, there was no longer anyone to stop him, more's the pity.

"Perhaps it was Fate!" wrote my brother in conclusion.

The following year, just after the Spring Festival, Xinchang came with my brother to my little house in the hills. Xinchang had grown even thinner in the months since I had last seen him. Sitting idly at home, he had heard from my brother that our family had a hill farm with plenty of bamboo. Just at that time the army was buying up great quantities of bamboo, so he was thinking of trying his hand at this business. This was the reason for their visit. Privately, my brother also told me that Xinchang was afraid it might be awkward for him to come alone, so he'd dragged him along. Not having any money, Xinchang was hoping I'd let him take the bamboo on credit, to be paid for when he sold it.

I couldn't help smiling at his courtly manners, but at the same time I could understand that a person who has suffered a blow to his self-confidence will often treat his friends differently from before: his psychology is somehow distorted.

That same evening we agreed on all the conditions, and so Xinchang began to negotiate with Army HQ, hire workers, and complete the formalities required by the town hall. Next, the bamboo cutting began.

But Fate can be treacherous, and its vicissitudes are unknowable. Legally our hill farm was jointly owned by gentlemen's agreement: my family's portion had never been formally divided from those of our two partners. Because of a boundary dispute Xinchang was prevented from moving the bamboo he had cut. Our co-owner said Xinchang's men had cut bamboo on the wrong side of the line.

On the day in question I too happened to be at the plantation. There were many of us and only a few of them, so, ignoring their protests, we went on loading the truck with bamboo. When it was fully laden, the truck began to move slowly forward. Suddenly my beanpole of a neighbor leaped out into the middle of the road, spreading his arms and shouting as if possessed: "You can't take away the bamboo! I won't let you take away the bamboo!"

The truck stopped. "Are you getting out of the way or not?" The truck driver was beside himself with anger. "If not, see if I don't run right over you!"

But the man showed no sign at all of giving in. He glared, round-eyed: "Run me down then, if you've got the balls!"

The driver shifted into first gear, the truck screeched angrily, and it began to nose forward. Gradually the distance between man and truck grew shorter. To everyone's surprise, the man suddenly lay down in the road, gesticulating toward the truck and his own chest: "Come on! Come on! Try and run me over, if you've got the balls!"

The driver kept going until his whole face was dripping in sweat, but in the end he had to step on the brakes. Now the worker who'd been tying the bamboo bundles came flying down from the stack on the truck and stormed up to the man. With one hand he dragged him up by his clothes, and then he bunched the other hand in his face and yelled: "Motherfucker! Wanna die, do ya?"

Li Xinchang rushed in between them. With difficulty he broke them up, saying, "Enough! That's enough!"

Then, using every possible argument and inducement, he finally persuaded the man to let them take away "the bamboo that had already been loaded onto the truck."

That evening I killed a big capon and opened a bottle of *sake*. My wife served the *sake* and acted as hostess. When I toasted Xinchang, he downed his cup of *sake* in one and toasted me back, also pouring a brimming cup for my wife.

"I toast you, Mrs. Zhong, to thank you for your kindness these past few days. Old Zhong! Let's drink to your good lady."

So saying, he flung his head back, glug-glug, and turned his cup upside down to show it was empty.

"A few years ago I might have killed that guy today, but not now!" Flames were burning in his eyes, but his voice was low and calm. "It's not that important, not worth coming to blows over, is it? I've had bigger business losses than this. You might find it hard to believe, but when I was in trade do you know much money I made? A whole truckload! I put the banknotes in gunny sacks topped up with a layer of chaff and stored them in a woodshed. If I hadn't been raided by the inspectors on a tip-off, even my sons and grandsons could never have spent all that money. You can imagine: when a man's been through something like that, why should he get het up about a little thing like today? Alright then! Tonight we're going to get thoroughly drunk, and we won't stop till we're soused! My dear lady, pour some more *sake* for Old Zhong."

And so we drank to our hearts' content and didn't mention the bamboo business again. Xinchang was very jolly, frequently losing himself in loud gales of laughter, sometimes to the point of weeping with mirth. He sang a few songs that he said he'd learned in the South Seas. After the songs came a grass-skirt dance. He swung his hips and shook his belly around in the dim lamplight.

It was eleven o'clock when the party finally broke up. Before going to bed I softly went over to Xinchang's window and saw him sitting quietly at his desk, looking gloomy and dejected. It was a sudden change from his behavior just now. I stood there for a short while. I just had no way of knowing which of these two attitudes represented the real Li Xinchang.

Suddenly, I felt guilty.

Unable to move the cut bamboo, Li Xinchang had no way to pay his men's wages, and so the workers pestered him every day for their money. Naturally no more bamboo was cut. I asked someone to arbitrate the dispute, but after a fortnight or so of to-ing and fro-ing there was still no acceptable solution. Xinchang was terribly depressed.

One day when he returned from the hill his nose was bleeding, there was a big bruised swelling on his right temple, and his shirt was torn to strips. He looked really terrible.

I felt myself go pale with shock. I rushed out of the yard to meet him.

"Xinchang, you . . . "

"Oh, it's nothing," he said indifferently. "I got beaten up."

When I quizzed him further he told me he'd got into an argument with the workers about their unpaid wages. Neither side would back down, and the men had worked him over. Truly it was just one piece of trouble after another.

That day Xinchang was more worked up than ever, but he kept silent all day. After dinner he sat bolt upright at his desk again, aloof and alone, a study in desolation. Whenever I recalled my own involvement in his misfortune I felt terribly bad about it, but there was nothing I could do.

The next day Xinchang got up very early, and as soon as he saw me he told me he was leaving. I was somewhat surprised and told him that the dispute should be settled within the next few days. Hearing this, he gave a thin smile and said, "Forget it!" I looked at him without speaking. It seemed that he had thought about it all night and in the end he'd seen through it all. There was no chance of changing his mind about leaving. He said I should do whatever I saw fit with the bamboo, but he hoped I would pay the wages he owed.

After breakfast he shook hands with my wife and me and bade us farewell. That was our last meeting as friends. The bruising and swelling on his temple were still visible, and there was a cut on his nostril. Although he kept smiling and did his best to seem cheerful, in his smile I could see sadness, loneliness, and regret. As far as I know, this was the lowest, roughest time of his life.

"I'm so sorry," I said. "This was all because of our land dispute."

"No!" he replied. "Perhaps it's the other way around: it was I who caused problems for you. I'm always in the wrong place at the wrong time."

Not long after that, my brother died, and I lost touch with Li Xinchang altogether.

I heard that he subsequently did a lot of things, and that later on he was running a chemical plant or something in Tainan. What fragmentary news I had of him was all second- or third-hand.

The flow of my reminiscence was suddenly interrupted by a great hubbub outside. When I looked up I saw several men alighting in single file from a minibus. A middle-aged gentleman walked in front. The others, who followed behind him, were all town hall officials. They walked into the office out of the sunshine.

Although I hadn't seen him for ten years I immediately recognized the gentleman as Li Xinchang.

I instinctively drew back and hid in the shadow of the bookcase. I didn't want to meet him.

Li Xinchang was carrying a leather briefcase, and he wore a silk Hong Kong shirt and a large gold ring on one finger. He looked elegant and dashing, grand and superior. What especially surprised me was the physical change in him. His face was plump, well fleshed out, and radiant with health. Although he wasn't yet what you'd call corpulent, he had certainly put on a bit round the middle. He had all the appearance of a real big shot. For the first time in my life I saw the close and evident correspondence between a person's physiology and success or failure in his career. Li's voice, intonation, and gestures were composed, calm, and full of self-confidence. This too was different from before.

In short, everything about him had changed into something quite different from ten years before. I looked at him, and then back at myself: shabby, impoverished, down on my luck!

I hunched back a little further.

Luckily everyone in the town hall had long since completely forgotten my part in that business ten years ago, and Li Xinchang himself would never have expected to bump into me in a place like this—that I would have become a common clerk in a rural town hall. And anyway, my appearance had completely changed in the past ten years: old, skinny, withered, feeble. . . . Even if he had seen me he would have been unable to recognize me.

Just then, wild laughter suddenly broke out among the men, and one voice could be heard shouting, "No way! No way!"

It was Li Xinchang's voice, booming and jolly.

"No way! No way! Your country women are no good: they're far too stiff and starched! Why not come to Tainan sometime, and I'll show you the women there. Ah, they're the ones to give you a taste of what you're missing! Even their eyes can talk! Have a smoke!"

His last words were louder, and with them a cigarette flew through the air and landed on my desk. Then another landed in front of Mr. Lin.

"Have a smoke!"

I noticed that he dispensed with even the basic courtesies. Indeed, his tone was contemptuous.

From the shadow of the bookcase I looked out intently. I saw that each of them had a cigarette, which they were getting lit at Li Xinchang's lighter. Their faces were flushed and there was a strong smell of drink; obviously they had just finished a rather liquid lunch. Soon they were wreathed in clouds of smoke, and the smell of tobacco, mingled with that of alcohol, wafted over to us in the corner.

Li Xinchang had not noticed me, but still I felt that the cigarette-throwing stunt had been uncalled for. With that action, everything between him and me was over and done with. The parabola traced in the air by that cigarette represented the distance between us that now existed. He was at one end, and I at the other; he wouldn't cross the space, and nor could I.

I experienced the most complex feelings, feelings I could not sort out or name. You could say this was the sadness of a man losing a friend, or perhaps the indignation of a man who finds himself dropped, or even the bitterness of a man discovering his own degeneration; it resembled all of these, or a combination of all three.

They sat for a while, and then all crowded upstairs in a huddle.

Lin picked up the cigarette from his desk.

"Wow! Double Happiness!" he exclaimed in delight. "Aren't you having yours?"

He stuffed the cigarette between his lips, got a match, and lit it.

A song drifted down from the gramophone upstairs.

"All a man needs is money," Lin went on feelingly, after a few puffs on the cigarette. "Don't you think so, Old Zhong? If you've got money, everything is fine; and you get respect!"

But by now I was thinking of something else.

—Perhaps he—Li Xinchang—had already remolded himself!

First draft completed in summer 1960. The author died on August 4, 1960, in the midst of revising the manuscript. First published in October 1960 in Zhong Lihe, *Yu* 雨 (Rain [and other writings]), Taibei: Zhong Lihe yizhu chuban weiyuanhui (Committee for the publication of the posthumous works of Zhong Lihe).

16. Rain

I

It was hot and oppressive. Even people sitting indoors were sweating, as if in a steam bath.

"It's going to rain!" they said when they looked at the sky.

The sky was gloomy and somber, and gradually getting more so. From early afternoon dark clouds began to congregate toward the northwest. In less than two hours they had piled up into a great black mass. The cloud clusters hung down low, almost kissing the tops of the hills beneath. Thunder rumbled continually, but very low, as though the sound were coming from a great distance.

The clouds hung lower still, and even more menacingly. The sky was so black it looked as if a thick layer of ink had been flung over it.

Suddenly the thunder stopped. Great, big, heavy drops of rain began to fall, making one hole after another in the light, powdery earth of people's yards and on the roads. Everywhere wisps of steam rose up from the ground.

"It's raining! It's raining!" The farmers cried out for joy, wide grins on their faces, their kindly eyes gleaming.

But no sooner did the rain start to fall than the wind began to blow. It blew fiercely, madly, gust after gust, rumbling across the fields like great heavy footsteps. Suddenly with a whoosh the rice sprouts and the astragalus[1] were bowed almost to the ground, where they stayed for a long time before lifting up their heads again.

Gradually the dark clouds dispersed, until finally they had taken the rain away with them.

---

[1]. *Astragalus adsurgens* Pall.: a tall, drought-hardy, soil-binding herbaceous plant; used for fodder and as green manure.

When the farmers came out to take a look, they found only a very thin, damp crust covering the earth, which turned to powder when poked with a toe. The earth underneath was a fine powder as before, and when you picked up a handful it was burning hot to the touch. Disappointment rose up in their faces.

The wind kept blowing. Slowly the clouds parted, revealing the blue sky.

The sun came out again.

And the wind stopped.

2

Huang Jinde had just completed an inspection tour of his land, ending up back in the shade of the hibiscus tree at the head of the fields. He sat down and lit a cigarette. The leaves of the hibiscus were really big, really round, really thick, and densely layered in the canopy. Beneath them were deep shade and a cool, pleasant breeze, creating the finest place hereabouts for the farmers to rest when tired and thirsty from work. Down from the tree there was a branch of the main irrigation ditch, but now it was dried up and neglected, resembling the backbone of a dead king-ratsnake.

Take one step out from the shade of the tree and you were in the world of the sun: under its roasting rays a semi-desert landscape spread out. Half of the fields had already been planted out with rice sprouts; some of the other half hadn't even been plowed yet, and even the fields that had been plowed were covered in drought-hardy weeds. Where rice had been planted out, the leaves of the sprouts had already turned brown and the tips had turned a burnt reddish color, because there was no water for irrigation. At their roots the earth was cracked like a tortoise shell and gradually turning white. Clearly, another fortnight without rain and the paddy would wither and die.

The land Huang Jinde farmed lay just below the hibiscus tree. He rented it from a local man named Fu. Originally it was 1.1 *jia*,[2] but he only farmed seven tenths, having made over the other four tenths to Xu Longxiang's widow. Now all of it was "375 Land"—"Land to the

---

2. One *jia* 甲 = 0.97 hectare.

Tiller" land.³ An irrigation ditch drawing water from the branch ditch lay before him at an angle. This was the boundary between his fields and hers, with his portion on this side and hers on the other. Of his seven tenths only four had been planted with rice; there hadn't been any water for planting the other three. Now, more than three months later, his remaining rice seedlings were still huddled together in the seedbeds, gasping for breath.

In Longxiang's widow's fields not a single rice sprout had been planted out.

The unplanted fields were a wilderness; those already planted were thirsty. Jinde was worried about both. The browned leaves of the paddy made his frown almost into a knot on his brow.

Another farmer walked into the shade cast by the tree.

"Damn it!" the man said, as he sat down on a flat stone and lit a cigarette. "Another false alarm."

Jinde didn't reply. Only after they had smoked silently for a while did he look up and say: "A-Xing, I heard the temples are planning to hold masses for rain. Is it true?"

"That's what they're saying. Maybe they will. Last night the Kings spoke; they had instructions for everybody."

"The Temple of Goodness and Enlightenment?"

"No, the Ping'an Gong."

"What did the gods say?"

"What did they say? They said they expect everyone to do some good deeds."

Jinde's eyes opened wide, and he sniffed vigorously. "What? As if we usually go round committing murder and arson?" He exhaled some tobacco smoke, noisily, as if in anger. "What else did they say?"

"Er, nothing."

---

3. From 1949 land reform in Taiwan aimed to control all annual land rents at or below 37.5 percent (375) of the value of the rice crop, landlords previously having taken varying rates, up to 66 percent. Furthermore, buying and selling of land was to be controlled by the government with the aim of redistributing land ownership. In principle, a landowner repossessing "375 Land" from a tenant ran contrary to this important national policy, which by the time of the action of this novella had already succeeded in transforming Taiwan's rural economy.

Jinde shut up and smoked his cigarette, and both men's gazes automatically fell on the fields before them. The sunshine reflected from the fields was so dazzling it hurt their eyes.

Longxiang's widow was in her fields. The weeds had grown very tall and were basking in the sunshine, apparently thoroughly enjoying life. Off to the south someone was spraying pesticide, the cylinder on his back flashing in the sun. The pump lever stuck up high above his head like an outstretched arm. He held the spray pipe in his right hand, while the left repeatedly reached up to pull on the pump lever, producing a dull metallic clanking. The unmistakable nauseating stench of endrin fumes drifted on the breeze over to the two men.

"Jinde," said A-Xing. "Have you heard about Sister Longxiang's land?"

"No," replied Jinde, pricking up his ears. "What about it?"

"Well, what I hear is they're going to return it to the landlord."

"Well that's strange. That's 375 Land."

"So what if it's 375 Land? The landlord just needs to give the tenant a bit of money."

"Mm, hmm," Jinde nodded. "Who's the buyer?"

"As if you didn't know. And I hear the middleman is Youfu."

"Tang Youfu?"

"Tang Youfu."

"So it's him up to no good again." Jinde spoke almost as if in soliloquy. "He's always going behind my back."

A-Xing looked at him and smiled.

Jinde threw down his cigarette end, picked up his bamboo hat, and put it on. The two men walked out from the shade and continued their conversation as they walked into town.

When they got to town they went their separate ways.

Jinde didn't know if what A-Xing said about Longxiang's widow's land was accurate. But he couldn't easily put the matter aside, because to him it was an affair of honor and duty.

Xu Longxiang had been his blood brother. During the Second World War the two of them had been conscripted together into the Japanese army as porters. They had served at the front line in the South Pacific. Once, their column had been attacked and Jinde had been shot in the shoulder. When he had lost so much blood that he grew faint and confused, Xu Longxiang put him on his back, and in this way they escaped. Longxiang had saved his life. With the injury to his shoulder it was often too painful for Jinde to carry his load. Again, Xu Longxiang came to his rescue by taking some of Jinde's load as well as his own. Longxiang had really looked out for him. Later, being the same age, they swore same-year blood brotherhood.

In the last stages of the war the Japanese went from one defeat to the next, and units became detached and dispersed, everyone fleeing for his own life. One day Xu Longxiang injured his leg. Jinde helped him along as they fled into the mountains. After a few days of flight the wound on Longxiang's leg became infected, then it got worse, and eventually it was in such a bad state that he couldn't move the leg an inch.

"Leave me," he said. He knew there was no hope. "I'm not going to get out of this."

Jinde knew that he spoke the truth, and although he could hardly bear it, in the end he set him down at the foot of a coconut palm. He picked several coconuts for him and gave him a bottle of water and a knife.

"When your leg's better you can take your time finding your own way back," he said. "Perhaps there are still units coming up from behind who'll find you."

Longxiang cut a lock of his hair and entrusted it to Jinde, along with his watch, a ring, and so on, to take back to Taiwan for his family. In particular he asked Jinde, as his blood brother, to be sure to look after his family. Jinde swore to do so and begged him not to worry. And so they parted.

After Japan surrendered Jinde was repatriated. Xu Longxiang was still missing, but there seemed little doubt that he had become a part of the soil of Mindanao. Now, fifteen years later, Jinde still often thought of his blood brother and comrade-in-arms, and he felt very sad. Now once more a vision of Longxiang appeared before him: leaning against the trunk of the coconut palm, looking at him piteously with sorrow in his eyes, just before they parted.

"Blood Brother, please take care of my family."

It niggled with Jinde that a few years after Longxiang's "death" his wife took up with none other than the Tang Youfu he and A-Xing had just mentioned. In Jinde's eyes, given his kindness to her and her children on his blood brother's behalf, no other man had any business coming out of the woodwork—no wonder he wasn't happy about it. He felt as if he had been tricked—taken for a fool. The guy always seemed to be lurking around her—in and out of the shadows like a ghost, or like a cangue[4] hung around her neck that even stopped her breathing freely. Through the woman that guy had become the true master of everything that went on in her household. The original order of things had been broken. But Jinde had no say in any of this; he had to pretend not to see.

Luckily Longxiang's two boys, Tusheng and Huosheng, were already grown up; Tusheng was married, and so was their sister. In this way the onus on Jinde was already somewhat lightened. These days he hardly had any dealings with the family, unless there was some particular business that needed discussing. He hoped the two brothers would take proper care of everything.

Jinde reached home and went into the hall, where he hung his bamboo hat on a nail on the wall.

"Pa!" It was his daughter, Yunying, coming out from her room. "Where've you been?"

Jinde wiped his upper lip with his palm, then used the back of his hand to wipe it again. "Is there a problem?"

"Ma says if you've got the time, why don't you repair the pig sty? It's almost falling down."

"Who says I'm not repairing it? I've just been to look at the rice sprouts." He didn't look at his daughter as he spoke but busied himself pouring a cup of cold tea from the pot.

"Pa," the girl said with a smile. "You wouldn't have been over to Uncle A-San's tobacco shed, now, would you?"

"Who says I was?" Jinde looked up now, glaring with big, round eyes. "And anyway, what if I did go there?"

"Nobody's accusing you, Pa." Now she was smiling even more pleasantly and her voice was even softer. "But I think it's best you don't go there; Ma will only get angry."

---

4. A cangue is an instrument of punishment and restraint resembling a portable stocks fastened round the neck and usually also both wrists.

"Huh! Your ma! Oh, your ma!" Jinde was getting a bit angry, but he kept it under control. Altering his tone, he said, "You're just like your ma, bossing me about!"

"Pa," she said, pouting now and stamping her little feet. "You're talking nonsense again. Who's bossing you!"

Jinde didn't respond, but he had softened by now. He wiped his mouth several times, alternating his palm and the back of his hand and each time wiping them off on his trousers. He looked a bit like a satisfied cat as he performed these actions.

Strangely enough, Jinde couldn't get along with his wife, and things weren't much better with his sons, but he had a lot of time for Yunying. When he was with her he lost all his backbone and became like a candle in a flame: her every smile or frown could mold him into almost any shape she wanted.

He finished his cup of cold tea, stood up, and prepared to go out.

"Pa," his daughter looked at him in surprise. "Where are you going now?"

"I've got some things to do. I need to go to a couple of places in town. Is that a problem?"

"Ma was asking if you had cut some of Uncle Dingrui's bamboo."

"I did cut some bamboo. I'll be needing some to fix the pig sty. But it wasn't his bamboo I cut. Who says it was?"

"Ma says Uncle Dingrui's really angry. He says it was his bamboo you cut the other day."

"It was my own I cut—it's nothing to do with him!"

And with that he left the hall.

"No, Pa, he says you crossed onto his land when you were cutting the bamboo."

"Hogwash!" Out in the yard Jinde stopped and turned back to his daughter. "You tell him to survey the land. If the bamboo was his I'll pay compensation."

Huang Jinde was a short man, not quite five foot six, but he was powerfully built. He dressed in black from head to toe, and his hair was black too, so that with his bright red face he looked remarkably like a locomotive, power in every inch. He had big, thick eyebrows, and although his eyes were small they looked really big and round when he glared at you, like a bird's eyes. His nose was very fleshy and always running, so that often while he was speaking he would be wiping his nose at the same time: first with one hand then with the other, and wiping them on his trousers in between wipes. Both his neck and his arms were short and thick, with big veins sticking out, and his hands were very hairy. If he was angry, or when he was talking excitedly, his neck got even thicker and you could clearly see each tendon straining under the skin. Meanwhile his arms would be gesticulating wildly in the air.

Jinde's mother died when he was four, and then when he was in the fourth grade his father died too. He and his little sister were taken in by his uncle. When he finished school he worked as his uncle's oxherd. Not until he was sixteen or seventeen did his uncle get him a job on a farm as a long-term laborer, and he was twenty-eight before he was married into a family named Lin. Marrying into his wife's family rather than taking a wife into his own deeply injured his self-esteem, profoundly affecting both his career and his emotional and intellectual life. He felt it as a huge blot on his reputation, a blot that was imprinted on his spine and could never be expunged. It was like the placard that criminals used to have strapped to their backs in olden times: no matter where he went it would forever prevent him holding his head up high. Now, with his father-in-law and mother-in-law both dead, he should by rights be the head of the family. But he was so in name only; the one who held the real power was his wife, not him.

Although they had produced quite a brood of children, Jinde and his wife hardly spoke a word to one another. Even when there was something in particular to discuss, their conversations were nothing more than (1) a question, followed by (2) an answer. If it got to (3), well (3) was the start of an argument. The end was sure to be unhappy for both parties: the woman would nurse her wrath to keep it warm while Jinde turned to drink and gambling.

Apart from all that, however, on the whole he was a happy man, filled with self-confidence. He was a tough guy, straight and upright, loyal and true; if you couldn't earn his respect, he'd rather die than give in to you. In his eyes the concept of "no can do" was very hard to understand. To him there was nothing in this great wide world that was worthy of a man's fear or subjection. When he was an army porter, his Japanese squad leader had boxed his ears over some trifle. He had almost killed the man, and narrowly escaped military prison.

When he thought about what his daughter had just said, Jinde couldn't help feeling angry, but the anger immediately subsided, and off he went toward West Street perfectly content with the world. When he got to his favorite haunt, the *bantiao*[5] restaurant by the town clock, some men inside called out to him in greeting. Almost all of them were gambling buddies of his. None of them were eating—they were only gossiping.

"I haven't got time," he said as he sat down at their table. "I'll come again tonight."

"Who said anything about gambling?" said a man with a long thin face whose name was Xinfa. "Jinde, do you want to buy some land? I'll sell you mine."

"Twenty thousand per *jia*?" said Jinde, half-serious, half-joking.

"Make it fifty thousand and you're on."

"What do you need money for?"

"Gambling," cracked Xinfa, but in the next moment he frowned and spoke despondently: "These days I'm crying out for cash. We haven't even enough to buy cooking oil. And damn it, every day my woman just goes on and on at me. It really gets on my nerves."

"Today I saw Youfu sitting in the legal clerks' office," said another man. "I reckon he's about to rake in another heap."

"A middleman's commission isn't that easily come by," put in another man. "I reckon it's six months or so since he made a fee."

Suddenly Jinde had an idea. All joking aside, he asked this man: "Do you know whose land he's brokering?"

"Who cares whose land it is?" replied the man offhandedly.

Jinde rose and walked out of the restaurant.

"What's your hurry?" someone called after him. "Stay and have a chat."

He crossed Mid Street and then went along an alley to Back Street, where his blood brother Xu Longxiang's house stood.

---

5. *Bantiao* 板條: the Hakka people's most famous staple food—thick flat noodles made of rice flour.

Neither Longxiang's widow nor her elder son, Tusheng, was at home. Just as he was turning to leave, Tusheng came home, and so he turned again and went back inside with him.

Tusheng politely invited Jinde to take a seat in the hall and poured him a cup of tea.

"You haven't visited for quite a while, Sworn-uncle," Tusheng said, standing beside the table. "Is there something particular today?"

"Nothing much," said Jinde. "Do I need a special reason?"

As he spoke he was sizing up the young man with his eyes. Tusheng was very tall, but his face was sallow and his eyes dull and lifeless, making him look like a simpleton. He was staring nervously now at the floor, then at the ceiling, as though he found himself in an unfamiliar place and not his own home. His overall demeanor appeared fearful and troubled.

Looking at the young man, Jinde hesitated, but eventually he spoke.

"Tusheng," he said. "I hear you're going to return that land of yours to the owner. Is that right?"

As he'd suspected, Tusheng knew nothing about it.

"Well, then," Jinde asked. "Where's your ma?"

"She's gone out."

Jinde stood up. The young man annoyed him, but at the same time he found him pitiful. Remembering his blood brother, he could not contain a sigh.

"Tusheng," he said kindly. "Young men should have a bit more vim, be a bit more on the ball. Just being a good worker isn't enough; an ox will always be a better worker than a man. You should take more care about your own family's affairs. Do you understand?"

3

"Yunying, Zhengang was just here looking for you."

When Huang Yunying arrived at Lizhuang Western Tailors and Dressmakers, a girl dressed in a white blouse and black skirt greeted her with these words. Yunying's face darkened, and she said unhappily, "Has he gone?"

"He just left."

"Did he say anything?"

"He said he'd be back after work."

Yunying said nothing, but took out her scissors and measuring tape and began to work.

The girl in the white shirt looked up from the material she was working on and added with a smile, "I'd say Zhengang's really interested in you. Why do you ignore him?"

"Huh!" snorted Yunying as she worked the scissors. "He's as sticky as toffee, and just as sickly too!"

Several of the girls laughed at this.

"Everybody knows where Yunying's heart lies!" said one of them, sitting at her sewing machine.

Yunying looked up from her work and said, "What would you know about my heart?"

"You have a sweetheart!" said the girl at the sewing machine.

"Nonsense!" said Yunying. Embarrassed, she tried to stare down the other girl, but at the same time she couldn't hide a certain complacency in her face that suggested she was actually happy for them to know she had a sweetheart.

"You deny it? Perhaps you won't be happy until I've told everyone his name, is that it?"

"Hah!" scoffed the girl in the white shirt. "Who needs you to announce anything? Everybody knows his name—Huosheng, hah!"

"You mean that boy who works at TTL?"[6] piped up another girl. "I saw him with Yunying at the picture house the other day. He's dead good-looking!"

"When are we going to get a piece of your wedding cake, Yunying?" said the sewing machine girl. "We can't wait."

"What pests you all are!" cried Yunying. "Do me a favor and shut up."

The girls only laughed harder.

Toward evening Yunying tore a strip off a piece of paper and quickly wrote a few words on it in pencil while no one was looking. When she had finished she folded the paper up very small, picked up her handbag, and made to leave the tailor's.

Just at that moment a girl wearing a striped dress happened to be leaving the shop, pushing a bicycle. Without a word Yunying handed

---

6. TTL: Taiwan Tobacco and Liquor, formerly a state monopoly.

her the piece of paper. Without a word the girl took the paper, stuffed it in her handbag, got on her bike, and rode off.

The streets of the town seethed with the hectic bustle that precedes nightfall; all around, smoke was rising from the kitchen chimneys of out-of-town farmhouses. An evening mist had descended, and the last rays of the setting sun lent a mauve sheen to the distant hills.

The asphalt road was crowded with cars, motorcycles, bicycles, and scurrying pedestrians. Yunying's long strides soon took her into a narrow lane leading into Front Street. This was a narrow, old street surfaced with grit and gravel. Here there were no vehicles of any kind, no noise, no smell of gasoline in the air. There were only quiet and tranquility.

Yunying slowed her pace to a sedate walk. Her body felt light and her legs strong: young life surged inside her like a spring tide. When she thought of the banter among the girls at the tailor's during the day, a smile rose once more to the corners of her lips. She thought the other girls ridiculous. But what they had said was true. She did indeed have a sweetheart, and his name was just as they had said: Huosheng. He did work at TTL. And she had arranged to meet him this evening at Twin Peaks Ice Parlor.

When her thoughts reached this point, the smile rose up to her lips again.

Huosheng was Xu Longxiang's younger son, and Yunying had known him for thirteen or fourteen years, since they were only six or seven. At the time, the war had just ended and Taiwan had reverted to Mainland rule. The countryside still bore the scars of neglect and chaos. The farmers were setting about rebuilding from the ruins, putting their land back to rights. When Huang Jinde came back from overseas he rented a big parcel of land from the Fus and made over four of the eleven tenths to Huosheng's mother.

From that time on Yunying and Huosheng saw each other all the time. They were innocent children and knew nothing of social strictures. The shade under the Taiwan hibiscus was their playground. While the grownups were busy working out in the fields in the heat of the sun, they would be under the tree playing with stones, playing hide and seek, or climbing the tree. If it was a busy season in the fields the two families would picnic together in the crisp, cool shade. The grownups would be laughing and joking, and the children would be more excited than ever. Those were really happy times. The sound of joyful laughter washed away the heat they were suffering along with any worries that they had. Above their heads the hibiscus leaves and branches would rustle from time to time and sway gently in the wind, as though the tree itself was also in a happy mood.

One time, in the fourth month, the two families were harvesting the winter rice. It was a Sunday, so the children had no school. The sky was blue as far as the eye could see, a light fresh breeze was blowing, wildflowers were blooming abundantly on the banks of the ditches, and bees were flying busily above them. All over the fields were people at work, while the sprightly song of the hulling machine could be heard all around.

Under the hibiscus the children were playing "getting married." Yunying took the part of the bride, and Huosheng was the groom. They had woven a veil out of grass stalks and hibiscus sprouts and made a big "bridal spray" from hibiscus blooms and wildflowers. The groom had a single hibiscus flower on his chest. But what was to be the bride's conveyance? This was a problem. Bridal sedans were out of fashion, and anyway our bride was against them on principle. But they didn't have an automobile, so what could they do? In the end they had to settle for two of the boys linking hands to make a sedan for the bride. At first Yunying absolutely refused, but finally she gave in under pressure from the others and sat down in the "sedan," wearing the veil and holding her bouquet. The sedan went round in three circles before delivering her to Huosheng. So that was that.

"Let the bridegroom knock on the door of the sedan!" intoned the matchmaker solemnly. Then: "It is time for the bride to enter her new home!"

Huosheng symbolically tapped Yunying three times on the head with a twig they pretended was a fan. The bride alighted from her sedan. Next the little couple knelt shoulder to shoulder in front of a stone to "do obeisance to the ancestors," and when that was finished they turned around and "did obeisance to Heaven and Earth."

Throughout this "ceremony" Yunying held her head low, a picture of shyness; Huosheng, too, had suddenly gone all awkward and dumb, every bit the panic-stricken bridegroom. Still, the two of them happily went along with the performance, never hesitating or hanging back.

Later, after the evening meal, Yunying accidentally slid down a bank into a ditch. Luckily the water was only up to her calves. Some of the others put up a clamor, teasing Huosheng: "Hey! Your wife's fallen in the ditch! Come on, quickly get in there and help her out!"

These words let the cat out of the bag. The "newlyweds" both flushed scarlet with embarrassment. Huosheng stood at the top of the bank, blinking and hesitating; Yunying climbed up the bank as quick as she could and rushed off to hide.

Everybody bellowed with laughter at the sight; the grownups in particular couldn't stop laughing. . . .

Yunying thought about the past as she walked. She also kept worrying she might bump into Zhengang. When she reached Back Street she finally felt safe and slowed her pace. Ahead were fields and farms; as she crossed a little bridge her home came in sight.

They had just finished eating when Zhengang appeared in the front doorway. Both physically robust and very self-assured, this young man worked in the Registry at the Town Hall. His limbs were strong and vigorous, like a basketball player. Today he was wearing a white shirt with a stiff, starched collar, gray serge trousers, and leather shoes. His father, one of the richest men in the district, owned a general store and a hardware store. His mother and Yunying's mother called each other "sister"; their relationship was actually quite distant but still passed for kinship hereabouts. So Zhengang addressed Yunying's father, Huang Jinde, as "Uncle" and her mother as "Auntie." Yunying's feelings about these terms of address were like her feelings for the boy himself: a vague distaste.

"Uncle! Auntie!" Zhengang called out as he entered, just like one of the family.

Jinde responded coolly, but his wife was all smiles as she rose to meet the lad.

"Aha! Zhengang," she said. "It's been quite a while since we've seen you here."

"Recently we've been checking the register household by household. We're run off our feet."

"Is that so? I thought you'd forgotten your old auntie."

Zhengang gave a laugh.

"There's a good movie on tonight at the old theater," he said. "I'd like to take you all to see it. Yunying, just now I went to your shop, but they said you'd already gone home."

Yunying kept her head low and smiled but did not reply.

"I suppose it's a foreign movie?" Jinde's wife screwed up her eyes as she spoke. "I won't understand it. I like movies from Taiwan."

"It'll have Chinese subtitles. I can read them out to you in Hakka." Beseechingly, earnestly he turned his gaze to Yunying and said: "You're free tonight, aren't you?"

"Oh, I'm sorry, Mr. Chen." Startled, Yunying spoke hurriedly. "I'm not free tonight."

"Really?" Zhengang didn't know whether to believe her or not.

"Yes, really," said Yunying in all seriousness. "A friend of mine from the shop asked me to go round to hers tonight to cut some material for a dress."

"Can't you do that tomorrow?" Yunying's mother came to Zhengang's aid.

"No! I promised her. I'm sorry, Mr. Chen," said Yunying, smiling sweetly. "Perhaps another day."

"Oh, what a pity," said Zhengang, disappointment showing in his face. "It's a really good movie."

"Another day, then, Zhengang," Yunying's mother said consolingly. "And anyway I don't like foreign movies."

Zhengang stayed a little longer, before going away with his tail between his legs.

Yunying went in to her own room to do her hair and face in the mirror.

She had a lovely slim figure, a heart-shaped face with a tiny mouth like a cherry, and perfect teeth. Her eyes were like deep crystal-clear ponds, with near-black irises; when they moved a cold gleam flashed in every direction, sharp enough to pierce the heart of whomever she chose—like daggers. Few young men would not suffer palpitations and lose their composure if they found themselves the object of that gaze.

Yunying applied neither powder nor mascara, because she knew that Huosheng preferred her as nature intended. She merely adjusted her hair with her fingers and put on a floral dress with a white Peter Pan collar.

She walked to the small ice parlor on the east side of the school. Just as she reached the door a youth came out, a handsome young man with a bright lively light in his eyes. The life and ardor of youth beamed out of him.

It was Xu Huosheng.

"Where shall we go?" asked Yunying.

"Let's go to the pictures," said Huosheng. "There's a good movie on tonight."

"No! No!"

Yunying seemed agitated, as if they were having an argument. Huosheng looked at her in surprise, obviously confused.

"It's too hot to be indoors," explained Yunying, making as if nothing was the matter. "Let's just walk around outside."

They met two girls from the tailor's who were on their way to the picture house. Each of them looked at Huosheng in surprise—their gazes were bold, even rude—and asked Yunying was she not going to see the movie? When Huosheng wasn't looking they pulled faces at her, but Yunying ignored them.

Avoiding the busy parts of town, they walked along streets that were mostly deserted. Here the street lamps were few and far between, and so it was dim as well as quiet. They came to a street with a stream along one side. Bamboo was growing on both banks. Across the stream the farmland began.

"I really don't like the way the girls from your shop look at me," said Huosheng as they walked. "The other day when I went there looking for you—you weren't at work that day—they all stared at me like something was wrong."

"Don't go there again."

"I'm not afraid of them staring."

"No, but you should hear their mouths."

"Do they talk about me?"

"Uh-huh."

"That's strange. Do they know me?"

"Yes, they do."

"What do they say about me?"

"They're really maddening."

Yunying didn't answer Huosheng's question directly, but he could pretty much imagine what they would say. Yunying's expression confirmed what he imagined, so he changed his tone: "You shouldn't pay them any attention."

"I don't pay them any attention, but it's embarrassing."

Yunying lowered her head and avoided his eyes as she spoke.

Later they started talking about the private lives of the girls at the tailor's: their families, love lives, marriages, and the way they dressed and made themselves up. Several of them were recently married, and were using the sewing machines in the shop to get free lessons in making up and sewing fabrics. These girls provided Yunying with plenty of romantic and dramatic material for conversation. She chattered happily and with relish. Huosheng listened attentively.

"There's a girl called Qiuju," she said. "Every day she comes to work, but instead of learning how to sew like the others, all she does is put her head in her hands on the sewing bench and cry."

Huosheng nodded slightly to indicate that he was listening.

"She has a sweetheart and the two of them have sworn to marry none other, but her parents say the boy's family is poor: they're forcing her to marry someone else. She'll be married in another fortnight."

"Why doesn't she resist?" Huosheng interjected.

"She is resisting! She's been crying for days now, and not eating, but her parents won't listen. Everyone at the shop is totally on her side: some of them are urging her to elope, others tell her to go to the Women's Association."

"How old is she?"

"Twenty. That's old enough for her to make her own decisions, isn't it?"

"Uh-huh," Huosheng was getting interested. "And what does she say?"

"She doesn't say anything, just cries all the harder. It's pathetic." Yunying was disappointed, sad, and indignant all at once.

"How can there still be parents like that in this day and age?" sighed Huosheng. "Really, it's too bad."

"Well, she should have a bit more guts herself."

"So you think they're too weak, do you?"

"Yeah. They should just take off."

"If it were you," said Huosheng, ardently looking her straight in the eye, "is that what you'd do?"

Yunying didn't answer, but from her eyes there shone two piercing beams of light that could not be mistaken.

They had reached a small, low bridge, beyond which the farmland began; this was Yunying's road home. They sat on the parapet for a while, then went their separate ways.

4

There was no change in the weather: it was very hot, and every day at nine or ten o'clock the sky would fill with gray rainclouds, which then gradually grew thicker and denser. The sun shone down on them from above, neither bright nor dark but murky and dim. The heat was oppressive; the uncertain light played tricks on the nervous system, making people irritable and ill-at-ease.

Straight after midday the gray clouds would pile up even higher and then spread out to cover the sky more evenly. Some of them were distinguishable as separate clouds, and these began to come lower and lower.

Then the wind would begin to blow. It blew fiercely and wildly, blasting this way and that across the fields, along the streets and through the woods, howling angrily. It tore up piles of dead and dying leaves from the trees as if it were plucking out stray pieces of wadding from a quilt. Now and then it created a miniature tornado, whirling from all sides round and round a focal point. Sand and grit, dust and leaves were sucked up and went floating high, high, and far into the distance. The heavens were thrown into a yellow, turbid chaos, while the sun grew even dimmer.

At night no moon or stars were visible, except for a few flecks of stars seen fitfully through the clouds, but they too were very dim, like underpowered lightbulbs.

Halfway through the night the heat slowly began to lessen. The air gradually grew cooler, and the dust dropped back down from the sky.

Little by little the sky turned from dim as ditchwater to clear as a bell. Then it went to crystal-clear, pure and pristine; and finally it was all over deep, deep blue again.

The moon and the stars came out again.

Next morning brought the return of the big, red ball of the sun, and so it all began again.

The paddy, the sweet potatoes, and even the astragalus were getting yellower, browner, and more shriveled every day. The cracks in the earth were increasing in number, width, depth, and whiteness. There wasn't a drop for watering, and the farmers were at their wits' end. There was no more need for fighting among themselves over water supplies; there wasn't even any need to check their fields.

In the fields not yet planted there was no longer any point in doing so; the leafy things in the paddy that had been planted just huddled together in the field, gasping, withering, and dying.

Even drinking water had become a problem in town. Because of the drop in water levels the flow of water from the cistern inlets was now as thin as a little boy's stream of pee. When the sun was at its hottest and highest in the sky, the flow would dry up completely and people had to climb into the cistern and scoop up water from the bottom. Squatting there, it took them half an hour to fill a bucket, half a ladle at a time. At every cistern in town there were long lines day and night. And from those lines there frequently arose the raucous din of disputes over the water—arguments, swearing, fighting, howling, weeping, and the shrill cries of women.

One evening, when the Huangs were at table, they suddenly heard the sound of gongs being beaten in the town. Several fields lay between their home and the town, so they could hear the gongs but not what the gong beaters were crying. The eldest of Yunying's younger brothers went to see what was going on; when he came back he reported that it was an announcement from the Ping'an Gong: the whole town was to say five days of prayers for rain, and during the period of prayers everyone in the entire township must fast. No meat could be eaten and no animals slaughtered or butchered.

"Too late!" said Huang Jinde with feeling. "The paddy's already burned dry; it'll be no use, even if the prayers do produce rain."

His wife snorted and said unhappily: "Maybe you aren't going to do any planting, but others surely will!"

He glared at her but said nothing.

Then she asked: "That summons from the Town Hall today: what do they want you for?"

"That was from the Township Arbitration Commission. Luo Ding-rui has put in a complaint against me."

"What's his complaint?"

"It's about that bamboo, isn't it! Damn him, I should complain about him, not the other way around."

"If you didn't cut his bamboo, why would he complain?"

"If I cut his, whose did he cut? You'll see, when the day comes I'm sure going to make him look stupid."

That night the sky was very turbid, with only two or three stars blinking weakly. The sky and the earth seemed to form a huge furnace. Whatever you touched was roasting hot, and the heat just kept rising from the ground.

Yunying finished putting away the dishes, took off her apron, and was getting ready to go out when her mother called to her: "Going out again?"

"A friend at work invited me to the pictures," said Yunying.

"You're always going to the pictures," said her mother with a stern look. "A girl like you, always gadding about town, aren't you afraid of gossip?"

Her daughter smiled. "I won't be late."

"You'll chop the sweet potato leaves for the pigs first, then you can go. I don't have time to do it."

It took Yunying hours to finish chopping the pig greens; as soon as it was done she threw down the chopping knife and ran out.

Huosheng was still waiting for her in the ice parlor.

"Have you been waiting really long?" asked Yunying apologetically.

He only smiled.

And so they set off to walk on the edge of town and stroll among the fields. Through the hazy night air Yunying saw many dark shapes to the west of them, heading north. They were people heading for The Temple of Goodness and Enlightenment.

"Let's go to the Temple of Goodness and take a look," said Yunying.

"Last night my brother and I stood in line all night," said Huosheng as they walked on, following a small farm road leading toward the foot of the hills. "It was dawn before we managed to get a couple of buckets of water."

"How come the two of you had to do it? What about your sister-in-law?"

"The baby's ill."

"You won't be doing it again tonight, will you?"

"Yes, we will."

"Well then, you'd better go get some sleep."

"I'm alright."

"Take care you don't get sick," Yunying said with concern, turning to look at him. "Lots of people are falling ill."

"That's because of this abnormal weather, isn't it?"

From the direction of the temple they heard the sound of gongs and drums, accompanied by the clamor of people's voices, but the latter was very low and distant and sometimes completely drowned out by the percussion.

"Saying their prayers!" said Huosheng.

"Probably some of them are saying prayers for the sick," said Yunying.

"Perhaps they're praying for rain."

At the roadside some of the fields had been planted out with rice, but there was no water for the sprouts to stand in, and they were all bowing their heads, motionless. The other fields bore only weeds.

Suddenly Yunying thought of something. She looked up.

"Huosheng!"

"What?"

"A few days ago," she said, "I heard my pa talking about your land. They said you were going to return it to the landlord to be sold on. Is that true?"

"Return the land?" asked Huosheng, baffled. "Surely not? Our fields are 375 Land."

"Haven't you heard anything about it?"

"No. I'd better ask."

"Yes, you'd better. My pa's very unhappy about it. He says you're being really stupid."

By now they had reached the temple. They walked inside.

5

After the evening meal Huosheng asked his elder brother, Tusheng, to come into his room.

"I've heard that our fields are to be returned to the landlord," he said. "Is it true?"

"Mm."

Huosheng was taken aback. He had actually thought the rumor might be false, but now here was the proof; he couldn't help feeling indignant, and also a little flustered.

"Why should we return the land?" he asked.

"It's Ma's idea," said his brother, scratching his ears in confusion.

Once again Huosheng was taken aback. He couldn't help being amazed at his brother for being so calm and offhand about a matter almost of life-and-death importance to their whole family. The more he thought about it the angrier he became. He just stared and stared at Tusheng.

"And do you agree to returning the land?" he said, after a long silence.

"I dunno," replied Tusheng in the same dull tone.

"How can Ma be so stupid? If we give back our fields what will we farm?"

Tusheng looked displeased. After brooding for a moment he answered: "It's Youfu who wants her to do it," he said, keeping his eyes on the floor. "If we return the land, the landlord will give us some money."

At the name "Youfu" Huosheng clammed right up. A faint expression of pain and resentment rose up to his face.

"But it's 375 Land, the landlord can't just take it back; he's not allowed, don't you know that?"

"Today I went with the landlord to the legal clerks' office; the land clerk told us to make an application to the Land Rents Commission to apply for arbitration; then when it comes to arbitration the landlord will make a statement saying we are four seasons behind in rent, which means he can take back the land. The commission will ask us if it's true, and then all we have to say is 'Yes!'"

"Do we really owe four seasons' rent?" asked Huosheng in alarm.

"No."

"So why should we say we do?"

"The legal clerks say if we don't say so the landlord won't be able to repossess the land."

"So we're colluding with the landlord to distort the facts?"

"Mm."

"How much is the landlord giving us?"

"Ten thousand yuan."

"Have you submitted the application yet?"

"Not yet."

"Ma's being so dumb; you're all really dumb!" Huosheng cried furiously, jumping up. "I'm going to see Ma. I'm against what you're doing—you should be against it too; we've just got to nip this whole thing in the bud."

As he spoke Huosheng was already on his way to his mother's room.

"Ma, I've just been talking to Tusheng," he said as soon as he found his mother, with no beating about the bush. "I don't understand why you want to return our land to Fu."

His mother seemed unsure of herself and ill-at-ease. She stared blankly at her son's face for some time. He seemed worked up and was clearly on edge. From his expression she could see that he already knew everything from Tusheng, so at least she was saved the bother of explaining it to him.

"If we return our fields to the landlord," said the young man, "what will we farm ourselves?"

"We still have our own two-tenths to farm, don't we?"

"What good is two-tenths to a farming family?"

His mother sighed.

"Huosheng," she said, looking at her son. "It's not that I want to return the land. There's nothing else I can do. Can you guess who wants to buy the land? It's Luo Dingrui."

"Luo Dingrui?"

"That's right, Luo Dingrui," said his mother. "You know full well that when Tusheng was getting married we didn't have enough money, so we borrowed five thousand yuan from Luo, with our two-tenths of a *jia* as security. The due date for repaying the loan is long past now, and he's pressing us for it. He says if we don't have the money he'll have the land auctioned to settle the matter. Several times I've asked people to speak up for us, to get us another couple of months. Recently Luo sent someone to tell us the landlord is interested in selling the 375 Land to him; all we need to do is ask Fu to repossess the land from us. Luo says if we do that he won't ask us to repay the five thousand, in fact he'll give us another five thousand—that's ten thousand altogether, and he's not asking for any interest."

"We don't need his ten thousand."

"Right! We don't need his money, but we can't not return the money we owe him, don't you see?"

"All we need is to fatten a few pigs and we'll have enough to repay him."

The young man spoke rudely. His mother smiled bitterly.

"Huosheng, don't you think I'd rather repay his money than return our land? But think about it seriously: how are we going to return the money?"

Huosheng was stuck for words.

"This is what we've been told to do," said his mother. "They say if we do this we'll actually do quite well out of it."

"Ma, you always believe other people's nonsense," Huosheng said angrily. "Whatever they say you obey—you're like grass bending in the wind."

When Huosheng had talked about repaying the debt with a few pigs he had spoken out of anger, without thinking it through. As soon as he'd said it he felt sorry and somewhat ashamed, but when he heard his mother talking about "them," he couldn't help getting angry again. He realized who "they" were: "they" meant Tang Youfu, the last name in the world he wanted to hear. Of course he didn't need his mother to tell him, he knew there must be someone in the background putting her up to all this, and he knew perfectly well who that someone was. However, in general he was a very dutiful son, so although just now in a moment of anger he had talked back to his mother, this was partly a way of venting the negative feelings bottled up inside him. Once more, as soon as the words were out he regretted it.

For his mother's part, she was perfectly clear that the "other people" Huosheng spoke of were none other than her own "they." Like a prisoner hearing her own death sentence pronounced, she was immediately beset with feelings of despair and pain, and her face turned pale.

She began to cry.

Huosheng stood up. He was remorseful and angry with himself. He tried several times to ask for forgiveness, but the words would not come. Silently he walked out of his mother's room.

The following evening, when he and Yunying were together again, she could see the depression and anger in his face.

As before, they were walking along dimly lit, unfrequented streets. Neither of them spoke. Yunying tried a few times to lift the stifling atmosphere but without success. They hadn't been walking for long when Huosheng said he had to go and stand in line for water, so he saw her home.

6

The Arbitration Commission met at the Town Hall. The Sun Yat-sen Room was transformed into a temporary courtroom by the setting up of a dozen or so long tables and chairs, stools, and benches for thirty people; between sessions the furniture was simply removed.

When Huang Jinde entered, there were only six commissioners and a dozen or so parties to arbitration, but as arbitration got under way another two commissioners and some more people involved in cases arrived. The eight commissioners sat in high-backed rattan armchairs at a row of long tables; in the middle of the row was an especially large chair with an extra-high back, in which sat an old gentleman of over sixty. This was the chairman, a man named Lai. His white eyebrows were very long, like an insect's feelers; they quivered whenever he spoke. His eyes were very small and his face gleamed red. He wore a white hip-length cotton overshirt with cloth fastenings. On his left was another old man of much the same age, who wore glasses and had a very dignified demeanor. The other commissioners were all younger men between thirty and fifty.

In front of the long tables were several rows of benches where the twenty or thirty people involved in cases sat themselves down without ceremony. Most of them were not much interested in anyone's case but their own, and so when they were not personally involved they would turn round in their seats and chat with people they knew; this meant that when arbitration was going on the commissioners and parties to the case would have to raise their voices. Sometimes there would be a call to order. It was only when a case involving members of opposite sexes was being investigated that everyone's attention would be aroused. Excitement and curiosity would show on their faces as they stared open-mouthed and listened with great appreciation to the words of the commission and the parties involved.

The first case was an application for medical compensation. The applicant was Li A-Gou, and the respondent Li Tianzeng. Li A-Gou said that his son had suffered grievous bodily harm at the hands of Li Tianzeng's son in a dispute over water and had been hospitalized for a full month. He had spent altogether five thousand yuan and demanded compensation in full. However, the hospital receipts that he held amounted to only eight hundred yuan. When a commissioner asked him how the other four thousand two hundred yuan had been spent, Li A-Gou gave a dozen incidences of expenditure, including travel costs, caregivers' expenses, manpower loss during his son's injury, and so on and so forth.

"If he hadn't been injured would he have been working?" asked the chairman. "We're in the middle of a drought, there's no work to be done in the fields: everybody's idle."

"He could've gone logging," said A-Gou.

"Oh no, that won't do," the chairman quickly put him right. "That's against the law."

In this case the arbitration fell because of the disparity between the sums sought and offered.

The next case concerned the intent to divorce of a couple who had been married less than three months. In a trice the entire hall fell silent. All eyes focused on the parties to the case, especially the young woman. She wore a peach-colored blouse, black trousers, gold rings, golden buttons, and a gold bracelet—she gleamed and sparkled from head to toe: very much the bewitching new bride.

The chairman asked her why she was applying for divorce.

The young woman rose to answer. At first she came over as rather shy, but she spoke clearly and didn't beat about the bush.

"His whole family maltreated me," she said.

Before she had even finished speaking an old woman suddenly sprang up from a corner and began yelling at her. This was the mother-in-law. The commissioners gestured at her and asked her to speak quietly, saying this was no place to have a row: everyone must wait his turn to speak. But it was no use. So the young wife turned round to face her mother-in-law and loudly defended herself. The two women were equally formidable, equally ferocious, equally sharp-tongued and foul-mouthed; truly it was an encounter between worthy rivals. The proceedings descended into chaos. The commissioners could only sit back in their chairs, completely stumped. A few times, when the ferocity of the exchange between the two women seemed to lessen somewhat, there was an attempt at recommencing the arbitration. But every time, after no more than a few exchanges, the women started quarreling again as if the commission wasn't there at all. The waves of noise created by the women's cursing and their onlookers' hearty laughter almost brought the walls of the Sun Yat-sen Hall crashing down.

This whole time, the young husband sat at his mother's side, a dumb spectator at the women's "debate," not showing any reaction.

There was no doubting that the husband's physiological state was an important contributing factor in the case.

Comparing his almost idiotic appearance to the young woman's vigor and fortitude, one of the commissioners shook his head and turned to the man beside him. "That's a real feisty mare," he said quietly. "She needs an able rider; that husband of hers ain't up to it."

Arbitration failed in this case, as in the previous one.

Next it was their turn: Huang Jinde versus Luo Dingrui.

Luo Dingrui only turned up half an hour before the case was called. All the commissioners were very polite toward him, rising halfway out of their chairs to greet him. One of them moved a rattan chair in front of the rows of benches for him to sit in. He accepted this honor without demur and sat himself down, as if he were not one of the parties to a case but rather some kind of juror.

Luo was a man in his fifties, and his hair was already gray and white. He was very plump, and the tails of his eyebrows fell to the corners of his eyes to give them the shape of tadpoles. His lips were very fleshy, but the lower one drooped, lending a base, mean expression to his otherwise noble appearance. He was rural gentry, a leading figure in local society. Many people showed him respect to his face but behind his back they spat in contempt when his name was mentioned. During the Japanese Occupation he had held important office in the Town Council's militia department. With such great power in his hands he had become a truly great figure in this township. What he said went, and none could touch him in his magnificence. After Japan surrendered, when those who had been unfairly or wrongly conscripted returned from the battlefield or from Japan's colonies, they went fully armed looking for Luo. Some said they wouldn't stop till they'd butchered this "running dog." So Luo ran off to hide out in Taipei and Tainan for a few years. He didn't dare come back until the hatred had dampened down.

The chairman first cleared his throat a few times, and then did his best to put on a smiling face. Rubbing his hands together, he looked first at one of the two parties to the case, then at the other, then back again.... Trying to speak as moderately and peaceably as possible, he first asked Luo Dingrui to explain the reasons for his complaint. When Luo had finished the chairman turned to Huang Jinde, again rubbing his hands together as he spoke: "Just now Mr. Luo said you cut some of his bamboo. I expect you didn't notice the boundary, it was a mistake, wasn't it?"

"No, I didn't make any mistake," said Jinde categorically.

Now Luo Dingrui spoke again: "That other time when you cut bamboo I thought, well, we're all friends here, so I paid it no heed. But now you've done it again: that's really very unreasonable of you."

Sitting back in his chair with his palms pressed together, he looked at no one, but conveyed a most magnanimous air.

Jinde turned to face him. His eyes glared, big and round, as he solemnly asked: "Hey, are you certain the bamboo I cut was yours?"

"If it weren't mine, would I say a word?"

"Did you get a surveyor in?"

"It's been surveyed in the past."

Huang Jinde leapt to his feet. He cupped his crotch in both hands and made to fling it in Luo's face.

"Pah!" he spat. "You're like my ****!"

The entire hall went into shock; in an instant a solemn hush filled the air.

"Mr. Huang, Mr. Huang," the chairman began waving his hands to stop him. "This isn't a place for brawling. Whatever is to be said, let's discuss it properly."

But Jinde's fury knew no limits. He was gnashing his teeth, his eyes were bulging out of his head, and with his right forefinger he kept stabbing at his opponent's forehead, swearing viciously. On his temples and his neck every single one of his blue veins stood out fit to burst.

"Luo Dingrui," Jinde was burning all over. "What did you say? I cut your bamboo? You're like my ****!" Again he made to fling his nether parts in Luo's face. "It was my own bamboo I cut. Even if I crossed the boundary, that would've been publicly owned bamboo, not Luo Dingrui's, so what are you so smug about? If I did cut a few lengths of public bamboo to repair my pigsty, that's no big deal. Even if I broke the law, I'm only a petty thief. But you, Luo Dingrui, you've stolen whole big truckloads of publicly owned timber, truck after truck. Do you think I don't know? I'm asking you, what happened to all those trees on the land I rent from the Forestry Bureau? Who felled them? Huh! You might fool others, but Huang Jinde won't be made a fool of. If the law takes a petty thief like me, I'll get three days inside at most. But for a great brigand like you, it'll be a year at the very least. If you don't believe me, just try it!"

Although Jinde spoke very quickly, there was no mistaking what he said. His words poured out like water from a bucket, and the quicker he needed to speak, the more Japanese he mixed in with his rudimentary Mandarin. Every phrase was clear and forceful, as if it would strike the ground with a ringing sound, or as if it would bounce. As he spoke his head, nose, and lips twisted to one side and his eyes started from his head. His whole person emitted a ferocious force, cowing his adversary. When he finished speaking he closed his mouth tightly: his lips were stretched thin and his eyes were fixed on the ground in front of him, blinking sternly. These facial contortions lent a further power of conviction to his words. This Huang Jinde was clearly even more vigorous and expressive than the Huang Jinde who made the speech.

The atmosphere in the meeting room became very tense. Everyone was riveted by Huang Jinde's performance; they wore the expressions of people who had just licked an ice cream on a sweltering day. A similar expression could even be glimpsed on the faces of some of the younger commissioners, try to hide it as they might.

Again the chairman waved his arms in an attempt to stop Huang Jinde, but to no avail.

"Think about it," Jinde began again. "How many people did you bully and humiliate in the time of the Japanese? If you hadn't scuttled off pretty damn quick after the Surrender, I for one would've cut off your head, or at least cut off your heels, do you know that? Yet you still have the nerve to go on living? Don't you understand shame? Huh?!"

At first Luo Dingrui tried several times to interrupt, but he was overawed by his opponent's powerful performance. And anyway he couldn't get a word in edgeways. All he could do was sit in his rattan chair, smiling superciliously from time to time, maintaining the serenity of the wise. Before long, however, the serenity disappeared: his face gradually changed color, and large drops of sweat began to pour from his adipose face.

"Enough, Mr. Huang," the chairman gestured to Jinde to stop. "Let's not bring up matters of the past."

"Haha! It may be 'enough' for him, but I won't be forgetting."

Jinde cocked his head to one side, drew his lips tightly closed, and then added: "You won't accept my words. So sue me! I'll be waiting." He stood up. "I don't have any more time now, excuse me!"

With a parting wave toward the commissioners, Huang Jinde swaggered out of Sun Yat-sen Hall.

7

That evening Chen Zhengang came again to invite Yunying to the movies. When he said it was a Taiwanese movie her mother was delighted and immediately accepted the invitation. Yunying had wanted to refuse, but because she had turned him down last time it seemed rude to do so again tonight. It was really very awkward.

She sat in a daze at her mirror by the window, uncertain what to do. Only after her mother had chivied her several times did she come out of her room, listlessly. Later at the picture house she couldn't keep her mind on the movie; she just kept thinking about Huosheng waiting forlornly for her in the ice parlor. She was sure he would have got fed up waiting—perhaps by now he would already have left and gone home. Or perhaps he would be wandering the streets alone. Oh! How lonely it must be for him, how solitary and bleak!

These thoughts made her as anxious as an ant in a hot wok; she was desperate to get away. Normally at the movies she felt the picture went by very quickly: it always seemed that she had no sooner taken her seat than the movie was over. But tonight she found the picture agonizingly long. On and on it went, scene after scene after never-ending scene. It seemed an eternity before the lights finally went up. She breathed a sigh of relief.

As they left the picture house Zhengang suggested a bite to eat. Yunying's mother was inclined to go along with this, but Yunying hurriedly said she had left something at a friend's house and had to go and fetch it. She left them and rushed off toward the ice parlor beside the school. But when she got there she was told Huosheng had left half an hour earlier.

Next day at noon Yunying finished work early and went to the TTL offices in the west part of town to wait for Huosheng in the arcade next door. She hadn't been standing there very long when he arrived.

"I guess you waited an awful long time last night?" she asked apologetically.

"Two hours," said Huosheng.

"Are you angry with me?" she asked. Then she told him that her mother had asked her to do something last night, and that when she finished what she had to do and went to the ice parlor, he had already left.

Huosheng seemed to believe her and made no comment.

Yunying was relieved.

Huosheng suggested they have a meal together and then visit the Ping'an Gong afterward. Yunying gladly agreed, which made Huosheng very happy.

The Ping'an Gong was not far to the east of the TTL office, past a gurgling river on the banks of which large green bamboos cast their dense shade. An altar had earlier been set up on the square in front of the temple and now an offering table stood in front of it. Above on the altar sat the gods—the Three Mountain Kings and the Bodhisattva Guanyin; below on the offering table were pure sacrifices, including fruit and candy. Incense smoke billowed up from the burner, pungent roiling clouds spreading far and near.

A few of the oldest men of the town knelt in the front row, dressed from head to toe in mourning; behind them and to either side knelt many more townsmen, every one of them bareheaded under the fierce sun. They knelt there with eyes half-closed, their faces brightly flushed to the tips of their ears. Drops of sweat the size of soybeans dripped down like rain from their skulls, their temples, and their necks. A sense of determination was written in their brows, kneaded in with a tragic heroism and reverence. It gave their faces an expression that was both hard and soft, humble yet stubborn. Their desire was that the naked, childlike innocence of their hearts would move Heaven and that their sincerity would move the gods to dispense sweet dew: give a little moisture to their parched fields. If Heaven did not receive their prayers, they were prepared to fall down with heatstroke where they knelt, to let the gods see how cruel and pitiless they were.

But Heaven seemed to be deliberately playing tricks on the suffering people. The last couple of days it had called in its black clouds and now the sky was an endless sheet of bright blue. The fierce ball of the sun spewed flame on the earth below, burning up everything. Everything either absorbed or reflected the fire, and even the wind was hot. The very air that people breathed was like hot water.

Some people surreptitiously looked up at the color of the sky; some of them were cursing.

The sound of chanting rose.

Somebody sprinkled a few drops of water on the earth.

Some people stood up, brushed down their clothes, and left without a word. No doubt these were people with things to do. Their places were immediately taken by even more people.

Women dressed in traditional smocks had for once turned down the sleeves to their full length and untucked the bottom hem from their belts.[7]

People spoke as little as possible, and at that only in very low voices. At the slightest hint of blasphemy or offense against good order, how-

---

7. The traditional dress for Hakka women, the *lanshan* 藍衫 (blue shirt), was usually worn with sleeves rolled to the elbow and bottom hem gathered up to the waist, even when the wearer was not working.

ever, they would immediately express the utmost indignation in the sternest of rebukes.

A man on a bicycle rode past at the edge of the square. His offense was that he was wearing his bamboo hat. Angry roars rose up from among the crowd: "Hey! Hey!! Get the hat off!"

The man seemed not to hear, or perhaps he heard but didn't realize it was himself that they addressed. He paid not a bit of attention.

"Hey!" the angry roars rose up again, now even louder. "Didn't you hear? Are you deaf? Get your hat off!"

The man stopped. Now it seemed he had heard, but didn't understand what it was about. He stood there, baffled, looking at the crowd, not knowing what to do. Obviously he was not from around here and didn't know that prayers for rain were being said.

A few men darted out from the crowd, roughly snatched the hat from the man's head and chucked it on the ground.

"Damn you, are you deaf? Are you blind?" Several voices roared at once.

The man flared up. He put his bike on its stand and went to grab the man who had flung down his hat. Just then an old man parted the crowd and stepped into the circle.

"Hey, Mister," said the old man, all smiles. "Don't be angry. We're praying for rain here."

Many voices rose up all around:

"Wallop him!"

"Send him flying!"

The masses were now agitated, ready to explode at any moment.

The man realized the situation and was overawed by the menace of the crowd. Meekly he picked up his hat, hung it on his handlebar, and walked away.

After that, in similar circumstances, they seized two umbrellas and countless hats.

The people had become volatile and irascible. The fierce sun continued to inflame the mood further. Their eyes were full of blood and shone with a fearful light; they were like a pack of hungry wolves.

"Is the rain mass over now?" asked Yunying.

"Yes," said Huosheng.

Following the crowd they made their way to the altar, where each lit an incense stick, bowed in prayer, and planted the sticks in the burner. As they were squeezing out through the crush they saw Huang Jinde. Yunying, walking in front, saw him first.

"Pa, are you burning incense too?"

Yunying's expression was somewhat unnatural and her voice sounded a bit strange, but Huang Jinde didn't detect this. He grunted a vague greeting.

Then he saw a young man appear from behind his daughter's back.

"Hello, Sworn-uncle," Huosheng said politely.

"Ah, Huosheng, you here too," was all Jinde said, rather coolly.

He'd always been fond of this young man for his intelligence and lively spirit, and he'd been pleased for his blood brother that he had a worthy heir, but right now he had a troubled feeling when he saw Huosheng.

Jinde and the two young people parted after a few words of conversation. Jinde had only gone a few steps, however, when something occurred to him. He turned back toward Huosheng to ask: "Is your ma at home?" But Huosheng and Yunying had already been swallowed up by the crowd.

Two hours later Jinde arrived at the *bantiao* restaurant by the clock. Inside, the stoves had not been lit, the kitchen was cold and quiet, and the owner, A-Geng, was in the middle of a lazy yawn. Three men were idly chatting at the table on the left by the wall, Li A-Xing among them. Jinde said hello.

"Not open today?" he asked the owner.

"It's the fast," the owner replied sluggishly.

"Do restaurants have to observe the fast too?" Jinde was rather surprised.

"There's no meat, so we've no choice."

"Strange."

"Aren't you fasting?"

"Fasting, my ass!" said Jinde coarsely, wiping his mouth with his palm. "But the last couple of days the wife's set on fasting this, fasting that; it's playing hell with my stomach. I'm dying for a proper meal."

A-Geng laughed. "Aren't you going to the Ping'an Gong?"

"Been already! But not to pray for rain—just to see the fun."

"Ah, everybody's there, kneeling and kowtowing. All the old folks, even the mayor's father."

"What a parcel of fools." Jinde lit a cigarette. "Kneeling . . . as if kneeling could bring down rain! Huh, damn tricksters!"

With that he rose and went over to the table by the wall.

"A-Xing," he said. "Is Longxiang's widow really going to return that land to the landlord?"

"Of course," said Li A-Xing. "They've already submitted their application for arbitration."

"Do you know who it is that wants to buy the land?"

"Luo Dingrui."

Jinde stopped short. Luo Dingrui! Him again! Why does he always have to cause trouble for me?

"He's bought several pieces of land," added Li A-Xing. "And each time he's used this same method."

"It's against the law."

"He's been very successful."

"When's the arbitration hearing?"

"Must be pretty soon now."

"You say Youfu's the middleman?"

"That's right. He's in for a pretty packet."

When Jinde left the restaurant he went straight to Longxiang's house at the eastern edge of town. The widow wasn't home, neither was Tusheng. Next, threading his way among the houses, Jinde came to Uncle A-San's tobacco shed. In the upstairs room he found two card games in progress. At one of them he saw Tang Youfu.

He sat and watched the game silently until it was over.

"Downstairs," he said to Youfu. "I want a word with you."

Youfu stood and followed him downstairs.

Youfu was middle-aged, average height, with thick eyebrows, a heavy beard, and a large nose. His eyes were constantly darting this way and that, as if there were always something on his mind. When he smiled, his eyes gleamed with a sly cunning.

When they got downstairs the two men stood facing one another. Youfu seemed already to have guessed what was on Jinde's mind, so he was mentally prepared. His face was alert with determination to deal with whatever was to come. His cunning showed in his eyes. He seemed to hold Huang Jinde in no special esteem.

"What've you got to say?" he asked haughtily.

Jinde made no reply and merely glared at Youfu. It was perfectly clear to him that Youfu's attitude was unfriendly, and he detected a certain tone of provocation in his voice.

He glared at Youfu again.

"I just want a word with you," he began. "I'm telling you, Youfu, I'm not happy about you colluding with Luo Dingrui to cheat that woman. For a long time now you've been feathering your nest at others' expense; enough now, you should stop. That land is the only livelihood they have left. You should let it be." He curled his lip and glowered at Youfu, his eyes flashing with venom. "That's all I have to say—you'd best mark it well."

He had said his piece without pausing for breath, giving Youfu no chance to interrupt. When he was finished, not caring whether Youfu had any rejoinder, he turned and walked out of the tobacco shed without a backward glance.

8

When the movie finished and the lights went back on overhead, Yunying remained seated. She forgot to stand up, as though intoxicated or in a trance.

She and Huosheng had been sitting shoulder to shoulder, so that she had been in a state of excitement from the very start. They sat very close, pressed tightly together, with only an armrest between them. From their shoulders to their feet they were stuck like glue, so that she felt a constant stream of heat coming from Huosheng's body and entering her own, spreading through her, making her breath come faster.

On the silver screen they'd seen the protracted leave-taking of a pair of lovers: in a garden under the starlight they clung to each other and hugged and kissed for ages. At this point Yunying had involuntarily leaned closer to Huosheng, her woman's heart beating as though it would burst out of her chest, and the blood surging up to the crown of her head. Her consciousness became blurred, and she fell into an absentminded, dazed state. Her eyes took nothing in, and her ears heard only a dull buzzing. Not until Huosheng said loudly, "Let's go," did she come to herself. Her cheeks were still ablaze.

She felt very embarrassed. She sneaked a look at Huosheng. There was a strange light in his eyes, but he appeared very calm, as though nothing had happened.

As they walked out onto the porch of the picture house, Yunying glimpsed a young man wearing a stiff-collared white shirt and gray serge trousers. It was Chen Zhengang. She thought of hiding behind a pillar, but it was too late.

"Oh, Miss Huang," he said. "Here for the movie?"

He also greeted Huosheng, but rather stiffly. His eyes were cold, you might even say hostile.

"Is the movie over?" he said, turning to Yunying again.

Yunying said yes and hurried off. She felt that Zhengang's attitude toward her this evening was rather unusual: she sensed a certain disaffection mingling with his intimate manner; his eyes seemed very polite and at the same time very impolite. His eyes and his attitude made her feel uneasy, troubled. Even when she had walked a good way off, she still felt the pressure of Zhengang's gaze on her back, like cold water pouring down her spine.

Coming onto the main street Huosheng suggested going for a cold drink or an ice, but Yunying said she was worried her mother would be cross if she were late and insisted on going home.

Huosheng walked her home. As they left the town behind, the lights grew fewer and further between and the sounds of the streets receded behind them. They had reached the seclusion and tranquility of the suburbs. Their two shapes dissolved into the shadows and all that could be heard was the scuff-scuffing sound of their feet.

When they reached the little bridge they sat down side by side on the parapet.

There were wispy rain clouds in the sky and a layer of dust in the air. The dust had not yet all fallen to ground, but it was spread very thin, allowing the gibbous moon and countless glittering stars to be seen, and their light to penetrate to the earth. The night was not gloomy, but soft and warm.

On the land there were a few lights thinly scattered all around, complementing the glow of moon and stars.

At any time the human world is beautiful, lovely, and full of tender feeling—and how much more so for a pair of lovers!

When she recalled the passionate scene in the movie Yunying's heart began drumming again. The blood rose up to her face and she involuntarily leaned in closer to Huosheng. Suddenly she felt her hands being taken in another pair of hands, her body being taken in a pair of arms and pressed against another body, and her mouth being subjected to a warm, sweet weight. In no way did she resist. This was exactly what she had inwardly been hoping for. She closed her eyes and gladly accepted it all.

The first kiss between lovers is an overwhelming, somersaulting joy. They kissed for a very long time. They kissed and kissed again and again. In this kiss they forgot themselves, forgot their troubles, forgot the world, and everything! They wanted to sink into this intoxication forever, never to sober up.

Some time passed before Yunying finally pulled away and broke the silence.

"Do you remember the girl I mentioned before?" she asked.

"Which girl?"

"Qiuju. From the tailor's."

"Oh. What about her?"

"She killed herself."

"Huh?!" Huosheng was shocked.

Then he added, "How did she do it?"

"Endrin."

"How ghastly!"

"We're all really upset."

"But how stupid she was! Did she really have to die?"

Yunying sighed softly. "When a woman can't see a way out that's what she'll do."

"That's so wrong-headed."

"Maybe so."

After that the pair fell silent, each sunk in their own thoughts.

Now and then footsteps went past on Back Street, not far from the little bridge. As of one mind, without a word, Yunying and Huosheng stood and walked into the farmland.

"Yunying," said Huosheng as they walked. "These days I can't stop thinking it would be best to get away from this place, to go out into the world."

"Where to?" Yunying hastily asked.

"Kaohsiung, or Taipei."

Yunying became more agitated. "Why?"

"Well, I find it hard to say why, but I just keep having these thoughts."

"You'd dump me here?"

"No! It's precisely because of us that I'm thinking about it."

"I don't understand you."

"I have a foreboding. I feel that our future holds many ordeals; things won't be smooth for us. Your father always used to like me a lot, but I know he's not going to like me anymore now."

Huosheng spoke with great certainty, as if he had given these matters deep and thorough thought.

Yunying didn't agree at all.

"It's true—he won't like me anymore," said Huosheng, a trace of pain flashing across his face. "Anyway, that's my foreboding."

"You're being too sensitive."

"Absolutely not. Yunying, I know I'm right about this. And your mother won't like me either. I know it." Again, Huosheng spoke with conviction. "Think about it. I'm only a minor clerk at TTL, with only a few hundred yuan a month, and no money in the family. Would they let us marry?"

"And so," Yunying retorted unhappily, "you're going to Kaohsiung? You're going to dump me here?"

"No!" Huosheng cried, beseechingly. "Let me finish."

"Don't bother." Yunying spoke crisply. "I've got just one thing to say to you: no matter how many reasons you can give, you just can't go!"

Huosheng fell silent, feeling that nothing he could say could change her mind.

"I'm afraid!" cried Yunying. "Don't leave me! If you leave me I'm finished."

She began to cry.

"Yunying," cried Huosheng in vexation.

"Don't say it." Yunying wiped her eyes with a handkerchief. "I don't want you to leave me."

All the way to Yunying's house the pair said not another word. Huosheng stood outside and watched her go through the front door before turning and walking off.

He felt exceedingly troubled, exceedingly remorseful.

9

The sun was heading west as Huang Jinde awoke on the spare bed in the *bantiao* restaurant. When A-Geng saw him coming out from the back room, he said in surprise, "Were you sleeping on the spare bed? How come I didn't see you come in?"

"I jimmied the door," said Jinde, smiling.

"Were you playing all night again?"

"Mm-hm."

Suddenly, the restaurateur lowered his voice and said mysteriously: "I've got some good stuff."

Going into the kitchen, he opened a drawer and brought out a selection of delicacies, including pig's trotters, kidneys, and liver, to show Jinde.

"See! Have a couple of trotters? Or will it be kidneys?"

"Oh! Good God Almighty!" Jinde's eyes were boggling. "That really is good stuff! Where did you get hold of it?"

"Outside."

The stove was already lit. Water was seething in the pot and steam was rising above it.

"So you're back in business, A-Geng."

"What the hell! If they want to pray for rain let 'em go and pray, but I need to sell my *bantiao*. If they ask me how I can just go ahead and sell meat I'll say I don't have any land to farm: selling *bantiao* is my livelihood, if I stay closed any longer my whole family will go hungry. Let the rain prayers say their rain prayers, let businessmen run their businesses! Isn't that right, Jinde?"

"That's right!"

"So I went outside the township to get some meat." A-Geng was cutting meat as he spoke. "In town everybody's fasting, no meat for them:

fine! But if I get customers from outside and I don't have any meat, how will that look? After all, this isn't a monastery I'm running, it's a *bantiao* shop."

The two men laughed heartily.

"I know you don't mind either way," said A-Geng. "You don't believe in all that mumbo-jumbo."

"Seems you're not much of a believer either!"

A-Geng placed a platter of sliced pig's trotter on the table, then brought a half-bottle of rice wine, a cup and a pair of chopsticks, and finally a saucer of soy sauce with crushed garlic.

"Me?" he said as he was arranging all this. "I have faith. But I still have to sell meat. Praying for rain and selling meat—I have to do both!"

Again the pair laughed loudly.

At the sight of the meat and drink on the table saliva was welling up in Jinde's mouth. Not wasting a moment more, he grabbed the chopsticks, picked up a large piece of meat, and stuffed it in his mouth.

"Hai!" he sighed as he chewed. "I've been so damn hungry."

Jinde had only just returned home from the restaurant when a woman came looking for him.

"Ahah! Sister Qingshou," Jinde exclaimed cheerfully. "What fair wind has blown you here today? Do you have some business with me?"

"If I didn't have business I wouldn't dare to come disturb you." Sister Qingshou wiped the betel nut juice from her chin and went on, all smiles, "I'm here to make a match for your daughter. Where's Sister Jinde?"

"Out back."

"What's she doing?"

"Feeding the pigs. My daughter's a tad young to be thinking of marriage, ain't she?"

"Oh, no. Do you know how old she is?"

"Um, seventeen?" Jinde replied uncertainly.

"Oh! What a clueless father you are! Your daughter's nineteen already."

"So, you know better than me!" Jinde said, raising his eyebrows and staring at her.

"Hee-hee, of course I know," Sister Qingshou chuckled with glee. "In this town I know it all: the ages of the daughters in every family, their looks, their education.... Otherwise, what sort of matchmaker would I be?"

"So you know what school my daughter went to?"

"That's easy! She graduated from the local junior high, didn't she?" Jinde laughed out loud.

After a pause, he asked, "What family is this you're making a match for?"

"A good family," said Sister Qingshou, calmly taking her time. "They have a general store and a hardware shop; the boy works in the Town Hall."

"Haha, come right out with it; don't give me riddles!"

"Chen Qichang's son."

"Zhengang?"

"That's right, he's the one!" cried Sister Qingshou exultantly, giving her chin another wipe. "A pretty good match, wouldn't you say? As for the boy: he's clever, educated, and has a good job. And the family: they have money, they have land, they have shops: all year round they have 'dry fuel and white rice, plenty of salt and ample vinegar'—they don't have to worry about a thing. Your family and theirs are perfectly matched, just right to be joined by marriage."

"How old is Zhengang?"

"Twenty-two."

"How come the son of a wealthy family is still single at twenty-two?"

"Don't you know? It's the wealthy families that find it difficult to get brides! Their boys have high standards: they might see any number of girls and never see one they like."

"So he likes Yunying?"

"Oh yes. Marriage is something that can't be forced."

"Did the Chen family ask you to come?"

"That they did, Brother Jinde."

"Alright then!" Jinde wanted to end the conversation. "Go and see Yunying and her ma. I have nothing against it. As long as mother and daughter are happy, it's fine by me."

After the woman had gone Jinde lit a cigarette and walked outside. By now it was quite late in the afternoon. The earth in the fields on both sides of the lane was scored deep with "tortoiseshell" cracks; the rice plants were covered in a layer of yellow dust.

Just then a farmer stepped up onto the lane from one of the fields.

"What does that look like to you?" he said, raising his chin and pointing to the south with his pursed lips. "Rain?"

Jinde looked in the direction indicated. He saw a dark, swirling body slowly but steadily traveling toward them at a constant speed. It was broad, deep, and tall, covering the sky and the land. As far as the eye could see it was swallowing up the ridge of hills, the villages, and the bamboo groves on the plain, wiping out everything on the ground. Wherever it went, everything disappeared; all that remained was a vast sea, dark and gray, like primordial chaos. But amid the darkness there was a hint of turbid yellow, and its swirling seemed not to go from the top down, but from the bottom up. Jinde could see that it was tumbling within itself, whirling and spinning round and round.

That wasn't rain!

"Do you hear anything?" Jinde asked, after watching for well over ten minutes.

"I can't hear anything," said the farmer.

"It's dust," said Jinde.

"I thought so too!" said the farmer, deeply disappointed.

As they spoke, the dust-laden wind reached the air above the town, and in another moment it began swirling all around them. Heaven and earth vanished before their eyes.

When Jinde went back indoors Sister Qingshou had already left.

The next person to arrive was Longxiang's widow.

Jinde sat upright in his chair in welcome and said, "Hello, Sworn-sister!"

After the greetings, the woman sat down on a low stool against the wall.

Jinde's wife handed her a cup of tea.

"It's so rare that we get a visit from you, Sworn-sister," she said with a smile.

"That's certainly true," said the woman. "I'm so busy every day of the year, I can never get away to spend some time with Blood Brother and Sworn-sister. It's awful. I heard that Blood Brother came looking for me twice in the last few days, but I wasn't at home. So I made this trip specially to find out what I can do to help you."

Jinde seemed to hear dishonesty and hypocrisy in the woman's tone and sensed that she was up to no good. He felt uncomfortable, but he did his best to put on a smiling face.

"That's very thoughtful of you, Sworn-sister," he said genially. "It's about something I heard somewhere. People are saying you're going to return that rented land to the landlord so that he can sell it. I hope it's not true. Perhaps someone with a grudge against you is spreading the rumor to make you look bad."

"Actually it is true, Blood Brother. And Huosheng is angry with me because of it. This is how it is: when Tusheng was getting married I was short of cash and borrowed five thousand yuan from Luo Dingrui, with my own two tenths of land as security. By now the repayment date is long past and I've nothing to give him, so I thought, if the landlord agrees and if Luo Dingrui is willing, I'll let him have the other four tenths. After all, that land wasn't originally in our family, so there's no shame in selling it."

"So Luo Dingrui wants land?" Jinde looked sharply at the woman.

"Oh, no! Why should he want land? It's me asking him to take it off our hands. He has plenty of land, far too much to farm himself." As she spoke she was looking down at the palms of her hands. "He said, 'I don't want land, I want money. As soon as you can pay me back I'll return the land to you.' But where am I going to get such a large sum of money!"

Jinde listened in silence and without comment, all the while fixing the woman's face with unmoving eyes. But she kept her head down, avoiding his eyes, and just kept examining her hands.

"Those six tenths that we farm: you know yourself that after the rent's paid we only just make enough to survive, no matter how hard we work all year long. We don't have the capital to go into pig farming. Whichever way you reckon it up, there's no way I can return the five thousand. It was you, Blood Brother, who were kind enough to get us those four tenths of a *jia*. You took pity on us for our lack of land. When Longxiang didn't return from the South Seas"—here the rims of her eyes turned red—"he left us behind: mother and children, the weak and the small. We were lucky to have you constantly looking out for us, and my whole family will always be grateful. It seems to me that with you being Longxiang's sworn blood brother, who else but you should I turn to? So that's why I swallowed my shame to come and ask you for help. You've helped us before, so please finish what you started! Blood Brother, I'm asking you to help us one more time. You have a tobacco shed, so a few thousand yuan is nothing to you. I must have committed sins in a past life, that my husband should die so young, leaving me behind, a mere woman. For nearly twenty years I've been carrying such a huge burden on these weak shoulders...."

The woman began to sob and could say no more. She wiped her eyes again and again on her sleeve.

"Oh! Sworn-sister, but we're like starving men pretending to be well-fed: times are hard for us too," said Jinde's wife, who had been sitting silently to one side all along. "We only have a few tenths more than you to farm. As for the tobacco shed, we only make enough to pay for our own labor, and sometimes, if the crop doesn't grow well, we even make a loss."

"Ah, Sworn-sister," Longxiang's widow looked up, "what convincing excuses you make! But at any rate you've got a lot more options than a poor widow like me. If only you'd be willing to help me out ... you could get four or five thousand with just a nod here or a wink there—easy!"

"I wasn't making excuses, Sworn-sister. Our families are connected, so if we could help you, why wouldn't we? It's just that we don't have the means! Please don't be offended!"

The woman stood and gave a few cold laughs.

"The truth is you aren't willing to help," she said. "I can see I needn't trouble myself any further. At least Longxiang won't be able to blame me, when his own sworn blood brother stands by and watches his widow sell the land. If there's blame, let him blame himself for dying so young. Otherwise, I ... " She burst out crying in great sobs. "I ... a poor ... widow ... "

Wiping her eyes with her sleeves, she walked haltingly toward the door, and was soon gone.

Beside himself with rage, Jinde raised a fist and brought it down with a crash on the table!

"Pei!" he spat. "You dirty bitch! What do you take me for? Think you can play your tricks on me too?"

The more he thought about it the angrier he got. Clearly her actions were a kind of threat or warning to him. He thought it must be the handiwork of Tang Youfu again, that he was using this as a way to mock him, make him a laughing stock. He wondered why he hadn't given that woman a few slaps just now, instead of letting her saunter on out the front door like that. "Hmph!"

Meanwhile his wife was smiling bitterly, her face taut with fury. "Well, you sure gave her a rod for your own back! You get involved in someone else's affairs and then it's you she comes to asking for money. So why didn't you give her the money just now? Your own 'sworn-sister,' ain't she?!"

Jinde ignored her, except for a dirty look as he walked out.

When he came back Yunying was home. As he passed her window he saw her at her mirror, fixing her hair.

"Yunying!" he called as he went past. "Come here!"

He sat in a bamboo chair smoking, his face looking utterly despondent, apparently deep in thought as he stared into space. When Yunying came in he didn't alter his posture at all, but motioned with his eyes for her to sit. The air in the room was stuffy; even before her father spoke Yunying was alarmed by the strangeness of the atmosphere.

"Yunying," said her father, removing the cigarette from his lips. "For a long time now I've been meaning to tell you, but I kept forgetting. I've been told that you are often with Huosheng. I didn't really believe it, but now I have to. I'm giving you a warning: from now on you'd better not have so much to do with him. I'm not saying Huosheng is good or bad, it's just that I don't like that family of his. That whole family, male and female alike, they're all spineless good-for-nothings. They're rotten through and through—there's no helping them.

"And another thing: it seems to me you're incapable of staying put in this house; you're always running off into town. What sort of behavior is that for a girl of your age? From now on I want to see less of that: I want you to spend more time at home. Do you hear? Alright then, that's all I had to say. Your ma had a visitor today: perhaps in a bit she'll have something to say to you."

Yunying just stood there looking at the floor, twisting the hem of her clothing. From start to finish she didn't dare say a word. When her father was done she went back to her room.

"No going out tonight," her father flung after her by way of an afterthought. "Got it?"

10

After the evening meal Huosheng went out and made his way to their usual meeting place—the little ice parlor—to wait for Yunying. He ordered a bowl of shaved ice topped with fruit, and went to sit in a corner. He waited for a very long time. He'd finished his ice and it was long past the time Yunying usually arrived, but there was still no sign of her.

He started to get anxious. He sat uselessly for another half-hour, then left and walked off toward the suburb where Yunying's home was.

On the way he tried and failed to think why Yunying might not have come. Although they didn't necessarily meet every day, today he had the strangest feeling: he felt she had had no reason not to come. At the back of this thought Huosheng had a rationale: their meeting yesterday evening hadn't been very happy, and he had ended by making her angry. He hadn't been able to get this out of his mind all day, and his desire to see Yunying again had grown all the more urgent.

He deeply regretted upsetting her, but he hoped she would eventually understand his dilemma. He wasn't being selfish, and was thinking only of their future together. However, in his motivation for leaving, once you took away the element of dissatisfaction with the status quo and with his family, he hadn't really worked out just how much of it was purely concerned with what was to become of them as a couple. Just as Yunying feared, perhaps his leaving would really be the end of their relationship. There was always that possibility.

His family had long been a headache for him. His stupid, incompetent brother lacked the ability to manage the family; as for his mother, it wasn't his place as her son to interfere, nor would he have felt comfortable doing so, but her decline could be seen on a daily basis. To Huosheng, the family was a cause of impatience and disgust. Only at the office or in Yunying's company could he take pleasure in life.

He had been hoping to meet Yunying on the road, but had no such luck. Before long he was standing only twenty meters from her house. Lights were shining brightly inside, and seeing their glow gave him a warm feeling, but he didn't dare go in. He stayed outside, pacing to and fro and looking on from afar. Standing in the road, he looked at the lights with yearning, particularly looking out for any movement in the room below the central hall. That was Yunying's room. She had told him so herself. But the door to that room stayed still and closed. He didn't see anyone come or go through it. He didn't know if Yunying was in there or not. Although the motionless, peaceful lamplight gave him a pleasant, tender feeling, it had no information to reveal.

As he walked up and down in the lane, his heart went from its earlier feelings of expectation to an intense anxiety, and from anxiety to vexation, until finally his thoughts turned to blame.

"Surely she can't still be angry?" This became his central thought, and circling this question all kinds of other things occurred to him.

Just at that moment he heard a woman's hysterical shrieking coming from inside.

"If they want to give the land back to the landlord that's their business, there's no call for you to go interfering." It was Yunying's mother's voice. No doubt husband and wife were arguing again. "I must have burned the incense upside down in a former life, to end up with a disaster like you for a husband: neglecting your own affairs to go poking your nose in other people's business."

Huosheng was taken aback, and the color drained from his face. Not daring to listen to any more, he turned and hurried away.

That night Huosheng was very troubled, so upset that he hardly closed his eyes. Next day he was still out of sorts as he went to work.

That evening when they met again Huosheng noticed that Yunying was frowning all the time. She seemed depressed and had little to say except to answer his questions, which she did as simply as possible.

They loitered for a while on the secluded back streets and the lanes among the fields on the edge of town, and when they came to the little bridge they sat down on its parapet once more.

"Are you still angry with me?" asked Huosheng gently.

"I'm not angry," said Yunying.

"Well, are you unhappy?"

"No."

Huosheng stretched out an arm, put it around her shoulders, and turned her face toward him with his other hand. Once again he advanced his own face toward hers. Yunying meekly accepted his kisses.

But when Huosheng was about to kiss her for a second time he suddenly noticed the sparkle of tears in her eyes.

"Yunying, are you crying?" he asked in concern.

Yunying said nothing, and Huosheng grew uneasy.

"What's the matter?" he asked her again. "Has somebody done something . . . ?"

Still she made no reply. Before long, they stood up and Huosheng took her home.

Next day after breakfast Yunying's mother told her not to go to work, saying that Zhengang was going to take her on a day out to Kaohsiung.

"I won't go!" she said.

"You're shy?" said her mother with a smile.

"I don't like him."

At first her mother thought she was saying this out of embarrassment, but gradually she stopped smiling and looked her daughter up and down doubtfully. Now she felt that this was nothing to do with shyness, and that Yunying was simply stating what she felt.

"Yunying," said her mother gently, remaining patient. "Surely there's nothing wrong with Zhengang?"

"There's nothing wrong with him at all."

"Well then, you . . . ?"

"I just don't like him." Yunying spoke bluntly.

"So you won't marry him, is that it?"

Yunying made no reply.

"Hey, come on, will you or won't you?"

Still Yunying wouldn't answer. She went into her room and picked up her bag, ready to go to work.

"Stay where you are!" It was a stern command.

Mother and daughter were now locked in a stalemate.

Yunying stood in the doorway and thought for a moment. Finally she turned and went back into her room and bolted the door. She went to bed and stayed there until well after noon, not even getting up for lunch.

At first her mother stood outside her window and angrily alternated scolding and persuasion. Later she went quiet, as if she had softened. Later still she began to call Yunying's name warmly and kindly, spoke with her, and asked to her to come and eat. Yunying ignored her throughout. Finally her mother came again to call her to table, but soon fell silent. Yunying turned and peeked out the window. She had thought her mother had left, but there she was still standing under the window, like a shadow. She stood there for ages before walking off. As she left, Yunying thought she heard her heave a sigh.

After her mother had left, her father came.

"Yunying. Yunying."

Her father's voice was full of amiability and mildness, but also carried a somewhat imperative tone, so that she was forced to get up and open the door.

"Yunying." He turned the chair round and sat at her desk with his back to the window. His face wore an expression of friendliness laced with dignity. "Why won't you come and eat with us? Do you plan to starve yourself to death?"

Yunying bowed her head, saying nothing. When she did look up, her father saw that her eyes were rimmed red and shone with a strange light.

"Silly girl," he said kindly. "If you don't like him, well, that's that. There's no need to get yourself into such a state about it. Come on, come and eat! You don't have to go to work today."

After her father had left Yunying quickly fixed her hair, got changed, and went into town. She had a bite to eat in a small restaurant, and then dropped in at the tailor's to make her excuses to the boss.

Chen Zhengang came to visit that evening. At first he appeared ill at ease, but soon he became as poised and natural as usual. No one mentioned the marriage proposal.

Zhengang said that the new theater was showing *The Butterfly Lovers* tonight: it was one of the better Hokkienese movies and was enjoying an excellent box office around Taiwan. When Yunying's mother heard this she immediately agreed to go. Yunying went along with the others, neither agreeing nor disagreeing. By now her mind was absolutely clear: no matter what they might try, she would just say "No!" But for the time being she didn't want to fall out with her mother, and so she had to try and humor her when she could, compromising in small things in order to achieve her big plan.

At the end of the movie they were among the last to leave the picture house. As they reached the street, if Yunying had paid attention to the arcade on her right she would have noticed someone suddenly darting out of sight into the shadows, then staying there and watching their movements. This person didn't emerge from the shadows until they had gone out of sight. His face deathly white, he staggered off like a drunken man.

Next day Yunying went back to work. She had only just put her things aside and sat down when a girl named Zheng took her to a back room where no one was around. She told Yunying she had seen Huosheng last night and he had been asking about her.

"How did he seem?" asked Yunying urgently.

"Very worked up."

"What did you tell him?"

"I told him you hadn't been at work."

"Did he ask anything else?"

"No."

"And you didn't tell him anything else?"

"No." At this an uneasy expression stole over Zheng's face, as if she had done something to be ashamed of. Yunying didn't notice.

An hour later, Yunying walked to the soda fountain on the corner of the street where the TTL offices were. She told a child who worked in the place to go to TTL and ask Huosheng to come and meet her.

The boy returned in less than ten minutes and said that Huosheng wasn't coming.

"He says he doesn't have time!" he said.

"Didn't you tell him who gave you the message?"

"I told him."

Yunying didn't believe this.

She told the boy to go again and told him very clearly and firmly that he absolutely must give the message to Huosheng personally, and tell him that it came from her.

This time when the boy returned Huosheng was walking behind him.

Not having seen her lover for two days, and especially after the upset that had occurred since they last met, Yunying couldn't help feeling a bittersweet sadness along with the surge of affection. This feeling almost caused her eyes to grow red-rimmed without her knowing it. Her heart burned for the warmth and comfort Huosheng could give her, which would be worth the pain she had suffered for him. But when her eyes met Huosheng's eyes, the strange light in them gave her a slight jolt. His eyes were cool and distant; this was far from what she had been looking forward to.

Huosheng sat down opposite her without a word. His whole attitude was cool and distant, as if she were a stranger to him.

Yunying's smile froze on her lips. She looked at Huosheng apprehensively.

After the waiter had placed two portions of ice cream on the table, he went out into the arcade, moved a hard wooden chair against a pillar, and sat down to watch the goings-on in the street.

They were the only people in the place. Huosheng lit a cigarette and smoked it leisurely. In the two days since he had seen her he felt Yunying had lost a little weight and grown a little paler, but these signs of sorrow had in no way diminished her radiance. On the contrary they lent added gentleness and subtlety to her beauty. He found himself more moved than ever by her charm.

Finally, he blew out a mouthful of smoke and said, "Congratulations on your lucrative marriage."

Yunying couldn't believe her ears. "What did you say?"

"I was congratulating you," said Huosheng with a bitter laugh. "Soon you'll be the wife of a wealthy man."

"Who told you so?"

Yunying watched Huosheng's face closely, but he was casually looking in another direction.

"Naturally I know your news. You can't hide a flame in a paper parcel!"

"Huosheng." Yunying's voice was beseeching. "Are you angry with me?"

"Haha, what a very strange idea! Why should I be angry? It's none of my business."

"No, it's perfectly clear to me. You're angry with me and you're deliberately trying to get me angry."

"That's just your oversensitivity."

"Please, Huosheng. Please." Yunying was pleading in all seriousness now, and she didn't seek to hide her sorrow. "Don't talk like that, please. Have you any idea what I've been going through?"

Now at least Huosheng stopped speaking. He shut up and silently smoked, but his face still bore a bitter, sneering expression.

"I'll tell you honestly," Yunying went on. "A couple of days ago someone did make an offer of marriage...."

"Come on, out with it. Be plainer; it's Zhengang, isn't it?"

"Yes."

"That's good," Huosheng laughed bitterly again. "Zhengang has plenty of money. You should say yes."

"Huosheng!" Yunying could hardly contain herself.

Huosheng fell silent.

"Please don't tease me. I'm trying to discuss this seriously with you."

"Hmm, and who says I'm not being serious? Doesn't Zhengang have plenty of money?"

Yunying was furious. All at once the flames of rage she had been damping down flared up, setting her whole body on fire. Her face changed color and she faintly felt the inside of her throat begin to spasm. She had never expected Huosheng to be so incredibly unreasonable, deliberately saying things to make her angry.

"What are you playing at?" she said, in high agitation but doing her best to keep her voice down. "They came with a marriage proposal, my mother's pressing me to accept, but I won't. I've been so upset these past two days that I haven't eaten a thing. And now I come here to see you and not only do you not comfort me, instead you actually say things to anger me. What: if someone asks me to marry him, is that my fault? Could I have prevented him making the proposal? Don't you think you should have found out if I accepted him or not before you got angry with me? What's gotten into you?"

The more she spoke the more difficult it was to keep her grief inside, and by now the tears were trickling down her cheeks.

"Ahah! If you turned him down," Huosheng was as stubborn as ever, "then how come you went to the movies with him? Do you think I'm stupid?"

Yunying tried to hide her surprise. She didn't understand how Huosheng could know everything; it was as if he had magic powers.

Huosheng's persistence in shutting himself off emotionally and his refusal to rethink his attitude only added a layer of heartbreak on top of Yunying's indignation. She pressed her handkerchief to her eyes.

"Huosheng! Huosheng!" she cried out in anguish.

She rose to her feet. But still she didn't want to leave with things as they stood. And so she sat down again.

"I went to the movies with him because I simply had no choice. Anyway I wasn't alone with him—my mother was with us. There's nothing for you to be jealous about. For the sake of you and me, sometimes I have to go along with things and be polite to him. You don't understand how hard it is for me, and yet you just take out your temper on me. If you keep pushing me, maybe I will accept him, and then what will you do?"

Drying her eyes she stood once more and smoothed down the front of her dress.

The waiter sitting in the arcade seemed to have noticed something out of the ordinary. Looking surprised and curious he walked in and stood to one side, gazing at them.

Yunying closed her mouth tightly and left without saying goodbye.

Then Huosheng got up too and silently left the soda fountain.

II

Huosheng felt as if he were walking in a dream; everything around him was covered by an unreal film of shadow, appearing misty, illusory, and bizarre. He walked back to TTL. Everything there was just as always, but now he saw it all through the strange shadow. He sat down listlessly.

By now he had completely calmed down and was in a frame of mind that gave him ample scope to analyze his behavior. He couldn't help feeling pain at his unreasonable and spiteful conduct. He truly didn't understand why he had been so willfully brutal. It was unforgivable: not even his death could atone for this crime. He realized that he had hurt Yunying deeply, and that the resulting damage to their relationship was frightening. When he thought of this he felt so remorseful that he almost wanted to dash his head against the wall. "If someone asks me to marry him, is that my fault?" Yunying's words had assumed a colossal weight that pressed down on his heart.

That night as he lay in bed the remorse he had felt during the day surged up into his heart once more and grew ever sharper. He tossed and turned, racked with regret and despair. He longed to go immediately to Yunying, to kneel before her and beg her to punish him as she saw fit. He would willingly accept any torment in exchange for her forgiveness. He was afraid that he had made her so angry she might refuse ever to see him again. What would he do if she left him? Could he carry on as normal without her? No! He must not lose her! Life without her—he was afraid even to think of it. He simply had to go and beg her forgiveness, and if she wouldn't forgive him, then let her see him die there on the spot. No matter what, he had to win back her heart.

Next day in the office he kept thinking about how to get to see her. Suddenly, the boy from the soda fountain on the corner came looking for him again.

Huosheng was so happy his heart seemed about to burst. Without stopping to enquire more closely who had sent the boy, he rushed out of TTL.

He was beside himself with joy when he reached the soda fountain, but there was no sign of Yunying. Instead he saw Huang Jinde sitting alone and smoking at a table by the wall. Seeing Huosheng come in, he smiled and nodded amiably in his direction.

Huosheng was so astounded that he almost forgot the proper greeting.

"Hello, Sworn-uncle," he said after a dazed moment.

"Ah, Huosheng," said Jinde, sitting up straight. "Are you very busy?"

"Oh no, no."

"That's good. Have a seat."

Jinde ordered two ice creams.

"Huosheng, you may speak plainly." Jinde sat with his head leaning forward, one hand resting on the edge of the table holding a cigarette. "What do you think of your blood uncle's character?"

This question was so abrupt and out of the blue that Huosheng had not the first clue how to answer. He was speechless.

"Alright! Let me ask you again," said Jinde. "How have I treated your family? Have I been considerate?"

"I've always been grateful to you, Sworn-uncle!" said Huosheng, very respectfully.

The young man's answer seemed to please Jinde. His head swayed a couple of times, and he blew out a mouthful of smoke in satisfaction.

"Your father and I took an oath as blood brothers," he continued. "By rights that makes you my nephew, so I am very sorry to have to tell you that I hope you won't get too friendly with Yunying. I believe you and she are only ordinary friends, and I realize that nowadays boys and girls can be friends. But after all, this is a small country town, and people do gossip, so I hope you will be careful. And now that someone has sent a matchmaker for Yunying you need to be all the more careful, to avoid embarrassment all round. You understand, don't you?"

A wisp of dark cloud floated across Huosheng's eyes, but he did not react in any way. Inside his closed mouth his top teeth were biting into his lower lip.

"Do you have anything to say?" Jinde was watching Huosheng's face closely for any change in his expression.

Huosheng shook his head. "No."

Seeing that Jinde had no more to say, Huosheng was about to rise and take his leave, but Jinde stopped him with a look and indicated that he should stay seated. Jinde took a puff of his cigarette, stubbed it out, and threw the butt in the ashtray.

"Stay a little longer," he said. "Do you know what's happening with your family's land?"

"No."

"You should know."

"Hmm. So what is happening?"

"It's just about to be returned to the landlord. The day after tomorrow the Land Rents Commission is having an arbitration meeting."

"Really?"

"You can go home and ask."

Huosheng was silent, while Jinde wore a bitter, deeply critical smile.

"I disapprove of your family's conduct in this," he said. "The lease on those fields was originally mine. It was because your family didn't have enough land to make a living that I made over my fields to you. Now you're going to get rich and won't need to farm your fields. You're going to return them to the landlord. Fine! But if you were going to do that you should at least have had a word with me first, out of courtesy. But no, you did it all behind my back. Don't you feel ashamed?

I can see it all very clearly. You and your brother are grown up now, you don't need me any more, your father's sworn brother. You can do whatever you like. Well, that's fine by me. I'll be happy to have nothing to worry about anymore."

At first Huosheng wanted to defend himself, but disgust and anger obstinately stopped up his mouth.

That evening when Huosheng went home he immediately went to his brother's room.

"You went ahead and submitted the application, didn't you?"

He didn't beat about the bush.

"Yes." His brother seemed very embarrassed.

"I thought you had agreed not to go through with it."

"It was Ma who told me to put it forward."

"So you just obey her in everything?"

"What else could I do?"

Huosheng scrutinized his brother's face. His stupidity, weakness, and ineptitude made him extremely angry.

"It goes to arbitration the day after tomorrow?"

"Uh-huh."

"And you're going to say what they've told you to say?"

"Uh-huh."

"Have you never thought for yourself whether it's the right thing to do or not?"

Tusheng didn't reply.

Huosheng realized there was no point in further conversation, and so after sitting there a little longer he left. He hadn't the heart to go and see his mother.

He went out and wandered aimlessly as far as the banks of the main irrigation canal, following it where it flowed among the farmland. Usually the main canal had running water in it, but now it was dried up and resembled a mummified corpse stretched out among the fields, utterly lifeless. Slowly he walked upstream, paying no heed whatsoever to the scenery around him. His head was empty, but his heart was heavy, wounded, and bleeding. Everything made him feel disillusioned and in despair: family and love had both abandoned him. All he had had was now lost. Life no longer held for him so much as a scrap of hope or a glimmer of brightness.

He thought again about his plan to leave. Now that he felt hopeless about his life, the plan floated into his mind with a new form and a new allure. He felt that leaving was the only way open for him.

He must leave this town! The town that had given him so much pleasure and richness in life—his birthplace—had now become the site of his heartbreak. It lay there as before, as beautiful as ever, sparkling with many lights, showing that human activity continued, but it no longer retained any meaning for him. All it held was alienation and indifference. Intimacy and warmth were gone.

He must leave this town. This was the only thought left in his head. He didn't care anymore whether his mother would oppose it or not. He must put his resolution into action at all costs.

12

Sitting at her sewing machine or standing at the cutting table, Yunying kept forgetting to work. She sat or stood in a daze. Her eyes would be vaguely focused on some far-off place, and then she would find that they were overflowing with tears, like a leaky tap. She would take out a handkerchief to wipe them surreptitiously, but sometimes she would have the handkerchief in her hand but forget to wipe her eyes, and just let the tears fall.

The girls in the shop watched her with a special look in their eyes. But whether they went out of their way to be polite to her, or put their heads together and whispered, she didn't pay them any heed. Her heart was broken, she was immersed in her own grief, and she had no time to bother with anything else!

Her mother's attempt to force her to accept Zhengang's suit had only made her angry—it couldn't hurt her—but this rift with Huosheng had plunged her into utter despair.

The buds of hope had been torn off and thrown away; the door to life had been shut tight.

She thought of death!

She thought of that poor girl Qiuju's suicide. Her place in the shop had already been taken by a new girl. Her story was like a shooting star that had flared across the sky and plunged into darkness: although it had aroused their interest for a moment, it had almost immediately been forgotten, leaving not the slightest trace. Was the world so heartless? If so, it might help her to make a clean break, but at the same time it was a blow to her thoughts of suicide. She felt that life and death, death and life were equally meaningless. She had the coldest, bleakest, mournful feeling.

She stood up, told the boss she wasn't feeling well and needed the rest of the day off, and then went home.

Next day she really was ill, with fever, a headache, and loss of appetite. She lay in bed with her gaze fixed between the dark roof beams. Tears once more stole into her eyes. She wasn't aware of them until they were pouring down. She couldn't be bothered to get up for a handkerchief, but just wiped the tears away with her hand. She had lost all control over the sluice gate of her tears. They flowed onto the pillow, soaking large areas of it on either side of her head.

The more she thought, the more heartbroken she became. She had gone to Huosheng as a child with hurt feelings goes to its mother. She had felt sure he would understand her and sympathize with her noble struggle: that she could count on him for the comfort, tenderness, and consideration that she needed. Then she could have gone on to tell him her plan for them to flee far away together if it came to the crunch. She not only had the plan, she had the determination. How could she have known that Huosheng would misconstrue her intentions, pour cold water on her sincere feelings, and even allow himself to mock her. She never would have thought it. She didn't understand how he could have been so utterly unreasonable. Did he think it was her fault that someone had proposed marriage? Did he think she had done wrong, even though she hadn't accepted the offer? How could he blame her so unjustly?

Her father sent for the doctor and brought her a one-day prescription. She refused to take the medicine, but her father would not take no for an answer. In the end he stood over her and didn't leave until she finished the full dose.

That night she awoke in the middle of the night when everyone else was fast asleep. The four walls stood silent around her and she heard not a sound. Before long the clock in the hall struck: one o'clock.

Yunying sat up and stayed sitting for a while, then got out of bed and went over to sit in the rattan chair by the window, gazing at the moon. By now the dust in the atmosphere had all fallen back down to ground: the sky was clear, and the moonlight silently caressed the earth below. The anger was now gone from her heart, as was the grief. What remained was a feeling of emptiness, like the kind of medical collapse a patient may experience after a long illness: a sensation of utter feebleness. Everything seemed hazy, as if she found herself in an insubstantial, illusory realm where the sense of time and space no longer existed.

She became aware of a moving light in the distance. The light was dim and tiny, probably some farmer's paraffin lantern, the kind made of a square wooden box with a pane of glass in one side. But because its appearance had seemed to coincide with the moment it came into her field of vision, she had the feeling that it had come from heaven, that it was not of this world. Listlessly she watched the moving light getting nearer, little by little. As it approached the corner of her own house, she could faintly make out a very soft, very slight but very regular sound. The sound grew clearer and clearer until eventually she heard it as footsteps. Just then the light disappeared. Evidently the light had gone behind the west wing of the house. Now the sound of footsteps was at its clearest, but then it got weaker and gradually more distant, then still more distant. Finally it vanished into boundless silence.

The mundane activity of the walker in the night pulled Yunying back to earth. Her heart began to experience feelings once again. All the things that had happened in the last few days swam back up into her consciousness. At first they were indistinct, but then they grew very clear. Her tears flowed again. Yet these things seemed to have been drained of all color and content. They no longer had any effect on her and were merely a cluster of incidents that were already dead and cold.

She opened a drawer and took out her photographs. She had filled a thick album, beginning with a family group taken when she was a little girl a few days before her father left for the South Seas, and ending with recent pictures. Then there was a smaller booklet with her junior high graduation photos: each student had received one of these booklets.

She opened the photo album at the beginning and leafed through one page at a time until the last. Each photograph was a slice of its own moment in her life. When she looked at each picture, the life of that time, with all its details, emotions, and thoughts was displayed anew before her eyes, as fresh and vital as it had been at the time. As she looked at one photo after another she found herself reliving her entire life history. It was a history that began in simplicity, calm, and innocence; then there had been a mid-section of hard work and diligence; finally her history had entered a rich, bright, and varied golden age. Who could have known it would be so fleeting, and now ...

It had been a lovely dream, but now she had woken.

She closed the album.

Her tears began to fall again.

She wiped them away with her hand and stood up with the intention of burning the albums. She wanted them to be consigned to nothingness, like herself. She didn't want any trace to be left behind in this world.

But just at that moment a faint thought flickered through her mind. She sat down again.

So was she really going to die now, just like that? As soon as this question occurred to her, her will to die was shaken, and even more questions came into her head. Was her situation really worth dying for? Was all hope truly at an end? Was there really no way for her to go on living? Had Huosheng really abandoned her?

As she dug further and further down in her consciousness, her will to die grew weaker and weaker, and the desire to live raised its head once more. No! She shouldn't die! She would try again. Opportunities were frequently grasped only in the last minute. Why shouldn't she keep trying, why must she choose death? She and Huosheng had gone through bad times in the past due to a misunderstanding on the part of one or other of them, but each time the bad feeling between them had been erased and their good relationship restored. She only had to explain to him clearly and sincerely the circumstances he had misunderstood and she could surely win back his understanding and forgiveness, so that he would be back at her side once more. This was not impossible, and it was well worth a try. If she made an earnest attempt and still failed to win back his love, well then, it would not be too late to die!

When she thought of this, hope returned to her breast once more. And so, brushing aside all distracting thoughts, she got back into bed.

Next day her father brought her another one-day prescription. This time she didn't need persuasion but took the medicine straightaway.

A few of the girls from the shop came to see how she was and sat with her for a while. By now she was recovered, and although she had lost some weight, her face had regained a healthy color. However, she asked the girls to ask the boss for another day off, and to say that she planned to return to work tomorrow.

At two or three in the afternoon she told her mother she was going into town for a while. She changed into a light blue cotton blouse with a flower print, a favorite of Huosheng's, and went out. When she reached the soda fountain on the corner she chose a seat, and then told the same boy as before to take a message to TTL.

The boy soon came back and told her Huosheng wasn't in the office. They said he'd gone to Taipei. Yunying hesitated, then asked the boy if it was someone at TTL who had told him. The boy said it was.

"Did you ask him what he went to Taipei for?"

"No," said the boy.

The boy's report gave Yunying an ominous feeling. She left the soda fountain to go and find out the truth for herself. In the past she'd been too shy to enter Huosheng's place of work, but she had no room for shyness now and just strode on in.

She walked up to the desk at the very front of the offices and quietly asked the slightly balding middle-aged man there if it was true that Huosheng was not at work.

Looking up from his desk to see a female there, the man replied very politely: "He's gone to Taipei."

"Is he there on business?" Yunying asked.

"No, he quit."

"Quit?" Stunned, Yunying spoke mechanically.

At this moment, the office manager looked up from his large desk at the top of the room. He knew Yunying and had a fair idea of her relationship with Huosheng.

"Miss Huang," he said, smiling in a friendly way. "If you're looking for Huosheng, I'm afraid he has resigned and gone to Taipei. Didn't he tell you?"

Yunying shook her head, turned around, and walked out of TTL in a daze. What she had learned struck her like a merciless axe cleaving into her brow. Her face was deathly white, but cold sweat was pouring from her temples and her hands were shaking. The world seemed to be spinning around her, and the light of the sky had gone dim. She felt as though grim, ice-cold, taut-skinned faces were leering at her from all sides.

Everywhere doors were slamming in her face, everything acting in concert to push her off the edge into an abyss.

As if plunged into an all-enveloping fog, Yunying walked on with no sense of direction. She walked unsteadily, but her feet led her step by step back to her own home.

13

On the day of the meeting of the Township Land Rents Commission, Huang Jinde was sitting in a small diner near the Town Hall. On the table in front of him were a dish of pig's ear, a pair of chopsticks, and a bottle of rice wine from which he served himself in a leisurely and superior fashion. He had sent the waiter to the Town Hall with instructions that Tusheng should join him when his hearing was over. Now he was waiting for Tusheng. It was ten-fifty in the morning.

Tusheng came at twelve-thirty. Jinde told the waiter to bring another pair of chopsticks and slice a dish of sausage.

Tusheng was fearful. "I don't drink," he said, waving away the offer.

"Oh, come on," Jinde insisted hospitably. "Just have a little."

Tusheng sat down on his left. When Jinde stood and raised the liquor bottle to pour him a cup he tried to cover the cup with his hand.

"Keep your hands to yourself," said Jinde. "I'll just pour you half a cup."

When the liquor was poured Jinde sat down again and lifted his cup.

"Come on then! Bottoms up!"

Jinde filled both cups again, and then stuffed some meat in his mouth.

"Do you know why I asked you here?"

His tone had changed, becoming very serious. As he stared at Tusheng, an awesome force seemed to shoot out from his eyes.

"Erm," Tusheng looked as if he no longer knew what to do with his hands and feet. "No."

Jinde's eyes glared wider than ever and his head jutted forward.

"Do you know what you should call me?"

"Sworn-uncle," said Tusheng.

In that instant Jinde raised his right hand and brought it strong and true right across the young man's face with a resounding slap. Five big, thick finger marks were immediately imprinted on his left cheek.

Tusheng was seeing stars, but still he sat staring dumbly at Huang Jinde. He seemed to wonder if he was dreaming and couldn't understand what had just happened.

"Hah!" roared Jinde. "Well, at least that's something: you still know who your sworn-uncle is." His throat was bright red, and beads of sweat were popping out from his head. "Let me ask you: who originally had the lease on those fields you farm? Now that you're returning them to the landlord, how come you didn't even mention it to me? Am I nothing to you anymore? Think about it: if you really didn't want that land anymore, no problem, just a few words from me and someone else would have taken on the let. The only thing is you wouldn't have been able to get your hands on that ten thousand, and after you'd kissed the land goodbye you'd've realized it was too late to regret.

"Now, that's probably the only time I'll ever hit you. From now on I won't be bothering with your family at all."

Tusheng remained silent, glued to the spot. He didn't know whether to stay or go, but in the end he did get to his feet.

"Go home and have another good think about things," urged Jinde, calling after him.

When the liquor was finished Jinde walked out of the diner. It was now already two in the afternoon, the streets were crowded, and from time to time he bumped into someone's shoulder, which sent him reeling and swaying. But Jinde was beaming all over his face with satisfaction, feeling light and easy in his heart.

Luo Dingrui's residence was on the same street as TTL. It had doors on two sides: one on the street, and the other overlooking the river. The door from the street led straight through to the parlor, via a small courtyard with an old sweet-scented osmanthus tree and several plants in pots.

When Jinde went in, Luo Dingrui seemed to have only just awoken from his siesta. He was sitting in a rattan chair, yawning and stretching, in a lethargic state of mind. As soon as he saw Jinde he gave a start, as if from an electric shock, and his sleepiness vanished. Not knowing the reason for this visit, and confronted with Jinde's fierce, liquor-flushed face, Luo was surprised and bewildered, so much so that he forgot to say anything.

Jinde swaggered into Luo's parlor and, without waiting to be greeted, went right on in and sat opposite the host.

"I beg your pardon," he said, with the opposite of humility, not even looking Luo in the face.

Thirty seconds passed in silence. Jinde kept wiping his lips with his hand, first with the back of the hand, and then turning it over and using the palm.

"I beg your pardon," he said with another wipe across his mouth; finally he put down his hand and looked up. "Mr. Luo, I haven't bothered you in a long time. I have one request of you: don't buy Xu Longxiang's land; if you've got the money you can buy land anywhere, it doesn't have to be those fields. If you do buy Xu's land, I have to tell you it will turn out badly. You know what I mean."

By now Luo Dingrui had composed himself and was more than capable again of thinking, responding, and counterattacking. He smiled cunningly and took his time about replying: "I don't want their land. I only want my money to be repaid."

"Whatever they owe you, I'll make sure they repay you."

"Can you guarantee that?"

With alacrity, Jinde slapped his own chest and said: "I, Huang Jinde, will be the guarantor."

Luo Dingrui laughed loud and long.

"Thank you!" he said jocularly. "It's not that I'm afraid they will withhold repayment. After all, I still have those other two tenths of theirs as security. However, I can allow them an extension on the loan. There: you'll be satisfied with that, I hope?"

Again, Luo Dingrui burst into loud laughter.

"Fine!" Jinde rose to his feet. "It's a deal then. Thank you for your trouble!"

Feeling extremely pleased, Jinde walked back to the *bantiao* restaurant by the clock. In the doorway he ran into the owner. A-Geng took one look at him and cried: "Oh, Jinde! Who've you killed now?"

"Haha," chuckled Jinde. "Murder wouldn't taste half as sweet as what I've been up to. And now I want a drink."

"Your eyes are already red with drink. You still want more?"

"I haven't had enough, not by a long shot."

"How much will be enough?"

"I reckon three bottles of rice wine should do it."

"Don't brag. One bottle's enough to put you in the gutter!"

Both men guffawed. Jinde walked into the restaurant.

"You want to sleep?"

Jinde grunted a reply as he swayed on into the back room.

It was dark when Jinde awoke. Other people had already had their evening meal and were sitting out on the roadsides enjoying the cool of the evening. Jinde ate a platter of pig's head and a bowl of *bantiao* washed down with a bottle of red dew wine.[8]

A-Geng sat beside him, smoking a cigarette.

"Weren't you there last night?" he asked. "Youfu and Quansheng really cleaned up!"

"I know," replied Jinde. "Tonight I'm gonna make 'em cough the whole lot back up again."

"If you ask me you'd be better just taking care of what's yours."

"You don't believe me? Just wait and see."

Uncle A-San's family's tobacco shed housed a gambling den run by Tang Youfu and Ruan Quansheng. The game tonight was chariot-horse-cannon, a roulette using Chinese chess pieces. Quansheng was the chief croupier, Youfu was the banker, and a great mass of gamblers crowded round them in a ring.

Jinde stood and watched for a while on the outer edge of the human wall. Then he parted it with a hand, shouting, "Make way there, make way there!" His voice was loud and his hand was heavy, and what's

---

8. "Red dew wine" (*honglujiu* 紅露酒, aka *honglaojiu* 紅老酒 ['red old wine,' the original name before it was Japanized in Taiwan]) is a rice wine, originating in Fujian, China, similar in strength and body to Shaoxing wine but with a reddish hue, produced by its main ingredient, red yeast rice, which is cultivated using the mold *Monascus purpureus* ("red yeast").

more his mouth gave off the strong acrid smell of liquor. The men hurried to let him through. He forced his way right into the middle and sat on the edge of the rush mat. Quansheng gave him an unconcerned glance and returned his full attention to the chess pieces. Youfu, on the other hand, realizing that Jinde was not here to deal in pleasantries, mentally prepared himself for trouble.

Quansheng was sitting cross-legged, both hands stirring about in a black bag. His eyes half-closed, he was the image of a conjurer doing a magic trick. Solemn and tense, his face was otherwise as devoid of emotion as if it had been carved in wax. After fumbling in the bag for quite some time he brought out a small metal box, which he pushed forward on the mat in front of his feet. As the gamblers placed their stakes, banknotes fell through the air like rain and there was a great hubbub of voices.

"Red horse five yuan."

"Black knight ten yuan."

"Red chariot . . . "

Youfu raised his voice above the clamor, shouting, "You can't take back a placed bet! Keep your hands to yourselves! If you take it the bet still stands . . . "

Jinde took out two ten yuan notes and placed one on the red knight and the other on the red elephant.

When all bets had been placed, the uproar died away and everyone held their breath as they fixed the little metal box with their eager eyes.

"Final bets now or never! The box is going to open! Keep your hands to yourselves!" Youfu was yelling all the while.

"Open!" The word was pelted out of a dozen mouths at once.

A tall old guy next to Quansheng whose nickname was Leggy reached out to open the box. You could have heard a pin drop, the men were swallowing saliva, and dozens of pairs of eyes were fixed on that long, dark-brown hand.

Leggy opened the box.

"Black cannon!" Many voices cried out at once, a few of them happy, the others disappointed.

"Keep your hands to yourselves!" Youfu was shouting again. "Anyone who grabs won't get paid! Whose is this one yuan? Here you are, ten yuan, take it! Whose is this five yuan? . . . "

Both of Jinde's ten yuan notes were swallowed up by the bank. Next, he bet on the red cannon and the black elephant, ten yuan each, and lost both again. Next again, he placed his full stake of fifty yuan on the black elephant.

"How about staking a bit less?" said Youfu amiably. "Or you could split your money into two or three different bets."

Jinde made no reply, but he did take back twenty yuan.

The metal box was opened, and Jinde's thirty yuan disappeared again.

Jinde kept losing, only once winning on a ten-yuan stake. But he gambled more and more audaciously, his stakes getting bigger and bigger. All the while his face was as taut as sheet metal, his eyes blazed fiercely, and sweat pricked up all over his body.

Once more the metal box was pushed forward.

Once more the rain came fluttering down.

"Place your bets! It's about to open!" Youfu yelled again.

Flames were spitting from Jinde's eyes, but he kept his mouth tightly shut. Then suddenly he took the ring from his finger and threw it down shouting "Red chariot! Red chariot, two hundred!"

The whole place seemed to go into shock; in an instant it was shrouded in an unnatural silence. But in another moment a great surging billow of commotion swept through the gathering. They sensed that a storm was about to break. Many of them withdrew their stakes at the last minute.

"Jinde," said Youfu, all friendly smiles. "Come on now, let's be serious."

"You think I'd joke with you?" Jinde's face was perfectly grave.

Youfu picked up the ring, quickly gauged its caratage, and placed it on one palm to judge its weight.

"It's genuine alright," said Jinde. "Two ounces. It can be redeemed tomorrow, no problem."

"Make it a fifty-yuan stake?" said Youfu, looking Jinde in the eye.

"No way! It's got to be two hundred!"

Youfu turned to look at his partner. Quansheng was looking away; the more perceptive observers could see beads of sweat breaking out on his face.

"Leggy, open!"

Every man in the room was bellowing for his bet to come out.

The old guy looked up hesitantly at Youfu and Jinde.

"Open it!" said Youfu.

In great trepidation, Leggy reached out a hand to open the metal box. His hand trembled slightly and was slicked with sweat.

All the gamblers stretched their necks forward to get a view; tension and excitement hung on every face.

The box lid opened a fraction at a time.

Five seconds, ten seconds, thirty seconds . . .

It opened: red chariot!

"Aaaah!" Everyone cried out together in amazement, many of them shouting words of triumph.

"Yes!" "Hurray!"

The crowd was going crazy.

All the color drained from Youfu's face.

Two hundred to pay two thousand. He counted out a thick wad of notes and handed them to Jinde.

"How much?" asked Jinde.

"Fifteen hundred," said Youfu meekly. "Five hundred short. You'll get it later."

"No way! You've got money!" Jinde angled his head, his eyes jutting at Youfu.

"I wouldn't lie to you. I really don't have any more."

Jinde grabbed Youfu's collar in one fist and shook it violently.

"Give it here! You give others what you owe, why not me?"

"But I really don't have it!" As he spoke, Youfu tried to pry Jinde's hand off.

Jinde gave him a great shove. "Fuck your mother! What kind of banker are you, with no money!"

Youfu staggered off a good distance. Luckily those standing behind him stopped him from falling.

Meanwhile Quansheng was struggling to his feet.

"Stay where you are!" Jinde barked angrily. "This has nothing to do with you!"

Quansheng stood stock still.

Humiliation turning to anger, Youfu was gathering himself for a leap at Jinde, but Jinde's eye and hand were too quick: he was already bringing up a fist and now he brought it down on Youfu's chest. Immediately there was pandemonium in the room. Many of the gamblers fled outside. Those who remained took hold of Youfu and Jinde and kept them apart.

"Fuck your mother! Open your eyes and take a good look who you're dealing with: Huang Jinde!" Jinde was struggling like an enraged lion in the grip of the men who held him. "You think I'm a soft touch? I'm Huang Jinde and from now on you'd better not get me riled. You get me riled and you'll be sorry. Fuck your mother!"

Just then, an urgent wave of sound swept into the shed. At first everyone thought it was a police raid and got ready to rush out. But now the wave of sound entered the room and became three words.

"Is Jinde here?"

Like a whirlwind, a man came hurtling up to Jinde, grabbed his arm, and began to pull him outside.

"Go home, quick!" The man was flustered and dismayed. "Something's happened at home."

"What's happened?" Jinde asked as he was dragged along.

"Your daughter's taken poison . . . "

Before the man could complete the sentence Jinde's face had turned ashen. He shook himself free and took to his heels. Without pausing for breath he ran all the way out of town. As he neared home he heard a great hubbub from inside the house. He could make out his wife's howling and wailing.

"Yunying—my child, if you didn't want—you should've said—Ma wouldn't have forced you—how could you go and—take your own life . . . !"

The woman's weeping punctuated her monologue. The sound made Jinde's legs turn weak and a lump come into his throat, but still he didn't stop. Instead he only ran faster.

His whole house—the yard, the hall, and his daughter's room, all were packed with people, all of them talking to one another, shouting, raising the very roof. Jinde ran straight into his daughter's room. Seeing him arrive, the crowd hurried to make a way for him to pass.

"Jinde's back! Jinde's back!" Many voices took up the cry.

Yunying was lying stiff and straight on her bed, smartly dressed from head to toe, as if she'd been about to go on a long journey. Her face was greenish, with foam at the corners of her mouth. One of her eyes was still slightly open. His wife was bent over their daughter's body, wailing. . . .

Jinde went forward, took his daughter's hand, and cried over and over, "Yunying! Yunying! Yunying! . . ."

Her hand was not yet cold, but no breath came from her nose; she was obviously dead.

Tears fell from the father's eyes.

"Did you send for the doctor?" he asked his wife.

"We did," said someone on her behalf. "He should be here any minute."

"She," he asked his wife again, "what did she . . . ?"

"She drank endrin."

It was someone standing by the table who spoke, lifting a bottle, which he shook and showed Jinde. It was the remains of the pesticide he used on his rice fields. He never dreamed his own daughter would use it to kill herself.

"Yunying, Yunying . . . " In his grief Jinde cried out to the daughter who would never answer him again. Tears streamed down his face. "Yunying, Yunying . . . "

"Yunying—my child . . ." The mother kept on and on weeping.

The doctor arrived.

14

The weather was abnormally hot and close, wringing great quantities of sticky, oily sweat from people's bodies; the trees bowed their heads and were utterly still, as though drained of energy.

Toward noon the sky began to grow dark as gray rain clouds spread over it. The clouds grew ever darker. By the time people were finishing their meals the scattered clouds had formed into cloud clusters hanging low over the earth. Then bursts of thunder began to roll: urgent, violent, shaking the window frames with great booming crashes.

The cloud clusters grew so dense that eventually they coalesced into a single mass, covering the sky. The sun had hidden itself out of sight, and at ground level it was as dark as night. Bolts of lightning pierced the black sky again and again, each followed by an earth-shaking peal of thunder: Kuang—lang-lang-lang . . . kuh-lalala. . . After each bolt of lightning the clouds regathered, dense, black, and thick.

The lightning flashed again.

Kuang—lang-lang-lang-lang . . .

Kuh-lalalalala. . . .

Still the trees hung their heads, as though waiting for something to arrive.

It's raining!

Farmers danced and gesticulated wildly, crazy with delight. Children ran back and forth in the streets, singing, "The wind doth blow, a-shrimping we will go; the rain doth fall, there'll be prawns for us all."

Anyone wearing a bamboo hat had it tossed to the ground; anyone using an umbrella had it torn to pieces. Such articles were taboo, and the people would not allow their use. The rain was the answer to their prayers.

No! It was more than that: it was pure gold! Heaven was showering gold upon them.

The rain fell heavier and heavier, turning the sky darker than ever; in no time at all the ground was awash.

The farmers quickly mobilized: some led oxen, some shouldered plows or hoes, some carried baskets. In the streets and on the lanes people were bustling, coming and going as never before. The whole town had burst into action. Within half an hour the fields were filled with human bodies in motion, and all around could be heard the sound of plowmen urging on their oxen: "Ho! Ho!"

Tense activity and high excitement filled the landscape.

The farmers were returning to their lives.

The rice seedlings might be past their prime, but the fields still had to be planted.

Some families mobilized their young and old to go searching for seedlings.

Favors, grievances, disputes, curses, fisticuffs—all of that was put aside.

Kuang—lang-lang-lang-lang-lang-lang . . .

Kuh-lalalalala ...

The thunder was singing. Then gradually it quieted down, until all that was left was the rain.

The rain was falling. Falling in sheets, falling ...

Everywhere was the sound of plowmen's cries: "Yah! Yah!"